Future Imperfect

Brooks' Adventures, Volume 1

J. Robert Maier

Published by J. Robert Maier, 2022.

This is a work of fiction. Similarities to real people, places, or events are entirely coincidental.

FUTURE IMPERFECT

First edition. August 4, 2022.

ISBN: 979-8201447762

Written by J. Robert Maier.

To all the people who believed in me to make this happen,
thank you all.

Prologue:

Alarms were blaring throughout the facility as a man wearing a lab coat and a very frightened disposition was running toward a communication terminal, clicking through several options before stopping at one name. After a moments' hesitation he selected it and waited for seconds that lasted an eternity before a bleary looking man answered with a slight cough.

"This better be good."

The man nodded. "Mister Stirling, we have a problem. We've had a catastrophic failure in the facility, unknown contaminants caused a reaction in sub-levels two and three; the halon system activated and subsequent venting has occurred."

There was a pinched expression on the monitor. "Damage?"

"Structurally, minimal. However, biologically sir - I...I can't really explain it, sir, you have to see it."

"Then show me."

There was a nod, and both men watched as the cameras showed several people screaming in agony as their bodies began to warp and change. Some held their heads as their bodies began collapsing on themselves stopping and leaving them as child-sized versions of themselves, with barrel chests and thick limbs. When it was over, they found themselves standing shakily and appearing confused and frightened, as if the worst hadn't yet come to pass.

The display changed to the outside of the building where two guards were undergoing similar transformations that were quite possibly worse. One was staring in mute horror as his legs and feet elongated, tearing through his uniform pants and shoes to become covered with fur, while on his forehead a pair of bumps appeared and began growing what could only be described as horns, extending and curling toward the back of his head. The view of the second guard was obscured, but his screaming told more of a tale than anyone would want to know. Several more views flipped through before a better one was found, and the second guards' trauma was fully realized – a different transformation was taking place as the guards' legs and torso began twisting and elongating, with a second pair of furred legs emerging as the screaming finally stopped. The transformation did not, with a tail and hooves beginning to emerge as the guard lay unconscious, twitching every few moments.

Mister Stirling, fully awake by now, addressed his colleague. "You said this was vented?"

"Yes, the automatic systems kicked in sir."

"How long before it's everywhere?"

The first man began thinking about it, not noticing his own changes beginning to take place. "I believe it may be as much as three days before it's hit through most population centers. A week, possibly two for full worldwide changes."

"Contact Legal. Prepare them for all the damage control they can muster. Call National Health, advise them of the situation, tell them that - " The orders cut off as Gerald began grabbing his own head and groaning, attempting to muster coherent thoughts that were, for the moment, failing.

The first man began staring at the screen. "Mister Stirling." A pause, No response. "Mister Stirling?"

The screen went dark.

"Gerald?!"

No response.

The newly changed assistant, looked down at his body finally and noticed his own fingers elongating along with his arms and legs becoming painfully longer, thinner, and more translucent. He took a shaky breath, reaching into his pocket for an old flip-phone, and dialed a very long phone number, waiting and hoping whatever was happening wouldn't keep him from finishing what was quite possibly one of the more important calls he'd ever had to make. Finally the connection completed and he whispered into the phone.

"Tell all of Jacks' friends to get ready for an emergency."

Chapter 1

The world used to be different. No fauns, no elves, centaurs, no dwarves running the internet. Cats weren't telepathic. I was married - and I wasn't a centaur.

But some things stayed the same. Take for instance the murdered lady I was looking at while my partner was talking to other tenants in the office complex. She was pretty, if Erinyes were your thing. She was a private investigator I'd hauled downtown for questioning a time or five when we needed answers.

Erinyes are good for that. Sure they've got the wings coming out of their back but they're almost impossible to see if they don't want to be seen. And catching them off-guard was a problem at best. Which was the first clue - no defensive wounds I could see, her posture didn't suggest anything other than she'd been sitting, and the bullets had gone through her monitor. Not your average walk-and-pop. The second oddity was that after the deed was done, the shooter had pulled the victims' hard drive from the computer - and for good measure had scattered everything to the four winds before leaving. This wasn't your average deadbeat client.

My train of thought was interrupted by my partner Devoin, giving me a look. I knew what was coming, but it didn't make it any better.

"You think she mighta stuck her beak where it doesn't belong?"

"Dev, that joke was old the first time you said it."

"Still funny though."

"It hurts my ears every time."

Dev bumped my wither with his elbow. "Come on. The Lollipop Guild's coming in to sweep the place before the meat

1

wagon can take her downtown, we gotta clear and do the paperwork. You giving me a lift?"

"Do I have a choice?"

"Not really, my knee's still giving me hell."

I sighed. "Fine. But remember the deal. You fart, I buck."

As we were discussing, four dwarves in police department jackets began tromping in with all their gear on a cart to start checking the scene over with their usual diligence. The Lollipop Guild nickname wasn't entirely out of place, but still. I went through the office complex, handing out my card to everyone I talked to, but I really didn't hold out much hope.

Once we got outside and navigated the stairwell, I got low and let Devoin get on my back, sidesaddle. I felt silly, since I hadn't gotten much taller as a result of changing, but Devoins' knee was bad. Really I didn't mind - in traffic, I was faster than most of the cars, and despite the fact that it'd been ten years, most of the cars in the department weren't exactly friendly to Neotypes. There was always something not quite right; for Dwarves the seats and pedals wouldn't really work with their three to four foot frames. The Erinyes were a little different - they had the height, but they also had wings which made seating awkward. Fauns, well, we actually didn't have any fauns at the station, but they had the problems of the Dwarves with regard to the height issues and on top of that the standard faun hoof was not exactly a pedal-friendly thing, so most cars were getting retrofitted with hand controls. And then the centaurs. There was some size variation, just like real horses; in my case I'd grown to seven feet six inches, which wasn't bad. What was bad was my front having to walk five feet to discover the final two feet-ish that encompassed my butt couldn't get through a doorway. But I digress. The real problem was clothes. Kilts were all the rage among centaurs, since they were practical and covered everything. The fashion-forward were into sarongs, but it seemed a bit much for me. Fauns were very much yoga pants fans, Erinyes favored loose shirts with short sleeves for their wings, and Dwarves just hit the "Husky Boys" section of the clothing shops.

The station house was busy, but not too bad for a Thursday. Devoin slid off with a grateful look. He wasn't a bad guy, but his sense of humor was typical of the people who hadn't been changed. A little speciesist and a little awkward - mostly because a lot of people changed, enough that everyone knew someone who wasn't what they were. The bad jokes were a coping mechanism for society's' stress of having a full half the population become something else. In theory, they'd taper off as society adjusted.

In theory.

The paperwork was routine but time-consuming, just filing the reports of what we saw, a section for anything that we thought was unusual, and then a section for additional comments. After that, it was time to turn in the weapons to the armory, get a harrumph from the new Erinyes working behind the cage, punch out, change, and head home. I slid into my vans' side door and buckled up. It was used, purportedly it had been tested against centaur crashes, and I didn't have the money to get something better. First I had to fold my legs under me so the torso strap would cinch down properly, and then the frayed five point harness for my front section.

Finally it was off to the section of row houses, warehouses, and converted warehouses that had been known as Little Italy since forever, and parked in the reserved spot in the parking lot of my home-slash-favorite bar, the Jolly Cholly. The bar itself was of the converted warehouse style, with two stories of red brick adorned with windows that weren't perfect, but workable. The second story access was a small entryway with mailboxes that led to a staircase, where the stairs led up to a fairly soundproofed hallway with a total of three apartments. One was fairly spartan and used as an employees' crashpad for when they may have had a grand old time with a few of the regulars. The second one was the managers' place and filled with paperwork and desks. The manager was a matronly sort of woman but quite capable of doing anything she put her hand to, whether it was plumbing, buffing the hardwood oak floors to a mirror shine, or grabbing one of the lead-filled baseball bats behind the bar proper to encourage folks with too much alcohol and too little politeness that when she said it was time to go it was in fact time to go.

I debated and finally decided that this day did in fact call for a beer. I took off my uniform shirt and tied it around my waist so that people didn't think I was drinking on duty, and squeezed myself through the door. One of the down sides of life was that most doors were just barely big enough for me to get through, which resulted in my entry being a practical but somewhat silly looking right-to-left shimmy. Easy enough once you learned it, but embarrassing when you were busy and tried to just keep walking.

For my trouble I got a wave and a small cheer from the regulars at the bar who were watching the game on the TVs nestled in the corners. The seventy foot long bar itself was oak and as legend had it was fashioned from timbers of a ship from the Revolutionary War. Which ship was a matter of debate among the bars' historians, and various contenders had been put forth, but the question was never settled.

In any event, the bar found more than a few veterans leaning on it as the years went by, and the mirror became home to a significant collection of unframed pictures with hand-written scribbles on the back. For the most part, they were of young men mugging for the camera before going off to do what their country had asked of them. More recently those pictures included women, but the smiles and poses were remarkably similar across the generations. I leaned in and found a large mug of stout in front of me, along with a smaller glass of whiskey to keep the mug company. I lifted the shot to a picture of a younger me and his younger friends lounging on a tarmac and carrying an unholy amount of equipment while waiting to go jump out of an airplane, and settled my lower half on a rotating padded plank that sufficed for a bar stool.

Now that I'd gotten comfortable, it was time to let the day dissipate into a few jokes at various patrons' expense and general disdain for referees, umpires, and all those who tried to enforce the rules of sports. After watching tonights' game, there was a spirited discussion regarding the potential ancestry of the officials, which wound up when we were collectively reminded the the rules were applied to make the game close, not fair. And with that, I finished up my pint and headed upstairs. It was late, and something about that Erinyes' murder was sticking with me. Call it cop instincts, call it whatever. It seemed like there was something more waiting to be found. I made a note to ask the dwarves about it in the morning. But first, it was time to deal with the cat.

I opened the door and surveyed. Everything was in the right place. Framed football jersey? Check. Second framed football jersey from the high school game where we scored four touchdowns? Check. Huge television and coffee table that scream "I'm single and not looking for a darn thing?" Check. Small fireplace with a mantle overflowing with multiple generations of Irish cop memorabilia? Check and double check. Picture frame encompassing the army career with umpteen medals and a lucky beret because I thought leaving an airplane in mid-flight over odd places was a great idea? Check and inner-shudder at doing that now. Spare bedroom with some decor, used every other weekend and during the summer when my son was here? Had not moved an inch. Twenty-five-pound cat was on the sofa that goes by the name Max? Furry and just waking up. He raised his head and blinked sleepily as I put my keys down and kicked the door closed.

"The hell, Brooks? You have a weird one?" Max's voice in my head was always a little sleepy sounding when I first came home. "Tell me about it while you feed me." He slid off the couch and sloughed toward the kitchen.

"Same old. Paperwork, murder. Couple speeding tickets, oat bars for lunch." I pulled out a little catnip, maneuvering around the cat who was promptly winding his way around my legs anticipating his bowl of crunchies followed by some heavenly catnip.

"Brooks, you're going to get drunk and try to forget about the dead person you saw today. Tomorrow you're going to go see the shrink, go over the paperwork, and then go walk your beat because the department always forgets to fix the Equa-car."

"Is it working?"

He shunched over his bowl on the floor. "For now."

"I'll take what I can get." I finished my first beer in the kitchen, popped a second one and started dinner. It was a quinoa salad with seasoned buffalo cubes and ranch. It was yet another oddity that I got used to, mostly out of necessity. I was never a small guy, but I weighed around seven hundred pounds now - and and all seven hundred pounds needed fuel. Since I was living what they called an active lifestyle, the docs said I'd need about thirty thousand calories a day to maintain my activity levels and not lose weight - about a ten-fold increase from what I'd been eating before the change. Apparently the inactive sedentary centaurs could get away with about half that, but I had yet to meet a centaur that wasn't doing some kind of activity. I settled into the couch and tucked my legs under me, watching the game and snorting as they inter-cut bits of the latest attempts at Neotype sports.

Max flopped onto his favorite napping spot, my hindquarters, and proceeded to give himself a wash. Cats were the focus of intense debate after the whole event thing. Their telepathic abilities meant that they were distinctly sentient and not simply pets, however they were still cats with all that entailed. They weren't considered citizens, so they couldn't vote. However, they were exempt from all forms of taxation, which after some heated debate meant that they wouldn't be subject to licensing. Then there were the 'working' cats, the ones who lived in barns or on ships for vermin extermination. Collectively, these cats felt that they were okay with their current jobs, and being paid in dead rats was quite sufficient, thank you.

Then there were the big cats. A few animal-rights groups made a very large fuss about zoos keeping lions, tigers and so forth until the cats there spoke up for themselves and for the most part just asked for more food, a little bit bigger space, and toys. Said animal rights groups were a tad confused by this turn of events, having worked under the presumption that all of the big cats were outdoor cats. There were certainly a few that were, but those ones had been problematic to the zookeepers beforehand and once they were able to make their desires known were properly re-homed.

Cats and their thoughts occupied my mind. I don't remember the end of the game, but that night I had the dream again. The Change. In reality, I went from having what I thought was the flu to being hospitalized to seven hours of agony interspersed with brief unconsciousness as the sedatives kicked in, wore off, and the process started anew. Finally after several days, less and less pain as my body settled into the equine shape and then started the first days of the rest of my life. There was no unconsciousness in the dream, just unending pain of torsion, growth, and then in the end of it there was the Erinyes that my partner and I had found. She was talking despite the bullet wounds, but I couldn't hear her over the screaming of my nerves. And the screaming in general.

When I blinked my eyes open, Max was staring intently at me from his perch on my chest. "You need to stop dreaming so loud.

See the doc. Maybe the head doc. You got problems that talking to me won't fix."

"Yeah, yeah if I can get the appointment. We ain't got an unlimited budget in the department, y'know."

"Good. Now, if you're conscious enough to be bitchy at me, you're conscious enough to feed me. We got any chicken gooshyfood left?"

"No, I had chicken for you last week, and you said you hated chicken." It was odd, talking to a cat. You felt more than heard, and talking back was a matter of focusing your thoughts. It wasn't easy first thing in the morning, but I'd learned.

"That was last week. This is this week. Chicken." Also of note, cats were still a little fussy and temperamental about what they like. Except now instead of just meowing, they could actually tell you.

"Speaking of not unlimited budget, mine. You're getting beef, whether you like it or not is up to you." However, while cats knew what money was, and that the rest of us had to work for it, they were lacking the leap of logic to understand that money was a finite resource. And with that, I glopped the cat food into the bowl for him and went to take care of the rest of my morning routine.

Uniform? Check. Badge? Check. Utility belt with everything I needed? right where it should be. Second bag over the withers with extra snacks and water bottles? Check and double check. My coat was getting a little long, which resulted in some extra time brushing - but I could make an appointment with the barber later today. Apparently being mostly Irish meant my equine side most resembled what was called a Gypsy Vanner. The horse part of me was covered in a dark red fur, with three white sections. The worst part was that my tail and ankles grew an exceptional amount of hair. I stood to my full height of just over seven feet tall and nodded at myself approvingly. Then I did a quarter-turn so that I could make sure there weren't any wrinkles on my kilt, and grimaced a bit as I realized I was definitely due for a chat with the barber. Still, it would be good enough for today. Thankfully, I'd gotten my winter coat blown out a few weeks ago, but I still needed to maintain my hair and coat. After that, I told Max to watch the house and went to the vehicle for commuting time.

It wasn't quite hell, but it was traffic. I parked my van in the designated lot, adjacent to the station, and sighed as I was about to play elevator roulette. As usual, the funding for the elevators had been deferred to the next fiscal year, which meant that we had a standing weekly appointment with the elevator repair crew. The elevators didn't have the "out of order" sign, so I rolled the dice. And no luck today, as I heard something grind pitifully and then stop with an expensive-sounding thunk. With that indicator of how the day was going to go, I made my way to the basement where my desk was so I could get the day started. It wasn't officially Centaurs-only but The Barn - as some of the more brilliant wits in the force had taken to calling it - was drafty, a little under-lit, and where every Neotype officer who was a sergeant or below had a desk. It used to be the armory and parts storage, but when half of the force undergoes various changes in size over the course of a year in various ways, changes are made.

I settled on my bench-chair and reviewed the email, and after some time made some changes for the beat so we could go check out the murder scene from yesterday. Then I checked out the voicemail just in case anyone had called to report they'd seen something. It wasn't like the crime rate was high, really - honestly looking at the numbers crime had gone down a pretty decent amount in the last few years, but there were a host of new crimes to consider. On the up side, it wasn't from the look of it being classed as a bias crime. Still, I'd be better off checking to make sure. To save the walk, I called up. It was answered by a profoundly baritone voice.

"Forensics, Ricky."

"It's Brooks. You got any followups for me on that Erinyes from yesterday afternoon? I got the case number if it helps."

"Yeah nah. Lemme check it." There was a pause while I was on hold. "Brooks? Something weird. File's gone. Like, gone-gone. Not even a Special Case Division flag."

The Special Case Division was a new department - specifically they took over cases that were cross-jurisdiction and involved neotypes. They were also to a one assholes. I suppose that comes with the territory simply because they overlapped everyone's jurisdiction and took arrests and investigations away from everyone else. And more to the point, they took away budget. However, they were usually polite enough to let you know when they were smacking you in the teeth.

"Hey Ricky? Can you check the system for any errors? I mean, the storage is getting kinda old, so it mighta just ate itself."

"Way ahead of you - it was an intentional delete by someone with way more access than me. You're gonna do the dumb thing aren't you."

"When have I ever done the dumb thing?"

"I have a spreadsheet for the dumb things your entire department does. I can send you a copy."

"Back-burner that."

I hung up, thinking things over. The first thing was that someone had intentionally deleted the file, but they hadn't cleaned up after themselves, in a manner of speaking. So probably someone who didn't know the ins and outs of the system. So there was that. It was time to go be a beat cop for awhile. Fortunately the weather was nice, so I didn't have to drape a blanket over me. Unfortunately, a new problem presented itself in that I had to visit the latrine. I sighed and cursed myself inwardly for that second cup of coffee. This wasn't going to go well.

There'd been mandates and requirements for awhile, and the city had been all pomp and circumstance when they opened the first new station in upper-middle-class suburbia with shiny facilities for everyone. However, retrofitting the old ones was going to take some time and budget, neither of which seemed to make it to where I was working. So as a workaround, my particular floor had simply renamed Mens' and Womens' to...NeoMens/Mens' and NeoWomens/Womens'. It was brilliant - and according to the budgeteering elf who took care of ordering the signage, had only cost the city twelve bucks per station house.

Which did not really solve the problem. I made my way to the bathroom and headed for the back stall, which was the only one actually wide enough for me to get into. Step one, back that butt up. Step two, raise the city-approved-for-centaurs uniform kilt over the legs and forward. Step three, reach back and lower the goods so that aiming isn't a problem, but not too low as to incur the wrath of the plumbing gods. Step four, accidentally mash the flush button with the butt and swear a bit. Step five, sigh as the first flush finishes, check to see what got damp this time. Step six, actually drain the lizard. Peruse the wall graffiti. Add another notch to the soaked berries board, wonder when the city is ever going to bother with relocating the damn flush button. Step seven, finish and step forward, shake the damp parts off before flicking the tail to get the kilt back in place, and finally gently tap the flush button again with a back hoof while contemplating if the city would relocate the damn button if I just hauled off and fired a kick through the button and into the wall.

Most likely they'd put a note in my file, put a new and sturdier button in the same place and reject the relocate idea as too expensive after an exploratory committee followed by hiring several consultants at rates that would make the most shameless con artist blush, completely ignoring the fact that my apartment was retrofitted to handle this same operation for about a hundred bucks. Thankfully this hadn't been a number two situation - it was an unwritten rule that if you had that problem, you needed to solve it by heading to the kitsch boutique three blocks away, as the station plumbing was ill-equipped to handle centaur-sized bowel movements. I reflected on small blessings in life.

As Devoin and I hit the pavement, we discussed what we could do as far as the case. Realistically, it came to "not much". The murder was in a part of town where twenty witnesses didn't see a thing, and that made it tough. Still, we had to try one more time, if only because whoever had removed the case from any visible jurisdiction.

We canvassed the building one more time, leaving our cards and stressing that we were available any time if it was important, and that there was also a line on our cards for anonymous reporting if they didn't want to have someone know what was going on. Before leaving, we took one more look at the scene.

We didn't even get to the door before we both groaned. Someone had spray-painted "G1:26" on the door. And that was all we really needed to see, to be honest. Genesis 1:26 - the biblical verse that gave man dominion over the beasts. There were variations, depending on the predominant religion of the area, but it was the same vein - the neotypes were animals because they didn't look like people. Never mind that they'd been born people and that after the first year of it hitting randomly the Neotype changes didn't happen until pubescence, the end result was that humans were supposed to be the dominant species on the planet. And their logical conclusion was what you'd expect.

Of course on the other side of the coin were the Evolutionists, Evolved, or Darwins' Chosen - fringe groups on the other side of the spectrum determined to put humans in "their place". Just as bad, and I was one of the lucky suckers in the middle. However, all of that was not material to what I was looking for. There was something here that I'd missed on the first look, and I was determined to find it.

There was more to be seen, now that the room wasn't dominated by a dead Erinyes. There was a stack of five laptops in a corner, all scorched and even partly melted. That meant something. I searched the desk carefully, leaning over and around the drawers when something shifted where it shouldn't have. A false bottom. Whoever had initially ransacked the place hadn't been looking too closely for anything. To be fair, I hadn't either. But under the false bottom was a removable drive.

The important thing was that I had it now; and I was going to be looking for someone to give it to. Evidence bag and sharpies were duly used, but the real problem was going to be figuring out who to give this to. In any case, more needed to be done, but not here.

Chapter 2

We left the building and continued on our beat. Our route took us through the downtown outdoor mall, which I'd all but confirmed was for show. Look at the forward-thinking city, with a centaur police officer walking a beat to make sure everyone's safe. On the one hand, kinda silly really, since it'd been a decade since The Event. On the other hand, there were tensions from a century ago that still hung over the world. So there was some logic to it. But that was neither here nor there. I'd gotten the job before I Changed, I could still do the job, so the city was happy to pay me. Not enough, but still enough for me to keep up with all the bills that came with being a divorced police officer with a kid.

Devoin nudged me out of my thoughts. "Hey, Earth to Brooks. Kid over there, looks hinky, yeah?"

I checked, and the kid he was referring to was a centaur, apparently freshly changed, but not exactly in a good spot as he was begging without even a cup for cash or a sign to tell anyone about his story. His hair was a wreck hanging loosely to about mid-back, tail was worse if that was possible, and I could count all his ribs from a ways off. For those curious, the total is thirty pairs. No real idea what color the coat was, but I could say it was heavily covered in about 3 layers of mud. As far as the clothes, a t-shirt that was probably white one upon a time had faded to threads and dirt. Over the back was, well, dirt.

I scrunched at Dev. "I got this. Call the socials, see if they got a spare bed for a hard luck case." And with that, I moved slowly over, staying visible the whole time and made my first reassessment. He was not a he but in fact a she, and that somehow made it worse.

She looked at me with what was a resigned fear that all the horrible things that she'd ever heard were manifest in me, and that the best case scenario was that I would be quick with whatever fate I had planned.

She swallowed a few times before her voice croaked out "Arrest me?" and held a pair of trembling arms out.

I raised my hands casually. "Hey. Ain't here to arrest you, unless you do something. Far as I can tell, you're sitting, and as far as I know there's no law against that." I settled my comparatively bulky self down, pulling out a liter of sports water and a couple of the emergency snack bars I had stashed in a side pocket. The water was half gone before I could warn her to be careful, and she promptly hurled it back up, and she started having what I'd politely call a fit of weeping and kicking at the sidewalk. Devs' hand was hovering over his taser a bit, and I waved him off.

"Alright, let's try it again, but slow sips, alright? By the way, I'm Brooks."

"R-Rebecca."

"Alright, Rebecca, I ain't gonna ask when you had your last decent meal, cause I ain't going to torture you like that. What I see, is someone eyeballing the rest of world and being afraid. So what happened?"

Rebecca's story was one I'd heard a few times in the last decade, and had read a few papers on from social workers and students. Kid changes, becomes a centaur, suddenly the food bill quadruples. Family life goes to hell as suddenly parents have to make a choice between feeding their kid and putting a roof over their head. Initially, in the massive chaos that was the Changing Times, everyone had a plan and nothing got done - which meant there were a few folks who got the short end of the stick. There were support groups of a sort, but more than a few neotypes wound up dying as a result of malnutrition and suddenly realized allergies. I was one of the luckier ones, since I had a little savings and was able to adjust. Not everyone was that fortunate.

It was a few months of absolute chaos as people realized something should actually be done, and that we really weren't going to change back, no matter what forlorn hope people had. After a few months, fewer adults began changing, and peoples' kids started changing. Finally after about six months, Changes started happening exclusively to teenagers as puberty kicked into high gear. The up side was that while the initial Changes happened over hours or days, the younger generations Changed over the course of weeks. Still not great, but more manageable - if you consider being hit by a bat swung by a Little Leaguer five times a day for a month more manageable than being hit by a bat swung by a major leaguer constantly for three days.

Overall, it went a little like this; after discovering that Little Johnny (or Jenny) was suddenly a Neotype and in several cases ruining whatever grocery budget they might have had, parents could apply for what was politely called Neo-Aid. Basically it was a kit with food and essentials (mostly painkillers and muscle ointments) to help alleviate the initial physical issues. The problem was the folks in charge of figuring out who needed what forgot to inquire with the respective neotypes as to who needed what, and so everyone pretty much got the same thing. Which did not help when Chuck Centaur received things that were designed to help Eric Erinyes. A decade later, and there was an ongoing industry online as folks would swap items they didn't need for things that did.

As an additional mitigation step, insurance companies had also stepped in with insurance policy plans. It started in Great Britain, when a company noted for insuring anything offered the royal family a policy against any additional expenditures if the latest Royal Baby became a Neotype. After that, several other insurance companies realized that there was a new revenue stream and began offering helpful plans. Well, helpful and profitable. Usually it was an additional charge for new parents who were thinking about preschool and college funds. However, there were more than a few exceptions buried in the fine print, generally limitations on the amounts paid out over the life of the policy. Overall, centaurs and dwarves were the most costly to feed and raise, and then in order erinyes, fauns, and finally elves being the least expensive. Overall, the insurance plans were a blessing for some, and a minor aid for others. And for some it was an outright scam.

Of course, for some folks even the governmental and insurance aid wasn't quite enough, so they could legally place their kids up as wards of the state. This was all well and good in theory, except that again budgets weren't infinite and the departments were overwhelmed at both local and state levels, and a waiting list developed. So to fix that problem, the option was given to simply emancipate the child, which gave them rights and responsibilities equal to any adult. All well and good in theory, until there was a realization that after the initial Event, most folks undergoing the Change were young teenagers; IE not many life skills or privileges prior to said change. Additionally, the final emancipation process took several months, by which time a family could easily be rendered destitute.

That part was politely ignored by everyone who just wanted to be able to say that there was a solution - and on top of that, the second part that was ignored was the fact that it might take up to a year for the paperwork to process. A few other solutions had been proposed and rejected over the years, as politicians realized that the solution wasn't going to miraculously fall from the sky and this was something that actually needed to be addressed. However, for the most part it was race between income and feeding a child. Feeding the kid (especially a Centaur) lost more times than anyone liked to admit, which led to a lot of young centaurs on the street. There were definitely others, as each Neotype had specific dietary needs - but it all added up to situations like the one I had in front of me.

I had a few numbers for people I could call, generally the emergency social services team. But at the same time that wasn't going to really help in the long run, and unless someone did something, wee Rebecca here was going to be in and out of the system until she turned eighteen, which did not bode well. For the most part, centaurs seemed to have their heads screwed on straight and a fairly well-defined set of morals. That said, it's easy to have morals when you have a full belly. Most of the Centaur criminal rap sheets were low-level stuff like shoplifting groceries and the occasional assault as a result of people not realizing that centaurs have a lot coming behind any kick, front or back.

At the end of the day, it meant that despite there were cases like Rebeccas', who's parents had probably tried every legal avenue before looking at six months to a year of poverty, loans, and possibly-probably losing everything before the harsh decision was made to send Rebecca out into the world to make her own way without the benefit of any legal paperwork, which ended with her starving on the street in front of a cop. From what I got, as of a month ago fifteen year old Rebecca had found herself without a home and no real skills to speak of. There seemed to be more there, but I wasn't going to pry that door open just yet. I suppressed a shiver as I remembered previous meetings that hadn't gone that well. On the up side, I had a number of people in my neighborhood I could call who owed me favors from helping them out with other problems. I went through my phone, found a number and dialed.

The ring was was answered with a gruff bass voice. "Fisticuffs, start talking." Fisticuffs was a gym in an old warehouse in Little Italy; it was a three-story affair, with the top floor being loft apartments for gym rats and employees. The second floor was equipment repair, storage, and administrative offices, while the ground floor was the gym proper, complete with a steam room, showers, and exercise equipment for everyone who wanted a workout. Paulie did brisk business for folks who wanted to sweat, and not just look good in gym clothes. The fact that it was neotype friendly was partly my doing. It was a few blocks from the Jolly Cholly, which meant I could work out and walk home. Overall that was a win for everyone.

"Paulie, s'your favorite cop needin' a solid." I forced lightheartedness that I didn't feel into my voice, and Paulie knew it.

"What, your mama finally break the pavement?" The reply was just as forced, getting the pleasantries out of the way before we got to the actual meat of the issue.

"Worse. Got a foundling needs a spot and a gig. And probably some character representation in about four-to-six months when the paperwork flows to get her emancipated." For her part, Rebecca was bracing herself for the inevitable bad news that she'd gotten used to as a constant in her life since she'd Changed.

There was a groan. "Another one? How many more of these you gonna throw at me?"

"You're just complaining because you like to complain Paulie, and you know you'da gone broke years ago without me pumping your tires to everyone. Besides, what happened to that last one I sent you?" I glanced to Rebecca who seemed to be torn between her emotions, on the one hand there was hope, and then on other hand there was what looked like either fear or shame.

"He ran out on me and went to college soon as he could. Becoming a physical therapist or something. Never calls." It wasn't entirely true - about half of Paulies' employees in the last five years had come from me or similar referrals. For the most part, they stuck around even after they reached the point where they could go out on their own.

"This one could be better. Come on, room and board for a week, tack it onto my membership if you gotta. Otherwise she's gonna starve, be in and out of the hospital, and then they'll raise your taxes to pay for it all. Save the system a dime." We both knew that a week was going to turn into a month, and then a year. But the proprieties still had to be observed.

"Brooks, you're lucky I'm a soft touch. We'll start her off as a janitor, and then we'll see if she got skills." Translation: "Get her over here as fast as you can."

"You're a prince - she'll be there in an hour, I'll be by after my shift for a quick one."

We hung up, and I nudged Rebecca gently on the shoulder. "Okay, so here's how this is gonna go. I got a friend, owns a gym. He's willing to take you in on the condition that you do some work for him after hours. Mopping up, wiping the gear down, that kinda thing. My condition is that you go back to school, we're gonna have some people coming who'll help with that. You go to school, you get educated, and you get your butt off the streets. I see you on the streets like this again, I'mma take it personal an' me and Dev here haul you to juvie and let that pile of bums deal with you. Deal?"

She nodded, and slowly sipped her water as the Social Services van arrived. They were legally required to show up, however nine times out of ten the spaces in the official state-run homes were taken, and this was one of those none. Figured. Fortunately, I'd already worked out the next step. I told them to drop her off at Fisticuffs, and that I'd be by later to check on her. I also slipped her a few snacks so she could eat something without destroying Paulies' fridge.

The rest of the day wasn't much to speak of; really it was a blur of citations and a few meet and greets; a new taco truck had made the rounds so we stopped there. Cheap but crap, and not much of it really. I was rather glad I'd filled up at breakfast - it made some people uncomfortable to see a hungry centaur. The phrase "eats like a horse" was not an idle thing - in the case of centaurs, it was gospel writ. Once I got back to the office I dialed up Forensics again, and got Ricky again, thankfully.

"S'ricky, whatcha want?"

"Ricky - Brooks again, with a hypothetical."

"Your hypothetical better be good, I got a dark ale and a hot date that you're putting me behind on, Sergeant Single Stallion - hey here's a thought you could help me, she said she had a cute centaur friend, we could double my chances of getting lucky if you came with, hey?"

I ignored the hint. "How about we answer this hypothetical, I go home and have a wheat beer, you ply your charms on the poor blind woman and strike out again and we meet up for lunch tomorrow yeah?"

"Buzzkill. Hypothetically...what?"

"Well hypothetically, there's a case that doesn't exist, and something fell from the sky into an evidence bag that looks like a removable storage of some kind."

There was silence on the line for a moment, as apparently I'd thrown poor Ricky a curveball. "Hypothetically? I wouldn't be telling anyone about it. I'd definitely make arrangements to have it fall into someone elses' hands, and I'd definitely forget I ever had anything like that. Cases stop existing for a reason. Don't get involved or you get like the case, yeah?"

"...yeah. You're a prince, Ricky."

"A prince with a hot date tonight. Have fun looking at your nonexistent thing and hoping nobody else can hear us talk."

I hung up the phone and checked the time. With everything that had happened, it wouldn't go amiss to head for Fisticuffs, have a nice solid workout, then go home, lock the drive in the gun safe, have a nice long shower followed by a good meal, and then head to the bar for some interesting discourse with some 70-proof idea generator, and maybe a snack. Quite frankly I wasn't going to eat anything at the bar - most places still didn't have a handle on what most of the Neotypes liked, so there were little niche bars just starting to crop up. Alcohol was always in style.

I still had things to do, and it was high time they started getting done. I handed my weapons into the armory, with the distinct feeling that the new Erinyes who'd signed off on the return was paying me more than a normal amount of attention. Who knew, maybe she'd never worked with a centaur before. Still, it felt weird. I made a note to catch her name if she was in the cage tomorrow as I caught a ride in a patrol van over to my van, and subsequently to Fisticuffs.

Entering the gym was like a bubble where the outside world stopped, and nice energetic music combined with iron plates to make a space where you put your body through its' paces. I'd been going to the place even before I Changed, and somewhere along the line someone decided that Paulie needed to join the neighborhood insurance program at an exorbitant rate. I had a very long talk with the insurance salesman who, after looking at a few of the previous salesmen who had visited Paulie in an attempt to convince him to join, decided that it really wasn't profitable to be in the neighborhood. A few years later, the head of the insurance company and more than a few of his lieutenants went to prison for a stretch as it was determined that what they called insurance was what the law called racketeering, extortion, fraud, and a host of other things that were decidedly not insurance.

That said, the doors were wide enough that I could walk in easily, the lighting was solid without being garish, and the equipment was both varied and easy to get to. It felt like a place where you could work up a sweat without having to watch out for people trying to pose for their social profiles or guys trying to show off to get a date. My reverie was interrupted by Paulie.

"Brooks, you godforsaken Navy puke - I got half a mind to wring your friggin neck." He knew I'd done nine years in the army, just like I knew he'd done twenty in the navy. He shifted his softened but still muscled body around the desk he was manning and smacked my lower shoulder with a gentle punch that moved me about a half-inch.

"Paulie, if I thought your Air Force arms were capable of wringing anything tougher than a mop I'd take it serious." I turned and swatted him casually with my tail. "How's y'new hire doing?"

He nodded over. "Kid's making a good impression to start off. Needs food. When I saw her condition, I mighta called Nona."

"You called Nona." I said flatly. Nona was the neighborhood Italian grandmother. She was somewhere between seventy and a hundred and seventy, knew everybody on the block, knew their parents and grandparents was friendly with most, and was a wizard in the kitchen. Her restaurant was on the other side of the street from Fisticuffs, and when the wind was right, you finished your workout fast just so you could hoof it across the street and fill up. Local legend had it that Nonas' nona had started the restaurant right before the Depression, and would feed all comers from dawn to dusk. Most of the original clients were the workers from Fisticuffs' original warehouse days. It served her well, because people didn't forget when times were better, but the tradition continued - if you needed a bowl of soup and some bread to get you through your day you could stop at Nonas', and they'd run your tab without asking. If you were smart, you did not refuse Nonas' food. If you were very smart, you paid your tab at Nonas' as soon as you got back on your feet.

Paulie waved a hand energetically. "Look at her. Kid lost 20 pounds after she showered off, and she ain't got much left. I got her a shirt at least, the socials got her a skirt for her back end."

I took a look, and with the dirt gone she looked tremendously different. Her hair and coat was actually a light blonde color, but she was moving around cleaning the equipment slowly. I could still count ribs under the official Fisticuffs employee shirt - a pair of fists punching together with broken handcuffs at the wrists - but she looked like she'd had a nap at least. Her face was screwed up with concentration as she applied a rag and cleaning solution to one of the benches.

"Point, but that just means I'mma have to do a breezeby workout, because-" the door banged open with authority as Nona made her way in with a small cart rattling behind her.

"B'cause why, Officer Arthur?" Nona was there, apron and three layers of wrinkles that told the story of a happy life with hundreds of fat children, who was about to have that family grow a little more and could not be more thrilled by the prospect.

"Because Nona, I don't want to be taking food from Rebecca." I shamelessly deflected.

Nona looked, and her gaze turned upon Paulie. "Paulito, why you got this girl workin' she so skinny she can't move!" And there was a wooden spoon in hand before anyone knew it to whack Paulie on the forehead.

"Nona! I can explain - ow - the social people dropped her off here cause Brooks here saw her on the street and they said she needed a job!" Nona had a habit of carrying the wooden spoon to smack people who had gotten out of line a little. Being smacked with the spoon didn't hurt that much, but the lectures that came with it were certainly unpleasant.

The wooden spoon was now waving in my direction. "Brooks Arthur, I'mma make you bend down so I smack you if you got no good answer in about two seconds."

I held up my hands. "Nona, she was on the street because her family couldn't afford to feed her after she Changed - I didn't want to arrest her for being on the street, I figured she could work for Paulie after school, earn a little pocket money and have a warm roof." The spoon wavered but didn't go down completely. "Nona, she needs family. I stop and look after her when I can, she learns she's got a place in the world, and...well, look at her." I pointed. "There's hope there Nona. Idle hands are the devils' playground, because now she's got something to think about other than her parents and where her next meal's coming from. Her name's Rebecca."

The spoon finally fell back into the apron pocket. "She need food. I smack you later for not sending her to me first." And with that she pushed the cart of food into the main gym, parked it and hustled her bustle over to Rebecca. I had just enough time to catch Rebecca and mouth "Nona" to her before Nona was on her in a whirl of hugs and kisses and compliments on her beautiful coat, and then came the mini-feast of Italian dishes in the employee lounge. Satisfied that Rebecca was in good hands, it was time to work out and find some form of inner peace.

I checked my workout schedule, and today was upper body day. It was going to have to be fast, since I couldn't count on Rebecca holding Nonas' attention forever. Pull-ups, sit-ups, and a few workouts heavily modified due to the whole 'your entire lower body has transformed into a horse' thing. It was going pretty well, until I was upside down and Nonas' face appeared in my field of view. Crud.

"Brooks, I think I found someone for you." This was the down side of Nona. She was a firm believer that everyone had to be married. Apparently the fact that I had been married and subsequently divorced did not sit well with her, and she was always arranging dates, brunches, and holiday parties with an eye toward getting me (and others) married. There was a complex formula in her head as far as when someone should start seeing other people again, and I had passed that particular time-frame long ago. Still, it was nice to know that someone was looking out for my dating life.

"Nona, you shouldn't have."

"It's been eight years, you need to find someone. It's not right for you to be alone." She lifted herself onto her toes briefly to poke my forehead with the Wooden Spoon of Discipline. "She's a nice girl, her mama's in my bridge club. You should at least go out with her once. She's not like that puttana you got married to." My ex-wife Ann had Changed as well, but she'd become a faun. After that, whatever it was that held us together was gone, and we both knew it. So we'd sat down with our son and explained it, filed for divorce, and I'd moved out of our two story condo and into a two-bedroom apartment above my favorite bar in Little Italy. Ann had done fairly well afterwards; she'd been a therapist before, and with the Change she began to work for the state, specializing in post-change psychology. It was a common field for fauns to be in - pretty much any field that had a lot of people contact had a dedicated faun employee base.

Unfortunately, the fact that Ann and I got along was lost on Nona, who was rather set in her beliefs - and one of those was that Ann was at fault. I sighed and extricated myself from the bench. "Nona...would it bother you if I said I'm okay with being single?"

"Yes. You're a good boy, you need to have two hearts and make your house a home."

"I have two hearts already." I pointed at my upper chest and then at my side. "So, do I get a pass?"

"No." And then she whacked my side with the spoon for being a wise guy. "Hurry up, get dressed, she's over there. Waiting for you. Lisa's a good girl, never been married. Never found the right man for her."

I sighed inwardly. Nona was an absolute master of the family ambush. Odds were good that the girl I was being set up with was also being coerced. Though on the up side, I didn't have to worry about paying for dinner tonight. I tried one last ditch effort to avoid this date that Nona had set me up on.

"I don't have anything to wear." Which was one of the weaker fibs I had at my disposal, and she knew it.

"So you stopped packing an emergency suit? Hah. I know you, you never forget to have nice clothes just in case." I'd been packing spare clothes since I was twelve and a passing bus had wrecked my shirt, pants, and chance at going to the arcade with Jennifer Gibson. She'd gone with someone else, they fell for each other, and last I'd heard, they were married with four kids.

My face fell a little, and Nona had a triumphant grin. "Come on Arthur. She's a nice girl. You'll see."

I sighed. No way out now. Unless..."Nona, what about Rebecca?"

"She's in her bed sleeping, you just stop worrying about other people and go meet Lisa." One of the blessings of Nonas' food was that it was highly filling - and if you weren't careful you would find yourself nodding off. Rebecca was not careful. One of the life lessons she was about to get in regard to Nona.

Shucks and other comments. I went back, showered, and changed into my spare set of nice clothes - specifically, my extra-long polo shirt with the 101st Airborne logo on it, a nice fitted blue kilt that got wrapped a few times to make sure that the goods were covered and remained covered, and some nice long boots that covered the hooves. Still needed to head down to the barber for a trim later, but that could wait until tomorrow.

I told myself to think positive. It was just one date, and given that it was at Nonas', I'd be able to put it on my tab. I walked across the street, contemplating all the ways this could go right (one, maybe two) and all the ways this could go wrong (infinity plus three) as I made my way in and asked the head waiter Steve to point me toward Lisa, because Nona was insistent.

I had a bad feeling about this that Steves' professionally neutral expression did nothing to ease. I'd known Steve going back to when we were in high school, and if he was trying to keep it neutral, it was not a good thing. Then we got to our table, and Lisa turned out to be an Elf. And a very solid representation of the type. Eight feet tall. Willowy. Ears that slid up to delicate points. Eyes that were large, brilliantly blue and a dainty nose framed by angular cheeks. Skin that wasn't exactly pale, but translucent. The expression that followed was rather pointed and spoke volumes about how she felt. I did not hear wedding bells. If anything, I heard the tolling of the condemned man.

"You are Brooks Arthur." Her voice was clipped and very no-nonsense. Pretty standard for Elves - whether by accident or group assent, Elves all pretty much spoke like they'd been professionally voice-trained by a monarch.

I nodded. "Lisa, I take it?"

"Yes. I'm here because my grandmother blackmailed me. I'm a librarian." She settled in with her napkin on her lap. Perhaps we were supposed to bond over our civil servant occupations.

"Here because Nona guilt-tripped me. I'm a cop." I didn't exactly have a lap due to the seating, so I basically covered my stomach with the napkin.

"You've had exactly one overdue book. Fine paid. That's good." She looked at me as if to probe for a weakness, guilty conscience, or other signs of moral weakness.

"I didn't get a chance to run your name through the system, or I'd have a witty comeback. I have a cat." I had to put that out there before we got too deep into any conversation.

The look at the mention of a cat would have frozen lava. "No need. I looked at all the books you've checked out. Single parenting, child psychology, and sports history. Nothing regarding adult relationships. Suffice to say, while I'm certain you're probably nice enough, I have no desire to pursue this beyond the required one date. I've been compared to enough ex's that I'm not interested in anything form of relationship, much to the dismay of my grandmother."

The problem with dating is that at a certain point, you're looking for the least broken toy in the second-hand store. And Lisa was broken in a lot of ways, based on that schpiel. And with that, the second date was not happening. Also, cats and Elves had some sort of war that nobody could understand and was shrugged off by both sides when others asked, as if you were asking why gravity existed. It was like a sports rivalry. I was Team Cat, and I'm pretty sure everyone on Team Elf was going to get the message by tomorrow morning.

I hmph'ed softly. "So awkward silence or meaningless small talk?"

"Meaningless small talk, I think." Essentially I was to be an interactive podcast that she listened to with dinner.

Meaningless small talk it was. That said, the food was awesome, I managed to keep my shirt clean, and Lisa was okay with a tiny salad and what looked to be two fettuccine noodles with butter and a small garnish. Apparently she enjoyed that. The small talk revolved around jobs and how things had changed. According to her, the library had finally managed to get the plumbing done for an all-types bathroom that was actually up to the task. Lucky dogs. I demurred and admitted we hadn't done anything like that at the station, but the budget was in theory going to be there for the next fiscal year. Nice enough as an individual, I suppose, but it seemed like she was determined that we not click. Which was another interesting phenomenon about Neotypes. After they Changed, they developed what the scientific-minded called "Instinctive Compatibility Sensitivity". In short, love at first sight was a very real thing with neotypes. For some it was scoffed at, until it happened. The dating industry had caught up, with a unique form of speed dating where folks would walk past each other and then back in various combinations while tapping a button or two depending on how they felt. It felt very industrial, and I was not a fan.

Of course the inverse and various shades of the spectrum were also real, which is one reason why my divorce proceeded as calmly as it did. We didn't hate each other, but it was clear that both of us were no longer the couple we were when we married. It certainly could have gone worse, as some couples suddenly realized that their partner had a very punchable face, and domestic disputes were called in. Those were the least pleasant calls, and they usually had Centaurs on scene to break those up.

Finally I picked up the check, and we left.

"I'll tell Nona thanks." I shook her hand politely.

She tilted her head slightly, nodding. "I will tell my grandmother that you were pleasant enough but not a spark."

Good enough. I did make sure she got to her car okay before hopping back across the street to where I'd parked my car.

The short drive home was a head-clearing thing. On the up side, I'd done my job. On the down side, Nona didn't seem to understand my whole perspective on dating. I'd done it, I thought that it'd work, but reality and time had decided otherwise. It's not like I didn't want to date, but my headspace was crowded with the more basic day to day. And frankly, being a cop was rough on the best days. It didn't seem right for me to bring someone else into it. Even another cop, because at that point you not only had your day, you also had to worry about someone elses'. Maybe I'd get married again after I retired.

Besides, I still had Max to keep me company. I popped the door, and the fluffball sauntered in long enough to sniff and then go directly to the couch.

"You stink of Elf. Go shower."

"Max, what the heck? Yes, I had dinner with an Elf, is that a crime?"

"It should be." He curled up in a ball with his tail covering his nose.

"And some day you're going to explain the problem with Elves." I cracked open a can of food and supplemented it with some crunchies in a bowl.

"We had a meeting." Max attended to some imaginary fluff on his back leg before washing it.

"And?"

"Elves are out. There's only enough room on this planet for one hyper-arrogant species and we were here first."

"Suck it up furball. She wasn't arrogant, she was a librarian."

"Second date?"

"Not happening." I grimaced, thinking about it.

"At least you were that smart." Thus placated, he wound around me and went to the the food dish. I went for the bourbon. A decent tumbler of that over ice and I was in for the night. Max was blissfully silent. In all likelihood, he thought he was punishing me for going out to dinner with an Elf.

The next morning was pretty well arranged. It started off with a call from my boss reminding me to bring the nice clothes, as I was scheduled for a pair of school visits for today.

I hated school visits. It was pretty much the same thing. A crowded auditorium of children who were, depending on their age, either more interested in recess or ditching class while I droned through a few canned scripts about the police, diversity, and how being a Neotype is improving. I mean it is, but at the same time the approved verbiage was so dry it desiccated the index cards it was written on.

Still, it was a nice change of pace from the usual day. Commute in, park it a little ways away, and then to the desk to see if anything new came in. Nothing new there, so it was time to get pretty for everyone and then to the back of Devoins' pickup for the ride in. The down side of it all was, well, walking through the station. Since the formal uniform was a rare thing, the folks in charge of designing it felt like it needed to show off the fact that centaurs were by and large a muscular folk. The back half was far more snug than I liked and left my forelegs uncovered. To top it all off, the top was wide in the shoulders, snug at the waist, and had splashes of color in the form of several service medals for various things I'd been a part of. The worst part of the whole thing was that there was absolutely no place to stash snacks without ruining the lines. After being inspected by the captain, I had to head downstairs past the bullpen where everyone congregated to see Devoin and me off. It was filled with wolf-whistles, catcalls, and sisters' phone numbers as I cheerfully flipped a few of them off as I left.

Yeah. If there ever was a time when I needed that, it was never. Especially after that date last night. Still, it felt awkward and I glanced around, seeing the new girl - an Erinyes had just been assigned to the armory; she was staring at me in a way that was odd - she was cheering and clapping along with everyone else, but at the same time she was looking at me like she was sizing me up for a fight. There was a flutter somewhere, and I shook it off as nerves from having to look forward to riding in the back of a truck. I glanced back and she was not there, which did not put my mind at ease.

Devoin was similarly attired, but he wasn't subjected to the same level of scrutiny as me for some reason. Quite possibly because he was a bit soft around the middle, but still. I did not like the attention. I mean, I just did my job, helped a few folks where I could, but somehow I'd gotten to where I was the go-to for any public appearances where a Neotype was requested or required for whatever reason. It felt like being the department show pony. Literally, in my case.

The ride was annoying, and my shoes were slightly scuffed but still theoretically serviceable. But not for me. I grabbed a cloth and buffed all four quickly before heading into the auditorium, where a bunch of teenagers sat with various calculated expressions of boredom.

As the principal stood up and told everyone to settle down, I scanned the auditorium and found the crowd pretty well separated out - Elves in the upper corner so they wouldn't block anyone out, fauns in the other upper corner so they could scatter and quite probably cut class as soon as the boring stuff was done, and centaurs up front as a practical matter. Top center were the Erinyes, who'd likely flown up there because they could. And in the midst of it, the half that hadn't changed. There weren't any dwarves, because quite simply after dwarves changed they acquired some sort of educational booster that made traditional school impossible. Instead, they went to specialized dwarf-only schools that had a curriculum on par with the top-end engineering and science colleges, with a lot of hard science with a few humanities and morals classes to ground them and remind them that science without moral boundaries can and does backfire in epic fashion.

I took a breath, looked at the index cards one last time before stashing them as the principal called out various students who'd distinguished themselves with their community service (oddly, all of them were unchanged) before turning the microphone to me. I looked down at the cards I was supposed to read from, looked back up and then I went totally off-script.

"So, again I'm officer Arthur Brooks, and I'm supposed to be following up your principal with congratulating you all on what you and your classmates have accomplished, but I'm not gonna lie, reading that almost put me to sleep, and if there's things you don't want to see, it's a centaur face-planting out of boredom. So with that in mind, I want everyone to get up and mix it up a little." I pointed at the fauns "and I see you getting ready to cut out early - c'mon, group experiment." They slowly reshuffled, but were confused as they tried to keep their collective distance. Eventually they'd mixed it up as best they were able to. Not great, but good enough for the point I was aiming for.

"So it's rough, yeah? The idea here is to not only get yourselves educated, but to get acquainted with each other; find groups you like, find common interests. I came in here, and I saw everyone in their own little knots. That's nice, but once in awhile, you're going to have to venture outside your groups and bubbles. Because some things you can't do yourself, and none of your normal group's going to be able to really help because you're always seeing things from the same perspective. So now that you're all thoroughly uncomfortable, it's time for fair play. We've got about twenty minutes, and the floor's open for questions. To me. I do however reserve the right to not answer any questions about my personal life and-or physique, so all of you who were thinking about asking that question, find out online."

There were a few snickers and points. Teenagers never change.

Finally there was a hand that came up from one of the fauns and I pointed at them.

"So, like, how do you wipe your butt?"

There was general laughter, and once it quieted down I answered; "Toilet paper." A few more laughs, but then I raised my hand up. "Okay, it does require a bit more of a sideways bend, but it's kinda like this." I reached back, twisted, and shimmied a bit to demonstrate. They were impressed, I suppose. Although the chorus of oh's could have been for a completely different reason.

Another faun stood up with a question I got far too often - even at work. "Boxers, briefs or boxer-briefs?"

"That's a go ask online question. Nice try though." I smirked, and there was a low wave of laughter through the auditorium.

An Elf stood up and raised his hand with a question for Devoin; interesting. "Does it feel at all awkward knowing that your partner is more capable than you in most respects?"

Oh wow, that was a harsh assessment. Very Elf-like, though. For some reason, their whole ethereal nature post-Change made them pivot straight to a highly developed sense of superiority. To be fair, they did seem to have a lot of advantages - they were analysts par excellence, which made them highly sought after for management positions, as well as frighteningly good chess players. The international governing body for chess had created a whole new division after a kerfuffle. There'd been a few studies on Neotypes, and it seemed like if you changed, the type was at least partly based on your personality pre-change. Which made for a sticky situation, as stereotyping was technically forbidden. That said, if a faun and a centaur were the suspects in a criminal investigation, I'd confidently lay a box of donuts on it being the faun and be right nine times out of ten. Centaurs seemed to have a core of honesty or honor or valor or whatever it was that made them adverse to criminal activity, while fauns were more morally flexible. To Devoins' credit, he grinned a little at the question.

"Well, y'first off, I've known Officer Arthur here since before he Changed. He's always been a bit ahead of the curve. See, before he was a cop, the army paid him to jump out of airplanes and do things once he landed. So for him, going to being a police officer was easy. He was the guy that we talked about at the academy as someone who'd make a damn fine chief if he got the chance. The fact that he's a Centaur don't change the fact that he's a good person. Centaur. So if it's uh, weird, it's only weird 'cause everybody wants to make it weird, ya know? And if I ever do feel jealous, I remember that he had to relearn how to wipe his butt."

The elf cocked his head oddly, seemingly unsatisfied by the answer but too polite to pursue the matter further. Finally, the question I was expecting and dreading came up; it was from a severe looking young man who was as close to dead-center as you could get.

"With the rising rates of crime committed by neotypes, do you think the proposal for homogeneous areas is a viable solution?" And the way he said 'neotypes' was rather similar to how you could imagine a nobleman of the Middle Ages say 'peasant' or 'serf'.

It was something I'd seen a few times on the news - one of the state senators had made a grand proposal whereby all neotypes would be compensated and relocated to purpose-built areas where they could live, socialize, and frolic among what was politely termed Hz's, short for Homogeneous Neotype Zones. Said senator was very much a friend of the Genesis-type organizations.

"Short answer; no. Long answer goes a little something like this; statistically, overall crime rates have remained about the same for a few years, even going down for certain classifications, and as neotypes like myself and your classmates become a greater percentage of the population, the amount of crimes committed by neotypes will naturally increase. We're not all saints in this big beautiful world we have. So, as the numbers of neotypes grow, that does mean a greater number of crimes by neotypes, and indeed they become a greater percentage of the whole, but those numbers as a whole are going down."

The young man persisted a bit. "But the rate of crimes committed by neotypes are going up annually. Wouldn't you agree that something needs to be done and that the Neotypes would be more likely to act within the bounds of law if they were in a zone where everyone they saw was a familiar shape?"

I held up a hand. "The crime rates are an excuse. A bad one, if you look at it in any depth. I assume they teach history in this school?"

The questioner looked a little awkward, but nodded. "There's a few things that keep coming up throughout history if you look at them. One of the big ones is that when you try to create a homogeneous enclave of a group, that group suffers. Whether by inattention or more unkind intentions, the group suffers. I'm sure your question is well-meant, but history teaches us the answer, and the answer is not in a camp, ghetto, or gulag with a pretty name like Homogeneous Neotype Zone. And in truth, the proposal doesn't address long-term concerns, which makes me personally suspicious of what the honorable senators' answer to that would be. If you think back a bit to when we first started this, that was part of the reason I asked you to mix it up a little. High schools where we learn to get along or segregate along whatever imaginary or not-imaginary lines there are. The alternative is that we congregate, talk, and learn that someone's a schmuck because they're a schmuck and not just because they're an Erinyes, Dwarf, or what have you." I checked my watch. "And on that bleh note, I've got time for one more question."

One of the Erinyes fluttered up; "What's your phone number, our math teacher likes officers." Oh good, a silly question to wrap. I rattled off all the general numbers to the department, took a look around, and headed for the exit with Devoin.

I hopped into the truck bed carefully, as our next stop was for lunch and a check to see how long it would take to our next appointment. Devoin started it up and we were just out of the parking lot when he floored it and laid on the horn. I got thrown to the back, with a little yelp. Devoin opened the window and passed me the bubble light they gave us as a just-in-case.

"Sorry, they just called us - armed robbery in progress, we're about a minute away. Hold on to your butt, we're making a hard right in about 3 seconds." Devoins' driving left a lot to be desired, as he turned hard right at a speed much faster than was recommended by any manual. Even with me as far to the right as I could get, the tires lifted off the pavement for a moment before slamming down hard onto the pavement with a protest at the abuse. After all four tires were in fact on the ground, I passed Devoin his belt with weapons and cuffs from the storage box, and snagged my own because this was definitely not a school visit with uncomfortable questions and snickering fauns.

We were hauling up to what was one of the odder things I'd seen - Three people total, two robbers and one guy at the wheel. The car itself was tagged up with a few gang markings from the west side of town, which was odd given that we were not on the west side. The driver - a faun - had apparently flooded the engine and was trying desperately to get it started again. Bad luck for them that we were here. I jumped out the back as Devoin was parking to cut them off and landed in the proper location for such things; basically I was sideways to him with my gun out and pointed toward the pavement. The theory was that my side would have protection for myself and my partner. Not the case at the moment, but it was a bit too late to hide.

I waved my hand a little to get the attention of the driver; he was wild-eyed and his hair was flowing colors of red and black, neither of which were particularly good. One of the things that made it easy to interrogate a faun was that their hair color shifted with their mood. Some fauns had learned to control it, but for the most part it was as automatic as breathing. Devoin was holding behind the drivers' side door to tackle anyone who went that way, while I covered the passenger side.

In case it was at all unclear, I barked it out; "Police, out NOW!"

One of the people in the back wrenched their partner closer, and I realized there was a knife at the partners' throat. Oh good, a hostage situation. Just like mom used to make. I took a breath to reassess what was happening. A wrong move and I was going to be grilled for weeks while dealing with the fact that I'd failed. Meanwhile, the fauns' hair went full disco inferno, cycling through the rainbow and never settling - he was freaked out. Given the situation, I'd say he was right to be freaking out. Still, I had to focus on Knife Guy.

"Hey, roll down the window so we can talk. Doesn't need to be far, but I need to talk and I need to listen. You're already in a bad spot, don't make it worse. So far I see kidnapping, and the radio says armed robbery. So roll it down and we'll talk."

He spewed invective at me before rolling down the window. "You're stalling so you can shoot me or so someone else can shoot me! No moves or she dies!"

He wasn't wrong about the stalling part; we were definitely not ready for a hostage situation at this point, but if Devoin was doing his part, he was calling for backup with a negotiator in tow. Hopefully one was around.

"Okay, I'm not going to shoot you unless I got no other choice. Right now I got a choice, and I'm choosing to holster." I slammed the pistol into its' holster to make sure he heard it. "Now, you got a choice. Come on, you know what's coming next. More people show up, and then you're going to be surrounded. You open the door, let her go, I'll say you were cooperative after realizing the situation, and you get a plea deal. You do some months, do some probation, life goes on. Hey, if you're clean up until now, maybe the DA has a heart and realizes you got a life ahead of you - you just get probation, fines, community service. But the longer she's there, the worse this gets. You get stabby, I got no choice but to yank the door off and yank you out. You might get hurt, bad. You saw that one video, right? Drunk guy tried throwing down with a Centaur and got his shoulder dislocated for his trouble. Clock's ticking on your chance to get out of this nice and neat." There were hundreds of videos like that, mostly under the "stupid people doing stupid things" category. Knife guy thought about it for a moment and then made his move. He shoved the hostage down to the seat and got out the drivers side, where Devoin got a nice shot off with his stunner, leaving the poor guy not having a good day. Meanwhile, the faun tried getting out the passenger side and bolted down the sidewalk.

Mistake. Fauns are fast, but they only have the two legs. I started a slow gallop, and in less than a block I had him by the scruff of his neck and was walking him back to the scene. Once cuffed, I sat him on the curb next to to Devoins' truck when the backup arrived. He did not attempt to run again. All the workouts at Fisticuffs were doing some good apparently, as I wasn't even breathing hard after that.

Devoin was in a good mood as the flashing lights and sirens arrived. "Oh look, they missed all the fun. How's our hostage?" Devoin nodded to the sidewalk, where the lady was sitting cross-legged with a foam container of something warm. She was shaking slightly, and her eyes were unfocused as she was quite possibly trying to make sense of what just happened and considered all the ways it could have gone poorly. I handed the faun off to Devoin before settling down next to her and psyching myself up for The Wraparound.

This was an odd but recommended procedure from the department shrinks as well as a few case studies from independent psychologists with more letters after their name than in it - according to them, folks (even most neotypes) felt comforted by the presence of a centaur-shaped blanket. Which had its' ups and downs. The up side was that we could help people and not have to worry about anything except the occasional allergic reaction. Yes, some people were actually allergic to neotypes. The down side, for me at least, was settling and having close contact with people. I don't know how the others did it.

Still, duty called - and I felt a momentary sensation of being watched as I did so. I settled slowly to my stomach before talking to her. "Hey, I'm Brooks. You allergic to anything?" After a beat, she slowly shook her head, and I assumed the position, hoping that the ambulance would get here quickly. "Look, I'm sorry I wasn't able to get things sorted faster for you, but I needed to say what I said. We have to give people in these situations an out, otherwise it gets worse fast. I wasn't trying to be nice to him for his sake, I was being nice to him for yours."

After all that, she was very silent. I was completely on board with this. and then she stopped being silent and started bawling into my lower shoulder. It was nice while it lasted, and it wasn't the first time I'd gotten some full on snot-rocket wailing into my shoulder. Still, expecting it to happen didn't make it easier, and I'd learned that more talking was not necessary. I flicked my tail a bit to get around her, and let her just cry. A lot. The problem was during this was that I couldn't really move much. And currently, there was a loose piece of gravel digging into my butt.

Finally the ambulance arrived and she was helped into the back to get checked for any potential serious injuries. I handed one of the medics my card after giving a quick rundown of what happened and possible injuries she might have, and then it was time to clean up as best we could and head for our second destination, a small elementary school. And we hadn't even stopped for lunch. To make things worse, if Devoin tapping his finger against his wrist could be believed we were not going to get to stop for anything of substance. Fast food it was, and since I was paying we hit Chargers, a nice place that had more than a few Centaur-specific item. I opted for the spicy tofu wrap with ranch in a quinoa wrap with a chocolate power-shake. That would at least get me through the rest of the day, since the shake itself was a blend of yogurt, several eggs, chocolate, and just enough milk to get it through a straw, and their advertisements guaranteed it would put pounds on anyone who wasn't a centaur. It was popular with the gym rats and Centaurs.

We finished just in time to park and complete a last-minute dusting of our respective uniforms. We were properly shiny and clean for the most part, and then get ourselves into a gym full of elementary children. It was a similar pomp and circumstance thing, the principal calling down half a dozen children to receive awards for doing nice things for the neighborhood, and then a slightly more raucous bunch of questions. A few girls who were definitely in their sparkly unicorns and rainbows phase wanted to touch my fur and oooh'ed about how it was so fluffy and soft, and then it ended with several of them using me as a jungle gym and me sinking to the floor as about forty seven-year olds tackled me to the gym floor. I resigned myself to the whims of fate and children, as keeping the little balls of energy still for any length of time was a miracle in itself. This was the sort of thing might keep them well-behaved for the rest of the afternoon. Or the rest of the afternoon would be shot as they talked about it. Finally order was restored, with two of the unicorns and rainbows girls having to be bodily removed from my legs. I talked to their teachers and was able to get permission to give them a ride back to their classes.

Devoin was smirking a bit as the two girls were giggling and shrieking at a very unholy volume as we went through hallways that were vaguely claustrophobic but still manageable. Apparently that was in fact the best day ever for them. Still, for me it was exhausting. Time to get back to the station, change into something less gaudy, tap keys for a few minutes about the whole armed robbery thing that wrecked my chance at a decent lunch, then gym and home. Unfortunately, this meant another round of whistles and cheers of admiration, because I was not allowed to write reports from home.

Having to choose which situation was worse was difficult. It was a coin flip between the seven year olds and this. I hated having to do these reports, because there was always someone who wanted to play armchair coach about two months down the line and that's when I remembered things that I hadn't noted at the time. So, I had to write the whole mess down as quickly as I could while ignoring the itchy sensation of being watched as I headed to the armory to turn in my gear and head to the lockers to change.

Once in something a little more decent, I settled at my bench and started typing and checking email, and also checking the local news feeds for anything interesting. Which was bad news, as Devoin and I had made the local newscast as hostage situation defusers. The hostage was interviewed while being treated for minor scrapes and had nothing bad to say about me or Devoin. This meant we'd probably have to do a followup visit for the cameras later.

Crap.

I hammered through the report and was going to try to get out when my terminal pinged out a message. I checked the message, and it was the captain wanting some time with yours truly to discuss recent events.

Double-crap. And then the phone rang.

I grabbed the receiver and immediately had a full-volume roar in my ear that lasted for thirty seconds before it ended by being summoned to the captains' office chop-chop and forthwith. Well, this day was just turning out to be a pile of nope with a need for Nonas' alfredo at the end of it. I took a breath, finished up my report because I had been previously advised that completing the report was job one, and then closed it out for the day. Plus, it was a legitimate reason to make the captain wait for a minute. I chalked it up as a small victory.

Heading to the captains' office on the third floor was a pain in the neck, because the stairwells still hadn't been fully widened to allow someone coming one direction and a centaur going in the other. So I had to pretty much announce my presence and direction at every floor while heading up.

Once I got to the captains' floor where all the administrative and executive folks were cheerfully stashed with their nice chairs and views, I was not in a good mood. It didn't help that the third floor had been fully renovated to allow the elves in the executive branch space to walk freely, while the centaurs who were mostly the grunts and low-end folks had to make do with non-functioning elevators and a bathroom that more theoretical than functional. Still, once I got through processing the emotional unfairness - I was still in a bad mood.

I found the captains' office, and he was politely on the phone lining up a golf game with someone for tomorrow. Once that wrapped up, he pointed to a human-styled-and-sized chair.

"Take a seat, Brooks." Apparently he didn't have time to remember that I was not human-styled-or-sized, or he was playing a power game as Elves were occasionally wont to. Most likely the latter. In addition to this, his voice was sailing from his standard Elven accent (which sounded like a genteel Belgian) to something much more akin to his pre-Change voice (a dockworkers' growl). Whatever I'd done, it was not good.

"I'll stand, thanks. Got no need to damage city property at the moment." Of course, as I said that I kicked the chair to a corner with a front hoof, then backed up a step to close the door casually with my rear hoof. Finally, I was ready to be chewed out for whatever sins I had committed. More than likely it was getting something dirty.

"Officer Arthur. I received a call from a high school principal today, praising your honesty and intelligent handling of questions from the students. I did tell her that we would have a discussion about it. This is that discussion. You went off-message. That message was vetted and approved by our public affairs group. You were not to deviate from that message. Was this somehow unclear?" He ran an immaculate hand through silver-blonde hair that was disgustingly perfect. I wondered if everyone else could call a meeting like the cats had before I reminded myself that elves were outstanding in their fields. The problem was they didn't hesitate to remind the rest of the planet of that.

"The message was boring. If we want to be heard, we need to engage."

"Ah, so we should re-write policy because it's boring?" He stood up to his full eight and a half feet of twigs and translucence, his brilliant blue eyes looking down on me with a scowl. "The only reason you're not being given a three day suspension is this." He pointed at the newscast, where the chief of police was holding a hastily put-together press conference with half a dozen reporters, praising Devoin and me and shoveling departmental praise on us both. "Congratulations, you're a good officer. Good enough that you and your partner are going to have lunch with the chief tomorrow and have a commendation awarded. You'll be in full dress tomorrow, show up on time and smile for the cameras. You'll get the menu tomorrow morning. Don't go overboard."

"Cap'n, permission to ask what the heck this is all about?"

He sighed as someone burdened with simple-minded fools sighs, finally regaining control of his voice to it's normal natural unnatural timbre. "This is another incident we can use to reflect well on the department, so that we can get some additional budget that we need in order to continue the retrofits that we've been working on for a while. Maybe if we get enough, we can get the Barn bathroom upgraded. Smile for the cameras, do not go off-script, mention how proud you are of your partner and your department, and do not under any circumstances play cowboy like you did today at that high school. And make sure you're presentable."

"Does that mean I can get out of here early and drop my uniform at the dry cleaners?" I was pretty sure I was pushing my luck on this one, but he probably wanted me out of the building, and I needed to get out of this place and get to taking care of the other important things - specifically, the cat, and also checking on Rebecca.

"Yes. Dismissed, Brooks." He did in fact want me out, as he was already turning his attention to his paperwork before I'd even gotten the door open.

As I left and went down the stairwell, several thoughts ran through my head. One, there was no way I could get my currently dirty as heck uniform cleaned by tomorrow without asking for a favor from someone. And in my world, that meant asking Nona. Which meant I was going to have to go on another date with someone from her bridge-knitting-cooking club. Nothing for it, really. I grabbed my phone and called. Nona picked up on the first ring.

"Officer Arthur! You big hero, you're all over the local news."

"I know Nona, but I need a favor. See, I'm having lunch with the important folks tomorrow and I got my uniform messed up. You know someone who can dry-clean it real fast while I go to Fisticuffs and talk to Rebecca and maybe work out?"

"Oooh, of course - how'd the date work out?"

"Nona - she's a nice girl like you said, but we're not seeing the world the same way. I'm sure she'll make a fine wife for someone, just not me." I couldn't come right out and say it was a train wreck, plus Lisa's grandmother knew Nona. Polite was the best route.

"Ohhh, I'm sorry Brooks. You need a wife though, you can't go through life with just your boy and your cat, you need a wife." The hardest part of all these dates was telling Nona. For some reason she kept thinking that I'd find the right woman if she just kept introducing me to them. She's probably seen a couple fall under the effects of the instinctive compatibility, and decided to help me out to get things rolling in what she considered the proper direction. The problem as she saw it was me, in that I did not see many people outside of my routine. The solution was obviously to bring in more people. I for one, greatly preferred my routine.

"I know Nona, and maybe I'll have a wife again someday, just not today." It was time to be optimistically neutral while I was walking through the station to the Barn to grab the rest of my stuff, waving off everyone who wanted to congratulate me by smacking my shoulder and in one case, my rear. I turned to eye whoever did that, but that didn't exactly work well, as the phantom butt-smacker had disappeared and nobody was going to fess up. Alas.

"I'll keep looking." And that was the most ominous thing said to me all day.

"I know you will. I'll bring my uniform by in a few minutes, I'm leaving for Fisticuffs now."

"Of course, we'll get you neat and tidy."

Chapter 3

Well, at least I had that going for me. I stuffed everything into my travel bag and booked it to my van, where again I headed for Fisticuffs. Still, I felt watched. Something was really not right. I even checked and looked up for any Erinyes on a payroll or just gliding. Nada, but the feeling never went away. Still, I felt better as I got toward the unofficial border to Little Italy and wheeled the van into a nice easy to walk from parking spot where I gathered my uniform up and went to Nonas'. Nona bustled and snagged my uniform, and I gave her a kiss on the cheek for her trouble, and I promised I'd be on time for the next date she set up. Then I headed across the street to work out. I'd had quite enough of the world and I needed Leg Day.

What I got was a near tackle from Rebecca as she blindsided me, hard. Her emancipation paperwork had been pushed through, probably as a result of several people in Nonas' bridge club making calls. Nona herself had been feeding her, and well, she was a growing kid. Still, her clothes fit better and she carried herself a bit taller than she did yesterday. It was interesting as she ran her mouth about a mile a minute and talked about anything and everything - except her family. That was probably going to be a sore spot for the rest of her life, and I made a note to check with the department shrink to see what sort of plan we could pull together. Heaven knows we didn't need another juvenile delinquent because the world couldn't figure out what to do with folks who Changed and suddenly couldn't afford to eat enough and eventually became a bigger problem. Mostly it was Centaurs, because the body changes were frankly ridiculous, but it was an issue for everyone. Still, I managed to get everything together, get a solid workout in, and shower off before Nona's friend at the dry-cleaner got everything together and I left the gym with a freshly pressed uniform and a good feeling about the world. From there, I had a plan. Go home, have a beer, settle in and contemplate if I could come up with an idea to help keep kids like Rebecca from making bad life choices in the face of worse life choices.

That plan was shot the moment I saw the scarlet-haired faun that until recently had been my wife. Okay, it'd been seven years since the divorce was finalized and about eight since we'd started it. Along with her was a familiar adolescent, who was apparently getting the stocky build of a dwarf standing at my door. I braced myself, since normally we would do the custody exchanges at one of a few parks in the area. In addition, it was not my weekend for such things. She looked at me with exceptional impatience before motioning to the dwarf.

"Jeremiah just started to Change this morning, you take care of him. I have a new job." Well. That took me back a few years, specifically to the time where we'd just Changed. Ann had actually Changed first, but her body alterations were not nearly as severe as mine - that said, her personality altered a bit. It was like becoming a faun ignited some part of her that thought I was holding her back. Or it was a part of her that'd been repressed for some time and finally came out. In any event, it took about six months for the dust to settle, and while it wasn't bad, it was still a divorce.

"Hello to you too Ann. Nice hair." Which was a polite way of letting her know I was paying attention.

"It's Aoife, now. It's natural." One of the other things that seemed to be happening, within a few years of people changing, there seemed to be a trend of changing their name, whether legally or just going by something else. In Ann's case, it was probably going to be legal, because as much as she changed directions, jobs, and everything else, when she was committed to something she committed.

"I write the child support checks to Ann, and you seem to cash them just fine." I couldn't say much else about it in front of Jeremiah, since we'd both agreed a long time ago that arguing in front of Jeremiah was a bad idea.

She rolled her eyes and walked away, calling over her shoulder, "It goes through next week - I'm already late, he hasn't had dinner so make something good." Her hair color fluttered from scarlet to a green as she left. According to the general guide to faun mood hair, it meant she was going from angry to relaxed. On the one hand this was a good thing, since she probably wasn't going to start throwing random objects from her purse at me. On the other hand, it wasn't a great thing, since she'd basically just volunteered me as the solution to her problem. That said, her problems were probably fairly severe if she was going to the extreme level of "Get Help From Brooks."

Which left me looking at my son, Jeremiah - his phenotype was showing itself. I didn't quite have the heart to tell him he was going to be shrinking soon. Seventeen was bad enough. The scientists had an explanation, something about how two neotypes would produce a neotype child with near-certainty, but the exact direction was random to a point - the natural tendencies and personality of the child came into play. His mother had been granted custody due in no small part to my schedule and job, but her job was full of late hours that didn't quite balance. And now he just got dumped on me because reasons.

She'd become flighty after her change, but this was something new. I unlocked the door, ushering Jeremiah inside. He hadn't said a word so far, which wasn't reassuring. On the up side, I'd gone shopping. Down side, I hadn't expected a weekend with Jeremiah for a couple weeks. I'd gone shopping for only me, which meant I only had energy bars and trail mix snacks to tide him over while I scrounged something together that would suit both us. I tossed my jacket on the table, went to the kitchen and started rummaging through, calling out to him while trying to remember just what the heck a Dwarf wanted or needed to eat.

"Hey whatcha feel like eating champ?" Probably the best way to start really - engage and then we can figure out what the heck was going on. Hopefully he'd clue me in on where his mother was at in her head.

His voice was muffled. "Whatever." Or not.

"Going once, champ." I backed out of the kitchen a little to look at what he was up to.

His voice was still muffled, and it sounded like he was digging around for something. "What-eveeerrr."

"Zucchini parmesan it is. Greek yogurt and lingonberries for dessert?" Not exactly my go-to, but it was relatively easy and filling. For me anyway. And he did like it. Or he had before, so it was a start point to see if old favorites were still favorites, or if we needed something totally new.

There was a long silence. "Uh...Dad? Could we maybe, uh...uhm...meat?" Finally, getting somewhere - my diet was going to have to change, or I was going to have to be a decent cook and make two meals at once.

"What?" Among the responses I expected was not an entire food group.

"Like, I'm. My, I'm..." His voice faltered and I found him behind my computer desk, re-cabling everything. "I'm eating a lot more meat." He blushed. "Mom said she couldn't really afford...she, and...stuff." His voice taking on the lower tones of 'I'm not crying' before he finally stopped and went back to rearranging the cables. Something that didn't get mentioned for the adolescent Changed - their diets started shifting about a week before the actual Change kicked in, sort of like the body was preparing itself for a new form. I for one had completely forgotten about it - mainly because I'd been hit in the early going.

"Hey, we can order in. Just be careful back there, and we'll go grocery shopping tomorrow." It sounded like the budget was about to get its' proverbial teeth kicked in.

He sounded relieved that I wasn't going to yell at him. "Thanks Dad."

I was picking up the phone to call the local pizza takeout joint when I heard a voice in my head. "The hell is that racket? I need my beauty sleep and you don't have a date tonight. Feed me and I'll forgive you."

I called down the hall. "Max, get out here if you want to get fed - Jeremiah's staying with us for awhile."

The tortoise-colored cat sauntered out; well, as much as a 25-pound feline could saunter. "I don't remember approving this."

"You get veto power when you start paying bills. Until then, your powers in this home are limited to being a solar-powered telepath and converting gooshy food into poop."

"You people are weird. You can't just pay me for being me? Ungrateful minion." Max stopped and stared at Jeremiah for a long time before a little trill escaped. "He passes. Also, he's scared."

"He's my son, of course he passes - because the other option is I hand you to Ann. Side note, she changed her name to Aoife. Curious, why's he scared?"

"Scared of a lot of things. He's turning into a dwarf, he doesn't know what that means, he's scared you're going to get tired of his meat-eating ways and kick him out in a week, scared he's not going to get a date at the next dance, scared that people are going to laugh at him because he's probably done growing." There was a pause. "It sounds like Aoife was in some serious money trouble. She was playing bill roulette even before he started changing, and it sounded like things were catching up in a bad way."

That was odd - Aoife may have been a few things, but she was usually good about the bills. "Well, I guess we're doing a meat-lovers pizza and a Sentahr Special, yeah?" I grabbed the phone and started dialing. Slowly, in case Jere had any second thoughts. Also, I absolutely hated the intentional misspelling.

Max sneezed by way of response, and there was silence. The lessons of an infant and partial custody came to the fore; when a kid is quiet, they're probably doing something they shouldn't. A low-tenor yelp from the living room confirmed my suspicions.

I scrambled with my taser out and looking for targets - nothing was there, but Jeremiah was typing furiously on my computer. And he was talking to himself; he was definitely not in a good place, which got worse when I saw he'd attached the removable drive. It took him a few moments before he looked up and started the I'm-not-crying as he yanked the cable.

"M'sorryDaditwasthereandIthoughtIcouldIcouldIcould   do something and I thought thought thought that it wasn't important but it said 'Unauthorized' and then it said 'data destruction in progress' and I stopped it from doing that and then then I shut it all down I'm sorry I didn't meantooooooo" - and then the rest of it was a snot-bubbling mess of a kid who'd gotten his hand caught in the cookie jar. It was weird, in a few ways. I mean it was just a computer. Granted it was my only laptop, but at the same time he acted like he'd taken the crown jewels out to practice juggling.

I sighed and put the taser away. "Jere, you're not in trouble. You're not in the clear, because you touched something that wasn't yours without asking. You meant good, but you did it wrong. Which means I'mma have to think about what I'm gonna do, and what I'm gonna tell your mom."

There was a flash of anger from him for a moment, but he didn't say anything. I cocked an eyebrow at him and continued.

"But the first thing you're going to do is make sure you didn't break my computer. Then, no computer for the rest of the night - you got school tomorrow, and you're not missing it. We're gonna talk and watch something goofy."

Max trilled in a bit; "Good job. I'll give you an eight out of ten."

"Thanks for the vote of confidence." I grabbed a box of tissues from the bathroom and set them down next to Jeremiah. He was silent for a time, and then took several to blow his nose. Finally he looked over at me.

"I like your cat." It was a start, at least. Jeremiah had known Max for awhile, so he was kind of stating the obvious, but he was talking.

"Max? Yeah, he's good people, if a little lazy and indignant."

In response, Max launched himself at my flank and started kneading in preparation for a mock attack. "I am not people."

"Close enough." Messing with Max was a bit of light entertainment that the world needed at the moment, which Max was able to pick up on, as he launched himself onto my foreleg and began to swat relentlessly without his claws. I took the break to glance at Jeremiah. "So before you get too deep into the laptop, I was in the midst of ordering pizza. You still good for that?"

"Ya-huh."

"Good. Get to fixing, I know you can."

Jeremiah smiled weakly and nodded, booting it up and typing things for awhile. Satisfied that he wasn't going to touch the removable drive, I found a beer and relaxed for the first time in several hours. Finally the door rang for pizza, and Max bolted to the door, highly enthused about the prospect of getting whatever was left over. I paid and brought in two boxes as Jeremiah was shutting down, looking relieved.

"Not ruined?"

"Not ruined." Jeremiahs' nose twitched a little. "But I had to do some stuff."

"Like?"

He started speaking another language. I blinked and held up a hand. "Uhm, could you repeat that in English?"

"That was English, Dad."

"Not to me."

"Ah."

Max chimed in. "Annd that's why I told you to take a computer class last year."

"Stop helping, Max."

"Whatever. Gimme."

We paused our discussions to inhale and watch a weird pseudo-documentary where someone with bad hair had evidence that the whole Event was an alien conspiracy. It was amusing because there was no mention of what the aliens were after, just...aliens. Eventually it got to be bedtime, so I pulled the couch out a bit and laid out the usual blankets and things for when Jeremiah was usually over and ambled myself to bed.

The dreams that night were an odd variation on the standard. I was in my jump gear, but I was post-change. I was still able to fling myself out on the plane, but the chute was still sized for a human. This presented the obvious problem of falling faster than a safe landing allowed. While looking up, then down at the rapidly approaching and damnably firm terra firma, I able to slow myself a little by throwing my weight onto one side which made me spin wildly out of control. It didn't help, and as I prepared to eat dirt the dream shifted and I landed in a large pile of iridescent feathers. Safely. I didn't question it, since it was a dream, I just went through the motions of getting loose, at which point I woke up with half my blanket kicked off and Max batting my nose to wake me up. Apparently I'd been dreaming loud again and interrupted thirteen minutes of his snooze time. Unacceptable in his world, and thus he deserved a treat for the suffering I'd inflicted.

The rest of the night passed with minimal incident, and in the morning we got everything together and got ready to hustle to places; first to school for Jeremiah, and then work for me. The first bad thing I had was a voicemail from Ann. I called my lawyer for a conference, and then he called her lawyer, and subsequently Ann.

"Hello Ann?" This was the part I hated with these calls. They were destined to end poorly.

"Aoife."

"...Aoife. I've got the lawyers on the line with us, and I'd like to know what the heck is going on."

There was silence for a long beat. "Brooks, I have a new job."

"I'm going to say this as politely as I can, but you've had a few new jobs and you've never left our son at my doorstep and acted like you did. First off, that was rude. You need to call Jeremiah and apologize for that."

"I don't *need* to do anything." She'd definitely gotten up on the wrong side of the bed this morning.

"But you should." I could hear the sounds of packing stuff in the background.

"Fine, if it'll keep you from being such a sanctimonious jackass." Annnd it was worse than what I'd thought.

"Your maternal instincts are where?" Okay, admittedly I was being snippy. But to be fair, she'd kinda sorta dumped Jeremiah on me last night without even calling to warn me.

Ann/Aoife snapped. "Right where they've always been. You think I like having to drop Jeremiah off with you? I've got a new job, and that means sacrifices for everyone - me, you, and Jeremiah. There's a NDA and some restrictions, one of them is no kids."

"Who the heck hires like that?"

"The Power Company." There was a weary triumph in her voice, like she'd finally gotten somewhere that fit her personality and had some sense of permanence to it.

That threw me. Several years ago a company had claimed the largest trash patches in the Pacific and Atlantic oceans, compressed each of them into islands a couple miles square, set up a set of tidal generators as well as a second set that somehow used pressure and temperature differences in the ocean to generate additional power, and then ran some high-efficiency power lines back to the mainland. The startup capital had come from a bunch of dwarves and elves who'd figured out some genius way to deliver electricity over longer distances than previously thought possible. Local utilities had a hard time with it, and there were still a lot of places fighting to keep them out. However, the prices were competitive despite the fact that it was essentially a startup, and their PR department was amazing.

The Power Company made me think something was up. There wasn't a single thing, but enough of what I learned didn't hang together. Whoever was financing it didn't seem care about money, at least in the short-term - but if I've ever learned one thing, it's that the richest don't get that way by not caring about where the money went. The other thing about The Power Company was that they didn't have a public face. Oh, they had commercials, went to trade shows, but it was always either a dwarf from the technical labs or a human from the Employee Resources group. But on the whole, they were either playing the long game with their investment returns, using the losses to get a lower tax burden from some more profitable company they were somehow tied to, or they were legitimate environmentalists. Or at least that's what the folks I talked to who knew accounting better than I did thought.

"Brooks!" Ann/Aoife's voice broke through my thought processes. "Were you even listening?"

"Not so much. Just thinking about what else is going on."

"Well pay attention; yes I'll have the paperwork to our lawyers today. Yes it's for temporary relinquishment of custody due to employment requirements. It's a three-year contract, and then we can revisit it. So get your dumpster house in order. Is there anything else?"

"No, guess not."

"Fine." The line dropped.

I took a long, calming breath. "You got all that, yeah?"

My lawyer chuckled. "Course I did. We'll have you set and it'll be legal inside a week, if what she's saying is what she's doing. Congratulations, you're a dad."

With that, it was off to drop Jeremiah off at school and haul it to the station to make myself presentable for the higher-ups who were planning to use me doing my job as a way to score some points. And if I had five minutes, I might be able to draw some attention to a problem before it became the next mayors' problem.

And as I got into the car after dropping Jeremiah off and signing off on more paperwork, that nagging sense of being watched returned with a vengeance. I didn't see anyone suspicious, but still every nerve was on alert. I'd learned to trust my instincts, but at the same time it made no sense.

Day Two of dress uniform was if possible even more dismaying than the first. More catcalls and whistle action, more than a few disparaging remarks made about me going soft, and the Erinyes from the Armory section was there and eyeballing me again. It was weird, her face was jovial but her eyes were not. Maybe I needed to talk to her.

Still, I didn't have a thing to do for a few hours. Time to call Ricky and see if he knew anything.

He picked up on the third ring. "Brooks if this is more hypothetical shenanigans I'm gonna stop liking you."

"So you don't want a hypothetical beer and free food from Nonas'?"

There was a pause. "I'm listening."

"You ever heard of a computer virus that can wipe a computer and kill the internals?"

"Yeah, but only theoretically. It'd need to be fast and break a lot of security junk. Computers these days have a few safeties involved to prevent the terminally stupid from melting a couple grand in hardware."

"Huh. So, hypothetically, if one did happen to find it's way onto my computer via means dark and flash-drivey, and my kid managed to salvage it and the drive, what would you suggest?"

"Buy him his own computer and tell him to break that. And then enroll his butt at an engineering school."

"Any chance it mighta left something behind?"

"Turn on your hypothetical computer and find out."

"I may have to."

"And Brooks?"

"Yeah."

"Walk soft, man. Something ain't right upstairs, you get me?"

"Gotchagotcha." Ricky might have been a desk driver, but that meant he was also far more aware of the ebb and flow of the station, and his warnings usually foretold drastic change.

Chapter 4

So with that I hung up and began the arduous process of twiddling my thumbs until the lunch thing. I called Nona and let her know that Ricky was coming in on my tab. I also called over to the social department and asked about Rebeccas' case. The fact that she had been emancipated was pretty much step one. From there, it was more paperwork and at least one hearing in front of a judge where character witnesses would attest that she did not need to be remanded to any state-operated custody. Between me, Paulie, and more than likely Nona, that was going to most likely be a formality. The system was awkward, as it always was, but it was slowly getting better. I hopped on my computer and typed out a few things for reference while getting ready to take my shot.

Eventually, the time to go be paraded was nigh, and I went to a very nice restaurant near the capitol building - it was where all the lobbyists and politicians and other assorted power-players in town went for a martini and a bill to be passed. I got my head together to make my own ham-fisted play and see how to make the world a slightly better place.

As I got things settled in Devoins' truck bed again - my van was not approved for public appearances - I began to run through a few things to try and keep things quick, clean, and hopefully discuss things with the mayor.

It did not go that well. It also didn't go that badly. The restaurant had obviously been rearranged for this session, and from the scuff marks on the floor it wasn't the first time. However, it wasn't quite standard, as they didn't quite make room for my back half. There was a very quick handshake and photograph session,

after which I got re-seated at the far end of the table with a
Mandatory Smile on my face enjoying a minimalist lunch. Okay,
they weren't used to Centaur-sized meals. I had to make an effort
to eat slowly. The press did ask a few questions, and I answered
with as much of the Public Relations-approved answers as I could,
and spoke out a little about ways the department would work with
other city departments to keep the city as peaceful as possible.
Finally during the post-lunch mill about and get to know people
time, I was finally able to corner the head of Community
Development. Okay so I might have used my back half to good
effect, but after the initial discussion he was able to be on board
with my idea.

To wit, the ward of the state process currently in use was being
overwhelmed; the process I gave him was simple. Giving businesses
tax breaks on their properties and state income taxes if they could
show proof that they had a Neotype ward in their employ. Said
wards would be required to attend school and do all the usual child
things, but in addition they could work for the employer not more
than three hours a day, six on weekend days. I tentatively titled it
the Apprenticeship Program. The way I wrote it felt a little weird,
but I had written it for what I thought would be broad base appeal,
not to reshape the world as I saw fit. The head of community
development read it like he'd never heard of such a possibility,
and said he'd take it up in committee at the next chance. As I
understood it, that was a politically neutral way of saying "maybe
in about five years." Not great, but not nothing. On the up side, I
had a few attachments showing it worked at least one time, and a
second trial was underway.

The rest of the day was a blur as I wrapped my head around
what was happening. But, things changed at the end of the day
when the captain called me into his office. This time though, there
was a proper chair for me to settle on. This was not good.

He had his standard 'not amused' face on. "Brooks, who did you piss off?"

"Everyone I wrote a ticket to, Cap'n."

"Not the time, smartass. The clownbrained dinks at Genesis are making the rounds again, so we get to protect them. And guess who's name got pulled out of the hat?" The captains' voice had changed, taking on a less-polished timbre. I wasn't entirely surprised, as sympathy for Genesis was non-existent among Neotypes. It was even worse with Elves - they were the ones who generally led the more extreme factions of Neotypes, preaching their evolutionary superiority to any who would listen, with just enough cherry-picked data to make it seem like the world would be a far better place under their benevolent eye. I pulled my thoughts to the present to give a hopeful answer to the captain.

"Devoin?"

"Neither of us are that lucky. Apparently someone thinks it's good press if the Genesis group has Neo's as their security detail. The fact that you just got done meeting with the mayor put a little halo around your name."

"Was this someone tested for drugs subsequent to this decision?"

"Didn't I just say not the time, Officer Arthur?"

"Sorry. Was this someone tested for drugs subsequent to this decision, sir?"

"For your information, yes, and they came up clean. So it's you and three others pulling the duty. We'll have several other plainclothes in the crowd just in case it gets wild."

"Thanks. I get anything from the armory?"

"You get defense spray and body armor."

"Seriously?" If something went wrong during this, I'd be target number one - somehow folks seemed to think that simply because I was larger than most, I could handle myself if I were on the wrong side of a fight against hundreds to one odds with nothing more at my side than a spork and a can-do attitude.

"Look, Brooks. The brilliant minds upstairs wanted me to send your ass our there with a uniform shirt and a smile. Be happy you got this much." And I was fortunate that I didn't have to share the spork.

I sighed. "For the record, I believe this is a bad idea. This is an idea so bad there will be documentaries narrated by a genteel Englishman in hushed tones. On the up side, we'll be played by the handsome but overworked civil servant types. Well, I will, anyway."

"Brooks, if you're trying to get suspended, you'll need to do better."

"And by better you mean...?"

"You are dismissed, Brooks. And close the door."

The next week was scheduled to be a whirlwind of commuting, homework, and doctors' appointments as we figured out how far along Jeremiah was with his change and I got a helpful brochure and nutritional guide. On the bright side of things, since he was becoming a dwarf, the change was relatively slow, taking about three weeks from start to finish. From a physical standpoint, there were a few things going on; his entire body was going to get denser, so to an outside observer he was going to shrink to about three-fourths the size he was when he started. At the same time, the compression was going to cause some minor-to-severe pain, depending on the exact order of things. Painkillers were recommended. Additionally, not everything came together at the same pace, so the phrase clumsy was going to be a common theme if the feet compressed before the legs. Also if the legs compressed before the feet. Arms, hands, same thing. In short (no pun intended) I was pretty much going to have to baby-proof the apartment. Meanwhile, I had to fill out a bunch of paperwork at his school advising them that he would be transferring to a Dwarven academy. According to people who knew more about this than me, the side effect of more densely packed brain cells was that they worked faster, with the net result being that dwarves were collectively some of the more brilliant minds in existence. Or at least they were wrong in faster and more ingenious ways.

The nutritional guide wasn't exactly filled with information, but the main things he needed were fish, meats, and dark chocolate. The psychological guide was bizarre - apparently a secondary effect of the brain compression was that mentally he'd start maturing rapidly; effectively he'd age about a year every three calendar months as he started processing events. This reportedly plateaued when his brain hit about twenty, and then from there it was waiting for the body and time to catch up. I started looking at the budget closely and after crunching numbers it was going to be tight this month, but by the next month it looked like I would have things sorted without asking my landlady for a little extra time to get the rent together. All the while there was the nagging sensation of being watched.

Still, in the midst of all this I was able to sort things and have my parents over for dinner. Neither of them had Changed, so they only had the normal older people problems to deal with. Pops' biggest problem was finding something to do. He'd retired from the force after thirty-plus years a few years back, and he was still looking for something to do. So far he'd built a koi pond, restored a forty year old car to mint condition, converted half the garage into a scale version of the Jolly Cholly, brewed several batches of beer and mead for Garage Jolly Cholly, and also rebuilt the kitchen so the he and Ma could cook together. For Ma's part, she was a computer programmer and technician who'd spent years learning every computer language she could, gaining passive familiarity with most forms of technology. With Pop retiring, she'd pretty much decided to do the same, scaling back to do consulting work and effectively becoming the repair technician for the cul-de-sac where they lived. Her stories were funny but also hard to understand if you didn't speak whatever mad language computer people used in place of English.

It was a little surreal in some ways, but at the same time it was almost expected. The Irish side of the family came from Pop, while the Italian side came from Ma, and how they met was story in and of itself. They'd seen each other now and again since Pops' patrol beat took him through Little Italy where Ma lived. There were some folks who wanted her to work for them on some things that were just a little shady. That's according to Ma, however I did look into it a bit and I found out that what they wanted her to do was, according to the dry prose of the prosecutor at the time, a lot shady.

Ma went to Nonas' for some advice. Over a large amount of Italian comfort food, Ma explained to Nona what was happening, and Nona saw multiple opportunities. One was to help scale back the local Mafioso who had watched too many shows glorifying their thing, and the second was to introduce Ma and Pop to see what would happen. The next night they met formally for the first time, and it was not great. That said, things started moving in a better direction after the second and third dates, which were pretty much working affairs where they were walking around the area with Ma pointing out all the highlights of the neighborhood. After a bit of time and Pop working a few things with his captain, Ma agreed to hide a few things in the custom builds she did for the local businessmen. The upshot of it was a lot of people going to prison and Pop getting assigned to a light protective detail, which rapidly turned into an unofficial close protective detail. And thereafter a wedding, with all the things that come with that. Specifically me.

Which eventually led to Ma standing at the door with a large slow-cooker full of chicken and Pop bearing a tub of things for grilling. Me and Pop went out to the patio to take care of the meat, fire and sharp objects while Ma and Jere talked shop about the latest and greatest in the world of computers. Listening to them talk was a lesson in how language can be utterly incomprehensible and yet perfectly understandable at the same time. They probably had the same thoughts about my conversation with Pop, which was a perfectly sensible and understandable conversation about batting averages, wins above replacement, and then moving on to sacks, yards after contact, and the all important touchdown to interception ratio.

With everyone in their own conversation, the afternoon progressed casually. Jere and Ma were looking at some new computer wizard thing, while Pop and I fretted over the latest trade rumors. Eventually, everyone wound up around the table for a high calorie feeding. Ma was quite happy to keep feeding her son and grandson until the two of us were full - an impressive feat for the both of us, given that Jere was eating everything in sight and I was, well, me. A good day, all told.

The next day began to shape up in a fairly normal way. The bus to Jeremiahs' school pulled up to the curb just as we were leaving, with the driver giving me a once-over to make sure that I matched the parental description he'd been given before Jeremiah hustled in to a chorus of new-guy cheers and what sounded like a thousand thumbs typing rapidly. Apparently this was cause for celebration. Or something. Still I went back, drove to work, and did not win Elevator Roulette yet again.

About mid-morning, my radio crackled with a request. Since I wasn't doing anything except walking with Devoin and keeping alert for pickpockets and petty theft along our usual beat, I figured I might as well answer. I keyed my microphone.

"This is Officer Arthur, what's up?"

"We have a request from SWAT, they're sending a van to pick you up, ETA one minute." Sure enough when I listened for it I could hear a van in the distance sounding their horn to get traffic to clear for them.

"Dispatch please advise of nature of request." I'd applied for SWAT a few times in the past, but the rejection letters were piling up at a depressing rate. Even though my marksmanship was consistently in the top five percent of the entire force and I'd previously advised them on additional urban tactical training, they kept telling me I was not selected. It did not help that the SWAT team was entirely made up of Unchanged, and that I would probably upset whatever in-jokes they might have had. Or at least that was what the rejection blurbs hinted at.

"Nature currently unknown, SWAT will advise en route." That did not help my mood. Their station was notorious for inhaling the police departments' budget at the expense of everyone else, which meant that they got all the latest toys, trips to special week-long functions where they would discuss the latest and greatest in police science for half a day and spend the rest of the time at the beach working on their tans and social life, and their elevators and toilets worked. Still, they needed me for something, and it did bring a little excitement to the day.

The SWAT van screamed up and came to a halt in front of me, with the doors popping open and a few tactically-dressed folks popping out of the back to secure the immediate area. Devoin and I glanced at each other and shrugged. Apparently they were in some sort of "always training" mindset, which meant they had a set method for doing everything. They were a little sloppy about it, but I couldn't exactly berate them on the street for it. Devoins' radio crackled and told him to get moving, while I hopped in the back.

The van groaned a little under my weight, but everyone piled back in and the van roared off, siren blaring and lights flashing. Once we'd taken off, the interior lights flicked on and I got to see the person in charge of this request. The face was familiar, and annoying. He'd been a part of my army unit when we were overseas. However while I was jumping out of planes, he was in charge of the laundry and showers. The laundry was bad enough that we took to washing our own clothes and gear by hand, and the showers only really worked when the base commander was checking them. After a week of hearing him whine that it wasn't his fault and it was the wingnuts that he'd been given that were causing everything to not work, we took to calling him Wingnut, and it stuck for the rest of the tour. He did not like the nickname.

To bring things back to the present, while he wasn't exactly the face of the SWAT team, he always knew where the cameras were and managed to look like he was doing something in the background whenever the cameras were rolling for the local news. He'd gotten enough time in front of the cameras and microphones that he'd received a few promotions. Unfortunately, he had not managed to cultivate any actual leadership qualities. Despite that, he'd somehow gotten tasked with leading this, and had apparently requested my presence for this job, whatever it was.

My thoughts were taking too long for his liking, so he harrumphed around an unlit cigar to bring my attention to his scowling face.

"Officer Arthur, are you waiting for something?" He adjusted his beret, which was just a slight shade off from a proper Airborne red and attempted to assert a measure of authority in the situation.

"Just trying to get a sense of what I'm needed for, Wingnut."

He pointed with his free hand to where a lieutenants' rank insignia was. "I have a rank here, and you might want to try using it."

"Will do Lieutenant Wingnut. What do you need me for?" Given that Wingnut had never gotten above private first class when we were overseas and we both knew it, I felt like I could push my luck just a bit on this.

"We are executing a search warrant on what we suspect is a large drug manufacturing and distribution facility. However, we're missing our door breacher." His face spoke volumes about who's fault it was, and who would take most of the blame once the reports were written.

"So, what you need me to run grab it? I mean I can run pretty quickly, so, sure?"

"Negative, Officer Arthur. The mission is time sensitive and requires an immediate alternate plan. That's where you come in. You'll be using your unique physical shape to breach the door." Translation, buck and boot the door.

"Do we know if they've planted anything to keep unwanted entry from occurring?"

"No, but we are confident that there will be no obstacles to entry."

"And do I have any additional gear?"

"Affirmative." He handed me a familiar piece of hardware, and I checked it over briefly. The rifle was well maintained, clean, and had absolutely no bullets. I glanced, and he smirked.

This was not shaping up to be Brooks Arthurs' best day ever. "So in short, I kick the door, hope it's not booby-trapped, and then get to cover?"

Wingnut nodded, having reasserted his command authority. "You understand the plan perfectly. We're almost there, so lets' get to it. Once we get out the door will be directly forward. Turn, kick the door, and then let the professionals handle it." I arched an eyebrow as he apparently he considered himself one of the professionals. Admittedly it had been over a decade since I'd been in combat, but I'd been policing - and that had been its' own adventure. I decided to ask a few questions, just in case I'd missed any parts.

"So, what channel am I putting my radio on?" Going under the logical assumption that these guys would not conduct operations on our standard frequencies, I reached down to fiddle it.

Wingnut rolled his eyes like I'd asked him for the most unreasonable thing on the planet. "We have our own. There's a spare over there." He pointed and I picked up the set and flicked it on. No power. I flipped it open and found that the batteries had been reversed. After re-seating them, I was in business and listening in. After seeing that little piece of competence, Wingnut decided to play nice with the battering ram. "Play this smart, Arthur, and we may have a permanent spot for you on the squad. Seriously, first neotype SWAT officer in the city - gotta be a goal."

Wingnut cracked open the dividing window, looking out and nodding before turning back to address us. "Alright, we're about thirty seconds out. Get ready, let's make this clean."

I still heard the siren going. "Hey, if we're trying to surprise the folks we're dropping in on, shouldn't we kill the lights and whatnot?"

Wingnut shook his head. "Nope. We pull up with full lights and sirens. Looks better on television." I craned my neck to look back and sure enough we were being tailed by two news vans. This day just kept getting better and better. The rest of the team seemed aware that Wingnut was making their job at least a little harder, but apparently this was something they'd gotten used to. Well, we were in it, and there really wasn't anything we could do except drive forward and hope we had the upper hand as far as training and weapons went. I slung the rifle they gave me, since it had still been issued to me.

The van braked and we were out. Well, sort of. The two at my rear opened the doors and smacked the TV van behind us. Which prompted a quick exchange about who was moving, and since the second van was behind them, it turned out that we had to pull forward several feet to make room for me to get out. This was not going by the numbers. Finally I got out and saw the door that I needed to boot down. There were several small wires running across the walkway. That was concerning, and I wrinkled my nose as a slightly pungent smell arrived. I pointed the tripwires out as everyone was smart enough to avoid them. It wasn't good, but at least the rank and file were disciplined, even if they were led by someone who earned the nickname Wingnut every time he drew breath.

I waved them to stack up and took a long look at the door. Booby trapped, and it wasn't exactly subtle. I radioed it in. "Command, door is trapped, send the demo team to disarm."

The reply filled me with dread. "No time. Proceed."

"Command, confirm you wish us to proceed." This could be anything. Explosives, gas, Nona with a date for me. I looked around and saw the camera crews doing live standups and panning around to get a good local shot of the area. Apparently Wingnut was helping to direct as the cameras swiveled and zoomed to finally come to rest directly on my happy face.

Wingnuts' voice hissed over the radio. "Don't argue, Arthur. Boot the door and get out of the way." On the up side, if the whole team did get turned into chopped steak, it'd be live and Wingnut'd be heading for the unemployment line. I looked to everyone else stacked up to enter, remembered that I had updated all my beneficiary forms, and turned around to get my rear hoof positioning correct. Once all that was done, I nodded to everyone to make sure they were ready and bucked to fire a kick at the door with both of my back feet.

The door disappeared and I landed with my rump just inside the door. The other team members surged before I was clear, creating what would be a very comic situation if we weren't in the midst of something potentially deadly. As I started to move forward to attempt to clear the door I heard five small pops. I didn't feel any pain, but adrenaline was surging and it was quite possible that I had actually been shot and I didn't feel it. Also, I was squishing the first guy who was trying to defy physics and get through me and the door frame.

Since I couldn't go forward I backpedaled hard, getting my sidearm out and then doing a spin, scanning while looking around. There was a great deal of action as the team swarmed the warehouse, shouting that they were the police and that a search warrant was being executed. There was a lot of echo as I was moving, and once I paused, I saw emptiness. The whole place was empty. Scrubbed clean. You could probably have performed an operation with the right equipment. I relaxed a little, trying to find the source of the pops I'd heard earlier. It was the door, and it had been rigged with glitter bombs. I looked at them, and at my back. Yep, my butt was all a-glitter. Both on and even under my kilt. I sighed, thinking about what fresh grief I was going to get back at the station once I got back. Meanwhile, the whole place had been gone over by the team, and the one thing they found was a slip that one of the local delivery companies used when they had a package for you and nobody was home.

I walked out to look around and survey the situation. Wingnut was controlled, speaking to the cameras still as if the whole plan was perfect and had gone off without a hitch. The group filed out, looking dejected as heck. I looked around, seeing a crowd of lookyloo's and workers from other nearby places. One of them I saw looking a little too interested, so I started winding toward him as Wingnut made pronouncements for the cameras to spin this trainwreck of an operation into something good.

Mister Interested saw my meander getting a little too close for comfort and he finally broke into a run. Which was probably the worst thing he could have done. I surged myself forward, telling the crowd to move and Mister Interested to stop - the crowd didn't need much encouragement, as eight hundred pounds of centaur moving rapidly in your direction is an excellent motivator to give way. Even for me, and I am eight hundred pounds of Centaur. And at a full sprint, we're kinda quick. It took me about half a block to catch up and bump him to the ground. Then I slid to a stop and backtracked to him, where he was groaning in pain from where I'd knocked him down. I picked him up gently as he started cursing my name, my family, my kids, and anything else he could think of. I gently put him against the wall with my front legs, frisking him and getting an ID out.

Funny story, I knew the name. He'd been suspected of a few things, arrested a few times, gotten bailed out a few times, and had only done a little time for an armed robbery several years ago. From what I remembered, he was moving up a little. And his phone was still recording. Apparently he'd been tasked with taking home movies of the SWAT team assault for entertainment or training. Probably both. After confirming that there were in fact several warrants for his arrest, I cuffed him and we put him in the back of another van that had arrived in anticipation of a whole bunch of arrests. Turned out, not so much.

At some point during all this, the TV crew noticed that a thing was happening and promptly ran over to me to get something other than Wingnut talking about how even though this wasn't a fully successful action, that he was quite happy with the way that his team had performed. Even as I was putting the suspect in the back of the van I could hear him droning on about the challenges overcome in the beginning with entry, but it was certainly something they were trained to overcome. It was his standard boilerplate, with not a few undertones of "Officer Arthur was horrible during this whole thing" - despite Officer Arthur being the only one to make an actual arrest on this whole thing.

I pushed the TV folks back a little bit, mainly to keep everyone from interfering but also because I didn't want my disco-ball lookin' butt on TV. Finally once the van peeled away, I glanced over at Wingnut, who looked a few shades of furious that I'd taken the spotlight off him. I was finally able to assess the crews. Both were a pair of faun reporters, with unchanged people running the cameras. Fauns were currently the go-to neotype for newscasts. They were almost as good as Erinyes when it came to balancing the empathy and hard-nose questions that local news demanded and as a bonus you didn't have to watch out for wings. Both of the reporters were wearing ankle-length skirts and sharp blazers with their respective station logos prominently displayed. Currently they were arguing amongst themselves as to who would get first dibs on the interview, and Wingnut took this opportunity to sidle over to me and give me a few words of what he considered wisdom.

"So here's how this goes, Arthur. You were picked for this last week; the team was ready, but unfortunately the people we were coming for got wind of it and left before we could come in fully. We've got the best forensics team coming to investigate and see if they can find anything that might lead us to where they are now. The door breach was your mistake due to being over-excited. Any other questions, you defer."

I quirked an eyebrow at him. "So basically make your team look good at my expense?"

Wingnut grinned broadly, like a teacher who finally got the slow learner to catch on. "Exactly. Do it right and we'll have a spot for you within the month. You're talented, don't let it go to waste."

The two reporters had finally settled their discussion via the ancient method of rock-paper-scissors. The winner grinned and fistbumped the loser, walking over to me while the loser started furiously writing on index cards.

The next challenge was getting a good position for both of us that also kept my butt well out of frame. We eventually decided for this one the reporter would be on my back, with me twisting in a less than comfy manner and using the SWAT van as a background. The cameraman was polite enough to keep my glittered bits out of the frame, while still showing that a centaur was being interviewed. It wasn't entirely orthodox, but it was better the other options which involved a box and/or me kneeling.

Finally, it was time for the second-worst thing to happen today. The reporter started her perky chatter intro. "We're back live with Officer Brooks Arthur, who today became the first Neotype police officer to become part of a special police operation; Officer Arthur, tell us how it felt working on this for the last few weeks?"

I debated for a moment before answering - the debate was brief since we were live. I racked back the bolt to discretely show the camera that I had a rifle with no ammo and an empty chamber before answering. "Well, I can only assume it would be an honor and a privilege to be selected ahead of time for this, as opposed to receiving a call due to being the closest Centaur available in a situation where the standard equipment was left behind."

The reporters' instincts kicked in hard - specifically that Wingnut had spit out a lot of things and that a few of them hadn't exactly been honest. Her hair went from blonde to pink and back as she worked out her next few questions on the fly. "So can you tell us in your own words how this day went for you?"

"The short version is that I was contacted by dispatch because the SWAT team needed me specifically. After which I was advised to get in the van for a briefing." I shrugged casually. "I mean it's not the first time I've been called in for something at the last minute, sometimes things happen. But one of the more important things with activities like this is that they are based heavily on surprise. I counted four separate tripwires along the walk-up. I would not recommend setting them off - they look to be explosive and dangerous. The element of surprise was nonexistent, which placed the team in jeopardy. However, we were ordered to continue and breach. The door was, as you saw, also booby trapped, however instead of a fatal result, it was more of an insult." I shrugged and took a breath before wrapping up. "In any event, after the breach the team was professional, well trained, and as you saw at the end the raid did result in an arrest, which I'm sure will lead to some additional actions in the near future."

The reporters' eyes sparkled and her hair was flickering blonde to orange. Apparently this was going to be her ticket to a few kudos back at the office. The second reporter was almost chewing her notepad up because she was going to be late to the party. The best part of it was that Wingnut couldn't do much except try to plead for a few minutes of time to explain away what I'd just said. The second interview was fairly similar, but I did give the second ones a bit more on the actual arrest portion, which would hopefully get a little bit more shine on the other neotypes in the office. Eventually everyone made sure the reports were filed and as they came in the explosives team made its' way on scene with a lot of gear. Wingnut came stomping up to me filled with fire and fury.

"Brooks, you think that what you just did was smart? I'll have your badge before the end of the day, and I mean it. You just torched a huge investigation. Huge. You made us look like we're some Keystone Cops over here, when we're not." He reached up to tap my chest with his forefinger for emphasis. "We. Are. The. Best." And to further drive the point home, he re-adjusted his beret, nodding.

His ego was definitely unchecked, but really it wasn't my place to bring him back to reality. That I was going to leave to the people who were good at that sort of thing. I nodded right back at him. "Well, if you're keen on it, let's go have a talk with my captain and we can figure this out. I don't know about you, but I'm still on the clock and my partner's been riding solo for a few hours. Shall we?"

He snorted. "Your funeral. Get in the back I don't want you wandering off and forgetting anything."

I hopped in the back and swapped out for my regular radio set. "Dispatch, Brooks is en route to station after assistance with SWAT. Advise the Captain that the lieutenant on-scene would like an immediate action review, and that he may want to have all the necessary paperwork ahead of time. Arrival time -" the van lurched and fired up the siren, throwing me backwards a bit. "- Arrival time will be soon."

There was an unfamiliar voice on the radio call back. "Brooks, dispatch confirms. Captain has been advised and will have the paper per request."

Chapter 5

The ride back was rough - I'm fairly certain the driver was told to make my life difficult. In the interim, I poked around a but and found that they did in fact have ammo, but Wingnut forgot to give me any. This was not going to be good. I was definitely going to be catching some angry words for my stunt with the reporters, but I was pretty certain that Wingnut was not going to have his day go any better.

Once we were back, I made my way up through the stairwells and to the captains' office, where he and Wingnut were having a slightly animated conversation. Wingnut being able to use the elevator had gotten there first. The grief had already begun on my way up, as some folks at the station had seen the live footage of me making the arrest - there was already a whiteboard dedicated to suggestions with vote tallies in progress. "Sparklebutt" had a commanding lead, followed by "Discoballs", and in third place was "Hollywood". My appearance on TV had apparently garnered some fans.

I knocked a few times to interrupt whatever was happening, and the captain did in fact summon me in. On his desk was a relatively thick file, next to a second file that was about half as thick. Somehow he'd pulled both mine and Wingnuts' personnel jackets in the time it took us to get here. The fact that mine was thicker was possibly a good sign. What was not a good sign were the chairs. Nothing for me to sit on, but Wingnut had a nice comfy chair. That said, Wingnut took the interruption as a sign that he should start talking.

"And here is a prime example. Insubordinate behavior. Not in proper uniform. It's disgraceful, and I fully believe that he should be fired. Actions like his reflect very poorly on the department as a whole."

"You seem to think that I will take your words at face value, without reviewing what predicated them. First, let's address his uniform." The captain steepled his fingers, turning to his TV, which was queued up to the video from both cameras. This was not the footage that had made it to the newscasts, and hopefully it wouldn't ever get on them. It showed me booting the door and subsequently looking rather silly as the swat team tried to barge in before I'd cleared out of the way. "As you can see, his actions that you had ordered him to perform - over his objection - were the immediate cause of this out of uniform situation. I remind you that if you do press forward with this as the specific charge, the review committee have access to this as part of the full record."

Wingnut was deft with the reply, I'll give him that. "That doesn't mean he wasn't insubordinate. Two occasions, one where he didn't break the door, and then the second one when he did not remain where he was supposed to, and then the third when he did not interview as I told him to." Wingnut rewound to the beginning where I was pointing out tripwires. "And here. He was supposed to pull these and move forward."

The captain raised an eyebrow. "Really."

Wingnut nodded affirmatively. "Yes. Based on the events at the door, he could have easily set those off and continued forward to the door."

"I believe I will reserve judgment on Officer Arthurs' actions until a full report is received from the bomb squad. That said, I have a preliminary report from the bomb squad. The sidewalk tripwires were rigged with a home-made high explosive. While not as powerful as conventional explosives, their technicians are quite confident in its' lethality. Your suggested course of action would have resulted in the entire team being reduced to nothingness." His eyes bored into Wingnut. "I strongly suggest that you re-evaluate Officer Arthurs' behavior, and learn from his example. If you have more that you wish to discuss, you may continue."

Wingnut did not pick up the hint that he should not continue. "The interview afterward. Look at what he did. All of it."

"Very well, let us review." Oh heck. This was the one part where I was worried. we rolled through the interview a few times in silence before Wingnut tried to start it all anew. "See? All of that was against my express, direct orders."

The captains' face was blank for the moment. "And those orders were?"

"He was supposed to admit to making mistakes due to the unique nature of what had been asked of him, and from there apologize for those errors and promise to move forward."

An eyebrow arched. "Was he at all dishonest?"

"He did not do what I told him to do." Wingnut was hanging on to that for all he was worth.

The captain sighed. "That does not answer my question." Oh, this was shaping up to be better than I thought.

"Look, at the end of the day, he didn't do what he was told. He made the SWAT team look bad. And that is justification for immediate dismissal."

"He made you. Look bad." The captain held up a hand to forestall argument. "Now, Leftennent -" the British pronunciation still tripped me up "- if you persist, I will be required to submit the entire record to the adjudicating committee. Including the reason for his assignment, which as I recall was that you failed to have required equipment. In addition to that, I will be forced to include the factual actions; that you not only failed to equip properly, that you made onerous requirements, that your recommended course of action would have resulted in injuries and deaths, and that the sole arrest in the entire affair was made by Officer Arthur. I do not believe that any inquiry will make you, or the team you command, look good. In fact I believe that any formal inquiry will result in your reassignment to a position far more in line with your particular talents. Do you wish to continue."

Wingnut finally picked up on the hints. "No."

"Very well, you may see your way to your own station. As the matter at hand did involve one of my officers, I will be reviewing all statements and reports prior to final disposition. I will annotate any discrepancies I find."

Wingnuts' ego took a beating, and I wasn't sure if he was going to be able to do much more. Neither did he, apparently, as he stood, nodded to the captain, executed a perfect left face and exited the office. Which was good and bad - good in that I didn't have to restrain myself from demonstrating to Wingnut exactly what several hundred hundred pounds of cranky Centaur looked like. Bad news because it was in fact my turn to get chewed out.

"Officer Arthur. I would very much like to hear what particular madness has infected your mind since you left this morning. The leftennant was quite incensed by your behavior, and he is adequate within his current position." The hands were returned to their steepled position, which was not good.

"Permission to speak freely sir?"

"Continue."

"Captain, that man has been a screwup ever since I met him when we were both touring overseas. Dodging work and grabbing credit were his two main goals in life. He stayed overseas after I shipped out, came back here and joined the force like he had to prove something, and now that he's finagled himself into the SWAT team, he's trying to make himself look like he's someone important. He leads from wherever the camera angles are best.

Today was a prime example of that. He coulda easily gotten people killed and the only things that saved that team from being turned into paste were me seeing tripwires and telling the team to not clip them, and the fact that the folks we were raiding wanted to flip us off after killing us. Other than the glitter trap, there was nothing but a note. He needs to be reassigned before people die. He'd be a great Public Relations officer for the sanitation departments' sewer division." I had raised my voice a bit during this, which became apparent to me when the captain moved his hand to readjust the nameplate on his desk.

The captain squinted. "Very well. Officer Arthur. In light of your service record, your recent family changes, and upcoming events for which you are assigned, I will be placing you on a paid leave for the next four days. I will be communicating this to the Leftennant, and will be making additional recommendations to his superiors. I believe you have earned a small amount of time off. You will report to the armory Friday evening to sign for what you will be wearing Saturday."

The look on my face said it all. Four days with nothing to do but work out and watch TV sounded great, but I had Nona to worry about. It was going to be rough for the most part. I left to about thirty of my fellow officers cheering me on and a last pass at the board indicated the winning suggestion to be Sparklebutt. I was going to need at least two weeks for that to clear. Hopefully. Still, four days to get ready for playing guard for folks who wanted nothing more than to see me relegated to an intelligent farm animal might just be what the doctor ordered. Plus, I'd get to pop in to the barber for a haircut and hoof trim.

I have been more wrong on precisely three occasions. The first was thinking my marriage was going to last. The second was later, and it involved me thinking a parachute landing at night wouldn't be too difficult to manage. The most recent was thinking the early symptoms of my Change were actually me overdoing it on leg day. Day One was spent at the Jolly Cholly catching up on sports. There may have been a special delivery of schnapps with gold flakes and glitter from the happy campers at the station. It may have been addressed to Sparklebutt. And a new picture was posted to the mirror - me at the raid, looking ready to rock, just after the door was kicked in but just before the glitter bomb went off. Day two was spent at Fisticuffs working off the aftereffects of Day One, after which I spent the afternoon talking sports at the barber shop. That was a couple hours in and of itself, because I needed hair trimmed from my head, and fur trimmed from darn near everywhere else. Every month it was time for a trim, and even then I had the occasional touch-ups. The touch-ups only took a half-hour, whereas the full body treatment was an hour at minimum. Two hours if there was a hot topic to discuss.

Day Three was three dates courtesy of Nona. Brunch with a Unchanged who was looking for many children, and apparently got cold feet as soon as I stood up to greet her. That was followed by a late lunch with the first faun who interviewed me. She was jubilant, as apparently that had fast-tracked her to a promotion, and she was buying while she talked to me about a few opportunities. If anything happened, it would probably be about one step above an arranged marriage. Professionally we'd probably be doing well, personally we would both acknowledge that whatever we did and whoever we did it with was to be kept very quiet. A nice concept, but not what I was looking for. The last one was another centaur, who'd been working airport security for a few years and saw my interview with said faun, which had encouraged her to finally apply to become a police officer.

We had a long conversation about that with Jere and Rebecca joining us - sort of. While we talked shop, he inhaled a couple of steaks with fries on the side and kept glancing at Rebecca. Rebecca was enthralled to have the chance to talk to us and discuss career options in between her own sneaking glances at Jere. Many ideas were discussed, and Rebecca seemed to be highly interested in the idea of being a personal trainer. A lot of professions had been upended by the Change, and a lot of the world was still stubbornly trying to fit square pegs into round holes with minimal success. It seemed like a good plan for her so I gently encouraged Rebeccas' planning and mentioned there'd be a lot of biology, because working muscle groups meant that you had to know what muscles were where.

On the whole, it felt like, well, a family meal. I had a small wave of nostalgia, remembering similar events from when Jere was much younger. Overall it was a great night, but not something that caused sparks or fireworks. At least not on the adult side of the table. I wasn't sure, but it seemed like Rebecca and Jere were playing footsie under the table.

We walked our new security officer/cadet interviewee to her van, and made sure she took off safely before we walked across the street. After she left, we started across the street to Fisticuffs with Rebecca in between Jere and me. Even though the night was calm, something in the back of my head was telling me to get ready for something because there was Not Right somewhere nearby. I didn't ignore it.

"Come on, let's hustle you back home Rebecca." I nudged her, with my voice taking on the tones that this was not up for discussion. The kids nodded and started moving quickly, crossing the street. I was last across, and the Not Right announced itself with a roaring engine and tires screeching on the pavement. I looked to my right to see that it was a panel van. It didn't take much to realize that it was going to hit me. Hard.

And everything had been going so well.

Chapter 6

I met the front grill of the van rather abruptly, and the impact prevented any further introduction. I was sent flying, but not too far. Fortunately, my bulk worked in my favor for once as I landed and was able to get rightside up and patted my jacket to ensure my wallet was still in place. I was going to need that in about ten seconds. I checked my phone. Cracked but functional. I dialed the department backline, and put it in my pocket with a pat, identifying myself and where I was with a request for some backup. I did a quick walking check of my parts to survey the situation. And it was not good. There were two people with video cameras strapped to their hats, and from what I could see of the lights they were rolling. For some reason. Jere was trying to fight them and holding his own to a degree, however this was not a fight he was going to win without help. Luckily for him, Officer Brooks Arthur from the city police department - aka "Dad" - was on station and was not about to let things slide. Particularly when one of them sucker-punched Jere, leaving him gasping for air. With Jere sitting and watching, while trying to get back to his feet. One had her in a headlock and was maneuvering her to the back of the van, while his compatriot was throwing the door up to open it. Rebecca for her part was oddly quiet, putting up minimal resistance.

I raised my voice loudly enough to wake the neighborhood; "POLICE. Both of you, I wanna see hands, and I wanna see 'em NOW."

The one operating the door turned to give me a gesture that was at best rude, but not illegal. "Mind your own business Gluestick, we're taking our sister home."

It was definitely not a new epithet, but it was odd, and I had to stall for a minute before the cavalry. "Fellas. Y'ain't going anywhere." Meanwhile Rebecca had come out of her fugue and was backpedaling awkwardly; it was quite possible that these fellows were not who they said they were.

In any case my job was clear. I spared a glance back to Jere who was getting up weakly but putting up his fists for round two. My boy. I waved him back to keep him from getting into this, mouthing "Don't worry" before returning my attention to this horrendous attempt at a kidnapping. I stepped around the front of the panel van and caught a whiff of antifreeze. It seemed as though when they hit me, they'd cracked the radiator. Hopefully it wasn't a rental.

A few things happened rapidly, as the doors to Fisticuffs opened and a cranky Paulie made his appearance. I came around to the other end of the van, and Paulie was kind enough to lob a taser to me. I caught it, but kept it down. Maybe I could pull something from my bag of calm the situation down.

"Fellas. Right now you're definitely in a bad spot. Hitting someone with a vehicle's bad news. On top of that, we got assault. And last, attempted kidnapping. Now, I'mma repeat myself. For the record, I'm a police officer so anything further comes with that added 'against a police officer' thing, which means a nice long stretch." I shrugged. "So, you boys let her go, get your hands on top of your heads, and the trouble you're in'll be a lot less."

For my trouble, I got a snort from the older one, while the younger one tried to wrestle Rebecca into the van again, although this time with much less success because she was becoming coherent and fighty. "Listen Dogfood, we don't care if you think you're a cop. That's our sister, we're taking her home, and we're gonna put her to work." The tone seemed to be that I was the slow one in this conversation.

I sighed, hoping the backup was on their way. "Okay, Let's take it from the top. One. You're both under arrest. Two. She's legally for all intents and purposes an adult. She's not going anywhere. Three. You're both under arrest. Four. Her boss and landlord - that angry guy with the shotgun - is right there; I dunno what he's got in there, but I guarantee it ain't gonna tickle. Point of interest, before opening up a gym, he spent two decades in the Navy as a Gunners' Mate. Which means if it shot, he took care of it. Pretty sure he won't miss. Now, what do you boys say to settling down and not getting into any more trouble?"

For my trouble, I might as well have been talking to the wall. Things happened very quickly after I stopped talking. The one who seemed to be in charge of talking pulled out a baton and cracked me with it. Something wasn't right, because I felt a full-body pulse and my left front leg went numb and tingly. In response, I turned and hipchecked Talky into his brother, which freed up Rebecca, who ran full-tilt toward the Jolly Cholly. That was a good thing, because there were more than a few people there who would help if the backup didn't arrive in a timely fashion.

Unfortunately the last thing that happened was not great. Ricky fired off the shotgun, and made a liar out of me as I got hit in the rear. From the instant sting, it was rock salt. I needed to have a discussion with Ricky once this was all over - and we were going to start with how shooting your cop friend in the butt with rock salt was frowned upon in civilized locations.

That said, the upshot of all this was clear - the two brothers were suddenly realizing that things had not progressed as planned. They were outnumbered, outgunned, and they had definitely exhausted the patience of the authority figures in the immediate area. As if to punctuate this, the backup arrived with lights but no sirens. I finally relaxed, disconnected the call, and with that a whole group of hurts announced themselves. I let the other officers take over, and from there the two began their whole thing again. After giving my statement of what happened, I made my way over to Jere who was leaning against the wall and was recovered, but worried.

"Should I go get Becky? I think she went to our, uh, place." He was breathing heavily, and I looked him over - he looked like he had gotten the worst of it with a little cut on his face and a stomach punch that knocked the wind out of him. Overall, better off than my first fight.

I nodded. "Go make sure she's okay, and we may need her to come back and talk to the guys here." Jere grinned and hustled, happy to be doing something. I made my way over to Ricky and settled for a moment.

To his credit, Ricky looked embarrassed. "I owe you a beer." In response I nudged his shoulder and looked back. Ricky got the hint and grabbed his handkerchief to wipe the salt out of my hindquarters and flank as discretely as possible.

"I feel like I got hit by a truck, man." Once the worst of it was out, the world was a better place.

"To be fair, you got hit by a truck. And you may have actually come out even, cause that Van ain't going anywhere by itself." Ricky smirked a little and hit my front shoulder. He was accurate. Still, it was odd watching what was happening as the two were protesting that they were in the clear and they even recorded it so they could prove they were clear. From their conversation, they thought they were clear right up until they were cuffed and dropped in the back of the squad car. From there they were protesting like nobody's business as they were driven to the station for holding and processing. And if they were lucky they'd be out on bail before lunch.

Finally the smoke started to clear, metaphorically. A tow truck was summoned and took the van to an impound lot. Ricky disappeared for a moment before coming back out without the shotgun but with two beers, handing one to me.

"Any idea what it was about?" I glanced at Ricky after a long pull on the beer.

Ricky exhaled. "I got suspicions. Every time we talked about her family she got scared and ready to bolt. I did some looking. From what I could find, her family's pretty much in the hip pocket of them Genesis folks. So having a kid change into a Centaur was probably a bit of a challenge."

"We better find out quick, cause if they've got a legal challenge it could make her life rough."

"Mmm-hm. And Nona'll be over quick. Make yourself scarce before you get to answer any questions."

I finished my beer and mad my way to the bar to check in and tell everyone to relax, and there was a visible wash as tension left the place on a wave of relatively good news. My butt was throbbing though, so staying for a quick one was out of the question. I went upstairs to find Max on Rebeccas' lower shoulder, with her head laying on Jere. She was very much asleep.

I was as quiet as I could be - not very - but at the same time, Rebecca wasn't waking up any time soon. I grabbed the spare pillow and blanket for those emergency nights when a regular wasn't going home in any way shape or form, covered her up, and eased Jere out from under so she could rest easy. Maxs' tail flicked as he settled in and regarded me before speaking.

"Why do you bring frightened teenagers into my house, and not gooshy food?"

I snorted. "Your house."

"Yes. My sleeping spot is in use by someone else. Fortunately, I am generous enough to share. Her breath smells like she ate something weird. Also, you're bleeding a little."

"Thanks for the reminder. Anything weird happens, you holler. Jere likes her."

"I know. She likes him too, which is helpful. If she gives me gooshy food and treats, I'll like her more." Max paced the blanket to make sure she was covered, and then resettled on her lower shoulder. for my own part, I went into the bathroom to finish cleaning the salt out of my rear. Which was its' own exercise in trying to keep myself from a noise complaint. Then there were a few band-aids used, and finally a little gauze to complete the patchwork. There were a couple I couldn't get, so those were going to have to wait until tomorrow when I could get back to Fisticuffs and have Ricky check them over for me. With that it was time for bed. I set my alarm for about thirty minutes before the usual so that I could get breakfast ready for everyone.

As I hit the bed, a wave of exhaustion settled over me. It wasn't like I was too old for this, but surprises like tonight took a bigger bite out of me than I'd like. Time to spend a few more hours a week at Fisticuffs. That was my last conscious thought before sleep overtook me.

In the morning, I found Rebecca already awake and making breakfast. For his part, Jere was still in bed, and max was happily plowing through gooshy food. Max regarded me for a moment before going back to it.

"I like her. She fed me first." Maxs' tail swished back and forth.

"You mean you totally lied about what I usually give you for breakfast." I knew a few of his tricks.

"I didn't say that. The fact that it happened like that is pure coincidence." His posture suggested that he was far too pleased with himself. In the interim, Rebecca had noticed my existence with a start and had pulled herself to the corner, looking very concerned bordering on frightened.

"I'm, I'm sorry Mister Arthur, officer Arthur, sir. I, I wasn't sure about breakfast so I started like I did at home and and you were there and Max said it was okay?" She was backing into a corner and making herself small. Relatively.

"It's okay as long as you don't burn the place down. But we do need to have a talk about last night." As soon as I said that, I felt like I'd stepped on a mine and I had about two seconds to clear it. Rebeccas' posture was anticipatory, like something very large and mean in the form of me was about to turn her world upside down yet again. I held up a hand to forestall any sort of imagined grief. "Nothing bad, I just want to know more, and if we can expect anything else like that in the future. First, I'mma check for anything downstairs."

I opened the front door to check for any sort of nastygrams as a result of the brothers making use of their phone call. There weren't any of those, but there was a bag of clean clothes for Rebecca. At lest she could get herself cleaned up before school. I brought the bag in and handed them off, shooing Rebecca to the shower, while I took over kitchen duties and had Max go wake up Jere.

Things proceeded apace after that with Rebecca coming out after a fast shower and with clean clothes. I made a note to drop the other stuff off with Paulie. But first, breakfast was served,

As soon as Jere and Rebecca saw each other, the mood changed - I won't say it was rainbows shining and bluebirds singing, but there was a definite lightening in the air. Rebecca was less of a frightened waif, and more confident. It was like Jere was a tiny lucky charm. I wasn't going to begrudge them that. It'd been a rough night all around. We found places on the couch to sit and eat, with minimal talking.

The big problem was that my day was going to be busy, despite it being the last day of my paid "You made Wingnut look bad" suspension. I was going to have to head down to the station house with Rebecca to make a formal statement regarding the events of last night, get a few things rolling with regard to Fisticuffs, and maybe look at getting my phone replaced. first things first, it was time to get Jere hustled to school and call Rebeccas' school to advise them they'd be missing her smiling face today.

Getting Jere to school was a little easy, and Jere looked a little awkward, shifting his weight back and forth. Finally, he looked at the sidewalk for a moment and then back up to me. "Do you think, uhm, we could get married?" That brought me up short for a moment. On the one hand, I didn't want to brush it off as some sort of puppy love thing. On the other hand, I could distinctly recall changing diapers and teaching someone how to walk. It was not that long ago.

"Well, sport, that's something that I would say we should wait on. Maybe get a few years under both your belts, and then we can have some more discussions. I mean you might find out there's things you don't like about each other. Just, y'know. Make sure the good outweighs the bad and you'll be okay."

Jere seemed to take this in and nodded. "Okay. I'mma go over there tomorrow." Hopefully Rebecca and Jere wouldn't disturb Paulie too much. And if they did, Paulie would not have a problem teaching them about what was and was not appropriate behavior.

Once back upstairs, it was time to make a call. Rebeccas' school took the news with minimal trouble, mainly because when I called them I introduced myself as Officer Arthur, and that Miss Rebecca was needed for statements regarding an incident that had taken place yesterday evening, however she would be in on Monday.

From there, it was a walk back to Fisticuffs to hand off the dirty laundry. Paulie was still a little apologetic for the whole thing last night, however the gym had not been vandalized. Yet. he did tell me he'd been on the phone with his lawyer, and restraining orders for the family would be granted on a preliminary basis by noon, pending confirmation of reports from us. That meant that our next stop was the station house.

Technically I didn't have to wear my uniform, however it really didn't feel right to wear anything else. Once I had everything where it needed to be, Rebecca and I piled into the van to make the short drive to the station, where things rapidly got interesting. First, I walked in to a dozen people cheering me as "Sparklebutt". Second was when I went to talk to the desk sergeant about making a statement regarding everything that had happened. We both got shuffled to the overworked assistant district attorney who had an office in the station for just such occasions. It was very enlightening, as her head stuck up among the piles of files. And then it got strange. Rebecca recounted what she remembered. she recounted the dinner in detail but couldn't remember anything from when we crossed the street to when she started running to the Jolly Cholly. Then I gave my statement, which filled in several blanks as far as what I saw happen. The security feed from Fisticuffs was already handed over as reasoning for the restraining orders. It was fairly quick, and we were able to confirm roughly what dates we'd be expected in court.

Once that was done, I had to go to the station armory cage to sign for body armor and pepper spray before I could pick them up in the very early hours of the morning. No helmet was on the list. The Erinyes was not there. The armory officer was not helpful when I asked him what they were thinking upstairs.

"Y'see Sparklebutt, the boys upstairs calculate only a twenty-four point seven percent chance that this'll turn into a riot. At twenty-five percent, they'd give you a helmet. Twenty-four point seven, they're probably going to be in the chucking rocks at you maybe, and the budget breakdown is thus; your head is so hard that any rocks thrown'll bounce off, whereas you put a helmet on your head there's a chance it might get scratched. Scratches cost money to repair, and so there y'are." There was a very non-committal shrug, and I was sure it was in the back of his head that I was going to get things thrown at me. We could only hope that they were soft.

I groaned softly. "I'm not sure if I should punch you or the accountant."

"Send 'em your dry cleaning bill if you get cut. I'll vouch for you."

I signed off for everything and made my way back down to the in-processing with Rebecca still in tow, because I had a question or two. I leaned in and asked if someone could do Sparklebutt a solid and show me the intake for a couple people who were picked up outside Fisticuffs last night. I got the intake sheet and looked at the list of personal effects that they had. One thing they had jumped out at me, each of them had a syringe of horse tranquilizer. That said, the amount would have put your average Unchanged teenager on their butt for awhile. Rebecca was certainly not that, which explained why she was out of it for a few minutes - they were planning to sedate her and then hopefully have her somewhere else before she came to. Hooray for a large body weight coming into the picture.

That said, there wasn't any reason to hang out, so we decided it was in fact time to go. And that was when the world got depressing. We were leaving and so were Rebeccas' brothers, having been bailed out by what appeared to be their father. I leaned down to her to whisper.

"I know a back way if you want it. You don't have to face them if you don't want to."

Rebecca took a breath. "I can do it. I can't run away."

The father looked very well-dressed, with a suit and watch that probably cost about three months pay for me. By contrast, the two sons looked like they were in some sort of rebellious phase, with counterculture slogans on their shirts and artfully ripped jeans.

The father gave Rebecca a look and waved her over. "Rebecca Ann. Come here." The 'we are not discussing this' tone was clear. Although honestly I don't think I'd ever used it to have Jere come over to talk. That said it worked initially, as Rebecca lurched forward and then back to my side, shaking her head once. I glanced at her and her eyes were wide.

He glared at her, while the two brothers took up a flanking sort of position. The battle lines had been drawn, it seemed. The older of the two spoke up. "C'mon Rebecca, we got a thing set up for you."

The father nodded. "Rebecca Ann, the Edens' Light Group has presented a very lucrative opportunity for the family. They are willing to pay a substantial amount for your immediate employment, as well as an annual stipend to us for continuing after you turn eighteen."

The younger of the brothers was rocking back and forth, anxiously waiting for Rebecca to say yes. Rebecca shook her head. "No, Papa. I'm, I'm an adult now, and I have my own job and I go to school. I'll be okay Papa." It was as if she was reassuring him, somehow - and also herself, as I could see this was not a good place for her, but I kept myself quiet and tried to remember everything that I could about the Edens' Light Group. It wasn't much - the press releases and promos that came to mind were full of Neotypes and Unchanged working in all sorts of settings, with the expressions I recognized as the Mandatory Smile one had on for the folks in charge.

A frown creased the older mans' face. "After everything we've done. You ran away. Do you know how much that hurt your mother? She was beside herself for weeks. It's only right that you apologize. And you should come home and do that."

Rebecca bit her lip. "Papa, I ran away because I heard you and Mama talking." She bit her lip for a moment, debating how much she should say. "I couldn't sleep but I couldn't move so I laid in bed, and I could hear you through the vent. You were talking about who would give the most money for me. You were talking about restructuring stuff so that you could use whatever money you got for me to pay off cards and stuff."

"And then you decided on the Edens' Light Group. I heard the man you talked to that night. They were gonna give me a nice stall in a barn so that I could adjust, and then find a good husband so that I could get married to him on my eighteenth birthday, and live the rest of my life as a good centaur mother. And all I could ever hear you ask was how much was going into your pocket for me. Like, it was like I'd become a thing. One of those assets from work you talk about."

Father reacted as if he'd been slapped. It wasn't a good thing because one, he'd been busted. And two, his authority was being publicly and directly challenged. "Rebecca. We can talk about this like adults. All you have to do is sign off, and the Edens' Light Group will give you a percentage as well as the family at large. And they'll train you for a career that's suitable for your interests and talents."

"Like what, pulling a plow? I looked around after I came here. I went to the library and checked things out. The elves game me a look but they let me use a computer for a bit. They're like a cult. They put the Neos in barns and treat 'em like smart farm animals. I saw stuff about 'em, and I didn't like it - is that what you want? Me gardening and pulling a plow and marrying someone I never met until the wedding day?"

"Rebecca. It's not about what I want. It's about what's best for the family - it's always been that way. You know that." Say this for him, he was a spin master. I had a hunch that whatever was best for the family lined up pretty well with what he wanted.

Rebecca took a huge breath, was silent for a long time, and finally let it out. When she spoke again, her voice was low. "Papa, when your lawyer wants to send something to me, make sure he sends it to Rebecca Ann Arthur, because that's my name from now on."

Oh. Hell. If they looked at my badge and nametag, they'd definitely put two and two together and get four. The only thing I could hope for would be that these guys were slow at math.

I looked around and realized that while the station hadn't come to a complete standstill, we'd attracted a few tourists who wanted to see how this particular drama played out. I waved them away, because if this kept going, there'd probably be another arrest or two. I started to shoo people away, clearing my throat and nudging Rebecca toward the door. She took the hint and walked out, head up and looking a little proud of herself as we walked back to the van.

Once we were in, it took a block for her to finally break down and cry a bit. I kept myself quiet during the drive, finally wheeling in to Fisticuffs to get things sorted out.

Once we were in her apartment, I poked my head in and took a look around. It was definitely an improvement on when I'd found her initially, but I was still a bit surprised. But, there were more pressing questions in mind.

"Rebecca Ann...Arthur?"

She nodded. "It was gonna be a surprise at the final judgment thing."

"Okay, but why?"

She shrugged a little. "Well, when your family wants to sell you to the highest bidder and call it vocational work study enrollment, it kinda lowers that familial caring a bit. I mean, it was a month. I hadn't even finished Changing and they were already having people over who couldn't wait to hand me over to them. I tried looking the people up on my computer, but they changed the nanny program on my computer so I couldn't look up where they were sending me to. At that point, they kinda stopped being my family and started being people I shared a roof with." She looked down at the floor. "I know it was a bad thing, but it was like, I could run away to live somehow or I could get my family some money and live a life that didn't sound good at all. And then, well...you saw."

I took it all in. "Well, I think we mighta done something good overall. But I think you might want to try and get some stuff after work for self-defense classes. If your old family's financials are bad enough that they'd try kidnapping you, they're probably gonna try again, and we may not be around next time."

She nodded a little. "I need to protect Jere-bear."

Oh. Oh man. She had a nickname for my son. First off, when did this happen. Hopefully whatever was happening could wait a few years. I didn't exactly have the wherewithal to come up with a good answer on that one, so I shrugged a little. "That wouldn't be the worst thing in the world. Maybe you should come over tonight if Paulie's okay with it, stay up late and watch bad movies or something?"

Rebecca perked up dramatically after that. "That'd be, uh, " she caught her enthusiasm and damped it down a bit. "I think I'd like that."

"Well, check with Paulie, and we'll expect you around seven."

Which meant my next stop was the store for extras. Despite everything I was worried, and one of the better counter-responses to that was a big healthy meal. After shopping for a big bag of popcorn and a whole bunch of other things that weren't a hundred percent healthy, I started cooking. I had about four hours to work with, and while I wasn't as good as Nona, I could hold my own. Besides, it was going to be a special night of sorts. We needed to balance out bad memories with good ones, and a night of movies and food seemed like the best way to make it happen.

Jere got home and seemed far too enthused about the evenings' plans. He even hurried through doing his classwork to start dialing up the movies for the night. I couldn't complain, much - the biggest problem was when he asked for help with his math homework, and there were no numbers to be found. According to him, he was supposed to calculate the orbital rotation of several planets of different sizes and impossible shapes. I pointed him at the laptop because that was far outside what I knew.

As soon as I heard the knock on the door, I checked the time and confirmed it was Rebecca, opened the door and saw her head straight for Jere, where they plopped on the couch and made themselves comfortable. After that it was bad movies, lots of finger food, and Max darting between the three of us to mooch. Jere was almost keeping up, owing to his youth and his own metabolism kicking into some fifth-dimensional high gear. It was certainly not what I was expecting, but it was bonding over high calorie diets with a lot of snacks and homework that was rapidly surpassing anything I could help with. Overall, the night passed, pictures were taken, and Max complained because he wasn't in every shot.

The next morning was a Saturday, and getting up early was not normally in the cards. But I did anyway, leaving Jeremiah a note to feed Max before he played on the laptop - assuming Max didn't tell Jeremiah himself. Once I was at the station, the Erinyes working the armory came in at the same time, winked at me and whispered that she had something extra for me when I got back to her area. My stomachs were already in bad enough shape, and whatever she had was not something I needed. But when I checked, there in fact was a little extra - a high-end trauma plate for my chest. Seemed like someone was concerned about my safety. I made a note to find out her name. If something happened, I'd definitely owe her a beer. But not a date.

And then I had to hustle to get on the bus with everyone else that had gotten picked to go play bodyguards to people who wanted nothing more than have me be their second class. Along with me were two other centaurs, a pair of Erinyes for flying looks, and no unchanged. Honestly it felt like someone had made the decision that we should be seen given that I'd had a few recent appearances with high-profile folks, and hopefully discourage anyone who had a beef with any of the speakers. No confirmation, but at the same time I and my compatriots were definitely sticking out in the crowd.

The whole day felt off. Or perhaps it was six hours of being declared unfit for anything except pulling a plow, racing, or stunningly indecent movies. On top of that it was a hot sunshine-filled day, and with the uniforms and body armor on, we were not in any way cooled off. We got breaks when our radio batteries ran dry or when our sweat shorted out the radios themselves, but past that it was a ripe slice of annoyance.

The day was not improved by Rebeccas' brothers showing up. They'd lost the counterculture gear, which made me think they'd bought it just for the kidnapping. Still, they did not impress. Especially when I got pulled off the line for a snack and water break. They decided that would be the perfect time to try to talk to me. And try to intimidate me. Well, I suppose two on one is usually intimidating on the school yard, but we were a long way from the nearest schoolyard. Since I hadn't had a chance to learn their names, they were promptly dubbed Older and Younger in the back of my head. They were leaning against the police bus in an attempt to look tough.

Older was the one who spoke up first. "Hey, Glue."

I quirked an eyebrow as I inhaled an energy bar. "Something you need fellas?"

"Yeah, our sister."

"That'd be Rebecca, right?"

"Yeah. Turn her over, and we'll be done. Promise, you'll never see us again."

Younger nodded his agreement. "Yeah. Listen, all we want to do is get her to sign off on joining Edens' Light. They said they'd give her a home and a job, and then they'd pay the family like, a ton for it until she turns eighteen, and then we'd get half and then she'd get half to give to her husband for the rest of her life."

"Is there an or-else here?" Part of me wanted to hear what they had for this.

Older spoke up, with a voice that took on the tones of unlimited self-confidence available only to fools and teenagers. "Obviously. That barn where she's living at now is gonna face some trouble."

I held up a hand. "Okay, listen - before we get too deep into this, I really need you guys to know a thing or two about a thing or two. First, pretty sure Rebecca's happy where she is. Second, her legal status? She's an adult - right now she's got one more hearing where it's written in stone. Free and clear, and I'm not sure if you've noticed but that means something. Third, I'm not your lawyer, but given that you're here, you've probably talked to a lawyer. I don't think anyone with an interest in your not being in jail with a criminal record is gonna want to have you two talking to me. So with that in mind, why don't you fellas go on your way and I'll get back to being over there?"

They did not pick up the gentle hint, as Older again took the lead. "No, you listen. You can either have the barn, or you can have Rebecca. You ain't gettin' both. So pick one."

I closed my eyes for a moment. "Guys. I'm gonna make this as simple as possible. You're threatening a police officer. That's a bad idea. On top of that, you're telling that police officer that you're going to be doing some massive property damage unless you're allowed to kidnap someone. That's a worse idea. Because that barn is also home to a few people. People like Paulie. You met him before. And then on top of that, there's about half-dozen gym rats living on the third floor. Two of them being mixed martial arts guys. I'll be honest, I wouldn't want to meet any of them in a dark alley, and I outweigh them by six hundred pounds. Our average response time is about ninety seconds to Little Italy. So before you you say another word, I want you to consider the scene. You've been busted trying to burn down someone's home. You realize you're in trouble and so you call the police. Meanwhile, several very large, very unhappy people have at least a minute and a half to use the two of you as punching bags. And kicking bags. Heck they might even make a game of it. You boys better hope your health insurance is good, because that's a situation where you find out."

Hopefully this would stick with them - finally I saw some apprehension at the potential for trouble to them personally. Older finally decided for them, as it was obvious they weren't going to get what they wanted. "Well...we'll see." He and his brother huffed and tried to walk off simultaneously, but it didn't quite work out as perfectly as they wanted. I sighed and finished drinking the gallon of water I had handy, before sending a text to Paulie advising that Rebeccas' brothers were keen on there being a round two.

And then I got the call to go up between the crowd and the keynote speaker, an epically handsome gentleman with an expression on his face that begged to be punched. Still, it wasn't my job to watch him, it was my job to watch the crowd. So I did. Not just the crowd but the buildings around it.

The speech was familiar ground, I'd heard it a lot of times in the past. The neotypes weren't people, they needed to be stripped of their rights and treated with all the care of animals, because they were taking jobs, upending the economy, spreading all manner of ills to tempt even the most stalwart God-fearing person. I'm fairly certain that nobody in the crowd saw the irony that the folks he was rabble-rousing against were standing in front of him to protect his skeezy butt. Quite frankly, I was having a hard time believing any of it, but I kept quiet, because if I started anything I would not only lose my time and a half for this thing, I'd probably also get suspended with pay, with nothing to do except dodge Nona, work out, and do homework with Jeremiah. And then the world went into slow motion as I saw a shiny gun barrel extending from a nearby window.

Never mind what the idiot behind me was saying, my body reacted. I reared up and called out the warning to everyone, and then my chest got punched. Hard. There was chaos and commotion, but my body wasn't doing anything it was supposed to. I struggled to my feet, and the punchable face was being hustled off by several suits with guns out. I looked down and then I felt pain radiating from my midsection - not quite my back, and not my front either. Someone was saying something in my earpiece, but it was fuzzy. Finally the world went blank.

Chapter 7

I woke up in the hospital with a very severe nurse looking at me. "Good. You're awake. I'll call the doctor."

A few minutes later an elf came in and looked at me. "Ah you're conscious. That's pleasant. Now then, I know you have questions, and I'll answer as best I can. You were shot in the chest, but fortunately the trauma plate absorbed most of it; unfortunately there was still enough for it to damage your upper thoracic heart before it stopped in your lung. Most of the damage has been repaired. You are quite fortunate, your lower heart took over for your entire circulatory system, which allowed you to survive."

I held up a hand. "Doc. My kid. Where is he, how long have I been laying here, and when can I get out of this slop joint and go back to doing my job?"

The elf wrinkled his nose at me. "Jeremiah is fine, four days, and I'm not at liberty to say."

"I'm damn well at liberty to hear it." I shrugged the blankets off and went to take off leads and managed to stand and walk three paces. "Now where's the bar. I need a friggin' beer..." And I promptly fell over as a lead I hadn't seen tripped me up.

"Alcohol is contraindicated at this time, Mister Arthur. You're on some elevated painkillers and you have several visitors outside."

I stumbled to my feet again and parked it as best I could. "Fine. But cut down on the painkillers or cut me loose tomorrow because otherwise I'll find a way home."

There was a very slight sniff. "I'm sure you will." He left and Jeremiah tornadoe'd in with Max, colliding with my chest in an unhealthy way. He had a 5 o'clock shadow and he looked like he hadn't slept in a week. He was also noticeably shorter, but hadn't gone shopping for new clothes. That was definitely odd. And the third visitor was even odder, as she was the Erinyes who'd been working the armory for a few months and slipped me the trauma plate.

For the first time, I got to look at her with more than a passing glance. Her black hair was tied back, and she was in a custom-fit charcoal power suit and pumps that reminded me vaguely of an up-and-coming executive. Even her wings were folded back in some sort of minimalist sort of pose. Someone did a study and found that Erinyes wings were distracting - which was something I probably could have told them for half whatever they charged.

As Erinyes went, she was tall - my foggy brain guessed she was close to six feet tall or thereabouts - with high cheekbones and coppery skin, black hair that was currently either in a braid or a ponytail stretching to her knees, if the wisps of hair could be believed. It was somewhat surprising for me after having seen her, admittedly in passing glances, to realize that she was probably Native American. In my defense, every time I'd seen her before I'd had several other things on my mind. And to make things worse, some sort of instinct in the back of my head was trying to sound an alert. She waited at the door with a briefcase as both Max and Jeremiah tried talking to me at once, while I tried to both figure out what the heck my brain was trying to tell me and keep a poker face in case there was a realization from the heavens that I didn't want to share. Something was definitely off - I realized I was moving my head back and forth and sniffing the air. For what I wasn't sure.

Looking more closely at her, it seemed that there was something similar going on with her, as her face was registering shock and surprise with her wings slowly opening to show themselves fully. Not gonna lie, the plumage was more beautiful than any I'd ever seen, dark roots flowing to a blue, then green, and finally at the edges they were a brilliant red. She finally looked at what her wings were doing and snapped them closed with an audible ruffling sound. Max and Jeremiah had in the meantime decided that Jere should go first, and he moved toward my bed hopping from one foot to the other anxiously.

"Dad, you're not gonna believe it but there's stuff going on and these guys came with Miz Elias and picked me and Max up and I rode in an airplane and we stopped and then we got down here in an army truck and then these other guys gave me a computer and they hooked up the one thing and said I needed to figure it out - " I hugged him and he squirmed a lot, apparently embarrassed. "But Daaaaaddd, there's more stuff and I can't say more cause Miz Elias said she needed to tell you."

Max was a bit more circumspect, keeping his voice low in my head. "Explain why I've had substandard minions feeding me for the past several meals." He paused sniffing around leads and several other things. "There was an Elf in here, we need to fumigate this place." However, the rubbing and weaving around me was enough to let me know that he'd had deep concerns. Finally he hopped from the bed to my back and started kneading before falling asleep. It was at that point that Jeremiah and Ms Elias shared a look. Jeremiah nodded a bit and went through a different door where I briefly saw what looked to be an adjoining room. Apparently we'd been given our own rooms.

Ms Elias pulled up a chair and a small desk for her briefcase, opening it and looking at me. The silence spoke volumes, as something was still trying to get a message through to my highly painkiller-infused brain, but I shook it off because there were questions on my mind. With that thought coming to the forefront, I spoke first.

"Soon as I get on my feet I'm buying you a beer." First things first. I probably owed her my life, and that was how the debt was acknowledged. It wasn't exactly a fair trade, but I couldn't very well rename my first-born after her.

An eyebrow arched, and she waved her hand. "Not necessary."

"Hey, without the trauma plate, I'm worse off. I owe you a beer at least." Or wine, or soda, or whatever it was that she preferred.

"If you insist. Let's get down to business." There was a shuffling sound from her wings. Possibly annoyance.

"Business?" That sounded positively ominous.

She reached into the briefcase, extracting a manila folder and opening it. "Quite. Brooks Arthur, neotype Centauris. One son, Jeremiah. Neotype Lilliputius, or dwarf. One now-ex wife, in the process of changing her name to Aoife. Neotype Faun. Patient Brooks Arthur is currently under medical care for fractured hominid ribs, pericardial lacerations of the hominid heart, a broken collarbone, a dislocated right equine shoulder, and multiple contusions of the upper lungs. Full recovery time estimated to be six weeks if he adheres to the prescribed regimen. Psychological analysis indicates recovery time of seven to eight weeks, as Patient Arthur has marked traits for stubbornness and refusal to admit to pain. Traits appear to have been initially learned during time as a paratrooper. Now that we have the basics out of the way, let me explain the situation."

"You mean beyond the apparent kidnapping?" The medication was only helping a bit, and I kept having to shift around to be comfortable.

"Oh it was an actual kidnapping, however there is a very good reason."

"Is this what the doctor couldn't talk about?" The fuzz in my brain was clearing a bit as I had something to focus on. Specifically that I'd been kidnapped.

"No wonder your reviews are all glowing. Even medicated you're making connections." She smirked a bit and fluttered her wings.

"My reviews are confidential." And that was something they'd drilled into us for awhile.

"Not if you're dead." She spread her hands almost apologetically, keeping an eye on me for a reaction. I did note that one of her hands darted into the briefcase, and I didn't want to think about what she had a hold of in there. I tried keeping it light, just in case there was something nasty in the briefcase.

"I feel pretty spry for a dead fellah." And I was supposed to be dead on top of it. This day could not stop being full of strange news.

"Oh, you're only dead on paper. To answer your next several questions. You and your son have become the latest Friends of Jacques. Jack, if you prefer. You're on an abandoned Air Force base in the middle of nowhere - specifically, we're in the southeastern part of Wyoming. The nearest town is called Uranium Hills, about two miles south of here."

That brought me up short. I'll be honest, I sat there for several minutes trying to figure out how to respond to that. I'm sure the security tape would be interesting, but I managed to get myself back on track.

"Why am I officially dead?" First questions first, really.

"Because your son plugged a removable drive into your laptop." Because that explained everything, really. I sat up a bit, realized I was in a hospital gown, and grabbed a blanket to cover my upper. Unfortunately, since the hospital I was in forgot that patient me was a big fellah that left my southern hemisphere feeling breezy. I grumbled and attended to that, finally managing to get everything decent before attending to the conversation at hand.

"You're joking me here. What the hell was on that?" I was quite confused, and I'm sure the look on my face was priceless - also, if this place was anything like the station house, it was going to be in the Christmas party tape.

"From what Jeremiahs' been able to piece together, it's several lists - some of it is seems to be technological, some of it is blackmail, and some of it, we're not sure. However, the security features on it are significant enough that we're having everyone who can work on it work on it. For one, there was a virus that would have destroyed your computer. For two, there was a tracker on it. And that's how we found you." This lady was chock-full of information, and was insistent on slow-walking it to me for some reason. Probably the medication, but also quite possibly because this was a bit of an unusual situation.

"You were tracking it? How? What about the Erinyes that got killed." It was time to start asking what might be some serious questions. Although I might not like the answers.

"Primarily, we created the security measures on it - someone lifted it from one of the companies we license it to. What they missed was that one of the passive features is a phone-home subroutine specifically for this sort of corporate espionage. We had an odd one phone home to us, so we started looking for it, but we couldn't get the exact location. I was assigned a job in the nearest police station armory, which left me a bit of time to look around." She spread her hands, almost apologetically. "We couldn't get to her in time. She kept buying laptops and destroying them, which only alerted us that the drive had been plugged in at a location, but it destroyed the computer before it could send all the data that we needed. I'm sure you saw the pile when you went back. She knew enough to break into it a little and she knew she was on to something. She was good. However, it looks like the drive has been re-keyed and without the correct code response, the drive activates a routine that destroys the hardware its' connected to. That starts within five seconds, so an enterprising individual can grab a little data before the loss of the hardware."

"Yeah. What about the rest of it. Why are we legally dead, and what the hell's next?" These were not insignificant moves being made by this group of folks. whoever the Friends of Jack were, they had some serious friends. You don't just get a job in the armory because you need a job. And getting two folks declared legally dead and relocating them to Uranium Hills, wherever it was located was something that took some doing. I was not taking her word that it was in Wyoming.

"Because whoever put this list together and put it on a drive has already killed at least one person for the information, and the only way to keep them from burning the Jolly Cholly to the ground was to have a team come in that night, ransack your apartment and leave a melted dummy laptop and drive in its' place. Which should be enough for them to mark it lost and move forward without it. Your funeral was lovely by the way. Rebecca was sad, and Nona almost threw herself into the casket. The station house closed for the day, the wake at the Jolly Cholly was traditional, and the mayor has promised that the plan you proposed at the luncheon is going to receive some personal attention and fast-track analysis. They're also very busy looking for the shooter." She kept looking down at her notes, apparently giving me some space to digest whatever was going through my painkiller-infused brain.

"Who's them?" This was rapidly spiraling out of the world where things made sense, but if this group was good enough to pull all this off cleanly, they had to have some idea of who they were up against.

"Them is unknown, but they're heavily invested in the Genesis groups. From what we have, they're multinational, wealthier than multiple nations, and aren't particularly concerned about

Neotypes. The rally you were protecting was supposed to end in a riot." Or not.

I blinked. "Should Max be hearing this?"

"Max is involved, since they were rather going to kill him. Jeremiah knows, and he's going to be in here as soon as I'm done. We have a room for him right next door."

"Okay, fine. Explain riot."

She opened her briefcase and flicked on a projector, throwing footage of the rally onto a blank wall. "Here's what you didn't see at the rally." She fast-forwarded to the last speaker and muted it. "Watch this and tell me what you see."

We watched in silence as the speaker ranted, raved, and kept moving his eyes to a spot until I reared and wrecked my day. And life apparently. I made a back up motion and asked for a pause. "He's looking at the shooter. Or where the shot's coming from. It's a setup."

She nodded. "You're a good cop, Brooks. We borrowed the key to his hotel room while he was enjoying a complimentary sauna and massage after the shooting. We found modified body armor, and from the placement he was supposed to get shot through his appendix. For the record, their body armor is much better than what I gave you."

I continued along her train of thought; "And then after that, they were going to immediately find a shooter, probably a neotype, right?"

She nodded, and her eyebrows moved up fractionally, accompanied by another wing flutter. "Right the first time. The police have already made two arrests. A bail bondsman had posted bail within minutes for one of them. The idea appeared to be that the one could be released and most likely lynched, and then the real fun would start, with a riot making it's way to your apartment where they'd send in a few people to break everything they could break, find the drive, and then burn it all down. Fortunately we were able to secure release and transportation for both of them. Neither of them appear to be the actual shooter, so we'll be providing legal counsel and confirming that the charges are dropped. In the meantime, we have a few people working to find the real culprit. The local police are highly enthusiastic about finding out who. It's likely that the actual shooter is going to be identified and we'll probably be working on an international scale to have them detained." The scope of the idea was breathtaking. Someone agreed to be shot to initiate a riot, all to find a piece of hardware no larger than my thumb that had some sort of secret information on it. If I hadn't been on an impressive amount of painkillers, I might have laughed at the whole concept.

"Okay this still doesn't answer several questions. Who are you, what the hell do you do, and..." I waved a hand "Why all this? Sure Jeremiahs' smart, always has been. But you're seriously telling me you've got all these resources, and he's better? I mean - this doesn't make sense." As I looked around, I noticed that there were a fair number of decorations from my apartment strewn about here.

There was a very light smirk. "I'm not sure how to tell you this, but your son is a genius - even relative to the Dwarven neotype. As in, we have five of the best programmers known. Their consensus was this would be weeks of work in a Faraday cage to even get it to where we would have something that wouldn't kill the computer it was attached to. He's already sorted a bit of it which is how we know how much we know. And now we have six of the best programmers known, which for us is a bonus, since only you were on our list. The problem is we don't have the person or people who originally created it. Which means there's at least one genius-savant level programmer out there that we don't know about who reverse-engineered about ninety percent of our security and added a few more things of their own."

"Still got questions here."

"Ah. Well, what we do is try to keep a world on the brink of exploding from exploding. Ever since The Incident, people and the Neotypes have been changing as their base needs change. Most have been able to find their niche, but, not everyone can. Which makes them easy targets. We fairly certain there's a group that's guiding it, but we don't know."

I held my hand up to forestall further talking. "Okay this all great but...what next? I mean, I'm a beat cop. My son's a genius. I'll accept that, but...what do you expect me to actually *do* here? And for the love of Pete do you have a real name?"

"You can call me Elias, but my name's whatever you want it to be, honey."

I reached for my non-existent handcuffs, which caused me to smack Max a good one and wince as I pulled something that didn't want to be pulled. Max complained, deeply. "Seriously, gooshy food. You owe me."

I hmphed at Max before continuing with Ms Elias; "Still doesn't answer the question of what I'm actually doing."

In reply, she dropped a file on my end table. "For starters, solve a murder."

"Great. So new question. Who in the name of all that's cute and fuzzy is Jacques, and why are we suddenly his best friends?" I waved an arm around my unfamiliar surroundings filled with familiar things.

"Ah. Usually that's the first question. Story time. There are in fact two Jacques in this story. The first is Jacques de Molay, the last Grandmaster of the Knights Templar. Short version, he and the Templars died because the King of France was broke, owed the Knights money, and decided the best course of action was to blow up the bank. So he convinced the Pope that the Templars were bad and needed to be done away with. Lots of history, we have several books on the subject. The second is Jacques-Charles Dupont de l'Eure, the first successor to the French monarchy who was not himself styled as a monarch. He was simply Chairman of the Provisional Government, and he retired after six months on the job."

She continued, setting aside whatever paperwork she was using as a reference. "We're certainly not pure and lily-white, and hopefully you'll be able to come to terms with that. In the past, we were focused on conflict prevention. We'd done a few things to help change peoples' minds, moving the world toward what we like to think of as an equitable arrangement where the world solved problems with equipment other than a gun. Then The Incident happened and we found ourselves fighting the same fight with new faces. Every so often we find someone with potential, and we arrange a meeting. If they seem interested, we offer them a job at one of our local shell companies in to more actively monitor them. In this case, you had been tagged as someone with potential, and I was monitoring you. We'd had the meeting, but we hadn't gotten to the offer point, so your recruitment was a little rushed. When you were being sent to the hospital, the section that does math did math and determined there was an eighty-five percent chance of someone related to the Genesis Group attempting to kill you while you there. We didn't like those numbers, so we gathered you, Jere, and Max up to come here."

"So I was being watched. But when was this first meeting?" I was fairly certain I would have remembered someone offering me a job with some shadowy group for an unknown purpose.

"That was during your lunch with the mayor. You were polite, formal, and yet you still found time to get a bit of your own agenda into the mix. You'll be pleased to note that your initial document has been rewritten for acceptability, and is winding its' way through the state government for what appears to be approval. Tax incentives do play well with the public, and having your heroic name attached to it is going to be very helpful."

I considered several things. One, that I'd been under surveillance and had only recognized it as a creepy sensation of being watched. Two, that they were watching me not date, and it was somehow favorable.

"That was a test?"

"Quite. So, now that you're satisfied with our processes, you'll be in bed for one more day before we begin the tour - doctors' orders. In the meantime, you have a few things to catch up on, and some reading." She tossed a thick manila folder wrapped with a bow onto the bed. "Do try to justify our faith in you." And with that she left me alone with Max, who looked amazingly smug. Cats.

Reading the case file was interesting on several levels. The first parts confirmed what I already knew, the victim had died from single shot to the head, very messy. Good thing the coroner knew what to look for. Ballistics reports were odd, however. Without getting too far into the gory details, the bullet didn't act like a bullet fired that closely would. No powder marking indicative of a close shot, and after asking for a few more painkillers and some coffee, things came together. I remembered that we had received a call about 30 minutes before we were summoned to the scene; noise complaint from the old lady who hated joy and thought the kids were shooting off fireworks. Which was possible, but there was only the one shot.

The down side of that was that I didn't have any way to ask for any incident report regarding the fireworks complaint, even if there was one. Dead bodies tend to have priority over what's probably some kid with a string of firecrackers. The rest of the report was full of questions. Toxicology report was nonexistent, given the probable cause of death. The usual reports for DNA analysis didn't bring back anything meaningful, as she'd had so many people in and out of her office there were hundreds of unique samples to run through. Overall, this was a report of what might have been a near-perfect murder. The key on this one was the toxicology - or maybe it wasn't, but it wasn't in my hands where I needed it to be. I made mention of this to Elias, and she pursed her lips and left my room.

The next day was the grand, but virtual tour of the place. For an abandoned airbase, there was a lot going on underground. Elias told me that this had originally been a base that was dedicated to nuclear missiles, which explained a few things regarding the design choices. After the missiles were removed, the Friends of Jack had first leased, then outright purchased the land from the government and set to work rearranging the silos to their liking. The place was an inverted fifteen-story office building complete with onsite living quarters, work sites and a medical facility - each in their own silo. Hopefully that was merely literal and not metaphorical. One other interesting thing was that the spaces appeared to be highly modular, as I saw a few people expanding a space for some additional equipment.

According to Elias, the power draw was massive, so they had their own experimental combination wind and solar farm a few miles away. It kept the lights on and everyone happy, and in an emergency there were several backup generators. In our quarters we even had satellite television with every channel. Literally - local, national, and international. At least I could watch football as soon as I figured out how to work the remote. On that end, I had two tablets, designated work and recreation. The work tablet was where I would be receiving all the communications from on high, as well as scheduling, requisitions, and other assorted things that I would be needing. The rec tablet had a listing of the Uranium Hills restaurants, including takeout menus, the liquor stores' current stocks and a section for any requests I might have, and the television listings. The nice part of the TV listings was that they had recordings of all stripes, and I quickly tested it by putting in queries for some of the football games that I'd missed this season due to being in uniform. They all promptly popped up. Maybe this wouldn't be so bad.

Regarding the decorations, I was mildly impressed to see that they'd cleaned out my apartment of all the important stuff. The memorabilia had been hung up, and more than a few of the favorite things were in a pile for later location assignment. I double-checked and the lucky beret was in fact in the right place. Don't ask me how, because they definitely could have put a different one in its' place, but it felt like the right one. The room proper was painted in a calming blue palette - it was similar to the ones we'd used in the interrogation rooms to put suspects at ease and subsequently be more willing to tell us things about what was happening. It wasn't extraordinarily large, but it had the necessities. A centaur-friendly couch and chair facing the large but not obscenely huge television, near that was a dining table that extended from the wall next to a kitchenette where I could make snacks and small meals when I didn't want to go to the chow hall. The refrigerator was full sized and stocked with the good stuff, and the bathroom was big enough to handle me comfortably. I asked and according to the nurse, there were no anticipated issues regarding the plumbing. If I thought about it, the only real difference between this place and my apartment above the Jolly Cholly was the paint scheme. I made a note to see about getting some paint to redo the walls in a color that made me happy, as opposed to this intentional calm they foisted on me.

In the adjacent room, Jeremiah had been given a top-end workstation with a direct connection what was officially designated Electronic Operations, but was more colloquially known as the Dwarven Mines. When we visited their section, it even had a sign made out of lights with the phrase "We dig until we hit Evil" gracing the top of the door. In addition to that, he'd been given a large selection of hardware to put things together, on the off chance he'd want to build his own system for whatever reason. He seemed happy enough, and the adjoining door was exceptionally soundproofed - we discovered this when he opened the door to show me how the search feature worked for the television and something that I could only describe as a demonic summoning attempt blew through my ears. Jere may have been tagged as brilliant, but they did not account for his taste in music. I tried shouting to get his attention, but that didn't exactly work. I looked at his monitor and saw what looked to be an aerial view of Nonas' and Fisticuffs. It looked like Jere was getting an aerial view of Little Italy, and it was really good quality. I also saw that he was zooming in on a particular centaur. Finally I braced myself against further assault on my ears and tapped his shoulder. He yelped and hit a button to turn the noise down to a reasonable volume. At least for him. For me it was still grating.

"Jeremiah Christopher Brooks, what in the world is that?"

He blinked and then realized I was asking about the music. "Oh, it's kawaii metal."

I recognized that those were words, but the look on my face apparently indicated that I needed context. "So it's like Japanese pop and heavy metal mixed into a thing."

Even after the explanation, it still sounded like there was no viable reason for this sort of this to exist. Which was probably writ large on my face if his expression meant anything. Still, instructions were needed, and I flipped the tablet around to show him what I was looking at. "Show me where the football games are from three seasons ago, please."

Jere eyed it, tapped two buttons on the tablet, and nodded. I looked, and there in all the spectacular glory was a football season to watch - even though I knew the scores, I hadn't exactly gotten to watch all of them. It was one of those "Someday I'm going to settle down and watch these" things. And now I had the time but only because my body had insisted.

Jere hid the smirk of 'fixed the muppet problem' pretty well. "Y'got it from here?"

I nodded. "Sure as soon as you tell me what's up with that." I flicked a finger at the screen, and I saw him tense a bit.

"I just, I was looking at stuff and I figured look at something familiar." He was looking at everything except his monitor for the moment.

I shrugged. Sounds solid enough." I cocked my head. "I think Rebecca just stretched out."

Jeremiahs' head snapped back to monitor in record time as if guided by some unknown force. Admittedly it was a little fun pranking him, but I was pretty sure I'd pay for it somewhere down the line.

"Not funny." He was sulking, but that was probably due to his imagination going full teen hormone for a moment before the letdown.

"Kinda funny." I grinned a little.

"S'not helping."

I nodded in reply. "Yeah, but you needed to realize that, y'know. You got other stuff to focus on. Rebecca's a big girl, she can take care of herself - and while you're at it, see about getting a switch in here that cuts the speaker noise when the door's open." I backed up slowly, throwing him a little something else for his ego. "It's not bad, it's just, y'know. Loud."

Finally I closed the door and was grateful. As I plodded back to the bed to settle and move Max out of the way, I checked the tablet with a new alert telling me that it was learning my voice pattern, and that I should speak a few training sentences to acclimate the system to voice commands. That would make this whole thing easier by a long stretch.

It took me a few days to get back on all four feet confidently, and a few more to be able to walk a distance further than to the shower. After that, I started to try sneaking out to find out what the rest of the place looked like. Unfortunately, centaurs do not stealth. First my doctor tried talking to me. That didn't exactly mesh well with me. After that, Max and Elias tried the same thing. After my third night of trying to get out so I could take a walk, a very healthy looking gentleman who looked at his taser and multiple spare batteries meaningfully was able to convince me I needed to rest.

For a day. After that it was take four. And subsequently take five. Max could not understand my need for activity, and became the alert system for everyone in exchange for treats and catnip. The little snitch. Elias rapidly became exasperated with my attempts to get up and walk, finally getting a hammock and installing herself in my room to make sure I wouldn't leave, which kicked off another conversation about what was and was not acceptable. She promised to leave me alone for showers, but apparently since I couldn't be trusted to not try to run off, she'd be right outside. In addition, she would use the shower right after I was done. It was a workable system, but it was still awkward as hell for a few days, particularly when the shower was involved. We never saw each other, but that was only due to the fact that we both liked hot showers and the bathroom was far too foggy for either of us to see. The bothersome part was that when Elias left to do whatever she did when she wasn't babysitting me, there was some sort of odd scent that I couldn't place and couldn't ignore, to my eternal frustration. It wasn't Max, and it wasn't my stuff. The only way I could successfully get it to the side mentally was to have the best-of from the previous football and baseball seasons on a loop.

The bathroom itself became a minefield of sorts, as Elias began invading the counter space with bottles and containers of unknown purpose. Apparently Erinyes needed four separate sprays and lotions for wing and feather care, as well as applicator hoses for those impossible to reach areas. There were similar things for centaurs, but I'd never really gotten into them. My coat was fine, I just needed the industrial sized bottle of shampoo-conditioner-grout remover.

All in all I wanted my body to cooperate when my brain said we were fine and less awkward "Hey, I'm in here!" moments. Fast. Outside of that, I needed to exercise somehow - I was not accustomed to sitting and doing nothing ever. After a lot of complaining, I was allowed use of the pool - the staff doc was against it, but at this point I was heartily sick of having nothing to do and raised my voice. Fun centaur secret - we have exceptional lung capacity, which means we can shout at levels that can be harmful if they are sustained.

I sustained. Max bolted and it took 20 minutes to corral him, and Jeremiah admitted he heard me over the noise of his stereo. The doc decided I could use the pool after that, but that supervision was required. I'd never been much of a swimmer unless I had to, and once I Changed, well, I became very self-conscious of my body. But at that point, I was ready to take anything I could get just to move my legs in a space that was larger than my quarters.

Of course, it had to be Elias supervising.

Chapter 8

The next day presented issues, as there was a distinct lack of swim trunks for me. I'd never been much of a swimmer outside of what was required for the military, and once I got out of that racket pools and beaches were a very optional thing. Proper swim attire was located in due course, and I approached the pool with trepidation. The walk to the pool had left me more exhausted than I liked. I'd been cooped up too long and I needed to catch my breath. Elias, on the other hand, thought it would be a lovely time to display what she looked like in a bikini. Given what I knew of her, it was probably some sort of mind game. Overall it felt strange looking at her. I was more interested in what appeared to be several sets of scars on her stomach and legs - the largest of which was partially covered with a tattoo of a childs' band-aid. Some were surgical, and others were definitely not. This sparked a conversation of comparison, and for the first time, she was more than just a bureaucrat with a talent for making me feel awkward.

She settled her legs in the water and pointed out a few of her scars before story time. "Helicopter crash, Somalia. Peacekeeping ops, and someone forgot to tell one side or the other. We were carrying some troops to a forward base, and someone with a technical - one of those small trucks, they mount a machine gun and drive 'em around - anyway, one of those had a missile launcher and an attitude, and they didn't think we should have been in the sky."

I perked a little. "You were the pilot? Good job getting it down."

She snorted. "Door gunner. I took care of the technical after the missile launch, but...didn't get the missile."

"Nice job on the technical but what happened after that?" I settled in next to her, checking out the scar and tattoo work, being mindful of the various dings I still had. To make things worse, there was an odd scent in the air from somewhere, and I kept looking around to place the source. Finally I decided it didn't want to be found, and looked at Elias closely while I settled on my stomach to get comfortable and catch my breath without looking like I was trying to catch my breath.

After I was settled, Elias gave me a look that suggested I'd been dropped on my head as a child. "We crashed, Brooks."

"After that, Elias. I was also a paratrooper, which means I have a very firm grasp on the concept of gravity." I leaned over and flicked water at her. "See? Water goes up, gravity takes hold, water falls down. Back to what you were saying."

"I'm told 3 hours for search and rescue to find us and retrieve us. The last thing I remember was shooting the technical. After that my memory picks up with tubes everywhere for a month. It was two months before I could walk. At the end of the day, four broken bones, lost a foot of small intestine and once all the surgeries were done, I couldn't have kids. Still can't - apparently there's some injuries that having your body rewritten can't fix. Count yourself lucky."

"Lucky? Did you actually read my Army medical history? High altitude - low open jump into a zone that Intel said was clear but apparently Intel forgot to tell the people we were planning to surprise. Jump went sideways about 5 seconds after we opened, my chute gets shot to hell and I basically fell through a tree into a crowd of unhappy campers. Sorted them, did the thing we came to do, and then discovered while we were getting hauled out that I'd been shot once, twice if you count the one stuck in my body armor, and I couldn't walk right. Got back, medic looked, called Dr Feelgood over, they ran xrays and scans, found out I'd done the whole thing with half a ligament for each knee and a dislocated ankle. Four months later, back at it until the Army decided they'd had enough of my face."

She snorted. "Forgive me for thinking there were worse things. And for the record, you whined for days about getting into the pool and now all you want to do is play Four Yorkshiremen with war stories? We could do that with beer in your quarters. Get your ass in the pool, or get in the shower."

I decided that nobody was going to talk to me that way, and I stood myself up and backed up a bit for what was going to be an impressive belly flop. It would have worked had my body cooperated like it was supposed to, however the dislocated shoulder didn't do what it was supposed to, and I went face first into the water, and by some trickery of that nasty bint named Physics, I wound up doing a handspring of sorts back-first into the water. On the up side, Elias was soaked to the wings. I twisted around and kicked to the surface to find a very displeased Erinyes looking at me.

"No running. No diving. Or you get to explain to your son why you're not allowed to go to the pool any more. Because I'm not explaining that his father's an idiot." She fluttered her wings to get the worst of the water off, and conveniently most of that landed on me.

"Finnne. So are there any specific exercises I'm supposed to do?" After my demonstration of shouting ability, the doctor had been relaying his medical advice through third parties. But not Max.

"None were mentioned, however we are going to have some restrictions. No gymnastics." That was a mild relief, as I couldn't do gymnastics even when I'd only had the two legs, so I wasn't missing out on much.

"Killjoy. Dare I even say...boo-bird." I began experimenting a bit to see what I could do in the water. Swimming was an odd sort of thing, as my usual swimming style of paddling with the legs and keeping the torso upright and dry was not happening with only three legs working normally. So I was left doing a bobbing up and down through the water that allowed me to use my arms to propel myself forward and around. It was odd and painful at times, but it was also time to get healthy again, and that meant it was time to work through the pain.

I got a splash of water to the face as I passed by Elias, who had remained in a supervisory sitting position on the edge of the pool to make sure I didn't drown. "No puns. And no war stories when anyone else is around."

"Duly noted. You getting in, or was the two-piece just a show-off and some psych game?" I slowed a little, treading water - this was something my body seemed to agree with, and it got me into a good workout sort of rhythm. But at the same time it was exhausting if I didn't pace myself, with my bad lower shoulder being the chief complainer amongst the group.

Elias' response to my challenge was to jump up, flap her wings twice to loft herself to the ceiling and subsequently divebomb the deep end and stay underwater while swimming the length of the pool, coming up next to me. "This is showing off. Now come on, swim or get out."

"That was a dive. Didn't you say no diving?" Now it was my turn to play the adult among us, and I wasn't gonna let it go easily.

"No diving for you. You're injured. See how I'm not injured? I can dive." Elias hopped up onto the edge of the pool and lounged casually, letting her wings flex a bit.

We swam, swapping stories of our respective times overseas, and after an hour I was actually tired. Which was a very annoying thing, as before I could exercise for a bit longer before I even noticed. Elias nudged my flank. "Relax. You've been out of commission for a month. It's normal."

"Even if it is, there's no regulation says I gotta like it." I remembered more than a few late nights at Fisticuffs when I'd come in after work and worked out until I was hungry, at which point I'd showered, and gone to Nonas' for a late night dinner and then home. But that was then, and this was now. And the now did have a nice shower, which sort of made up for everything else that had happened.

"I assume you'll be wanting your usual for dinner?" Elias threw an elbow into my lower ribcage gently. Even though we were out of the pool and back into our normal clothes, Elias seemed a little different. Maybe it was the story time.

"You're deflecting. But yes." I still hadn't quite figured out how to work the cafeteria menu, so I'd been sticking with 'Doctor Recommends' for choices.

We came back to my room where Jeremiah was waiting. "Dad! You got email." His look suggested I had been mostly forgiven for yanking his chain with regard to Rebecca the previous day.

"I got what?" One of the small benefits of this new thing I was part of was that I didn't have an email address for people to send advertisements to - it was not easy to wade through forty emails at a time when thirty of them were advertisements for various products of dubious quality and veiled cost. At least they were somewhat targeted, as I had no need for Dwarven "Height Enhancement Supplements" or faun hair dye. In any event, I'd gotten something and it seemed to be important.

"Well, I...just in case, we set up a thing to get your old cop email. and, uh, you got a big one today. Here! I didn't look at this one."

"Meaning you looked at other emails." I lifted an eyebrow slightly.

Jeremiah did look down a little. "...yeah. It...well, a lot of it is weird. Stuff for dating help, and then people are writing to you like we're both dead."

"Well, kiddo we kinda are. At least folks think we are. Anyway, let's get this email and some food and see what's going on." I flicked my tail a little, since this wasn't exactly a great thing.

He looked up at me. "But, what about Rebecca?"

I nodded. "Even Rebecca." I sighed a little. "I know it's bad, but it's better for her if she doesn't know what's going on with us right now."

Jere looked at his feet. "That sucks. She was nice."

With that unhappy thought, we walked to the Dwarven Mines as Elias disappeared to do whatever she did when she wasn't being the warden of my one-man luxury prison, and every 15 or 20 steps I stopped to get a good stretch in. Going from beat cop to indefinitely bedridden was not good, and I could feel the muscles in my back protesting the abuse. Also, I did let Jeremiah know that we needed to talk to the erstwhile Ms Elias about what the heck her plans were once I was done with my current assignment. Finally, we made it back to a room of blinking lights and horrible music.

Jeremiah kicked on his computer and clicked places, and then I saw the face of a dead woman. Specifically, the Erinyes that Devoin and I had found in an office several very long weeks ago. She was different - not that anybody looks good dead, but she looked refreshed and alive with something, and as she spoke it was familiar but not.

"So hey. You're Brooks. I mean you know that already, so why am I telling you that? Oh I should introduce myself I'm Jesse. I mean you know that cause you and your partner hauled me in a bunch times, but anyway I got a friend who says you're the definitional clean cop. So if you're watching this, I haven't checked into my backup for a month - so I'm either dead or I might as well be, but let's hope for the latter, hey? I like being alive and I've seen you walking the beat outside my office when you're not being a pain and bringing me in for questions about stuff I don't know anything about, and you look like a good guy so maybe I asked and maybe someone told me but I'm rambling and I usually don't do that. "

"So. Like a month ago, I was working for a client who was getting her house egged and graffiti'ed - outside your beat, but the cops there weren't helping. So I was flying around a little to see who it was and maybe see if I could catch 'em going near a friendlier place and they mighta seen me but it was someone I knew was a Genesissy, So I flew little higher so they maybe wouldn't see me and then they didn't but I saw them going into an abandoned place and then right back out again, and they kept doing it, like they were mailmen or something, so I kept track of where they were going and doing, and then I mighta visited one of the places at night."

"I found stuff Brooks. I hope you can follow up on it, legal-like. I found a jump-drive in one of their computers, so I mighta stolen the drive. Well, borrowed it really, I'll give it back when I'm done. Promise you won't arrest me if this becomes something big, I'm trying to stay clean. Bye for now Brooks."

I looked at Jeremiah. "That's...huh. Was that it?"

He nodded. "I'm gonna check the video for anything else, but there wasn't any other attachments."

I elbowed him gently. "You done good. Keep me posted if something happens with that drive."

Jeremiah grinned and nodded as I made my way back to my room, sliding onto my bed heavily as Max hopped onto my flank and settled in. "You're back."

"Never went anywhere, you dopey feline."

"You know what I mean. You got a good workout, and you got more pieces of the puzzles in front of you. You should be exhausted, but you're full of life. I can feel it." Max began wash his face. "So what'd you find."

"Well, the Erinyes murder case has a new twist. Apparently she wanted me to take the jump-drive once she figured out what to do with it. Like I was the only honest cop she knew of or something. And I finally got to do some pool therapy with Elias."

"She likes you." With his face clean, Max turned his attention to his paws.

"Not the time, catto." Of all the things going on in my life, I did not need Max channeling Nona.

"When's the time?"

"Not now. I'll tell you when."

"Fine. But she watches you when you're having bad dreams. And when she has her own bad dreams, she looks at you as soon as she wakes up. Bet you a can of gooshy food that twerp of a doctor came up with the idea of her sharing a room with you - and that's probably the first smart thing he's ever done."

"Max, be nice."

"That was the nice."

"And it's not happening, so quit trying to play feline matchmaker."

"You, are no fun."

The door clicked open, and in came a pajamaed Elias with a manila folder. "Few things before rack time. One, your new ident just got cleared, and we have an unofficial toxicology report on Miss Jesse." I was a touch perturbed, as her walking from wherever her pajamas were to here seemed like it was an unnecessary thing. That said, I couldn't really comment on her choices in attire, given that I'd been reduced to hospital gowns and only a few shirts and kilts from my previous closet space.

"Unofficial how?" I could play fashion critic another time, for the moment there was information to be had.

"The kind where we pay out of the discretionary funds to exhume a body when nobody's looking and do things that are highly unethical. Don't ask too many questions unless you get real chill about things real fast, former Officer Brooks."

I exhaled. "Fine - what's the upshot?"

"Well, when she was killed, she had about four to six months to live, even with the most aggressive treatment. More likely two to three months. We looked closely and found evidence that she had multiple cancers in her body. We checked against her medical history, and these all showed up in the last few months. So either this woman had the worst luck or she was targeted."

"Targeted?"

"Yeah - like she knew something, and someone was trying to kill her quietly, then when that wasn't working on their timetable they hired someone to zip her lip rapidly. Frankly, I don't think we need to pursue the shooter that much. The cancer...that's interesting."

"Define 'interesting.'"

She smirked for a moment at some unknown joke, but continued. "According to the reports, the docs suspect she was dosed with a few carcinogens that were aggressive. Given the state of her body at death, I think we can forgive the coroner for skipping any detailed analysis."

"Great, but what does that actually mean for us?"

"It means things just got really awkward. And given that Genesis was ready to take down your entire apartment complex to get at what's on that drive, I'm going to reiterate my last request to the boss for an exceptional amount of resources."

"Okay, new questions - where the heck does our budget actually come from, and does budget mean I get paid?"

"There's a few sources. Investments both traditional and non-traditional, and we'll take on information-gathering jobs for certain specific clients. They pay quite well. As for you, both you and Jeremiah are on the books as employees, and you're getting paid a small salary but room and board are included. You'll have a bank card in your wallet when you go out. Meanwhile, in good news, the doctors are ready to give you tentative clearance for full activity, if you keep up with the pool therapy. They're tired of you being grumpy."

"They ain't seen grumpy yet."

"Lights out, Brooks. Tomorrow's going to be busy."

She was not wrong. Right after breakfast, we hit the pool for an hour, and then I received my new identity. Peter Brooks, professional secure item courier. There was a bit more to it then just that, but it was fairly easy to memorize - it looked like they'd written up my fake life story to match up the real one enough that details wouldn't trip me up. Then I got to meet my boss through a video call, who was not pleased about anything. Especially the part where I requested that Jeremiah and I be allowed to go outside for a walk. By the time the conversation was finished I was certain that he had not smiled since he was about seven. Even for an elf, he was lacking. He insisted that we wear little wrist straps for our walk, and since there were other things to be done today, we were going to get buzzed after about 90 minutes, after which we'd need to come back down for more briefing and discussion.

Then I took Jeremiah outside. He was not pleased because he was onto something with the mystery drive, but hammered keys and finally grunted a little at the monitor before we took a very long elevator ride up to the surface. And it was a beautiful view. We could just make out mountains on the horizon, but closer we saw trees surrounding airstrips and a few planes. In the distance I could just make out the aforementioned Uranium Hills. Picking Jeremiah up was hard, as he'd picked up a few dozen pounds since the last time he was on my back. Still, it was invigorating to have sun and fresh air in my face.

"Dad...?" I looked back to see Jeremiah with his "I'm not sure how to say this" look.

"S'up champ?" I jogged my elbow into his side gently to get him out of whatever funk he was in.

"I'm sorry." He looked down at my back.

"For what?"

"Well...this I mean if I hadn't plugged in the thing, we wouldn't be here. I mean, this is nice, and there's good people, but..."

"Hey. I picked up the drive in the first place. Blame me if you're gonna blame anyone. So how's the school?" I skipped the part where some people had planned to have a riot to get the drive back. That was just not something I needed to tell him about at this point.

"Well...the ones in charge of my education said I should start writing my Masters' thesis. I got some tests they want me to take and then I can go back to trying to figure out the drive. I mostly got it, I got it so it doesn't kill the computer immediately but it's like each file has a different encryption set on it, so I gotta go through everything again before I can get useful stuff, but then they won't let me see the good stuff before I get to the next one. I guess they need to talk to The Elf about my security clearance or something." He was starting sentences off with some hesitation. That didn't exactly bode well. The Masters' thesis part brought me up short. It was strange, I remembered vividly the Changing of the Diaper, and it was not that long ago. "Bless his heart?"

"Yeah." He fell silent for a minute. "Are you and Miss Elias dating?"

"Where'd that come from?"

"Well, she's sleeping in your room, and Max thinks you should, and maybe...but...what about mom? Maybe you should talk to mom. You could maybe date her again when she comes back from her job?" It seemed like he was nibbling around the edges of something.

"Kiddo. I know you think it'd be great, and there's times when I miss her too. But we're not getting back together because we both have new lives. And I don't think The Elf would approve of bringing your mom in on the off chance that we'd be able to be a family again."

"But I want her to know that...that I'm okay? And that, you know. You're still around if something happens and you and mom could get, I dunno, remarried or something?" And there it was. It seemed like Jere was still holding out hope that we'd re-marry, even though both Aoife and I had agreed to disagree many years ago.

"I know but the way this is shaping up, the odds of us ever getting to see her again are not good." I didn't want to directly remind him that we'd been declared legally dead, and that as much as we were okay with each other, his mother was not interested in being with me. "So...did they get you your new name?"

"No, they said they wanted to wait on that. They're pretty keeping me busy, and they said there's no need. Why, they get you something new?"

"Yeah. Sounds like maybe they're going to kick me out the door to do something."

"Does that mean I'mma keep Max?"

"Yes. And you'll need to feed him. Not just meat pizza. Or gooshy food. He needs crunchies and exercise, and you are the one to give it to him."

"Fiiiiiiine."

We walked in silence for a bit, checking out a few of the buildings before the wristwatch buzzed and we clomped back inside. I dropped Jeremiah off at the dwarven mines and was about 3 steps away when I hear him exclaim and move fast.

"Dad-dad-DAD!"

"Where's the fire man?"

"We got it, we got it, and and and we neeeeeed to talk to the boss."

"Elias?"

"No...the...The Elf."

"Whoa, slow down, take me through it."

He dragged me back to his nest of papers, knickknacks, and soda cans to point at his monitor. "So I was doing a couple things while the file decryption stuff was running and I got bored, and there were some more files from the lady Jesse, and...it's kinda weird."

"Show me."

The screen lit up, and there she was again - and she was looking bad. "So Brooks, I gotta tell you this is weird. I was following up on some of the stuff from earlier, and I mighta taken a couple shifts at the G Club. You know the one, popular with the Genesis crowd because they only hire Neotypes and they have a high turnover because they treat 'em like crap despite the high pay? So I mighta grabbed a couple shifts there, and they...they had a new thing. It was a old-school burlesque thing, and then there was a fog machine in a couple spots. I think they put something in it, because the fog smelled, well, wrong if you can believe it. Me and other staff noticed it, but I guess it must be something only neotypes can catch on to because all the customers thought it was awesome. After that, I started feeling sick. Me and everyone else working there that night - Brooks, I think we got something. I went to the doctor, and he's doing some tests. We'll know more in a few days, but I really think that Genesis is doing something. Back at cha."

Then the screen went dark, and lit up one last time. Again it was Jesse, and she looked even worse. Her voice was cracking as she spoke. "Brooks. The doc said he didn't believe the test results. He's running more, but I think I'm out of time. I put everything I've got on this file. Whatever's on that drive, it's big. And I talked to the other Neos who were working at the G club. They're all sick like me. Funny thing though, the regulars aren't. We're gonna look." A list of names and numbers scrolled on the screen like credits. "Here's all the people who were working that night, and as many people as I could find who were patronizing the place. Brooks...I dunno what you can do anymore, cause this is, this is big." There was a pause in the recording, and when it restarted, there were flecks of blood around her mouth that hadn't been there before. "Brooks, I want you to know - I'm not scared. That you're a good cop. And you'll find a way. Every time you brought me in, you were a good person about it. If there's any one else who can do this, I don't know 'em. But someones' trying to kill Neotypes and make it look natural. Till the other side Brooks."

Oh this was a very bad thing. "Alright kiddo, let's get another copy of this for the boss, and then let's go find Elias to make sure we can get a meeting with The Elf."

Elias' reaction to the videos was odd. She was in turns almost weeping, and by the end of it I heard a fluttering sound from somewhere - looking around, it was Elias' wings vibrating like crazy. It took about a minute for her to get everything under control, but she finally got things sorted out and excused herself to change and likely punch a wall or three. Not gonna lie, I wasn't happy, but I had learned that me getting excited would get Jeremiah wound out. I nudged him gently.

"C'mon, young man, head to your room and clean up - get the nice clothes on because we're gonna have a meeting with the boss. Quickly."

We quickly changed and Elias was working on the comms while we walked. There were words used that made me highly concerned, but by the time we made to the administrative offices we were allowed entry to the main office. The Elf, officially the head of our particular branch, was a gentleman with the face of a hatchet and appeared to have been created right out of central casting for antagonistic bosses. His office was decorated in early "Look At Me I'm Awesome" with pictures of himself standing next to famous people of every stripe, and directly behind him were multiple framed degrees. Unfortunately I was taking a bit too long with taking the scene in, and there was a harrumph.

"Missster Arthur." The way he drew our names out was a bit disconcerting and also signaled that whatever we had needed to be good.

Jeremiah and I both answered "Yes?", which caused The Elfs' eyes to narrow.

"I was advised you had something of critical importance, which I have allocated precisely fifteen minutes for. There are now fourteen minutes remaining. Had I been aware that this critically important item was in fact you gawking at my office, I would have ignored the request."

That brought me back to the moment. "Sir, my son was able to retrieve information from my former employer. And that information may be useful in determining the means and method of a future event coordinated by the Genesis group."

There was a slight eyebrow quirk. "Go on."

Jeremiah handed over the drive with hands that were very shaky. The Elf seemed nonplussed, and as he watched it his eyes narrowed fractionally. It was quite unusual to see, as elves did in fact have the standard emotional range, but the one in front of us seemed to be an odd one. By the time the last video was done, he copied the contents of the drive to his own computer and sent them somewhere before swiveling to look at us.

"I fully expect the three of you to not disclose this meeting to anyone. Young Arthur, if anyone asks, you may direct them to me as you continue working on your current assignments. Older Arthur. Continue your rehabilitation, and advise the doctor when you are in fact fit for duty. Agent Elias. You are reassigned effective immediately. Supervise both of these gentlemen in their respective tasks. That is all."

Thus dismissed, we all hurried to get somewhere else. Jeremiah glanced at me once we were out of Executive Alley.

"Dad...that was, uh, is he okay?"

I nodded. "Yeah - pretty sure he is, and isn't. We just threw a grenade in his lap, and when you're in charge of stuff, sometimes you have to put things away and focus on your job. Which, y'know, his job's like, making sure that we can deal with this."

There was a pause. "Oh."

I leaned down and ruffled his hair a little. "You did good. Keep doing good, and we'll make ourselves a good name."

My stomach rumbled a bit, which served as a reminder that in all the fuss of everything, I had completely forgotten to eat. And it was well past midday snacktime. I did glance down at my betraying stomach as a couple snickers escaped from both Elias and Jeremiah.

"Elias can you take Jere to the Mines so he can do some stuff? I'm gonna go find myself a nice thick milkshake and somewhere I can figure out how to heal up faster."

Elias smirked. "Better idea, we can call it a day early and order in. The cafeteria does some wicked sesame beef."

Chapter 9

The idea had merit, but at the same time I wasn't quite keen on it. It felt like there was a lot more at play than just take-out and an evening in. I recalled The Elf directing Elias to continue supervising, and the idea that there was more involved settled in pretty solidly. All of that was overridden by my stomach, which once again reminded me that there had been nothing for it to do for hours, and we should be addressing that concern in a priority fashion.

We all trundled to my quarters, where Elias had apparently had some folks hard at work redecorating. The corner where her hammock had been slung was now slightly fuller, with a small desk now in place; she touched a wall panel and a drawer full of her clothes slid out from somewhere. In amongst them were items that looked silky, and I promptly went over to my desk to locate a menu on the tablet. After a beat, Jeremiah followed, while Max looked up from his napping spot on the couch and looked far too smug for his own good. I eyed the little furry cat with disappointment. Meanwhile Jeremiah parked it on an office chair and started to zone out a little.

"Max, when were you going to mention the drawers?"

"I thought you were a highly trained observant police officer. You're supposed to know the space you're in, so I thought you had that covered."

"No gooshy food. Two days." That was the normal punishment for when he was misbehaving.

"You do realize I can totally get around that by telling Elias stories about you, right?"

"You wouldn't even dare." Cats put a lot of work into not working, mostly by being cute.

"Then I'm not telling you about the conversation I had with Elias the other night. When you were passed out that week, she spent a lot of time in here watching you." And also by telling you just enough enough that you'd be interested to hear more. I knew this play from Max, and about half the time he got extra treats out of it. The other half he was disappointed.

I sighed inwardly and tapped in my order to the cafeteria before parking it on the couch, passing the tablet over to Jeremiah so he could order while Elias went to the bathroom to change.

"Max, where are you going with this."

"I'm helping you. I mean we don't have Nona to get you food and dates, and I can't cook so I'm taking over with the dating thing."

"I don't need help dating. I'll date when I wanna date." It was kind of annoying, honestly.

"Suit yourself Brooks, but you are going to get a surprise in the near future and my only hope is that I can be there when it happens because I will enjoy the look on your silly face."

Our conversation was interrupted by Elias, who came out of the bathroom in oversized flannel and plopped down on the couch a comfortable distance from me and was handed the tablet by Jeremiah for ordering. She tapped out a few things and sent it, setting things aside and settling in. And there was an odd smell in the air yet again, that I couldn't identify. I looked around a little for it but still couldn't identify the source. That was a pile of annoyance for me and amusement for Max, so I finally shoved it out of my mind and focused on the TV, scrolling through the tablet until I found football.

I brought my legs in close to get some distance. Max was not helpful, settling himself in next to Elias and nudging her closer to me. He was never getting a treat ever again. I tried to politely ignore the distance and nudged back only when absolutely necessary.

Jeremiah finally broke the awkward silence. "So, uh, I'm working on my doctorate."

That perked my interest. "Didn't you just get your masters? Seriously, let the ink dry on that one."

He blushed a little, looking down. "Well, I mean, I don't have one. A doctorate, I mean. And everyone else has a bunch, and they're mad at me because I'm pulling the average down, and I guess the headquarters is making fun of us."

"Headquarters?" I glanced at Elias.

She nodded. "The headquarters building is on and under the Ile de la Cite in Paris. Places of note on the island include the Conciergerie where Marie Antoinette was held for her trial, Notre Dame and most importantly for us, it's where Jacques de Molay was executed by being burned at the stake. Helpful hint, start learning French if you ever want to be re-assigned to the HQ division."

I hrmphed softly, changing the subject by looking over at Jere. "So what's your first doctorate going to be in?"

Jeremiah squirmed a little. "Well, mathematics. Then I was thinking about a specialty in cryptography."

I grinned. "My boy the codebreaker. Nice."

The conversation was interrupted by a soft chime indicating that food had in fact arrived. Everyone grabbed and found a place again. I tried to hint that I had dibs on the couch by stretching out all of my lower body, however that was apparently the cue for Elias to settle herself on my lower chest. Max was snickering softly as he went to his bowl of nibbles.

There really wasn't much talking at this point, since everyone was going to work on food, but the blissful silence couldn't last. It was Elias who killed the mood after checking her tablet for some information.

"So tomorrow Brooks - last day of rehab, assuming the doctor gives you an upcheck."

I moved slightly to get myself more comfortable. "And then we're on to next assignments?" I may have sounded a bit too hopeful, as Elias gave a slight snort.

"Yes. But we are going to be paired up for a bit. I've been designated as your on the job trainer, which means the hammock ain't going anywhere."

"Do you do this with all your trainees?"

"Only the exceptionally hard-headed ones. They've been looking over your records, and you appear to be prime for field work. Once you're fully rehabbed to the doctors' content, this place is going to double as a classroom. We're going to be going over the finer points of the job and the not-quite legal things you'll need to learn."

"Not-quite-legal sounds like illegal. Not sure I like that."

"Well, most of it's legal. Some things, like lockpicking, will depend entirely on your level of talent."

"What about Jeremiah?" I nodded over to him, as he appeared to be deep in thought about something - he'd stopped eating and was poised with his fork half-way to his mouth for a time before he remembered that it was in fact food time, whereupon he went right back to eating at an amazingly rapid pace. Elias observed this all with a slight smile before answering.

"Well, he's being educated at the Dwarven Mines, which if it were an actual college, would probably be one of the top three engineering schools in the world. He's got a pretty good support team around him - the biggest issue is that the current staff is made of post-pubescent Changes, which means they're having some trouble dealing with some aspects of his personality."

Jeremiah chimed in. Apparently he was fully back with us. "S'annoying. I just...think about a thing for a bit and then I look at the clock and it's 20 minutes later and someone's standing next to me like I was supposed to be listening to them. Weirdos."

I leaned back on the couch. "Anything we can do for it?"

Elias scrunched her face. "Well, really not much we can do. It's almost a biological trait more than anything."

"So, we let 'em know that he's not ignoring them, he's just having a heavy thought or five?"

"More or less."

Once we finished eating, we headed out to do some shopping for things that we all needed. This meant a trip to Uranium Hills, and that was a bit more of a production than I'd thought it would be. First we needed to actually get permission, which after some discussion with the right people was granted, after that we needed to sign out a vehicle from the motor pool. Then we needed to turn it back in and sign out a different vehicle that had enough room for me. Finally, we gave it a once over, confirmed we were okay, and then signed out at the front gate. Once we were actually off the base, the trip was fairly quick. First there were a series of bars, a few apartment buildings scattered in with houses, and finally we made it to the town proper. It was very similar to a lot of the base towns I'd been to in the past with most businesses built around the entertainment of the people who lived on the base. It almost felt like a homecoming of sorts. Still, Elias knew where to go and how to park, and we hit the mom-n-pop shop in the stores and markets section.

Apparently beard oil and a better shaving kit were items high on Jeremiahs list, as well as some other sundries. I ran over to the grocery section for the goods to make my own energy bars, because the mass-produced ones seemed to forget that centaurs had some serious calorie needs. Or the manufacturers were accounting for one of the unchanged folks buying one and trying it on a dare - an Unchanged person trying Centaur-specific foods never ended well, and was the subject of more than a few videos in the "people doing stupid things" section of various websites. Damned silly.

Also on the list, gooshy food and a new toy for Max; I needed to bribe the furball to firstly keep quiet about me and secondly start spilling more about Elias. Meanwhile Elias disappeared and came back with some sort of industrial strength feather care items. The last item on the list was a trip to the clothing section to find a few shirts and pants sets for Jere, as well as expanding my own collection of shirts and kilts. We finally found things that worked for us, and then it was off to pay for it all. To their credit, the cashier didn't have much to say about the diversity of purchases, and just rang it all up, tapping my credit card when prompted and then sending us on our way. And that was the end of the night, really. Not exactly exciting times, but the basics still had to be taken care of.

Once back at my quarters, Jeremiah ducked through the side room because he had an idea. Which left me with Max and Elias, and an awkward feeling from somewhere. I mulled it over briefly and decided it was pretty much a nerves thing due to tomorrow being the last day before I was once again allowed to re-enter healthy society, so I went ahead and flopped on the couch, tapping on the tablet until I found a classic football game, and mellowed out. Elias, for her part, went to her hammock and started tapping on her tablet. I glanced over every so often to make sure she wasn't dying or anything, and I saw that she was researching the rules of football.

She could have just asked. But I figured she didn't need too much help from me, so I focused on the game, with appropriate anticipation of watching everything come down to a single kick.

After all of that, it was finally time for bed. I went, changed into one of my old football jerseys and settled in, getting mentally prepped for "no matter where the doc prods, show no pain".

That night, the dreams were odd. I was back at my last jump before I went into the hospital, reliving it and trying to find what I could have done differently. So far, every time I'd had this dream it went badly - even worse than what really happened. This time was different. When I hit the trees, for some reason they were soft and flexible, bending gently instead of treating my knees like a mob enforcer dealing with someone who refused to pay their insurance. The mission proper was me running and doing what I'd done, except that every time I hit a wall, it was filled with feathers that exploded in my face. Somewhere along the line while I was motoring through everything and headed for the pickup spot, I heard Jeremiah calling for me loudly. That was definitely not part of the program.

Finally I blinked awake to several things happening. One, there were feathers on my face. I sat up a little bit to discover the source of the feathers. Elias had at some point in the night decided my bed was more comfortable than her hammock. Couldn't blame her for the decision, to be honest. Two, Elias' state of dress - specifically, she had her large hockey jersey on, but it had shifted around to reveal that she was wearing alarmingly sheer items under it. Three, the prime witness to this was Jeremiah; he was hopping up and down and looked excited as heck about something, despite having no sleep if the bags under his eyes could be judged. Lastly, the secondary witness to all this was Max, who was at the foot of the bed rolling and chattering in a way that I'd discovered meant he was seeing something he found utterly hilarious.

First things first, the feathered interloper in my bed. I nudged Elias gently, receiving a slight grunt and a face buried in my abdomen for my trouble. On top of that, I felt oddly queasy about the whole affair. Something needed to be done. A second more solid nudge gave better results; she blinked herself awake and stretched her arms and wings simultaneously with a happy sigh.

Then she took stock of the situation, looking at me, the hammock, and then the bed before she snapped her wings around herself and padded off to the bathroom. Jeremiah, for his part went from hopping about to slightly stunned by Elias' casual use of my bed moving his eyes from me to the empty spot where Elias was, and then back to me.

I for one, was rather interested in moving forward and ignoring whatever fever dream had possessed Elias to think there was free real estate where I slept. Also, I already had the two of them playing some sort of bizarre game where they were trying to make sense of the world. I moved to occupy the spot where she had been, and was rewarded for my efforts with a mental alarm ringing some sort of alert that brought me fully awake and determined to discuss anything and everything that was not Elias.

"Young man, don't tell me you pulled another all nighter reading under the covers again." After he'd learned how to read at the age of three by watching Aoife and me read and asking a lot of questions, he spent a lot of nights reading books under the covers at night. We made sure his flashlight never ran out of batteries, even though there were some days where he was cranky and needed a longer nap than usual.

Jeremiah snapped back to reality as I spoke, the blush disappearing as he pointed at his tablet. "I figured it out. And I haven't read it all, but I-I-I think we need to go to The Elf with this."

"Figured what out?" There were a few options on the list. Shaving, how to get clothes that fit right

"The drive that kept killing computers." Now that we were on track, he was hopping up and down excitedly.

I looked at him sternly. "All-nighter?"

He squirmed a little. "Well, yeah. But I uh...well Max told me that you'd gotten some autopsy stuff back, so I uhm, accessed the files from it to look at the cancer stuff to see what it was doing. Or how they were able to do it. The sequence is the exact same on all the samples, and I checked into it and it shouldn't happen like that - like the whole base for this is somehow chemically made. I looked at the DNA, and it's always the same structure no matter where they pulled it from. So I had an idea, and I fed the DNA sequence into the jump drive as a decryption key. And it decrypted. Clear, Dad."

I blinked. And blinked again. Apparently he wasn't just math and code-breaking, he was a biologist as well. "Oh, we are taking this to The Elf. Did you print it out?"

"It's printing now at the Mines' main. And I made a digital copy." Jere was hopping side to side a little.

"Get yourself presentable. Then we're going to interrupt whatever The Elf's doing and probably ruin his day." Jeremiah scooted, after which Elias came out prepared for the day, with what appeared to be her executive grade power suit and hair back in a serious ponytail. It seemed that she'd heard our conversation and agreed with the plan. She motioned with two fingers that the bathroom was in fact mine. It was time to multitask, so I grabbed the one suit I had and the tie that went with it and walked into the bathroom to change, leaving the divider open just a bit. If she could make me uncomfortable, turnabout was fair play. Also it seemed like she was in her own head a bit, since she hadn't actually said a word so far this morning. Time to figure out what exactly had happened.

"So I thought you had a perfectly serviceable hammock for sleeping." I got everything together, pausing for a moment to focus on the tie. I thought for a moment before tying it in a trinity knot - it wasn't too complicated, but the effect was a nice even three-part look at the knot itself that made most people take a second glance. Frankly, it was also a bit of a power move on my part, as most folks only knew a few ways to tie a tie. The jacket was shrugged on, and we were ready to make a move.

There was a pause before she answered that got my hair standing slightly. "It's not serviceable at this time."

"What?" I poked my head out after checking my look in the mirror one last time. I definitely needed a haircut once this was done. Not just my hair, but my body coat was getting a little shaggy. I double-checked and the hair around my ankles and feet had gotten far beyond respectable without my realizing it. My hair actually covered my shoes, which brought a grunt of disappointment from me. I was going to have to check for a barber after this meeting.

"It's not serviceable." She pointed and sure enough the hammock was a wreck. I didn't inquire further, but I did glance at Max, who sneezed and padded over to his empty food bowl. The hint was taken, and as I donated to his food supply and slipped a treat into the bowl, he muttered at me.

"She had a bad dream. Worst one I've seen yet from her." And it was back to eating for him.

"It's been how many days?" The thing about cats was they considered themselves experts in every subject, and carried themselves as such. Occasionally I had to remind Max that he wasn't.

"A few. But as soon as she got up she bolted to you like you were a nine-hundred-pound stuffie and was asleep in a minute. You have an aura." He worked on the cat food with a purpose, tail swishing the floor behind him.

"An aura of what? Most broken toy on the island of misfit toys?" Max was a fan of half answers and cryptic comments - mainly so he could get more treats for information. I wondered if other cats were like this.

"Nothing like that. I'll tell you more when you get back from your meeting. Jeremiahs' coming."

And on cue, the adjoining door slid open, with Jeremiah in a shirt that fit him perfectly not long ago but now hung off him like it was too big and too small at the same time. It would have to do. We hustled to the mines, where I took the catwalk over to the printer, while Jeremiah wove and dodged through the aisles below to the same place and Elias apologized and smoothed over the rough feelings left in Jeremiah's wake. Say this for Jere, when he was focused, he was focused. He pulled reams of paper from the printer, and spent a few minutes trying to figure out the magical workings of a three-hole punch before Elias slid in and showed him how to work it, after which we all gathered at the entrance and made sure every little thing was in its' place. As we left with Jeremiah and Elias on my back I distinctly heard someone call out "Hi-o SILVER!"

I made a mental note to punch whoever said that. The weight of Elias on my rump was an ever-present low warning, like thunder on the horizon. I wasn't sure why she couldn't just walk, and then I looked back to see her speed-reading a chunk of the printout.

Two could definitely play at that. I grabbed part of the documents that had been printed out so I could read a little while on the way. The part I had was focused on their homegrown carcinogen. It detailed an overarching view, with potential delivery systems for what they were terming Operation Patmos. There were also some very disconcerting things in there, environmental and economic impacts discussed in clinical terms that made me cold. We were moving rapidly toward the administrative side of the complex, where we were given looks that were startling. Apparently I wasn't supposed to be here. It may also have been because a centaur was speed-reading through reams of paper with an adolescent dwarf and an Erinyes perched on his back. That alone should have given me an upcheck from the doctor. To add to it, both of them were reading papers as well and giving directions so the centaur didn't bodily knock aside anyone who had the bad luck to be in my way. Knockdowns were still delivered to a few unfortunates whos' oaths and curses were noted academically. I was very busy reading and walking and carrying.

Finally we got as far as the two secretaries who looked at us disdainfully. "He. Is busy."

"He's gonna wanna see this. It's about the drive taken from the Erinyes' murder scene. Jeremiah got it decrypted, and we have an initial contents brief. We're going to need about ten to fifteen minutes, and I got all day to get those minutes." I didn't have anything on my schedule except rehab today, and the two secretaries looked at their screens, tapped a few keys and shared a glance as they had apparently pulled my file and realized that I would stand in front of them all day if needed. I hoped it wouldn't be needed.

We were admitted after a very short consultation.

"Misster Arthur." The Elfs' hands were steepled, and he drew each word out like a spooled thread.

Me and Jeremiah did a simultaneous "Yes?" again. This did not amuse The Elf.

"This is our second meeting in as many days. You are either highly fortunate in your findings or in need of guidance. The next few minutes will in fact tell me which, and for your sakes I hope it is not the latter. Agent Elias, I note that you are here. If it is the latter, an explanation will be required." Elias simply nodded. The good news was we apparently had the sort of leeway needed to walk in with an emergency. But if it wasn't an emergency, the consequences seemed unspecified but dire.

I knelt for Jeremiah to slide off my back and took a moment to mentally collate everything I'd read on the way. "Alright, executive summary; Genesis is going to release a genetically engineered agent that will induce cancer in every neotype with a one hundred percent fatality rate. It keys off DNA sequences found only in neotypes. My son has the full data here. There is additional information within the hard copy here, as well as unrelated information concerning other activities. Additionally, the group that created it has very high security measures - the decryption key is the DNA sequence of the resultant cancer cells." The Additional Information was placed on his desk with a thump. During this, Elias simply sat patiently.

The Elf looked at me dryly. "If this turns out to be correct, the minutes were not wasted. Mister Arthur - the older one, you will be taking a copy of this information to the MidPacific Power Island for further analysis. Agent Elias will be accompanying you. Mister Arthur the Younger will be continuing analysis of the data locally. Exact methods and travel arrangements will be made available to you both shortly." He then looked back down to what we had laid in front of him, before glancing up briefly. "Excellent work. I expect to see more soon. See yourselves out, I have other matters to attend." Through all this, Elias was still sitting on my back end and I almost swore I felt a wriggle of sorts. It was odd, and I glanced to see a very slight reddening in her cheeks. It felt like I'd busted her for something, but I still wasn't certain what.

Jeremiah looked at me quizzically for a moment before I picked him up and parked him on my back and we left The Elf to deal with it. Jeremiah shifted a bit as we left and passed the two elves handling secretarial work.

"That was weird. We did all that and all he said was 'excellent work.'"

There were a few blinks from the secretaries in the foyer, so I leaned down a bit so one could properly keep whatever was being said between us.

"In five years, the best thing he's ever said to either of us is 'adequate', and that's as good as anyone's ever gotten. You three watch out, he'll expect miracles with whatever he gives you both next."

Jeremiah and I looked at each other with our eyebrows raised. "Noted."

Once we'd left the Executive Alley, Elias took off to do something while Jeremiah and I went back to the Dwarven Mines, where the crew had prepared a cap and gown ceremony of sorts. While I had been working on physical rehab, Jeremiah had run through approximately twelve years of coursework, and his masters' thesis had not only been accepted, it was spawning a few new projects with regard to data encryption and decryption. It felt a little odd, to be honest. I could distinctly recall helping him through long division, and here he was with a degree in some level of mathematics where numbers were apparently optional.

The other problem was the mines were banks of servers and workstations created with dwarves in mind, and other types were an afterthought. Which meant I had to scramble up and maneuver a few catwalks that they'd installed for others in order to watch anything. But I still whistled maniacally when the head of the department gave Jeremiah his diploma and a small silver hammer - according to the lore of the department, percussive maintenance was always an option, and the hammer was there to remind the recipient. Jeremiah blushed red at his dad embarrassing him, which was enough to make me snicker. We retired back to front of the mines where there were a few drinks available in celebration of what we'd done. I was offered something that they claimed was beer but tasted like a mix of motor oil and stout. I was able to keep it down, but barely. Eventually we were able to wind things down and I was able to exit as discretely as I could.

For the next order of business, it was back to my quarters for a change prior to visiting the doctor and telling him yes I was fine. Doc was very uncertain, looking at timelines and the paperwork he'd accumulated on me, finally order a full body scan. I hated those things, and requested to be shoved in backside-first. Going in headfirst gave me claustrophobia, as I'd discovered a very long time ago. After that, he looked at his notes, looked at me quizzically, and then shooed me out.

I still felt pretty good, so I went to the pool to swim a bit before bed. I got changed, and since nobody was looking I decided to break to 'no running' rule. Which didn't work out too well - hooves and wet tile do not mesh - but I did manage to hit the water. After a quick check for bumps and bruises, I started paddling about and seeing just what this old body of mine could do. It could do quite a lot as it turned out, as I finally tired and looked at the clock, discovering an hour and a half had passed. Even though I was fit to do whatever they needed me to do, I wasn't exactly fit as far as I was concerned. I got out a bit more gingerly than I got in, deciding to check and see if the folks who'd built this were able to keep everyone in mind when they built the hot tub.

In point of fact they had, but in doing so they may have advertised it as a location for low-key romantic actions, as I found one of the secretaries and her dwarven boytoy in the middle of some form of water-based eye exam. And it was a very intense exam, since both of them were completely ignoring me; I decided discretion was preferred and a hot bath in my own room would be better for everyone.

Entering, Max crinkled his face at me while winding around my legs. "You're late, you're damp and there's no gooshy food."

"You're on a diet and I've had a day. I'm taking a bath and going to sleep. You can take the problems up with management. Also, tomorrow I'm probably going to be on a trip, so you're going to want to head over to Jere's place for a bit." With that I went to start the water and grabbed a couple beers, waiting for the tub to fill while I leaned and though about the day.

"So they're going to get you earning your keep? Nice."

"If you can call playing mailman earning my keep, sure." The good news was that whatever weird scent was around had disappeared for the time being.

"Good enough. So where's Elias?"

"Not my day to keep track of her. She might be out on a date. She might be out doing recon. She might be doing prep work for whatever's coming up next from The Elf. Heck if I know." I was quite happy to not have her hovering over my every move, at least for a few hours. While I'd certainly learned how to survive and even thrive in close quarters with a bunch of people around me all day every day back in my youth, there were times now when I needed a minute to walk around in solitude. Even if that walk was a metaphorical one in my head.

There was a feline growl. "Well, I suppose it's better than thinking she's dead in a ditch somewhere."

I slid into the tub with my second beer in tow. "Don't put that evil on me, cat. You're the one who's worried, not me. She can take care of herself, and has. Quite well before I came along."

"Whatever."

"Max, this is not a debate I'm having, and it's insane that you think we should." Also, there was a beer in hand that required my attention.

"Can you at least keep the current sleeping arrangements? That hammock freaks me out." Max was pacing the length of the bathtub, deciding if he wanted to jump up to have a serious conversation.

"Because you can't jump on it without falling and looking goofy?"

"I never said that."

"But it was hinted. Meanwhile, I believe you said something about more details about this supposed aura thing I've got?"

"I did. And yet, there is a severe case of no-treats happening which is taking over my concerns at the moment."

"I am not getting out of the tub just to give you a treat."

There was a rustle and rolling sound from outside as the door slid open with Max pawing the treat canister toward me, and finally he sat with anticipation as it came to rest within arms' reach. "Oh look. There's the treat can."

I hmphed softly, using the magic of opposable thumbs to open the treat can and deal out several. After all, I needed some information and I was not above bribing my source. There were happy nomming sounds, and finally Max sat back.

"So, remember the Wraparound Policy?" He hopped up on the tub to keep an eye on me. And probably gauge my reactions.

"All too well." I wasn't a fan of it, but the policy wonks said it was good.

"Good. That policy existed because you and the rest of the Centaurs have a very unique quality, in that you radiate some sort of eye of the storm calm. And you have it to a greater degree than any other one who was currently on the force. We didn't get into the why of it, but someone had a theory that it was your background - like you were doing what you loved, and that kinda came out in everything you did."

"Who's we?" I looked down and sighed, realizing my hair was reaching a distressingly shaggy length. I needed a barber, soon.

"We being me and Elias."

"How'd she know?"

"She wasn't just hanging out in the armory all day when she was checking you out for recruiting into this fancy gang of theirs and trying to chase down the lady who was our start point for all of this. According to her, she was going through the files and cross-referencing, and she found that people who'd the wraparound as performed by you needed about thirty percent less after-event therapy. You're a shining star. A shining star with treats." Max padded over to the treats for a moment, as if his hint wasn't enough.

"That's not entirely important."

"That is the most important thing." Max hopped onto the toilet tank to regard me. "Maybe you haven't processed this yet, but you could very easily be one of the better agents this place has. I'd start thinking about learning French."

"And yet, I'm still divorced."

"That's the down side of being you. Some folks can't handle the supreme calm you bring to the table. They want chaos. Hence the more chaos oriented run like hell from you, while others are unnaturally attracted to you and curl into you when they have bad dreams."

"That is a dangerous assumption."

"Exhibit A being Elias herself. She's got three categories of sleepwear that go under the hockey jersey. One, minimalist. Two, flannel. Three, soft and smooth."

I decided I did not need to ask how he acquired this knowledge. "Cut to the chase, fuzzbutt."

"She never wore the soft and smooth until last night. She changed into it after she wrecked the hammock." I really did not need to know how that knowledge was acquired either.

"How the heck do you know she changed?" Okay, I was a little curious about that.

"I looked. Obviously. It's like you forget that I'm a cat sometimes."

I really didn't have an answer for that, so I settled and finished my beer. Elias didn't come back into the room for the rest of the night, and the beer ran out and the water got cold, so I found a bed.

Chapter 10

The next morning was full of surprises. First, reveille was being played at an unholy volume, which launched me out of bed and headed for the dresser for all the things I needed to be decent for the morning formation and run. And then I remembered I wasn't in the Army and I slowed down enough to throw on a shirt and a butt-cover. Second thing I noticed as I went for my coffee, the wreckage of the hammock was gone. After that, I saw Elias was standing at the door with a grim look, baggy eyes from pulling an all-nighter, and what appeared to be a traveling sort of outfit. The suspicion that we were going somewhere was confirmed by far too much luggage on a cart and the fact that Max had disappeared. Fifth, I looked at the clock, and it was far too early to be doing anything that wasn't sleeping.

"Reveille, Brooks. Dust off in thirty, make sure you have a copy of the goods you had at the meeting yesterday. Max is in Jeremiah's room, and Jeremiah's in the Mines with the rest of them doing some demonic Dwarf code to see if we can find out where Genesis is with this plan of theirs."

I blinked a few times, stumbling into the shower. "Okay, breakfast?"

"On the plane. Move with a purpose already."

I moved, but as was the ancient right of the soldier, I was griping and moaning the whole way. "Okay, but why are we going to...wherever we're going?"

"Communications and start laying the groundwork for a contingency plan. The islands each have an underwater habitat with living space, worst case scenario we evac as many as we can and negotiate from international waters." Elias put a cup of coffee in my hand and I sipped. And then blinked, as she'd somehow figured out how to make coffee the way I liked it. Either she was a wizard, or she'd watched me make coffee at some point - the latter was more likely.

"And we can't just call them?" Seriously, all the wizard-like technology that was around, and nobody could pick up a phone and dial.

"Not with something like this. There's a reason your new identity is secure courier. Quit stalling and start moving." She swatted my shoulder to get me into the shower and we both flinched. There was a look of confusion on Elias' face, and probably on mine as well. We looked at each other and decided that we were not going to get anywhere by discussing, so I hustled to the shower.

"Elias if you hadn't noticed there's a lot of me that needs a wash. Unless you're getting in here to help, lemme do my thing and answer questions as they come to my mind." As the words left my mouth I realized that I may have opened a door that I would have greatly preferred to remain closed.

She did not get in. Pretty sure that was a relief to both of us. It was at least for me. Once I got out and toweled off I threw on the usual loose outfit and grabbed the handles of the luggage cart. "Where to?"

"Follow me, we're heading to Hangar One. And put these on, it's the package and the cover for it." She handed me a wristband and a gaudy watch.

"We have more than one?" As I fastened everything, I realized there was no way I'd be caught dead wearing this timepiece normally.

"Several, this is an old air base remember? Now freaking move." That said she jogged three steps and took off for low level flight. Crap, we were in a hurry. I put my back into shoving the luggage cart. I was slightly winded by the time we got to the hangar, where a small business jet was waiting. I made a note to do more swimming, as my conditioning had gone the way of the dodo, and that was absolutely unacceptable.

Elias gave me the quick tour as I tossed all the luggage in the cargo hold. "Since we don't have a bunch of planes handy, our aircraft fleet here is highly modular, capable of passenger and cargo deliveries, and can be reconfigured to airdrop said cargo and personnel if needed. Also capable of aerial recon duties in the right configuration. Good times."

I hadn't actually flown since I Changed, so it was awkward as heck at first. Instead of the seat belt rig, I had a cushioned section of floor and a comfortable net was draped over my lower half.

"Cargo netting?"

"Would you rather get flung about on takeoff? Relax, you can unstrap once we hit cruising altitude, and then we can fully set up for what's happening. Bathroom's up front." Elias had a nice normal seat where she strapped in.

It was after takeoff that more surprises began. Elias took out a folder for me to read.

"Since this is your first field gig and we really didn't have time to prep, we're making this simple. You're still Peter Brooks, licensed and bonded courier, however you are traveling with your wife-slash-business partner Elizabeth Smythe-Brooks - me. The business is legit, but we have our own back line to call HQ if things get dicey. If things get amazingly dicey, the luggage has several addons that you do not get with your average carry-on."

"Wait, *wife*?" Nobody said a thing about me having a wife. And that smell that was in my room was back.

"Yes. Wife. We're married - I'm here to oversee and confirm delivery of the package you're carrying to Gerald Stirling, CEO and head of R&D for the Power Company. Background, just in case you forgot; Stirling's 55, dwarven phenotype, and utterly brilliant. Also, a bit of a recluse. He's been alerted that we're coming with a package, but the contents haven't been disclosed. Only that it's from Jacks' friend, and Jack's friend would like to keep it quiet while we research solutions. Also, if there are any solutions his team can come up with independently, we'd be grateful to hear them." She paused to look up from her notes. "You're still hung up on the wife thing."

"Uh, yeah." I was certain this was another test of how I could react to a fluid situation and new information. Although to be honest if I'd been thinking about it at all, it would have been logical.

"Well, you've got six hours to get used to it. Suck it up." Elias smirked, apparently pleased to have thrown me for a loop.

"Any other surprises in that packet?"

"The Power company's been heavily recruiting lately - through shell companies and contractors; there's a major construction project going on and we're not sure why they're being quiet about it. Which leads us to our secondary job, find out why."

"Any speculation?"

"Normally, I'd say they're opening up a fourth island for additional power generation, but with it being off-the-books, I'd say there's something else amiss. We don't know for certain, and that's the worrying part."

I undid the cargo net holding me down and stretched. "This fancy rig got a bar?"

"Yes, but it's self serve. We got two pilots and us. Also, try not to drink too much, we still have to clear security and that's problematic if you're hammered to the gills."

"Yes, dear..." I glanced back to see her start at that. "Get used to it?"

"Brooks, you're an ass."

"Thanks." I grabbed a beer, considered, grabbed a spare, and started pacing a bit. "They're on an artificial island. Three ways they can go - up, down or out. They're doing it on the sly, so logically, they're building down where nobody can see."

"Except that they're not focusing on underwater specialists."

"So, we got anything to prove it one way or the other?"

"Nope."

"Do they have enough current personnel to build underwater without hiring additional help?"

Elias glanced through her notes and flipped through a tablet for a moment. "Just, if they worked their current personnel list as efficiently as possible."

"Well, then we can sit and debate the pros and cons, or we can wait for our arrival and figure it out once we're on the ground."

"Agreed."

"So, new question - whatever my first gig was, you were always coming along with as my wife, right? That's why you had a hammock in my quarters." I settled back down on the cushions and started going through the files, pausing to have a sip of breakfast beer.

"Penny for the smart boy." Elias smirked a bit as her wings fluttered.

"So why all the secrecy?"

"One, you're still being gauged for field work versus a desk gig. Two, it's easier to maintain the fiction with someone you're already familiar with. Say we'd sent one of the secretaries or one of our other centaur fieldies. You wouldn't have any rapport, and you'd have to fake it. Surprisingly, it doesn't work, and the cover's blown within minutes. If you can keep it together with a milk run like this, you'll be getting language training and we'll get you ready for more fieldwork. After that if all goes well, a nice long career with a decent retirement."

"So what's the retirement package?"

"Assuming you make it, we've got a few communities set up in various places. Baja California, the Keys, Hawaii, the Maldives..."

"Isolated islands where the old folks can be watched?"

She looked at me like I'd said something I wasn't supposed to before continuing. "Yep. On the up side, the food is great, the views are spectacular, and the bridge clubs are very cut-throat."

"Oh. Good." I'd never played bridge and had no desire to learn.

"Trust there's other things to get up to. Sometimes they call the retirees up for a consult."

"One last hurrah?"

"Something like that. Now if you don't mind, we're going to practice being married until we land." With that, she got up, looked at me carefully, and flopped on my cushioned floor space before finally laying against my flank. It was unexpected and horribly nerve-wracking. From what I could tell in my light haze of 'what is going on here', she was similarly affected - at least initially. She settled in quickly, adjusting her wings to drape over my back. Her face was determined as she read through something on her tablet, but every so often I felt a flutter from her wings. I was going to have to figure out what that was about. I had suspicions, but at the same time those suspicions were leading me to a door I wasn't sure I wanted to go through.

"Brooks. Relax. Or collapse into exhaustion." Elias glanced at me, trying to get me to settle down. And possibly get herself to settle down as well.

"This is so not comfortable right now." A bit of a lie - after the initial shock, my nerves settled a little bit, with my mental state currently at 'not okay, but getting to okay'. A stray image of a frog in a pot of water came to mind for some reason.

"When was the last time you had someone lounging comfortably against you?" Elias was concerned for some reason, and that reason may not have been entirely professional.

"A few weeks before my divorce started." I stared at the tablet and files in front of me, looking for something distracting.

She sat up a bit; there was concern writ large on her face. "Welll, crud. Once we get back, you're going to see Oscar. You're gonna get a few acting lessons."

"Coulda used those before. And a full-body haircut." My undercoat was starting to shed, and I felt it - still, I could suck it up for a day or two before getting back to base. That said, the longer I waited to get my coat raked out, the worse it was going to be.

"Hindsight. Alas. For now, suck it up trooper. Get used to the idea that we're married for the next twenty-four hours. Also, get used to the idea that you make a nice pillow. And it's better when your coat is fluffy."

I blinked a few times. "Okay seriously, that's a curveball I didn't need right now."

"Are you that bad at taking compliments? For crying out loud, your jacket is full of them."

"I was doing my job."

"Better than anyone else out there." She flopped back down against my side with authority. Whatever odd feelings this was causing for both of us were going to have to be set to the side. "Plus, you're letting me indulge my inner horse girl."

I was really not sure how to respond to that one, so I changed the subject. "So, the construction project. Whatever they're doing, I think they're building something designed to go very high up or very far down. Ordinarily I'd say very far down, but if they're doing this on the sly, what the heck does that mean?"

Elias didn't respond, so I continued on with my thoughts as I finished the beer. "If they're doing it secretly, it means they're either unsure about this and they want to keep it quiet in case it goes bellyup in some spectacular fashion, or they are sure it's going to work and they're going for the biggest PR splash they can get, or lastly they're sure and they don't want anyone to know because they're doing something horrible. That about cover it?"

Still no response. I finally looked back to find that Elias had decided my flank made a nice place for a nap. Well, at least one of us was comfortable. Sort of. Elias' wings were fluttering about once a minute against my side. I couldn't exactly look back at her expression during this, so I couldn't tell if she was having a good dream or a bad one.

The flight progressed, and I read up on the file packet while my second beer made its' way home. Everything I had kept coming back to some sort of underwater exploration; they were recruiting for labor and engineering, as well as some materials science people. But it was quieter than their last projects, and the worst part was it was a money pit. From the financial data, there wasn't a dime being made on this so far, but looking at the last publicly declared bits, it didn't seem like this was hitting their core business. Which made my tail twitch in a bad way. The money was coming from somewhere, and investors did not like negative numbers. All in all, it was interesting enough that I almost forgot Elias taking a nap and using me for a pillow. Almost.

There was a chime as the fasten seatbelts sign kicked on, and Elias stretched in a way that was disconcerting on several levels. After shaking her wings out, she looked back at me with an expression that wasn't readable before she belted in. At the same time, I sorted my safety net, stowed the files and got my legs under me for what would hopefully be a smooth landing. There was a slight chuckle from Elias that seemed somehow forced.

"What's that about?" I glanced over with an eyebrow up.

"Just thinking if this is your third or fourth time actually landing with an airplane."

"I haven't counted. That said I hate landings, which is why I usually left the plane early." It was an old joke of sorts.

"I'll make a note of it."

I looked outside, and a few things struck me. First, it didn't look like it was made from trash. Second, it was...small. It had a landing strip, boat dock, and some domes for what I assumed were control centers, but that was it. Outside was a orange-haired faun looking a little bored.

We disembarked, and saw a few porters with our luggage while the faun introduced himself as Drustan, and he would be our guide for this visit. Mister Stirling sent along both compliments and apologies, but he would not be available to receive our package for two days, which left us the option of leaving the package with him or staying a few days in guest accommodations until he was available personally. I gave him a Cop Look, which made him stammer out that guest rooms would be prepared immediately, but we would have to pass through security first.

Security was not in any way shape or form a breeze. First it was a pair of Oni asking both of us an exhaustive series of questions, and then they proceeded with a thorough pat down search. I hadn't run into very many Oni, so I took the opportunity to observe. In legends, Oni were the truly evil sent to hell and transformed into demons who delivered punishments to others who were evil enough to be sent to hell, but not evil enough to become Oni themselves. Outside of the legends, they were large in the seven feet tall and four feet wide way, red or blue skinned, possessed of very good eyesight, a set of hair-hugging horns that ran from forehead to neck. The one odd-ish thing, female Oni were referred to as Kijo. Same boxes ticked off as far as look and personality.

The Oni were also a study in superstition. In their home countries, their legal status was disputed; when they changed, they didn't maintain their birth ID. That person was considered to have died of natural causes, and the Oni that took their place was given a government identification number and subsequently re-homed with whatever their former families allowed. From there it was apparently an arduous process to get anything done, as very few people were willing to interact with them on any level. For the most part they became petty criminals in order to get even the most basic necessities, which then looped them back into the criminal system and created one of the odder chicken-or-egg scenarios the world had seen. There were noises about helping them in some manner, but the governments in question were very reluctant to even admit that the Oni existed due to the aforementioned bad luck.

And now The Power Company was hiring them for security. This sent up a few warning flags in the back of my head.

Fortunately I wasn't carrying anything more dangerous than what I'd been given when I Changed, and neither was Elias. Still, the strip search was to my mind, excessive. After that was completed, we were given our clothes back in slightly rumpled condition. and then the two security folks left us to dress - which was odd, given how well they'd gotten to know both of us not five minutes before. Somehow, that made it worse, and we decided by unspoken accord to both turn to face an opposite wall while we dressed.

"E..lizabeth?" I was throwing on my suit in what might have been record time. She was not nearly as fast with getting dressed for some reason.

She grunted.

"That's not normal, is it?" I'd been through a few security lines and even been on a few for various city functions, but this was well above and beyond the normal patdown and questionnaire.

She shook her head and glanced around, and then she did something very surprising, getting up on her tiptoes and wrapping her wings around us both. I was rather obviously stunned.

"What the heck?!" In order to keep from collapsing, I locked up my legs and arms to make a very lifelike statue of myself.

Her face was all serious as she hissed in my ear. "Brooks, our clothes are bugged. Act normal but this is not normal."

I kept my eyes on hers for a moment before my peripheral vision saw loose straps and made the brilliant leap that there were things I was not supposed to see if I looked lower. I resolved that by looking up to her forehead and keeping my gaze locked there and whispering back. "Okay, but ah, we're still on the job here. Could you maybe close your bra before getting this close?"

She released the wing embrace, her face taking on a look of a wife who's heard a in-joke a few times. "You can do that later, Mister Brooks. For now, this." With that she turned around, sweeping her wings up in an invitation for me to clasp her bra together. Something I hadn't done for some time, but I was able to manage it on the first try - not easy, as anyone who was looking closely would have noted we were both trembling. Score one for me, I suppose.

Once we were decent, we left security to find our faun tour guide Drustan waiting patiently to escort us to our room, explaining all the amenities. As we were guests, we would be given the appropriate quarters and room service would be provided as well as a laundry should we need it. The most interesting thing was that every possible effort had been made to generate power and allow the station to be self-sufficient. As a prime example of this, the beds had small pipes that used body heat to move fluid through generators attached to the outside wall. A second example was the walls and décor; it seemed like most of the walls were effectively aquariums, with sea life and plants densely packed in. Drustan mentioned that the plants were supplying a large part of the oxygen utilized by the stations' lower levels, and the fish and plants were regularly harvested to provide various foods required. The exercise areas were in another wing, and there was a bar available if we wished to mingle a bit. One additional item that Drustan seemed to lean into was the efficiency of the place. According to him, each station was entirely self-contained and could survive for an estimated fifteen years without any need for resupplies of food or water. He was uncertain about how they managed that, deferring to the pamphlets and other promotional materials in our room.

Once we were in our room, a multitude of problems made themselves immediately present. Firstly the bed, in that there was only the one. It was an Alaskan King-sized bed; roomy enough for two Centaurs. Three if they were really comfortable with each other. But that didn't change the fact that there was only one bed. Second was the fact that our clothes had been bugged, making conversation difficult. Fortunately, our respective military time helped a bit, and while making idle conversation about the bar, whether we were going to dine in tonight, we were able to signal out where the video and audio bugs were without tipping our hands too much as far as what we were doing. From what we could see, the microphones were probably sensitive enough to pick up conversation even if Elias did the wing-hug trick. Either way, we weren't taking chances.

Which led to our next problem, which was of the good news bad news variety. The good news was that there was a place where we could talk without being easily overheard. The bad news was that said place where we could talk for any length of time was the shower. And the least awkward way for us to talk was her on my back. For a first field mission, this was rapidly turning into some horrifying boundary-free stuff. Time to act married. My heart sank as I finally got a few moments to process that not only was I going to have to keep this up for a day, it seemed quite possible that a few more days were being tacked on for good measure. I was pretty sure I was being punished for some unknown sin.

The shower itself was glorious. Three showerheads - front, back, and middle, all with independent controls and flow settings. Looking down, the flooring was some sort of plastic material that let me sink my hooves in and get a nice grip. I grimaced as I could almost see my hair growing long enough to trip me up. While I was looking at the floor, Elias slid in and hopped on my back as the steam rose - apparently she liked the water set to sauna-hot. I was not comfortable, at all.

"This feels like the part where the cheesy background music kicks in. What's our next move?" I looked down at the drain to see how that worked, and curiously there didn't seem to be a single drain. It looked like everything drained into the flooring, which seemed odd. I glanced back to see if I'd missed the drain and saw that Elias had packed a bikini and was wearing it - this was someone who truly believed it was better to have and not need than to need and not have. I found myself approving on a professional level. Also, I was relieved to note that she wasn't so fully committed to the married couple bit that we needed to be unclothed. I did regret that I couldn't sneak a pair of swim trunks in for my own modesty.

"Brooks, you are horribly mission-focused. We like that." Elias was maneuvering on my back to get comfortable while she actually showered, which was sending a ton of messages. On the one hand, this was the job. On the other hand, her touches were lingering on my back longer then was strictly necessary - it seemed like she wasn't fully aware of it because I felt her hand jerk back a few times. To make things worse, once I was past the initial shock, I didn't mind. Which was a shock all its' own.

"Isn't that why you hired me?" Time to start talking. anything. Hopefully the distractions would cease and I could mentally retrack myself.

"Yes. So the security has tightened up considerably since the last time I was here; and there's only one reason for security to ramp up like this."

"They're hiding something horrible. If it was something beneficial, they'd let it leak and get a boost from the press as they played footsie with their favorite reporters after running some press releases denying the confirmation of their denial. Free advertising buzz."

"Very good. Now, with that in mind, we have a second mission. Find out what else is going on. And hopefully we'll be able to report it back. That said, back up a bit. And act like I'm your wife." Elias scooched down my back to perch on my rump and as I backed up under the second showerhead, she did some hair and wing care. At least that's what it sounded like. I maneuvered as best I could for the shampoo with a not-delicate but definitely smaller than me person sitting on my butt like it wasn't a thing. For my own part, I kept my eyes straight forward and focused on the wall, humming a few old running cadences to keep my mind occupied.

Elias hopped out after a long time, and as I finally looked back I caught her giving an appreciative look at all of me while she was covered with the benefit of wings. It wasn't like the looks she gave me when she was working the police station armory. These looks were different in a definable, meaningful way. That may have been the most uncomfortable part of this whole affair. After I was rendered unattached courtesy of Aoife, there were more than a few people who were highly intrigued by my new physique. And my reflexive response was still intact, flicking my tail at her dismissively.

"Now who's the killjoy, Pete?"

"Later, Liz." I did have to do some coat-work, and frankly it was time consuming. Still necessary, since I had to play the part of a professional courier - one part butler, one part mailman. And there were a lot of things running through the back of my head, all of which were awkward and unnecessary. It took a few minutes before I finally reminded myself that this was a job. Like running a sting operation. A couple days, and then we'd be back in our own rooms and relaxing for real. I wouldn't need to worry about waking up with feathers in my face or awkward situations. That was something to look forward to.

After cleaning up, I hopped out of the shower and found the Centaur towels. They. Were. Awesome. Big enough to cover all of me and fluffy enough to be part cloud. I made a note to check where they got these and order a few. Maybe more than a few. I found Elias deep in the luggage, nodding and pointing at a tablet that had been hidden in a false wall inside her luggage. There was a message written on it "Act interested. They didn't find this. We have comms with home. Initial report sent, confirmed recon go. We check in regularly, but max ten hours."

I chuffed. "Liz, I didn't think you'd bring that along. Feeling playful?" As soon as I said that I felt very awkward, like there was something I shouldn't have said that couldn't be unsaid.

"More than you realize, Sparklebutt." She nudged me with her wing and gave me a look for the cameras that was filled with emotions I wasn't entirely sure how to process. And whatever odd smell was in the air at my quarters was back with a vengeance.

"Mmm...that's a look of someone who wants to order in. Pizza?" So we put those emotions right back on the back burner to simmer for a bit. They needed to be addressed tomorrow. Or even the next day, once we were back at base. With some helpful friends from the liquor store.

"Yes please; remember that one place we went to that had the quinoa pizza crust? see if they have one of those. If not, you know. Whatever. Don't forget the beer." It occurred to me that I wasn't entirely sure what Elias ate or drank, so this would be a learning opportunity for me too.

"So, we got two days on the Power Company's dime before we meet the boss." I parked it on the couch and flicked through the list of amenities for VIP's, which apparently we were. "What time is it anyway? My stomach thinks it's food time."

Elias looked up from the desk. "I think I'd like that, we can play tourist tomorrow, right? They have massages and a sauna. Almost seems like the boss is always busy, so it's like he set this up to keep people comfy. We could almost run the whole business from this place for a week if we had to. and for the record, your stomach always thinks it's food time." She stretched languidly and moved to resettle herself on the bed, looking over paperwork.

I grunted. "I'm a growing boy. And couriers don't make much unless they're on the move. Something about the job description, what was it? Oh, right, couriering."

I got a pillow thrown at me casually. "Hush and turn on the TV. I know you're dying to check out the scores, now get over here and be a palomino pillow. I've gotta call and let some people know we'll be here for a bit so schedules are going to need a rearrange." I smirked a little and hopped onto the bed, settling my newly found pillow at my back and kicked on the remote. Elias parked it against my flank again, lounging comfortably and keeping her wings thoughtfully out of my line of sight as I checked out the baseball scores and highlights. At least that's what it looked like. Under the covers she was bouncing her leg in an apparent nervous tension.

Whatever she was saying was muted, at least to me. Okay, I was ignoring her. Or trying to, at least. I kept my focus on the TV and tuned out whatever she was saying. That said, whoever was listening in on the room and our conversation wasn't hindered by having merely mortal ears. I tried to relax, but it was not working well, until a discrete knock at the door announced that room service had arrived.

Even though we'd only ordered pizza and beer, it was served on china and silver. It was a slice of awesome, really. And one of the better meals I'd had in awhile. We re-retired to the bed after ordering breakfast and a wake-up call, in order to maintain ourselves for the benefit of whoever was watching the security cameras. Then she started drawing on my hand with one nail, which brought a whole new level of tension until she tapped my wrist and started over.

Then I figured out that she was writing letters on the back of my hand out of camera view, and the baseball game was far less interesting. It was a decidedly one way conversation, but it was full of information.

"Jeremiah is good. He's putting on a brave voice. Said 'Don't hurt my Dad' - Max wants gooshy food." She glanced over and gave a me warm smile that threatened to be borderline genuine. "The Elf wants us to find out everything and have a full report to him tomorrow morning. We've got some extras for electronics. Lights out in fifteen, we've got a long day."

Against my better judgment, I started relaxing a bit as information was passed along. It was either that or the exhaustion of the flight, the conversations, and getting ready to do a few things that I was used to doing with a badge to back me up - though this time I was without the benefit of having a badge. It was those thoughts in my head as I backed into my pajamas and flopped into the bed. Unfortunately, I couldn't fall asleep easily. Several thoughts were running through my head. How to find the information that we needed, how to get it out without tipping off security, or worse the boss. And above all, how to fall asleep comfortably while Elias was sound asleep and pressing against me like I was some sort of oversized teddy bear. And I could barely move, because when I did, Elias whimpered and moved herself closer. I dozed off at some point. Somehow.

Morning came, and with it, the scent of a properly sized bowl of oatmeal with cinnamon and sugar on the side for me to take care of. Elias was already awake and having cod with scrambled eggs, and between the two of us was a pot of coffee. After that, we started getting ready for the day with another shower conference that felt a little more relaxed. I was still more interested in the shower wall decor than Elias' state of undress. Her being parked on my back was awkward enough. I let my thoughts drift for a moment and ran through what I was going to do today. Since we hadn't discussed a formal plan, I figured I'd wander and tourist it up a little in preparation for the meeting. No sense in me rubbernecking like a fool when there was work to be done. After that, I could hit the gym for a solid workout, and then see where the rest of the day went to.

"Okay Brooks, here's the plan. First, we find out where we can and can't go. Second, I'll see if I can't find a maintenance area with network access, see if I can get anything on their project. Meanwhile, see if you can't get a route to Geralds' office. No reason for you to rubberneck, and you might see something. Third, we hit the gym, which gives us an excuse to meet up here in the shower afterward. Then we hit the bar in the evening, see if we can hear anything amiss. Finally, we get back here, see if they have anything else for us, and then tomorrow we deliver, take the day to see if anything else pops up, and then we fly ourselves home and cash a paycheck."

"Sounds doable. Got a timetable?" I glanced back at her to see her eyeing me like there was something very not right, but whatever wasn't right was also not definable. She collected herself with a wing flutter and turned to face the shower door.

"Play it by ear, but call me if you make a mess. We have a lot of things in our luggage and with our luggage that'll help in an emergency." Her fingers were tracing along the entirety of my back and not spelling anything, which woke me up much faster than any coffee ever would.

"Can do. Call me when things have gone sideways." I lifted my legs to work out a kink and I felt her pull her hand back rapidly. There was a lot of what the hell in my mind.

"Obviously." She slid off my back and got out. As soon as the door closed, I flipped the shower to cold for a ten-count, then got out myself and threw on shoes and some tourist-y wear for todays' excursion. I probably wasn't getting a trip to the barber today, and the current state of my lower half was definitely shaggy approaching unacceptably bad. Still, the job took precedence over my look.

It was interesting. Drustan was highly concerned that we were going in different directions, but finally decided to follow Elias, which gave me a little free reign to walk around and see what amenities were available. There was a full Neo-friendly cafe to go along with the bar, a few other accouterments, and the administrative and actual working sections where the power plant things were happening. I was advised in no uncertain terms that the working section was off limits by a fussy card-reader.

Alas. However, I was able to finagle a dime tour of the administrative section, as I wanted to not get lost on the way to the CEO's office. For this, I rubbernecked like a good tourist, but unfortunately their love of security extended to the admin computers, and I couldn't see a thing until I looked in an open door to a meeting. For a few seconds I saw what looked like a tower with cables attached, and then it zoomed out to show an animation that made me blink. It looked like they were building a tower underwater, and then launching it into space - the final bit was some sort of ring arrangement that made regular appearances around the central tower. I moved on before anyone noticed.

I took four long strides and caught up with my guide, who looked a little miffed about having to escort me around. That said, I did learn quite a bit from the canned schpiel about the current power output as well as projections for future use - even in their worst case scenarios, it sounded like the Power Company could be providing about eighty percent of the worlds energy in less than a century.

I'm not sure why, but some of these projections felt odd. It may have been that the numbers were hard for me to really wrap my head around, but it seemed like they were making assumptions in a vacuum without accounting for all the usual hiccups - not the least of which was the fact that world peace was still a concept only realized in the optimists of fiction. Still, I didn't throw any wrenches in the works yet. Partly because I hadn't fully grasped what was fully going on, and partly because someone was going to be interested to see what was happening.

Another thing that came up as odd for me was the feel of the offices themselves. On the one hand, it felt like there was something going on that I couldn't see - privacy screens abounded and when I tapped someone to play dumb tourist, they gave me a look that was half grumpy, and half worried that I'd seen something. My erstwhile guide interceded rapidly, keeping the fuss to a minimum. I began to get a nagging sense of something being not right.

As far as the walking portion I kept pace easily and listened intently throughout the tour before politely asking where the gym was, as I felt the need to stretch my legs. There was a knowing smile from my guide, as he pointed me to a wall, tapped the screen and then selected a button for the gym. A series of lights formed arrows for me to follow. He gave a code and told me to punch it in at the gym to tell the system it didn't need to light the path for me anymore, and to let me in. I nodded and set off at a trot to the gym, where I was given some sweats and a code to the lockers.

The gym was top-notch; honestly it was quickly becoming what I was starting to expect. Rooms, food, equipment, everything was luxurious and functional without going overboard. All the exercise equipment was resistance-based and each machine had counters that gave me pause for a moment until I realized they were tracking power generation. They were obsessed to the point of mania, but then again it was named The Power Company. There were even a few machines I didn't quite recognize, but the two things they didn't have were free weights and a pool. Frankly that was a damn shame, but I suppose if someone really wanted to swim, the Pacific ocean was right outside, and free weights were a problem waiting to happen. Still, I got a few miles in on the track, and the universal was good enough to sweat in.

After an hour of this, I left, making sure the workout gear would eventually make its' way back to the proper place and got back to my room for a shower conference with Elias. Ten deep breaths, and then focus on the wall, just business. Just talk. We were both professionals, and this was the best way to get information to each other for further analysis.

As I walked into the room, Elias was already there with her wings facing me, and a robe dropped to the floor; "Join me for a few, Mister Brooks?" I closed my eyes for a moment before moving to the shower myself, being careful not to show off or look too closely at anything that might have been seen as improper. I didn't need any more complications before we went out.

I heard a giggle as Elias got herself situated while we were waiting for the shower to get uncomfortably warm. "Okay Brooks, what'd you learn?" As I told her, I couldn't see her face, but she went "hmm" at a few points, before finally tapping my head with a feather.

"What's that for?" I was a touch annoyed.

"I have a theory. They're building a space elevator." She did the happy wriggle thing on my rump for a moment, which did nothing to set my mind at ease. I glanced back at her and she froze, looking like she'd been busted again.

"Are you kidding?" It was insane on the face of it.

"Nope. Think about it. No weights, because exercise gear based on gravity wouldn't work in orbit - and how do you keep water in a pool when there's no gravity? And that clip you saw was a demonstration to some engineers probably. Good thing you didn't ask, or people might have freaked out. It jibes with what I found and saw."

"Keep talking." She needed to explain, because I was pretty sure The Elf was going to ask, and she needed her logic to be solid.

"Well, I mighta gotten lost heading to a few places; and I saw miles of cables - superthin, and I have no idea what it's made of, but it smells weird and it's really strong. I might have found an end and cut a few feet off for analysis when we get home. I can see why they'd be keeping this under wraps. It's a total game changer on several levels. Aerospace, and the materials science by itself would rewrite construction."

"Okay first off twenty bucks says you're wrong - someone would have said something by now. With that in mind, now what?" Something odd was happening, and it felt like we needed a breath to think about what was happening.

"Now, we go out to dinner, Sparklebutt. No need for formal-wear, but you should wear that green silk button-down and that black sarong. It brings out your eyes."

I stammered a bit. "Wait, I don't have anything green." My favorite sports teams did not have green in their color scheme, and a few of the rivals had green in theirs. Thus it was that green was not a favored color in the household of Brooks Arthur. Or Peter Brooks, as I was known now.

"I packed it for you. Just in case. Now hurry up." She slid off my back and got out, trailing questions in her wake that I was not ready to ask. Still, I finished everything as rapidly as I could and covered up in a towel, finding that in the interim she had changed into a flowing electric blue dress that redefined the phrase "plunging neckline".

"I thought this was a casual thing. That...does not look casual."

"I like to look nice for my husband. Sue me."

That hit me for a moment before I remembered we were playing characters, and that was my cue to play along. "You would have to take several steps down to get to just 'nice.'" I slipped on my shirt and fastened my sarong properly, continuing past her minor blinking; "Hopefully this'll get us a few looks and someone'll give us more work to here, this place is fantastic. Wouldn't mind seeing what it takes to be here permanently."

"Maybe we apply to come here when we're close to retirement. Spend a few years in communications, then we retire to that nice place my parents have for us, and watch the grandkids roll in."

"I can smell the grass already." The conversation was almost too automatic, but frankly part of me knew that if I stopped to think about it whatever flow was present would be broken.

"Let's hurry up, we don't want to be late." She fastened her jewelry, and with that, we went to the bar, making use of the guide wall.

While it wasn't super formal, Elias had chosen my outfit well. The seating was minimalist and beautiful, with abstract art delicately lit as well as multipurpose chairs everywhere. Our waiter was quite interesting, a Japanese woman in full kimono, who instructed us to stand still while we were quickly scanned and then led us to a booth that morphed as we approached to form a Centaur-suitable couch and chair for both of us.

I spoke softly after she left. "That's the first unchanged I've seen here."

Elias quirked an eyebrow. "Wait for it." And than pointed as our waitress appeared to grow ears, and I could see several tail-tips under the hem of her kimono. "Kitsune. They're kind of like fauns as far as attitude, but don't make the comparison in front of them. Unless you like the idea of getting bruises."

"Noted. So, what's the menu looking like?" As soon as I said that, the table lit up with several menus for me to start ordering. In a word, holy crap. Still, I was able to navigate the menu and order a few things that were nice, but not too expensive looking. Meanwhile, Elias was indulging her seafood junkie side it seemed. In the interim, we watched and listened. The oddest thing was the lack of Unchanged; everyone was something else. Elias noticed it as well, giving a running commentary. Kitsune and nekomata, oni, a bat-winged popobawa, and even a lamia. It was enlightening and concerning at the same time; it felt like the company was pulling in every Neotype they could for some reason. Elias nudged me to bring me out of my reverie.

"Trade? I wanted to see what that was about, but the surf and surf was just too tempting."

I smirked a bit. "Be careful - it's spicy lamb." She smirked but tried it and her eyes watered as she reached for her water with flushed cheeks. "How. How do you eat that stuff."

"Kinda like this - " I demonstrated. "And then feel the burn all the way down."

She swatted me. "You need to warn me, you goof."

"I did. But do you listen to me, nooooo..."

She gently punched my shoulder, and I started relaxing. I was either getting more comfortable, or the ouzo and beer was way more powerful than I remembered. The lights dimmed, and the head waiter came on over the loudspeaker. "Everyone, put your hands together for Aoife, our latest singer, for your entertainment."

It couldn't be.

It was.

Her mood-hair was a soft red as my ex-wife began singing a gentle love song; her expression of someone with raw passion and love for her job. On the one hand, I didn't understand why they'd need a lounge singer here, so she probably had some sort of day job as well - and from what I saw of the operation, resource management was an important process here, even to the point where there weren't any children around in this huge facility. Still, all that was second to the real problem. My ex-wife was supposed to think I was dead, when I was presenting her with conclusive evidence that I was not.

"E...we need to get out of here. Now."

"What's the hurry?" Elias looked at me oddly while Aoife finished her song and looked at the crowd, her face registering shock as she saw and recognized me.

I took her hand and very gently began spelling out "Ex-wife" on the back while staring at her with what I hoped was an expression of something other than blind panic. She got the hint and started leaning into me very closely while waving for the check. We charged it to our business account, and hoped The Elf wouldn't freak when he saw the tab. And then we tried to leave as discretely as a centaur and erinyes couple could.

We were not successful. Aoife caught us as the waiter was bringing the bill. She was bubbly and happy after singing, and slid in beside Elias to look at both of us.

Eternal seconds passed before Elias finally spoke. "Hi, your singing was beautiful, can we get you something to drink?"

Aoife waved it off. "Nah, I just saw you both here and just, well...he looks so much like my ex-husband I had to check." She pointed at me.

Thinking quick time to play the part, I extended my hand. "Pete, and yeah I get that a lot. Something about my face I guess. I'm sorry if I brought up bad memories?" I pitched my voice down a little, which hopefully threw her off a little.

She shook my hand, uncertainty on her face. "No, not bad, but well kind of? I'm sorry where are my manners, Aoife." Aoife glanced at Elias, looking for something. Elias seemed completely at ease with the situation, as if her 'husband' was accosted by lounge singers all the time. Aoife looked down at the tablecloth for a moment as a drink appeared by her side.

Elias grabbed the lead in the conversation. "Well, Aoife I'm Elizabeth, and my husband and I are couriers. Have been for awhile, but if there's something you needed to talk about...?"

Aoife hesitated, then nodded. "Well, my ex was a cop. He...he passed a few months ago in the line of duty, so this is one those weird things. And then that night our son was killed in a break-in. Some people my husband had raided a few days earlier." She ground her hands together, her hair flickering through several shades before settling to a deep violet. "I was working here, and I didn't get to go to his or my sons' funeral. We watched here on TV, it was a big thing, at least locally. And, well..." she stopped for a moment. "I guess seeing you both here brought up some memories. Good ones, mostly."

I let Elias do the talking. The less I spoke, the less chance this whole thing would be blown. Elias thankfully seemed aware and kept the conversation flowing, moving us to the side so folks could keep walking around us. "What was your husband, sorry ex-husband, like?"

Aoife leaned back a bit, sipping her drink. "He was a wonderful person. Good cop. Our son was so smart. We, well Brooks and I Changed and we didn't click anymore. So we split up, and I never...never got the chance to apologize to him. You see, I'm a therapist normally, and for about four months before I got this, I was just getting by. Clients, jobs, everything was drying up. I got a final eviction notice and the offer letter for this job the same day. Now I'm a lounge singer and an occupational therapist. I'd packed everything I could into my car, and I told Jerry it was going to be okay."

Aoife looked up at us. "It was supposed to be okay. This job, it was going to be my way to give Jerry everything he'd wanted. And a college fund so he could go to a good school and use that smarts of his, and then he became a Dwarf, and everything was just...it was a crisis and I didn't handle it well, and now it's going to be years until I can do...anything." At the end of it, Aoife seemed like she was looking through me to some imagined future where we were friendly neighbors.

Elias was calm throughout it all. "I'm sorry we can't do anything about your husband, or your son. But here." She fished a business card from somewhere. "If you need something delivered to make things better. Call us."

Aoife smiled weakly. "Thank you, both. If you'll excuse me, I have to go to my room and cry before seeing my patients tomorrow." She left and the check was delivered to us. Elias glanced at me and we got out of there and back to our room. The had barely closed before I flopped onto the bed and groaned, not even bothering to change into anything else. "Ohhh, what else could go wrong..."

"Don't challenge the universe like that. It'll find something you'd never expect." Elias dug into the suitcases to change.

"At this point, I'm not sure what else could happen."

She looked at me with an unreadable expression for a moment. "Whatever happens, you know we'll face it together. Just like always." And then she slithered up to my chest with an uncomfortably warm look. "Now how about we find a hanger for those clothes and a shower for that hair, hm?"

Chapter 11

I assented numbly, trying to keep myself together for at least a minute until the shower started and I settled into the shower. Elias was too close, or the shower had shrunk in the past few hours. "Brooks...focus. We just need to go to the office tomorrow, wait for his reaction, and then we're going to be on our way home. And then we debrief, relax, and wait to see what's next. And then we can talk openly. But for now, we need to rest." She paused, then hugged me from behind with her arms, and then added her wings to the hug, which shocked me back into reality. The hug lasted an eternal moment before she drew back. "Do your part Brooks."

I was stock still and hoped her eyes were looking at my back and nothing else, but I didn't freak out too badly, keeping my breathing shallow as Elias began to massage my shoulders into submission. Eventually I began to relax, after which we got out of the shower and headed directly for the in-suite minibar. Shots were taken by all parties, and the night passed in comfortable fuzz. Elias checked in, keeping what she sent very brief and skipped over our dinner events. I was a bit grateful for that.

The morning was too damned early. I was nervous, trembling a little as we got ourselves set for the meeting. I shaved closely and checked every thread on my suit as if I were about to pass a general inspection. I checked my tie, re-doing the trinity knot four times before it passed. Meanwhile, Elias was getting herself into a dark blue power outfit and makeup in impressive fashion. Finally before we left, we locked up all the luggage and dropped it on a cart to get ourselves out as rapidly as possible - our plane had a scheduled arrival time, and we didn't want them grumpy at us because we were late. While I could have carried all luggage by myself, I was not keen on how that would make me look. I'm not a pack animal.

As we led by Drustan, we were quiet, but we were the subject of no small amount of attention. Mainly because our light-strip was blue and going straight to the CEO's office; subtle but informative, as people seemed to catch on the we were in fact Very Important Personages. The walk seemed to last for awhile before we finally got to the office proper where one Gerald Stirling met us at the door. His tie was loose, but it was in the familiar trinity knot - we shared a very brief nod and acknowledgment of style. The rest of his look seemed to be of your typical high-grade executive; tailored suit and shirt, cufflinks set with three purple gemstones, and a watch that looked like it cost slightly less than the budget of a small city.

Gerald seemed to fill the room with his presence, as I glanced around the room. Gerald himself was your typical dwarf insofar as physical look, with a slightly balding head, a full but neatly trimmed beard that smelled like cedar, and a body that looked like it would have fit quite easily in a barrel. There wasn't a lot in the room that featured him, no wall of famous people he'd been photographed with, but at the same time there was more. An old soda dispenser from the 1950's, an antique gas pump, and a few knick-knacks I couldn't quite discern. As I looked in the room, another thing began to stand out - everything was grouped in threes. the items themselves were different but they had a theme, and there were always three of them. Even on his desk he had a pair of pyramid-shaped paperweights flanking a box that looked like a large collection of gears that formed a hand-turned something or other.

"Antikythera mechanism." Gerald's voice resonated; and with that I could see how he'd helmed this company to the position it held. At my quizzical look, his beard parted to a brilliant smile, looking like a scale model Santa delivering presents. "It's a reproduction, but the original dates back to the year one hundred BC; historical references can be dated back as far as four centuries earlier - the time of Archimedes. It reminds me that brilliance can be found in old things as we look forward to new things." He held himself up. "But, I digress. I'll be here all day and I won't find out what you have for me." With that he went back to his desk, which again seemed to be some sort of ancient stone thing with a wood-looking top.

I took a breath. "Well, we've found something that is deeply concerning to Jack and his friends. We'd like your opinion to see what can be done." I took off my watch and undid the compartment, handing the sliver of a drive to him, which he accepted with a curious look, and then seated it into his almost out of place computer. He read in silence, and watched the recordings at double speed, his face a mask until he got to the last one before I saw his eyes getting moist. It took him a moment to speak after he finished absorbing everything.

"Well. Thank you for this. Let our friend Jack know that I'll have something for them very soon. Now you, you have a plane to catch?"

Elias smoothly acknowledged the dismissal. "Of course. We'll be leaving within the hour, assuming air traffic control is amenable." Gerald nodded, already picking up his own phone and talking to it, keeping his voice low and in control, saying something I couldn't quite make out as the door closed, but Elias had on what I could see was a professional mask while her face was turning to an ashen pale. she began moving fast, almost power-walking to our room.

As soon as the door to our room closed, Elias was moving fast and doing one last sweep of the room to make sure we hadn't left anything behind, her whole body tense. At my quizzical look, she stopped for an explanation. "I heard him tell whoever was on the other line to activate 'Genesis Six'. It's not good."

"What the heck..." The fact that she'd dropped the discretion was not lost, but the lead ball forming in my stomach was severe and inexplicable.

I was interrupted from further questioning by the television trilling and coming to life with an image. It was Gerald, looking red-eyed but still very much in command of himself.

"Everyone, please. Could I have your attention. I know for some of you it's very late, and for others it's very early, but please." He paused for a minute, appearing to compose himself before going on, sliding to the side to allow for graphics to fill. "Many of you have been working on Project Enterprise under a non-disclosure agreement. At this time I am releasing you from that agreement, since I am telling everyone about it now."

His face changed to that of the Santa bearing gifts. "Project Enterprise is our companys' newest gift to Earth. In summation, beginning in the next hour all three power stations will begin finalizing the necessary procedures, and in two days we will begin magnetically launching thirty-one thousand miles of cable to match up with our satellites that are currently lifting themselves out of geosynchronous orbit to reach their new orbital points at a final distance of sixty-two thousand miles from earth, approximately a quarter of the way to the moon." He paused. "Yes, we're making a space elevator. With them, we will be delivering everyone what we've collectively dreamed of for centuries - the entire solar system. Stretching out our hand to grasp what has been denied for so long, powered and fueled by the very energy we harvest from the oceans, we will be our generations' explorers."

"There will be more to follow, but the most important thing is this. Sixty percent of our current facility will be used in this endeavor, and at the end of it, everyone who wishes to will be taking our first trips up to orbit, as each power facility will also take on a new function as the orbital counterweight to make this possible. I myself will be going up with the first group to ensure its' safety, after which everyone else who wishes to do so will be coming up. All of you will be receiving a survey of one question. You will have two days to decide, as that will be how long the cable construction will take. Please know that there will be no punishment for staying, but those of you who come with me will experience first the orbit, and then stars. Security, please set Condition Two. I thank you for your time, and encourage all of you to consider carefully." With that the screen went dark.

We both looked at each other, and simultaneously said "Whoa."

Finally things started to make sense. We went to our door and started to move out at Elias' pace, and it was going swimmingly until we made it to security, where guns were pointed at us by a pair of very not-nice looking Oni guards.

"We're to escort you back to your room." the larger one seemed almost apologetic. "Your pilot has been instructed to return in four days."

Elias shook her head. "No we're leaving immediately."

"Don't make this difficult." Oh, it looked like someone had some police training besides me. However, it was not helping him, as Elias and I were determined. Her body was radiating "I'm about to ruin some days" so I instinctively shifted a bit to cover the rear. Fortunately, nobody was there to approach from that angle. The Oni took another step forward, attempting to use his size to his advantage.

"Condition Two has been set - nobody in, nobody out. We have been specifically instructed, and we must insist." I felt something in the back of my head that said 'go time' - oddly, the voice didn't sound like anything authoritarian in my past, but this was not the time for introspective navel-gazing.

"So do we. Sorry." With that, Elias sent a wingtip into the taller ones' eye and raked it, blinding him and causing a reflexive shot to go off toward me. Oh good, just what the doctor ordered. I launched myself at the smaller one, tackling and knocking the wind out of him as we crashed in a heap of ouch, but I was able to get him unconscious. Elias nodded in approval as I hogtied him and stripped them of their weapons, and then she pulled a harness from somewhere amongst our luggage so that I could carry everything without a whole lot of worry. The luggage got fastened and latched to me in a few moments; it was very self-explanatory.

"Can you explain while we're running?" I shouldered the gear we'd recovered and started off fast.

"Genesis Six." And there was that ball of fear in my stomach again, that I had no idea why.

"Great, explain it to me like you're talking to someone who has no idea what that means, because that's what's happening."

She sighed as we were approached by more two more security guards who appeared to be named Trigger and Happy from the way they acted - they sprayed the hall as Elias went high to wing-sweep them and I took the available low path, sliding into them and hitting each of them with my back legs. The cold analytical part of my brain was complimenting us on our ability to work with Elias as if we'd been part of a unit for years. It was a pleasant surprise. While we were stripping, hog-tying, and getting their weapons and ammo from them, Elias explained.

"Genesis chapter Six is the story of Noahs' Ark. You know, great flood, humanity wiped out because God was righteously pissed off at mans' evil ways?"

"Aw...crap." That would definitely explain the lead ball feeling in my stomach.

"Yeah. Geralds' got some sort of contingency plan he's activating, and it doesn't sound good for the Unchanged. And we probably kicked it into motion when we handed him the data pack from the Genesis Twenty-Six crew. On the up side, our luggage has a lot of things built in to help us get out of here."

"This day's going to get worse, isn't it." I shifted things around a bit for comfort. There was going to be running soon.

"Oh...probably. I hear six behind us, closing fast."

I nodded, taking the corner that I remembered coming from when we first arrived and stopping. "Six ahead. They're loaded for seriousness. Aim low, yeah?"

"Confirmed Brooks. No killing if we can help it. Get low."

"Hate to break it to you, but I do not do 'low'." Still I was able to crouch a bit. My crouching was vigorously aided by someone trying to shoot me from the front.

I returned fire to the front, with me twisting and forming a barrier for Elias to shoot at the group coming at us from behind. I was rather pleased that my skills at shooting hadn't gone to heck, as they all fell down clutching legs and knees within a few moments. Elias was also a really good shot, hunkering down and firing at the ones behind. The problem was that the folks who were shooting at Elias had no problems shooting at her cover, to wit my hindquarters. I felt several sharp stings as said hindquarters were abused by bullets that were probably listed as non-lethal, but they still dug in hard and painful.

After she saw what had happened, Elias said a few things I couldn't quite understand and returned fire in a very undisciplined fashion, reverting to a style that would be best described as spraying and praying. When I looked back, there were four empty clips on the ground and a smoking gun in the hand of Elias, wearing an expression of raw fury that I'd never seen. I flicked my tail at her to get her out of it, and the expression faded as she looked at me with a very weak grin. "Brooks, have I mentioned how much I like your ass?"

"Not the time Elias!" I'm not sure where that came from but we were in no position to have a workshopped discussion about it.

"I really do, but okay. I'll get a hold of our ride out." She popped an earpiece in and checked her phone for a signal. Tapping a few more times, she finally got through. "Eyeball One, Thunder and Argento calling. ETA fifteen minutes, hot LZ. Touch and go if we can." She paused for a moment. "Understood, too hot, advise." Another pause, and then "Confirmed we have equipment for skyhook; it's his first time, be gentle." We rounded another corner to find that the elevator to the surface was decidedly not going to play nice. Elias grabbed a few things from a suitcase, re-purposing then to open the elevator door. I was gimping on three legs as best I could, which was probably still relatively fast but in the back of my head I kept thinking I was not fast enough.

"Cover me while I fix the elevator." Elias was digging through and finding a few more things to cajole the elevator into doing what we wanted it to.

I complied, but I did have to stop to discourage a few more of the security guards about halfway through. I also learned that my clothes were highly resistant to bullets, but still I was going to need a few days off once we were home. More guards joined the fracas, which made my job as point defense very difficult. As I was dispatching targets as I saw them, there was a blind shot from one of them and I heard Elias cry out in pain. I glanced back to check on her and I saw red on her wings and the back of her neck.

"Just a graze, it's nothing." She smiled weakly at me and tried to go back to what she was doing.

I didn't say anything in reply, because my entire being was infused with an anger I hadn't felt in a very long time. Here we were, trying to do a job and these people were violently trying to keep us from it. They'd shot at me. I was okay with that, however they'd also shot at Elias and hit her. That was unacceptable, and there was one response, and one response only.

I said something and charged the group of Oni who were attacking her. I saw clearly there were about a dozen of them, their expressions turning from satisfied to concerned, and then a realization that they had in fact made a large tactical error somewhere along the line. I didn't exactly take notes of who got what dished out to them, but it was quick. I had more limbs and more weight to bear onto each of them, despite their numbers advantage. Once it was done, I was short of breath, so I actually had to rock back and forth a bit to help get the fire from my lower lungs out. And I'd taken few more hits which was slowing me down further. As I looked around and listened, there were no more guards coming - but there were a large number of guards on the floor who were in various states ranging from not happy to not conscious. I looked around for anyone else, asked if there was anyone else who wanted to try something, and did not receive a reply. It was quite possible that they had seen what I was doing and made a healthy life choice.

There was a crash behind me and I whirled to see that Elias had opened the door and sent the elevator car to whatever afterlife awaits elevators, and she had also attached a clip to the back of my harness that ran to a smallish looking spool of what looked to be a thin bungee cord. "Get everything together and strap the luggage to your fine ass tight. Then get ready."

I was about to reply, but my repartee was cut off by her launching herself into the elevator shaft and up into the darkness. Things became very frantic as more guards arrived to see what had happened to their compatriots. I began firing out the last shots in my clip as someone finally decided that bullets weren't working for them, so gas was the next step up. I saw the pops and canisters and kicked as many of them as I could either back toward them or down the elevator shaft, but still the air was getting decidedly gross. And I did not have a mask.

My vision started to swim a bit and the world was becoming decidedly unstable before I felt a tug, a second tug, and I was thankful that we'd already secured everything as I was yoinked into the elevator shaft rapidly to ascend to what appeared to be the landing strip where we'd originally started this mess from two days earlier, with Elias looking up at a sky that was rapidly filling with something rude and dark.

"Elias...is that antiaircraft fire? That looks like antiaircraft fire."

"Then yeah, it is antiaircraft fire. They installed it as a counter-piracy device. We appear to be pirates now." It was at this point that my vision cleared more fully and I saw that she was wearing a harness similar to mine.

"Well, yo-ho-ho and bottle of rum, then." I paused, as what appeared to be our plane was descending and then stopped descending to take a level path. Meanwhile, Elias was rummaging in an untouched-until-now piece of luggage. "Forgive my ignorance Elias, but the plane does not appear to be landing. What gives with that?"

"He's not landing." She fired what appeared to be a crossbow connected to a second reel of bungee cord upward, and I saw a large balloon inflate a few hundred feet up. "He's gonna catch that and pull us up. When I say run, you run as fast as you can in the direction I'm flying."

"Wait, you packed all that?! Where?"

"Yes. Just in case. There's three pieces of luggage we carry when we can for things like this. Be glad, otherwise we'd probably be stealing a boat or swimming."

"If this is a joke, Elias, I'm going to be cranky as hell."

"No joke." She paused, and gave me a kiss. On the lips. "Just for luck. Now *run*."

I saw the direction she took and sprinted as hard as all three good legs and one gimpy leg could go, before I was unceremoniously dragged forward and up at a speed that was not quite ludicrous, but it was certainly unexpected.

The new problem was that I had been lifted into the sky that was also being filled with lead. And I was being tossed about like a house in a Kansas tornado, leaving me with only luck to avoid being hit be anything as my life was quite literally dangling by a thread. Elias was managing far better than I was, since she had wings and could maneuver a bit while while we were approaching Warp One. I was not entirely lucky, as I felt my left side explode in fire. I looked back and was able to see that it wasn't too bad, and that I'd been solidly hit on the rump with something while a second something had drilled a furrow along my side, leaving a nice scorchmark. On the up side it hadn't hit the luggage, so nobody's dainty underthings would be spilled into the ocean below. As we ascended it was getting hard to breathe, as the plane was pulling us and climbing to try and not get shot itself. This was a fine thing except I liked breathing and wanted to continue doing so.

Finally after what seemed an eternity, we were both brought into the rear of the plane, with Elias working the door and sealing it, allowing me to breathe freely and fully examine everything that had happened. For the record, I was still not happy.

Once we were actually safe in the cabin, Elias threw her arms around me for a full thirty seconds before looking at me. "You're bleeding. And you owe me twenty bucks."

"You should see the other guy. And so are you. I left my cash in my other wallet, so I'm gonna have to wait to pay you back."

"I did. Nice work, but don't do it again." Our plane leveled out, and she got her professionalism back on. "We're outside their firing range. Hopefully they don't have anything else, or maybe they assume we've already reported. We should do that. I'll be right back." She left and went forward to the flight deck, leaving me to take care of myself for the moment. The first thing was getting out of that gods-forsaken harness, and taking a look at my butt.

Yep, it was a butt. As the post-adrenaline rush started coming down, I realized that there were a lot of places that hurt. There was the near miss from a bullet designed to kill an airplane, the half-dozen or so shots from where Elias decided my ass would make a fine bunker, my knuckles, face, upper ribs and both elbows were scraped and bruised from the three minutes I decided to have a donnybrook on the wrong side of many to one odds, and my entire spine felt like it had been used as a xylophone by an angry god of music courtesy of the extraction. But other than that I was fine.

Elias came back to interrupt my reverie with a bottle of whiskey. "Second strongest painkiller we got. Two shots only, because The Elf wants a full debrief as soon as we land."

I gritted my teeth before speaking. "Elias, I may need more painkillers. It's going to be a long flight and in case you hadn't noticed, I got a lot of extra holes here."

Elias blinked, examining me from stem to stern and blinking. "Oooh. Yeah. Those look painful. One sec." she went up to the front of the plane and came back with a syringe which promptly went into my rear and made it feel no pain. Whatever it was, I needed a few more, as aches were beginning to assert themselves. "Local. Should last at least a couple hours, so you're just gonna have to deal with it until we land. Then we'll be getting some medical people and probably debriefing at the same time. What we've got is not going to wait."

"We both have to be there for debriefing?" I started flexing and moving limbs to make sure no other wounds were hiding.

"Yep. Even in your state, you're probably going to have some insight. In the meantime, more painkillers and brace yourself. We have authorization for a rapid return."

"Authorization for what?"

"Rapid return. Wait for it."

I waited and felt a very slight bump, as Elias relaxed a bit. "Congratulations, we are now supersonic. We're going to hit Mach two before this is over, we should be home and have you on the table in about an hour and a half. And that, calls for some additional painkillers."

She dropped the tray table in front of me, setting the glasses down and pouring out a few shots. We both tapped the glasses on the table twice before she started. "May the supply sergeant forget to count when you're there." I chuffed a little before replying "And may the platoon sergeant never hear you say you've got nothing to do."

Once the traditions were adhered to, Elias gave me a look. "Alright, start talking." She looked a bit of a fright herself, with her hair a complete haypile, one of her wings was crooked somehow, and there was dried blood from where she'd been shot. I felt a mild surge of anger at seeing it, but it did go away when I recalled the rest of the action.

I blinked. "Talk about what?"

"What in the name of all the good and pretty flowers made you think that going against a dozen Oni was a good idea? Those guys are seven feet tall minimum."

I waved a hand to dismiss her concern. "Nah. They were only seven metric feet tall, not seven actual feet. Were you counting them?"

I got a look from Elias like the painkillers and whiskey had done more damage than anticipated to my brain. "Yes. Yes I was. And you still haven't answered the question."

I shrugged. "Seemed like the thing to do." I tried rolling my thought processes back to what had predicated it. I'd been shot, so I was already in a bad mood. Then the elevator didn't arrive after we pressed the button and we weren't in a position to wait, and with no stairs available we got creative courtesy of our emergency gear. To top it all off my...my partner had gotten shot. That may in fact have been the tipping point. My thought processes were definitely slowed. Elias nudged me a little to bring me back to reality.

"What were we talking about again?" I didn't want to answer a question that hadn't been asked, so I fell back on being dumb.

"You did a very dumb thing, Brooks. A stupid, stupid, brave thing." And then she fell onto my lower shoulder and started smacking me a few times. "Don't. Ever. Do. That. Again." She punctuated each word with an open hand smack on my shoulder that hurt on a couple levels. Then she raised herself up to her knees, composing herself a bit and grabbed the bottle for both of us to pass back and forth to while away the time until our winged taxi took us to the hangar for a doctor.

Whiskey never tasted as good as it did on that flight. And I was finally starting to relax more fully. Either that or everything was starting to make more sense than it did. Maybe Elias was more than just a working partner. That train of thought was one that I examined for a moment before shutting it down. I wasn't anything special, just a regular guy who caught up in things way outside his pay grade. I'd had a wife, and she was currently a therapist pulling double duty as a lounge singer in what was appearing to be some kind of evil madmans' lair.

There was no way anything was going to work between us. Everything Elias had done was a show, because she was a professional at this, and she was just helping one of the new guys get his bearings. She hadn't even told me her real name. I took several deep breaths to keep the train of thought from going completely off the rails. I hadn't done too badly, and maybe we could keep it friendly. Less shower time, more analysis. Quite frankly we needed our heads straight, because chasing a bogus relationship wasn't helping anything.

Obviously the whiskey wasn't helping my thought process, as Elias was humming something to herself. She seemed pretty content after her last outburst, settling herself in on one of my uninjured parts and writing on a scratch pad between taking shots of whiskey with me until the chime came for landing. The oddest part was every so often I could feel her looking at me and when that happened I felt a full-body tremble that started in her feathers. As much as she'd said we were limited to two drinks, we'd both had more than two by the time the chime for landing sounded. Trays were stowed, whiskey hidden, and nets dropped down. We hadn't even finished landing when the door was opened and a very disheveled Jeremiah came rushing to tackle me, bringing all the aches of the past few hours anew. He'd gotten a respectable beard, but he was still working on trimming it. Following him was a medic for immediate investigation and a motorized cart/surgical table so I wouldn't be in too much agony once the doctor arrived.

"Dad, The Elf wants to see you he's got me working on a bunch of stuff and I can do it but it's kinda scary but it'll be okay...right?"

"Yeah. We'll figure it out and celebrate. Alright? Now, come on we gotta scoot." Jeremiah disentangled himself before giving Elias a bit of a look, and then we gathered our stuff and headed in, changing into some fresh clothes on the way. In the interim, the doctor came around and was highly unamused, muttering something about the damn cat not being here at least. He then poked and prodded and after pulling extra and unnecessary metal from me declared that I'd be mostly fine in a couple weeks, despite microcontusions all along my spine, six fresh bullet wounds on my right rump, and a second degree burn on my left side, three cracked ribs and other minor injuries. He recommended not sleeping on my back, left side, or right side without a trace of irony. He also gave me some burn cream and what appeared to be some very nice painkillers before moving on to Elias with two serious bruises from being shot, another minor but messy-looking graze, a mild concussion and two dislocated wing sockets - repairing those made me cringe. She was also given painkillers and told no self-propelled flying for a week. Finally, we were sent to Executive Alley, wherein awaited The Elf. Quite frankly I would have rather been talking to the Oni.

The Elf was having a very intense video conversation with someone, that quickly became apparent when we recognized the voice on the other side. Gerald Stirling, aka the guy who'd requested we be detained and shot.

"Gerald. Listen to me. I can't condone this course of action. You and I both know that the One-Two-Six doesn't have the manpower to pull this off any time soon. We'll be able to keep this under control if you don't go off half-cocked."

"We've been over this. What you've uncovered in and of itself shows that they can, and if they can, they will. If we don't do something now, we won't be able to. There's no control, no negotiation. People are dying for the crime of being different."

"And what makes what you're doing any better? I know you, you're going to make some grand show that, in this case, is going to backfire tremendously - the Unchanged will unite if you present any form of threat. Do you need the data, the models from my sociology department? Every predictive model that we have tells us that even if we have the moral high ground, a violent response will cause repercussions on scales we don't have charts for. One-Two-Six will lead the charge to genocide, and every Neotype will be forcibly relocated to the most barren wasteland available. Is that the future you want? Mass graves and empty space, with a possible hope of something?"

There was a sigh from Gerald. "Mass graves are happening now. Have you seen what's happening? Outside the Bunker? I mean really. Ask your field agents to report fully on what they see, what they experience every day regard Neotypes. Then tell me I'm wrong. Call me when those reports are on your desk. And think about this. When is enough going to be enough?"

"Speaking of people reporting, do you have anything on your desk that you could pass along to me regarding why my couriers had a very uncivil departure?"

There was a pause, and when he spoke, Gerald sounded quite embarrassed."That was my overzealous Security head. We've already spoken about it, and he's extended a formal apology and a request for where you pulled those two from. Looking at the reports from my infirmary, I should very much like to have those two as friends. I'll send you the security video after this, it is, well, it speaks for itself." Gerald paused for a moment as it sounded like he was gathering himself before continuing. "But please, we'll talk about that tomorrow. Get the data I'm asking you to get, and then we can get on the same page, and you can do your thing while I do mine."

I'm not sure I was a fan of that, but my opinion wasn't exactly front and center as The Elf countered.

"The antiaircraft fire is also similarly explainable, I presume."

"Again, Security head. Your aircraft had disabled its' radio transponder code, quite frankly what was he supposed to think?"

"Point taken. Still, we know you're doing something. If we think people are going to die from what you're planning, we're going to have an issue. Are we going to have an issue?"

"Not today." There was a sigh from the other end. "Next time I'm in DC, I'll make a reservation for us at the Palm. I'll try to understand where you're coming from if you try to understand where I'm coming from."

The Elf nodded. "Very well. We'll talk in a few days." The call disconnected and he turned to both of us, scowling. "You should have cleaned up, but no matter. He's lying. He's planning something big, and that something is going to involve a lot of death. Now report and be quick."

Elias stepped forward, distilling our trip into rapid sentences. She was polite enough to not mention our exact method of communication, and The Elf was polite enough not to ask. Elias also deposited the cable she'd filched onto his desk.

The Elf scowled at it, finally looking up. "Explain why Genesis Six is an area of concern."

Elias cleared her throat, as apparently the booze and her own batch of painkillers had done a number on her. "As I'm sure you're aware, within the Bible the Book of Genesis chapters Six through Ten detail the story of Noahs' ark, and the Great Flood that destroyed mankind. If I were to speculate, he has a four-stage plan, destroying the earth, or somehow wiping it clean of what he would consider 'sinners', and then re-shaping the biosphere in some way before his triumphant return with the righteous."

"Anything to add Brooks?"

I considered for a moment. "All my instincts say something's happening, and more than just a space elevator. People with a secret that's good want to tell the secret. They're excited. People with a secret that's bad don't want anyone to know. The people I saw while walking around in the administrative sections looked like they didn't want to know what they knew."

He nodded. "Find me proof of his plans - and find that proof in a way that does not require you to avail the doctor of his services. Prior to that, find a shower and make use of it."

We took that as our cue to get gone, finding our way back to my room and changing into something at least a little comfortable. Once we'd each (separately) showered off and gotten ourselves in a not-quite-ready for bed dress, we had a knock on the side door. It was Jeremiah and Max, who both looked far too pleased for their own good. Jeremiah was a little more gentle with the tackle-hug, while Max and Elias appeared to have their own discussion going.

"So how was Max?"

"He kept complaining that I don't know how to feed him properly."

"His highness is like that. Anything else?"

"Well...the guys are hurrying through my education, or the rest of it. The, uh...they're kind of amazed. I guess? I'm good at the computer stuff. So, they well, they put me on some problems they we working on, and I guess I kinda solved 'em."

"You're a prodigy. But don't let 'em run you down too hard. Take a day now and then. Otherwise you'll be burned out at twenty and no good to anyone, least of all yourself. Sneak out and see if there's anyone else your age around."

"Well...I mean. There are but none like me." He squirmed around awkwardly like the subject needed a change. I eyed him and decided that was acceptable.

"Your beard needs a trim. C'mon." I slid off the bed and winced a bit as everything painful reminded me that it was still there.

"Dad, I'll be okay."

"No son of mine is walking around another day looking like he shaves on a trampoline. No arguing. We're gonna show you the difference between shaving and grooming."

We shuffled over to his room, which had been decorated in Late Electronics Warehouse. Bins, hardware with no discernible purpose, and a workbench with an array of tools neatly laid out and a pegboard with each tool surrounded in various colors of tape, with the tape apparently signifying what the tool was for. Impressive as heck, really. Pretty sure he was controlling as much as he could, since there was a lot of our collective life that had been thrown in the proverbial blender. Even Max had a cordoned off area with a cat tree and crinkle toys in what had been labeled "Max Zone".

"Kiddo..."

"I like it. Stuff's gotta have a place to go."

"Well, I'm not gonna say it's bad. Bathroom, this way. You got a spot for the kit we got you in town?"

"Yeah, but I never, uh, used it. I keep forgetting." He looked down a bit.

"Perfect chance to learn." And over the next twenty minutes, we went over the basics of beard grooming and styles, as well as what looked good on him, how to keep things neat and conditioned.

"So, uh, Dad..." Now that he finally looked respectable, he had some questions. The first one was obvious, so I tackled that one head-on.

"I'm not involved with Elias. She's like my boss, okay?" We were not going to mention any feelings. That was a road that led to trouble and divorce. And whoever was in charge of the living arrangements was going to get a stern talking to. Sure the hammock might be too spartan but an actual separate bed would not go amiss.

"Oh. But...what happened?" He glanced at a few places where the bandages and gauze were secured.

"We had a message, and some people got the wrong idea, and it got interesting after that." I did not feel like scaring the hell out of Jere with the full details.

"The pilots' report said you got shot." He was looking at me oddly like he was just making the realization that his father was not an immortal god sent to provide guidance and time-outs. A

The fact that he was reading reports was concerning. "Who let you look at that?"

"Nobody, uh, let me. I just sorta mighta made a new user with superadmin permissions."

"Did you name that user 'God'?" The guilty look was all I needed, and I quirked an eyebrow.

"Actually, uh...I called it mother." Jeremiah looked down at his shoes.

"And did you look at anything else while you were poking around?"

Jeremiah blushed deeply. "I, uh, I mighta looked at Miss Elias' search history and some of the notes from someone named Lambert - I guess that's her therapist."

At this point I was a little torn. On the one hand, I was quite interested in anything that would help me get a read on this bizarre situation. On the other hand, this was definitely some boundary-wrecking stuff. On the other other hand, she did kinda shove herself into my life. And bed. And really, I kinda was curious to know what sort of person was shoving their feathers into my face. "Okay, but this is a one-off. Try not to do this again."

Jere popped the file open and found out what Elias was searching for recently. There were a lot of queries related to The Power Company before we left, including a few conspiracy sites. Aliens seemed to be big on the list, chief among them an alien-dwarven conspiracy to create ships with photonic sails in order to send the unchanged to Alpha Centauri and broker a peace agreement between worlds that would end with the peacemakers being eaten because of reasons.

Still, moving through the list there were a few references and apparent deep-dives regarding centaurs and centaur-based relationships. Instinctive Compatibility was something she investigated heavily, and the notes from Lambert suggested that Elias was heavily resistant to the concept, and was only becoming comfortable with the concept after evidence - to wit, jumping into bed with me after a nightmare. However the notes continued, indicating that Elias' mental state was such that further evidence would be required for her to feel at ease with what her subconscious mind appeared to already accept.

First off, it would have been nice had this Lambert advised me of what was happening. Second off, Max could never know. He'd be insufferable.

In any case, we had a few other things going on that were taking precedence over whatever personal angst we may have been feeling. And there were other things to address as well.

I looked at Jere quietly. "So first off, I'm going to have to talk to your boss about this, and maybe you should let them know that their security needs some beef. In any case, do I look shot?" I needed to allay concerns as quickly as I could.

Jere frowned. "Yeah. The, uh, the report said you got shot in the butt. And you got shot on the side." Not inaccurate but at the same time that was probably more information than he should have read.

"Naaaah. This isn't shot, this is 'almost shot.' But if it makes you feel any better, we might have some jobs for you and the rest of your team. Of the sneak into computer systems and find out what they're doing variety." I elbowed him gently.

"So that'll help?" He glanced at me, looking a little hopeful.

"Mmm-hm. This isn't superspy license to kill stuff. This is keep people from hurting each other before they have a chance to do hurtful things. If the choice is saving a hundred lives from a keyboard or killing folks with a gun, I'd rather you save lives." I politely skipped over the part where we were very much involved with shooting and being shot at.

"Oh."

"Chin up. You're getting your legs, and growing up. I like that."

"Okay dad. I'll, uh...see you tomorrow?"

"Yep. Bring breakfast over. Remember we get up early."

He gave me a hug. "'Kay."

I went back to my room, where Elias was showering and Max looked unreasonably smug.

"Do your Dad Deed for the Day?" He even sounded smugger than usual.

"What gives?"

"Just that I was right."

"About? Hurry up already." I re-arranged the cushions on the couch so Elias could sleep there, as she still didn't have a replacement hammock for her own sleeping area. Something to get tomorrow.

"Everything."

"I will absolutely shave you bald if you don't get to the point."

Max licked his paw to wash himself. "She asked about Aoife."

"Yeah, we saw her when we were out and about." I was still trying to wrap my head around that one, to be honest.

"She wanted to know if there was something there."

"And?"

"There isn't. I mean she did walk out on me." Max paused. "Us. I was a kitten and Jeremiah wasn't much more, so she's a part of your life, but not much more, yeah?" Admittedly, he was a kitten, so he may have had a skewed vision of what happened. Or the early part of the divorce and single life was not what I'd expected and there may have been some rough nights.

"Yeah." I popped a couple of the painkillers.

"And yet, you still haven't dated. Aside from the times Nona cornered you."

"We're not doing this again." I slid into the bed, turning until I found the least uncomfortable spot.

"You. Need to get out and strut. Get hammered and come back home three days later with fifty cents, a can opener, and some great experiences you'll never remember."

"That works for cats - I have to keep my job. You know, that thing that keeps you in treats, toys, and food?"

"Whatever. You're the new golden boy. They love you here."

"You haven't talked to The Elf."

"And I never will. So what was with you taking on a dozen Oni?"

"Everyone's making a fuss about that for some reason." I understood on a theoretical level why that would be considered odd, but at the same time in the moment I was just trying to do the right thing.

"Because it's not every day anyone walks out of a fight like that, much less comes out on top."

"Look, I just wanted to talk to them is all."

"Talk? About what?"

"Well, one of 'em had just shot Elias, so I wanted to have a discussion with the responsible party about right versus wrong."

"The way Elias describes it, she got a crease on her neck and then you pulled an impression of an Irish Warhorse out while she was working on getting the elevator door open."

I really didn't feel like talking about it much more, so I shrugged. "She was my partner. You take care of your partner."

Max chuffed softly. "Yeah you do. Now figure out that she's your partner."

"The heck's that mean?" I did not like the conversational turn this was taking, even schwacked out on painkillers. Max didn't reply for a long moment, just looking at me like I couldn't see my nose in front of my face.

Elias interrupted us by coming out of the bathroom in some sort of oversized sports jersey I didn't recognize that fit her like a tent, trailing lavender scent to the couch. That was new and odd. I hadn't known her to wear perfume, so maybe this was a new soap.

"If you boys are done, I think you need a bed."

"Yeah, it's about that time." I reached and killed the lights.

Max snitted. "If you need me, I'll be in my tree. Judging you."

Chapter 12

After the excitement of the day, I was winding down and realized the painkillers were going to town on me, and that despite my size I was going to be useless in about ten minutes. Maybe I should have only taken one, but then I'd be in worse shape. In any case, sleep came and was blissful.

I had a different dream that night. It was weird, filled with space, violence, and lavenders. Running through hallways, fighting while hearing Gerald talking about making the world a better place through extreme violence.

Finally I blinked awake to a knock at the door and Elias' face pressed into my abs. This was weird on several levels, made all the weirder by Jeremiah coming in with what was apparently a dwarven version of a healthy breakfast. Eggs, hash browns, bacon, and sausage covering a bunch of pancakes. He didn't drop anything but he did hustle to set the plate on the table while I was blinking the sleep out of my eyes and realizing there was hair that wasn't mine or Max's in my face. I absently wondered if he'd ordered it from the kitchen and realized he probably had, since our apartments only had a bare-minimum kitchenette. Also, he couldn't cook much beyond oatmeal.

Elias' nose twitched and she rose to sit stretching her arms and wings with a little yelp at the end as apparently her wings were still healing. "Mmm. Morning Jeremiah. You're early." She looked at where she was and hopped up off the bed. She padded to the bathroom quickly without so much as a backwards glance, leaving me confused, Jere gawking and then looking at Max accusingly, and Max with an exceptional smug look.

"She jumped into bed with you about an hour after you fell asleep. She woke me up with her damn nightmares, grabbed her blanket and hopped into your bed. She slept sound the rest of the night. You're good for her, deal with it."

"You set this up."

"I'm not saying I told Jere that he should see for himself that you're okay. I may have hinted it was okay."

"No treats today, Mister."

"Come on. We're on a time crunch, and you two need to figure yourselves out and get your heads clear before your next job. If what I'm hearing is right, it's gonna be a doozy. So I hit the fast-forward on your emotionally frozen butt. Unbunch yourself, get the gooshy food, and get breakfast going for her."

"Fine..." I started to get the coffee ready for both myself and Elias, and then limped to get Max his gooshy food.

"It'll work out. Trust me." The self-confidence of cats will never cease to amaze me - even if they've just had the living heck scared out of them, they're back to being lords of the realm in ten minutes.

"The last time I heard that, I wound up getting shot in the chest. So...hush."

"This is not that." Max leaped om my back to get me to move as Elias came out of the bathroom wearing some old Army-issued sweats, and went to the door where the kitchen was delivering breakfast for us. This made me highly suspicious, but it was probably the mad doctors' orders. I made it slowly to the bathroom to take care of the routine. The good thing was the bathroom wasn't retrofitted but custom-built for multiple Neotypes, so I could get the business done rapidly. The bad news was the same.

I finally came out to see everyone going through their usual respective food in a silence that wasn't tense, but more...anticipatory. Conversation was light while we were eating. and Jere had apparently learned the ancient soldiers' habit of "Eat it now, taste it later" as his rapidly disappearing plate would have brought a tear to any sergeant's eye. I know it did to mine a bit. Amazingly, none of his breakfast landed in his beard - still neatly done from last night, or he'd woken up and followed my instructions. He then excused himself to go to do his latest project, whatever that might have been, leaving the three of us alone. Max hopped onto the back of my chair and made himself comfortable on my flank, carefully avoiding where I'd been dinged. Finally I took a breath and started to forge ahead with something that might have been uncomfortable. My coffee was damned interesting, so I started talking to it more than her.

"Elias. I. Listen, I'm not sure what you're thinking, but before we have any more mornings with surprises in bed, I want to make sure we're clear. I'm a package deal - I mean, you should know." I pointed at Jeres' chair. "But I want to be sure you know what you're getting into. Jeremiah deserves more than me introducing him to a new 'mom' every other month, and you deserve more than someone who's going to ditch you in favor of someone else first time and every time."

I glanced up to see Elias similarly entranced by her coffee. "Brooks, that works in the rest of the world. I'm not the rest of the world - I have access to your personal history. That first night at the power company was the first night I've gotten a good nights' sleep without booze or painkillers in...years." She paused herself, gathering her words for more return fire. "I don't know what all this is. I know I like being around you, and it feels like I'm giving up something. So we both just need to deal with it until we can decide what this is, which is not going to be soon." She sipped at her coffee without looking up. "And you appear to sleep better next to me. At least Max thinks so. So, keep things as they are, and we'll sort this later."

I was silent, trying to digest all of this. Max kneaded my back with his paws. "Toldja."

"Max, stay out of this. I don't even know her real name."

"You didn't put me in your schpiel. I'm hurt."

"That's what you got out of that? Remember those treats you were gonna have, ever again?"

"Fine, suck it up and realize you two need each other. You can't handle it yet and neither can she, so make a deal with her or something so you two can at least get something." Max broke the connection and launched himself into his cat tree, where he began grooming himself - and somehow he was able to radiate some self-righteousness while doing so.

I looked down into my coffee as if it had the answers before I said anything. "Listen, Elias, you gotta understand this is new. I need to wrap my head around this, so how about this; on mission, we do whatever we need to - I mean, I'm going to be presumptuous and say that the folks in charge are going to look at what we did and keep us together for these jobs. Off mission, we can share a bed, but we're there to sleep. That's it. No flashy pajamas or lingerie or...y'know. Anything."

Her expression was one of relief at my stammering words - it seemed like this was uncharted waters for both of us. "Deal. Now hurry up, we're debriefing today. The Elf's offsite, so we're taking our time."

"Offsite?"

"I know when he's in, and when he's out. He never tells us why unless it's operationally required."

"Huh. A desk jockey without his desk."

"He wasn't always a desk jockey. But that's not important. What's important is we have to head upstairs for debrief in about 20 minutes. We can wear whatever today. Doctors' orders."

I finished the coffee and threw on a t-shirt and a wrap that would cover the bandages without pulling too much, but the real problem was my shoes. When I tried lifting my left rear leg to slide my shoe on, my leg did not cooperate in the least. Elias huffed and put my shoe on. And then she smacked my non-bruised butt cheek. At least it was gentle, but it still sent a large wave of something uncertain through me. And from the looks of it, her as well.

"Come on. We're late."

We should have called in sick. The next six hours were full of questions and answers as we repeatedly described everything that happened for various teams of folks in suits. The Dwarven Mines department was highly interested in the technical aspects which we were not able to provide, which led to a lot of questions and more answers, with us providing a lot of guesses. The other departments were less excited, security asked us a few questions about weapons, while operations mostly chewed us out for not leaving sooner - as if we could have left any sooner than we did.

Then there was a second round in the afternoon where we were both individually questioned about our actions. The questions were fewer, but more pointed. Apparently the operations group was comprised of armchair quarterbacks and swivel-chair generals who seemed to think that a firefight was some sort of video game you could pause to check everything and menu-select the proper action. I had to explain that it was otherwise, and a few times the questions went far out of bounds. The best of the worst was when someone who was the spiritual inheritor of Wingnut asked why we didn't simply surrender after they started shooting. I educated him.

Still, everyone got their questions answered, and then after another round of pool therapy, we had the evening to ourselves. I was planning on settling in and letting my brain not work on anything more meaningful than finding a barber who wouldn't charge an unholy amount to make a centaurs' coat neat and tidy.

Elias mentioned that she had to get some more things from storage and that she had some additional physical therapy scheduled, and took off. About ten minutes later the doorbell chimed. Which was odd from the get-go, Elias usually just walked in. I punched the button on the tablet to let the door open, and in walked a faun I didn't recognize, but seemed to be radiating ease.

"Uhm, hi...you're lost or something? Sorry I don't know my way around this place all that well, so you might want to check your map." The painkillers were working, but I did notice she was not dressed casually, and her dark blue hair was in a bun. Whoever she was, she was going to work.

"This is the residence of Peter Brooks?" Her voice had a soothing quality to it with a light French accent weaving its' way through the syllables. Something about this did not put me at ease.

"Er...yes, but I don't think we've been introduced."

"Check your schedule, Mister Brooks." I did, and apparently there was an appointment with a Counselor Lambert. I scrunched my face a little, feeling less at ease.

"Shoot. I didn't look down far enough. So, what's this about?" Max blinked himself awake from his spot on my flank, stretched himself out dramatically, and made his presence known, batting at the counselors' shoes a bit.

"Well, Mister Brooks, I am here to assist with your mental health. Much as the Doctor attends to your body, I attend your mind."

"Mind's fine. Thanks. That all?" I did not relish the thought of my free time being taken up by someone trying to blame my current mental state on a fall I had taken when I was a child. To be fully honest, I didn't need a counselor when there was a liquor store in the building and if was really bad, there was a perfectly good bar not fifteen minutes away. I made a note to head to said bar.

"Non. I have read the reports from The Elf and Miss Elias. There are concerns." Of course there were.

I sighed softly. "Fine. Ask your questions, but I reserve the right to not answer. And I also reserve the right to grab myself a freaking beer for this."

"If you insist, Mister Brooks." She seemed nonplussed by my attitude. I shrugged myself over to the kitchenette where a cold beer awaited. I took a deep pull from the bottle before heading back, mentally preparing myself for this assault. I resettled on the couch and shifted to make myself comfortable. Once all that was done, I spread my hands a little.

"Let's get this going then." I was trying to be accommodating, but it was difficult. And to make things worse, Max had decided he liked the counselors' lap for the time being.

She glanced down at her notes again. "Very well. The Elf has raised this concern - specifically that you have an awareness of the chain of command, however you have disregarded it. The incidents he has cited confirm that this was a correct action, however he has concerns that you will become overly familiar with circumvention of procedure."

"In other words, I did the right thing, but don't do it again?"

"It seems so."

I exhaled softly. "Look, I got brought into this joint for a reason. I'm assuming at least one of those reasons has to do with my abilities with judgment. I'm quite aware that there's a reason organizational structures exist, however there are times when things need to get done, and there's information that needs to get to the boss without the benefit of massaging, editing, or other similar actions. If I thought it would get done in an easier manner, I'd go that route. Anything else?"

"Very well. The area of greatest concern for Elias was at the end when you," she looked down at her paperwork to read, "said 'Let's have a go you leg bastards' and proceeded to engage in hand to hand combat with a large number of Oni security personnel." She looked up from her notes to wait patiently for my answer. Or in my case, non-answer.

"Why is that a big deal?" I was genuinely confused. It was like nobody'd ever been on the bad side of long odds and managed a win before.

"Your actions seemed foolhardy and out of character. Your preliminary reports are that you are effective, rational, and empathetic to the needs of others. The worst thing that has been said about you is that you are remarkably stubborn. Also, for my own education, what is a 'leg bastard'? I've never heard the term - frankly I believed that Elias was playing a joke on me."

I shrugged. "I was a paratrooper. It's an insult. Folks who don't jump out of planes get around using their legs. Hence, leg."

She nodded. "Ah. I understand. So, what preceded this activity?"

I took a drink from my beer. "Combat."

She quirked at me as Max hopped down, wound around her legs for a moment and then hopped back into her lap. "Could you expand on that?"

"I could." Whether the good counselor knew it or not, she was intruding on Beer and Football time. I wanted whatever this was wrapped up in a hurry.

"Will you?" It sounded like she knew it, and was not overly concerned.

"What do you need explained? Combat's not exactly the nicest thing." If she wanted to know, I was going to spare her the worst of it. For time purposes.

"What had happened in the minute prior?"

"Elias and I were running for the elevator, using scrounged weapons and ammo to keep them from advancing while we borrowed an elevator to get up top where our ride was hopefully going to be picking us up. Then Elias got hit and, y'know. They learned about consequences for poor life choices."

She and Max regarded me for a few long moments while considering. I was not in the mood to have my actions picked apart yet again, so I stared right back at them. Finally the counselor broke the look by glancing down at her tablet, moving a few things around, and then she spoke.

"Mister Brooks, have you ever heard of Instinctive Compatibility Syndrome?"

I snorted. "Who hasn't."

"It doesn't sound like you believe in it."

"I refer you to my marital status for more details."

"I have. Mister Brooks, I'm going to make a suggestion, based on my reading of the reports as well as observations from Elias and Max. You may want to consider the possibility that you and Elias are compatible, on an instinctive level."

"I don't wanna." I had had quite enough of everyone telling me who I should date, and I was getting cross.

"May I ask why?"

"Because things are happening, me carrying on like some love-struck teenager does not help a bit - tack on that I have Jeremiah to care for, and this is neither the time nor the place for any sort of speculation regarding my personal life. I leave that sort of thing to Max. Next?"

She took a slow breath. apparently I was stubborn enough to make a counselor go to a breathing exercise. Chalk that up as a win for Team Brooks. "Mister Brooks, I would very strongly suggest that you consider it. ICS has a large spectrum of emotional reactions; some react to it in a very subtle way, others are more overt. I believe your subconscious mind has already accepted it." She smiled very slightly, which was worrisome. "If it helps, Miss

Elias is in a somewhat similar frame of mind. She only began to accept it after consistent realization that being asleep in your presence places her mental state at greater ease. Good evening, Mister Brooks." She gently set Max on the floor and rose, leaving my room.

Elias came back a while later and flopped on the couch next to me. We were both in our own little worlds, which seemed to be where we wanted to be, and Max was looking at both of us rather smugly until we went to bed. Elias was a bit forward, not even waiting for the lights to dim before climbing into bed. I didn't have the energy to object, and given the conversation, maybe it was time to consider the possibilities that Lambert had raised. For at least a second. Those questions and possibilities were rapidly sent to the bin. Mainly because Elias didn't bring anything up, and I wasn't exactly keen on having any more deep conversations until I was off the painkillers.

The next morning was supposed to be a day off with a visit to the medic and then just lounging and watching sports while fighting over watching football or something that was not football. Operative word, supposed. Reality decided it would be hectic from the word go. Jeremiah banged on my door (I couldn't bring myself to think of it any other way, as that opened up other doors that I preferred quite closed) to rouse us early as we were missing something. And the comm tablet was lit up with twenty messages from various people to move it to the main presentation theater and whatever we were wearing was fine.

For the record, I did not think that what I was wearing was fine. I didn't ask Elias' opinion, nor did I offer one on her choice of sleepwear, which was another unrecognizable sports jersey. For the record, I had a nice blanket and a large airborne shirt. We went to find available spots in the back and grabbed coffee and donuts as the broadcast kicked in, showing Geralds' office and a faun from some major new network.

"We got rolled out of a nice warm bed at this hour for a puff piece?" I grumbled and made noises.

"Mm. Probably. I'mma take a nap. Wake me if there's anything interesting." Elias lumped herself into her seat, and after a long moment she began leaning on me.

"Do we get to shoot whoever's responsible if that's the case?" My pre-coffee self was in a mood, and my healing was not going to make this an easy day.

"Nope. But we'll get the day off if it is, and whoever sounded the false alarm buys a round for all the departments." She sounded like she was going back to sleep already. Either that or my arm made a very comfy cushion.

"Good enough." The faun dominating the screen was smiling as I started paying attention for both myself and Elias.

"I'm here with an exclusive interview, the first ever public appearance by Gerald Stirling, CEO of International Power Supply. We are live at the trash island northeast of Hawaii, now a power plant renamed Poseidon Island that currently supplies forty percent of all electricity to the eastern Pacific rim - Mister Stirling, when we were speaking before the cameras began rolling, you said your company is taking the next big step, what do you mean?" The office was almost exactly as I'd seen it before, but for the moment Gerald was seating confidently, his hands fiddling with the Antikythera mechanism like it was a puzzle cube.

Gerald had a look I'd seen before - it was when Max had discovered the treat bag was open and thought nobody was around. "Well Deidre, I think we can safely say that we've done a fantastic job providing clean and efficient electricity to a significant portion of the folks on Earth who need it. Not only do we Poseidon Island here, but our two other plants, Raijin station in the western Pacific and our newest one in the North Atlantic, Njǫrd station are equally as effective." His face took on wistful look of sorts as he continued. "But one night I looked up at the sky and remembered that there's junk in orbit as well. So I did some research, had some folks check my math, and realized just how much more there was for us to take care of. Not just down here, but up there as well. So, I've had teams working on this newest venture for some time. And now I'm ready to share our latest success with the world." He touched his desk, and the windows which were opaqued became clear, revealing that the whole office was rapidly ascending through the clouds, with the sky brightening as they rose through the air. An altimeter was also visible, and the numbers were climbing rapidly. The broadcast was bleeped. Repeatedly. Gerald stood, setting the mechanism in his hands down and leaning confidently against his desk and filled in for the gawking Deidre.

"If I may. International Power Supply has been working on a space elevator for some time, and we're using it now for the first time. Once we've established ourselves up there, we'll be sending out collection grids and drones to capture all the junk in orbit, in order to repurpose it."

"Uh...Ah. Re, repurposed to what?" The fauns' hair was in panic mode for about five seconds before she got her game color on.

"Whatever we can dream of. Living quarters, exploratory vessels to research permanent outposts on the moon. From there going further to find things we never could on earth."

"If you don't mind me asking, how much junk is there?"

"All told, about ten thousand tons. That's just the things bigger than my finger. It'll be a job, but I'm confident we're up to the task, and within the next month, we'll have everything collected and sorted for various repurposing..." I didn't hear the rest of it as a realization hit me. And I jogged Elias' side with my elbow.

"That's the play."

"What is?" Elias stopped doodling on my arm long enough to look up.

"Genesis Six. Ten thousand tons of junk, wadded up and returned to sender like a big snowball from hell." It sounded better in my head, to be honest.

She paled before I'd even finished the sentence - it was like she only needed a tiny push to get where I was going. "He could literally hold the planet hostage. Quick, we gotta go."

I grabbed my coffee and another donut on the way out of the auditorium, hustling as we went to the Dwarven Mines where the head of the department was looking at a video feed of Geralds' interview on one monitor and then rapidly tapping on several keyboards in succession and eyeing the outputs suspiciously.

Despite her just got out of bed attire, Elias was moving with purpose as she spoke down from the catwalk. "Kardar. Got a thought experiment for you." She grabbed the stair rails, sliding down the stairs as she finished.

The dwarf grunted, keeping his eyes on the monitors. "I'm busy checking their math."

"Finnne, I'll just get someone else to figure out the impact results from ten thousand tons of metallic space junk hitting various locations on earth. Brooks, you think Jeremiah could crunch the numbers and get a map together?"

I nodded, following Elias' train of thought easily. "In a heartbeat. Heck, I think for that I'd even give him a raise on his allowance."

That brought Kardar up short. "Do WHAT now?"

Despite the lightness in her words, Elias' voice was tense and her wings were fluttering a bit. "Last gig, we're pretty sure that ol' Gerald's smiling face has plans for that junkball he's planning to gather that aren't as benign as he says. We want something for The Elf when he gets back from wherever he's gone to."

He looked at her. "You're joking."

Elias looked right back. "Access the field reports. We got our asses shot at because someone took their lockdown orders very seriously, and my ohp-" she stopped to compose herself at something "My...partner." she paused again, apparently having to actually think for a moment before settling. "Brooks. My Brooks. He got shot in the ass. Several times. Do us the courtesy of considering this."

I was apparently the only one who thought that Elias had gone off in a weird direction for a minute. Whether she was tired, medicated, or some mad combination of both, she was not her normal self. Kardar didn't seem to notice - apparently working with Dwarves and being a dwarf meant there were personality quirks. He leaned back in his chair and blew air out in a manner that suggested deep thought for a moment. It also ruffled his beard out a bit.

"Wellllll, if he's being task and energy-efficient, he'll be splitting the work among the three elevator capture devices, so top end each mass is going to be three to four thousand tons each. Fire 'em, let gravity do the work, assuming no re-entry shields - a percentage'll get lost, which would be variable based on the angle of attack..." He hrm'ed and considered some more, falling silent. "Probably wreck a city, easy. Exact effects would depend on the city but if he's going for a big showy display of power, one prime spot off the top of my head'd be the coast direct south of Jacksonville, it'd probably put the entire state of Florida underwater, tsunami'd probably hit as far as east Texas. Southeast US'd be hosed for awhile, probably have to evacuate it. Crisis on all levels, but probably not horrific. Basically that'd be a warning shot." He paused for a minute. "Goin' the other end of the scale, drop one about a hundred-fifty miles northwest of Brest France, he hits the majority of the underwater fiber cables and plays merry hob with transatlantic communications on top of a similar trainwreck as the aforementioned Florida. Could also play the same card in the Far East, drop something just southeast of Singapore - if he hits it just right we got the cable destruction as well as putting most of southeast Asia underwater. Now the real fun one is if he fired it at the Yellowstone Caldera."

I blinked. "The what?"

Kardar gave a grim smile. "Someones' about to learn something scary. The Yellowstone Caldera. Kinda in the northwest part of Wyoming, basically it's a huge volcano. If he hit it in a way that'd make it explode, the entire country'd get hit with the ash fall, even ships at sea off the Atlantic seaboard'd get hit. Ash'd get everywhere, short power lines, kill crops, and if it was bad enough it'd basically cause a year or two with an endless winter. I'd want to be in orbit at that point m'self."

"Holy hell." I put my coffee down. "Could he make it worse?"

Kardar nodded. "Oh, easy. He could be anxious and help physics along by accelerating the mass before he dropped it. He's got the space elevator to send stuff up. What if he sends it down?"

Kardars' doomsday speech continued. "He could use smaller masses, for starters. Still lose something from the re-entry..." The dwarf trailed off. "Not enough data to give you a good estimate. I can worst case it for you - if he goes for the Singapore/Brest/Yellowstone trifecta, we're talking global catastrophe that wipes out, say about thirty percent of all life just by itself. Then the secondary effects kick in; society breaks down due to minimal communications capability, there's probably at least one nuclear exchange as there's fights over resources, at least one attempt to destroy the space elevators out of spite...y'know. Armageddon. On the bright side, even with that it's still only a fraction of the impact mass that caused the dinosaurs to go extinct." Kardars' deadpan expression was betrayed by the sweat forming on his forehead as he began internalizing the absolute scope of the damage he was describing.

I rubbed the bridge of my nose as Elias took over. "We'll see if we can get more data. Meanwhile, see if you can get people in to model some possibilities, and for now, compartment this. When you get rough numbers, let us know. We'll be putting a briefing packet in front of The Elf." She nudged me. "Brooks, let's go home and ruin some days around here."

The fact that she was calling my quarters 'home' felt awkward as hell. After all, the only thing she'd moved in was her (now-destroyed) hammock, some clothes - possibly most of her clothes - and some stuff from the store. Maybe a couple pictures in what I thought of as 'her space', but it certainly didn't mean we were living together. I mean if that was the bar then technically I was living with five other guys for two months during basic training lo those many years ago. Still, we made our way back into my/our quarters, stopping for some more coffee and donuts.

Once there, I settled into the couch and flipped on the TV to see what else was being reported as Elias started hammering on the comm station to send message traffic to exactly three people. Max apparently realized we were busy, and kept himself out from underfoot. For once. I was simultaneously grateful and unhappy with this, as any distraction would have been welcome - the things I'd thought of were unpleasant, and I wasn't sure I really wanted to go through them to any sort of conclusion.

I took a pad and started making notes about the technical details that I could glean. The numbers were stunning. To start, they were using their own power supply, not affecting any of their current customers. They were projecting that after completing their first mission of cleaning up the debris, they would repurpose the junk to remotely piloted craft for asteroid exploration. Based on projections, the next step was finding silicon and other materials for solar panel creation, which would be brought back and anchored to the elevator and used to power the next phase, tourism. As a secondary announcement, they indicated that once the elevators had proven to work and be stable, they would begin building monorail lines servicing coastal municipalities with garbage collection where regular trash would be repurposed, and hazardous wastes would be launched into a decaying orbit toward the sun.

Timeframes were at about a year for that, with the collection completion targets being set at a month. The interviewer Deidre had gotten herself composed and probably had someone from the network science team firing questions at her through her earpiece. Throughout it all, Gerald alternated between sitting on his desk with the backdrop of the earth and walking around the office to make a point that he was particularly animated about.

There were a few questions he adroitly sidestepped, mainly regarding legal matters. With those he deferred to his legal team who had advised him that they would be held to the same standard as any earth-based corporation, however he did insist that it would not be an issue, as they had always held themselves to a much higher standard than the law required. I'd filled several pages with notes by the time they'd descended back to the surface for the conclusion of the interview, while Elias had enough tabs open on her laptop that I was highly concerned. She was using my undamaged front right section as a pillow and making occasional noises as she typed something.

Chapter 13

Lunchtime came and went, as we got up to make use of the coffee machine or the bathroom, and as the day got later, we both looked up and realized we'd forgotten to eat, work out, or answer our door (my door) when someone knocked. And we had also missed our doctors' appointments, which was the lone positive out of all this. When I looked, there was a stack of papers that had been shoved under the door. Two invitations for a working lunch, one for a working dinner, a very stern note from the doc reminding us that we'd skipped our follow-up for today and we had darn well better be presenting ourselves tomorrow, and a scrawled note from Jeremiah saying The Elf would be back day after tomorrow and we should have a good explanation for stirring the collective pot.

There was a slight chuff from Elias. "We're getting tomorrow off. Officially no work, but with The Elf coming in hot the next day, that pretty much means we're going to need to get some good foundation for what is at this point, a theory with only the smallest amount of evidence."

"Does that mean we get to lounge around in sweatpants and watch TV? Because I'm down for that." I groaned slightly as I lifted myself off the couch for more coffee.

"Well, we could. However that would leave us unprepared to talk to The Elf, and he'd be grumpy at us. Not to mention Doctor Feelgood would be beside himself." Elias occupied my couch space casually, waiting for me to come back.

"Suggestions?" I came back with two cups, handing one to her and then resettling in the remaining space.

"Lounge around in sweatpants and watch every frame of all the interviews from today while I invade your personal space immediately after the doctor checks us over." I had apparently gotten her coffee the way she liked it, as she looked happy and then a little confused for a moment.

"That's a lot of hours of interviews at last check, not counting the fluff staff interviews and analysis." I paused to pull up all the interviews, science discussions and other related programs that were talking about this absolute bombshell. "About thirteen hours of stuff so far. I'm okay with that if you are, minus the invasion."

She smirked. "You obviously think you have a vote here, Mister Brooks. Max agrees with me, and you are being outvoted."

"Max doesn't pay rent." Although he was valuable, the rules were clear. No rent paying, no vote in the decision-making. While he certainly had a voice and wasn't ashamed of using it, my house meant my rules.

"Neither do you." That said, the rules may be in need of amendment.

"Killjoy."

"I revel in it. Okay, let's call it up. And call the cafeteria for some pizzas and soda."

The day passed intensely, with several boxes of pizza being devoured as we started by going through the interviews and looking for anything.

Eleven hours later, we found what we were looking for. Gerald opened the door to surprise one of the engineers, and we saw a reflection for three quarters of a second before it switched to a wholly different desktop, which was showing lift capacities, and after a few moments the interviewee slipped into a canned discussion about all the scientific theories that could be properly experimented on once the space junk had been cleared. It was amazing to look at what was happening. On the one hand, they were doing amazing work in repurposing space junk, and if they were going to do that it would be amazing. But then on the flip side, it was looking more and more like they were planning to weaponize a fair chunk of it to do some truly unkind things.

We reversed the image and zoomed in until it got blurry. Then we backed it out a little, and finally we called Kardar to come take a look at something interesting and related to our last discussion. Kardar arrived, sniffed at the wreck that was the place, and yawned impressively. Apparently he'd fallen asleep on the keyboard, as his face had a nice keyboard imprint on it. As soon as he saw what we were looking at, he plugged in his laptop and ran some sort of dark magic on it. We blinked, as it showed large numbers and a series of rings indicating acceleration points. After an oath of some kind, he was able to get it added to our report and then he left, muttering about needing a lot of whiskey to get to sleep tonight.

We looked around a little and realized we had a ton of empty boxes and soda cans strewn about from our PR blitz-watch. We looked at each other and promptly began cleaning up and feeding Max, as he'd been snoring on my backside for most of the day, with occasional trips to the litterbox and Elias' lap for a change of pace. Once the place was decent, Elias flopped onto the couch with a grimace.

"Pool tomorrow morning?" I reached into the fridge for celebratory beers, handing her one to open.

"I'm okay with that, but are you really trying to give me that to drink?"

"Why? It's beer." I checked the label to make sure I wasn't giving her a bottle of ketchup to celebrate. It was definitely beer.

"It's your beer." She took it back to the fridge and grabbed a bottle I hadn't noticed as I settled in with slight groan. "Which, I hate to break it to you, tastes like someone took a perfectly good batch of bread dough, seared it, and dropped it in a tank of sewage.

Try this." She handed me a bottle of something that said it was stout.

I swigged and gagged. "Someone filtered a perfectly good Guinness through a jock strap. That is foul, lady."

"Right then. Next trip through the store, we're getting Guinness. Sounds like it might be the one thing we can both drink."

"Why wait? We're celebrating, sort of, and let's be honest, I ain't got much to spend my pay on." And with that, we both trundled to the in-house store for a unseemly amount of beer. By the time we got back, a few bottles had gone missing as I attempted to lighten the load. A few more had gone missing as Elias was being helpful. Max was waiting at the door.

"Whatcha got there, gooshy food?"

I hiccuped. "Guinness. It appears to be one of the few things that meets with both our drinking palates. Didja know elves can't drink this?"

Max sneezed. "I can't be sad about that."

I put the case in the fridge, making my way to the couch to watch something that wasn't going to make my brain melt from trying to sort out what was useful and what wasn't. Sports it was. Elias made a noise that I was learning was her not-happy-noise.

"Hush. Brain break."

"Yeah, but...football?"

"Football."

"One, this an old game. Two, hockey's on."

"Hockey. Seriously?"

"Hockey." Elias nodded firmly. "Y'know, stick, puck, facepunching..." She snagged the remote and flipped it to another channel that was showing this hockey thing. "Hush, drink your beer, and when I say something, your line is 'The hell was that guy thinking?' The refs are biased, the other team is made up entirely of bums and scrubs, our team only has one bum."

I hushed and drank my beer as she parked it in front of me. Max plopped himself between us, as we were apparently warm and he needed a snoozing spot. After three bottles, the game started to make sense. Or I was pleasantly buzzed and didn't care. In any event, once the game was done, I found that Elias had fallen asleep. I carried her to her section of the bed and fell asleep myself, ignoring Max as he grumbled about not having a nice spot anymore.

The next morning brought with it a slight ache in my head and breakfast. Jeremiah wasn't coming over since he'd gotten some new stuff and skipped off to his school and work early. Apparently his lack of doctoral work was bringing the average number of doctorates in the department down, and Jere was not okay with that. Elias and I grabbed our swim clothes and casual wear because in theory we'd have time to change before the meeting.

We had walked no more than five steps from our (my, darnit, my) door, when there was a set of running feet and a very angry oath being sworn at us. We both looked at each other and then back to see the doctor chasing us and remembered that we had conveniently forgotten that we needed to go see him today as well.

There were the traditional scowls as we fell in like recalcitrant children. We were poked, prodded, and grumbled at in ways that made me wonder what the heck had actually happened with all the shooting and yanking my body from place to place. We were then advised that recovery was happening faster than anticipated, and we would be expected to be at his office promptly in one week for a second checkup. We did not get a lollipop afterward.

It was refreshing, to be honest. We'd spent two days on, well, not quite bed rest, but it wasn't anything physical, and frankly I needed to work out. The pool wasn't perfect, but it was good enough. I slipped in and yelped as the chlorine reminded me that I still had a nice long open wound along my left side and several on my right. Elias laughed a little as I squinted at her.

We got our laps in and headed off to shower, changing and looking at least a little respectable as we went to The Elf. And promptly cooled our heels for half an hour while he talked to several other people and finally wrapped everything up. We were allowed entry, and parked it with his traditionally peeved look.

"Kardar had some interesting things to say about you two this morning. Would you care to elaborate." The lack of questioning tone was our cue to start talking over each other for about ten seconds before he held up a hand. "You are not elaborating, you are wasting time. I have already exceeded my limitations for foolishness. Agent Elias, as you are senior, you may begin. Agent Brooks, you may occupy space." Apparently I'd been upgraded to Agent after we got back, and nobody told me. In any event, Elias distilled the entirety of yesterday's events into two minutes of rapid fire verbiage that made The Elf raise an eyebrow.

"Do you have a timeframe."

"Collection timeframe, from what we understand about a month. The solar collection and magnetic acceleration rings, unknown. Depending on their materials sourcing and construction - two months at most, possibly less if he's been planning this in advance."

"I see here that you are certain there will be three separate impact sites. Can you be certain in your assessment?" The Elf looked at us coolly, waiting to find a whole in the logic.

"I can't be a hundred percent certain, however if you look at Geralds' office and decorations, he does everything in threes. His tie, trinity knot. Cufflinks, three stones. Paperweights, two pyramids and some ancient Greek doo-dad I can't pronounce. Heck, even his power generators, three of 'em. He's doing three because that's how his mind works for some reason." I wasn't a hundred percent certain, but it was the best guess I could give him.

"Impressive deduction, Agent Brooks. Very well. You both now have a new assignment. Agent Brooks, do you recall the initial events that led to your hire?"

I blinked. "Like it was yesterday."

"Excellent. You may be enthused to know that your initial efforts have not been forgotten." He turned his chair slightly to light up a display. "We found that one of the largest fireworks manufacturers on this continent has a employee list that is quite heavily invested in the ideals of the Genesis 1:26 organization. This in and of itself is not interesting; what is interesting is that they have significantly reduced their pricing for the Neo Day celebrations next month. With these two items, we believe that they are going to use the fireworks celebrations as a medium for large scale deployments of the carcinogens that were initially discovered by your late Erinyes investigator. We have developed a counter-agent, however we require personnel to deliver said counter-agent."

The Elf clicked a button, displaying two buildings in a three-dimensional render on a side screen. "You have a pair of taskings for this. First, neutralize the shells that have already been manufactured and are prepared for delivery. You will need to infiltrate a warehouse" The display changed to a map with a nice red circle, "here for this. This will be the more difficult tasking - you will have to deliver the counter to each individual firework compartment in order for it to be effective. Agent Brooks will infiltrate by ground, Agent Elias will infiltrate by air. Stage one, Agent Brooks will connect to the primary security panel, and feed a loop to their off-site security. After that, other assets will cause a power outage in the area. You will have precisely fifteen seconds to introduce a false video loop and enter before their backup power restores emergency lighting and surveillance to the building. Power restoration efforts will take approximately one hour, and so you will need to complete this within that hour. You will be using this injector to neutralize each shell. The agent-counteragent reaction produces a small blue light flash upon contact, that is how you will know you have succeeded. The fireworks themselves will not be damaged, so Genesis will not be alerted, merely disappointed."

"Your second tasking involves infiltrating the manufacturing facility onsite to deliver the same counteragent to the raw materials storage. Each storage area has a damping system to prevent dust buildup and explosion. You will introduce the counteragent to the damping system holding tanks and then force activation of the systems multiple times in order to confirm the proper delivery. Do be careful, as an explosion would cause issues. Mockups are being constructed in Echo Hangar above ground, and will be completed tomorrow. Mission prep will begin at that time. The respective architectural drawings have been sent to your quarters. Study them today."

He turned his chair slightly and began ignoring us. That was our cue to go find somewhere else to be. We got the heck out and went to the cafeteria for lunch, which was a quiet affair if you could ignore the occasional stare and glare from a few places. Finally after we'd finished, we started back to the room to study. Finally we looked at each other quizzically.

"What was that about?" My tail was flicking a bit from annoyance.

"If I had to guess, we frosted their cupcakes with sewage. I mean think about it. One of the greatest scientific achievements ever, built on top of the most successful clean energy projects, and we basically told them it was all a smokescreen for the most epic heel turn since Brutus shanked Caesar. Even for us, it's a shock."

"It is a chore being right."

"You'll get used to it. Get the blueprints up, let's see if we can figure out a good route for this fireworks place."

The day was spent on tablets and proposing and rejecting routes. It looked like no matter what route we took, it was going to be a good 30 to 40 minutes onsite servicing the thousands of shells for the dozen or so fireworks shows that the place was purportedly going to be shipping to. That wasn't good. We needed some gear to speed up the process, which meant we had to visit the supply closet after doing some math to figure out what we needed.

The supply closet was run by a cranky-looking man about my age with a slight beer belly covered with a t-shirt that said "Cheap, fast, right. Pick two." and an explosion of brown hair beginning to frost with gray speaking around a massive wad of chewing gum.

"whaggyawant."

I stepped to the fore this time. No reason I couldn't right? "So we need a rig to deliver several shots of a liquid mix to individual containers, like hundred, hundred-fifty at a time. Need two of them, need to make them collapsible and mobile. By day after tomorrow."

"Y'fuggingcrazy?" He spit his gum out and got a fresh stick out while berating us in a rapidfire Brooklyn accent. "I need actual specs for one, and then me and the boys are gonna be double shifts working on this. We got other projects to work on too. We ain't like you Field Rats, we do the job right and then we get on to the next."

"This is my second job. Last one went weird, I'd like to avoid that. We want this one to go smooth, so we're here. Can you do it or not?"

"Course I can in a week, mebbe two." He shrugged, looking unconcerned by whatever else might have been going on in the world.

"We don't have a week."

"Course you don't, you never do. Fuggers always realize y'gonna need something right before they fire y'butts out to go play in the mud, and me and my boys gotta pick up y'slack. Gimmeabreak."

Elias leaned forward, giving her wings a little flutter. "Sammy. You know we're not asking this just to make your blood pressure go up. We're asking because we have some needs over here. We're asking you because you're the one who can do it." She leaned forward over the divider, activating some feminine cheat codes that made me feel a little awkward. "And I know that cute dwarf who was eyeing you would love to hear you talk about how you and the boys did the impossible over steaks and ale. You remember Dhara, right?"

Up-up-down-down-left-right-left-right-B-A-start. Sammy took a breath, as he apparently did remember. "Come back t'morrow."

We took that as our cue to exit, sliding out the door as Elias hopped delicately onto my rump. "Next stop, the dwarven mines and cash in a favor from Dhara."

"So Dhara doesn't like Sammy and we're playing dirty?" I was trying to wrap my head around how this helped us actually get what we needed. And what it was going to cost us.

She leaned forward to swat my back. "Not even. Dhara likes him, but she's terminally shy about everything but work. She just needs a nudge, and that's what this is for."

"Ah. You planning on riding all the way there?" It wasn't uncomfortable, but her weight was noticeable. Very. Noticeable. It wasn't bad really, but it felt like something had changed. Like she'd had a discussion with Lambert and was trying something.

"Mmhm." And she apparently took a delight in my mild discombobulation, punctuating her sentence with a full-body wriggle.

The next line was reflex more than anything. "You fart I buck."

"Mister Brooks! I would never." I received a swat on an uninjured section of my butt for my trouble.

I blinked and stammered a bit. "Sorry. Old habit. My partner back on the force had a trick knee. He had to ride my back to the station about once a week."

"Ahhh. In case you forgot, I like your butt. Sparklebutt." There was a second swat that confirmed the "talked with Lambert" theory. At least for me.

"My butt still hasn't healed from the last time you said that."

She hmm'ed happily about something, but whatever she said was interrupted by our arrival at the Dwarven Mines. Elias slid off, humming a happy tune as she went in and around, looking for Dhara. It was not pleasant. Everywhere I looked there were empty cans and wrappers, and there was a distinct odor about the place that reminded me of three weeks in the field without a shower. I went up the catwalk looking for Jeremiah. I was able find him, and he was in some sort of mad zone of typing. I wasn't entirely sure what he was working on, but there were cans of energy drinks filling his trash can to overflowing, and from what I could see on his monitor, he was crunching numbers on a few specific things, and then punching in numbers on a second monitor, and then looking at a third monitor to look at a few other things. The singular clean spot on his desk had a printout of a picture of Rebecca. Admittedly it was a good picture. It looked like tedious number work until I took a closer look.

He was crunching numbers on scenarios where the space elevators were being used as weapons. it looked like he was trying to calculate a defense protocol, without much success. He chugged another energy drink and looked around, not sure where he was being watched from. I coughed a bit to get his attention, and he looked up at me, some odd look of hopelessness fading and coming back to a smiles and a rush up to give me a shoulder tap and then a lean into my lower shoulder. I picked him up, which was probably embarrassing as heck for him, but he looked like he needed it. I let a little grunt escape, as he was getting heavy, and he looked like someone who hadn't slept in a day or three. Apparently Elias and I were the only people in the building who'd gotten any sleep, and that was more than likely because we'd each had several drinks.

"D-dad...they got me calculating stuff and it's, I'm scared. Kardar's got me running simulations on stuff, and, I'm...scared. They, he, it...and Rebecca. She's, she's there."

He was getting in his own way with his thoughts, so I ruffled his hair a little bit to get him to relax. "It's okay kiddo. We're here to keep it from happening. You're gonna help, but you probably gonna need some sleep tonight. I know this is a big thing, but other people are going to be putting their brains to work on it too."

Jeremiahs' sniffles subsided a little. "It's like trying to catch a baseball at a billion miles an hour. You can't catch it." He wriggled out of the hug to stand and look up at me to try and make it all make sense.

"So...maybe make it curve?" Job one was to give the little genius some options to work on.

"What?" He blinked at me like I'd just told him the earth was really a cube shape.

"Remember when we watched baseball, and you were always amazed by them throwing a curveball?"

"Yeah."

"Maybe if the ball curves enough, it doesn't hit anything and nobody gets hurt, right? It sails off to the backstop like a wild pitch."

"But...that'd be...we'd have to..." his face screwed up into concentration. "How do you throw a curveball?"

"I dunno. May have to check that out."

"It might work but we would have to...uhm, I'mma go back to look at stuff." He looked like he was already working out the math in his head.

"So what's the deal with Rebecca? Sounds like you've been keeping tabs on her." Time to clear his head of the big problem and give him something else to think about for a minute.

"Only a little. I mean, I don't think it's anything creepy but, I mean...her family was awful mad about her being free, so they kept coming by Fisticuffs and making trouble and a couple of 'em got arrested. I found out more about the place they wanted to send her to, and it, it's bad. They do stuff to Neotypes. Like, they should be in jail stuff." It was working, as I could see his demeanor change from a kid staring at a mountain to an avenging dwarf of old - all he needed was a comically large axe.

"So she's there now? At the Poseidon one?"

He nodded. "Yeah. From what I could find, they showed up after her family broke a bunch of windows. Couple days later she was packed up and left." He glanced around and looked guilty. "I uh, I mighta been borrowing time on some satellites to find out what was happening. They got her as a administrative assistant in the physical therapy department."

"What about her family?"

"They stopped hassling Fisticuffs and now they're suing the city for an exceptionally large amount of money since they can't sue you. Something about improper procedure for Neotype emancipation, and lost value. Nothing much about Rebecca, just what she was going to bring in from a money standpoint."

"I'm gonna assume you've looked at their financials?" Theoretically, I could get him on a positive track, and then lateral that to the big problem he had in front of him, courtesy of Kardar.

He nodded. "They're in trouble. They've got enough coming in to stay where they are for now, but they're heavily in paper debt.

It's like the dad made some bad investments, did some really cagey stuff to cover, and now there's a bill coming due - I'd have to go to Accounting to see if it's illegal or what. The total they owe is about ninety percent of what they're suing the city for. And then when they were trying to get Rebecca to go to that Edens' whatever, it was about half of what they were going to get from that. So that's a thing."

I scrunched. "Well, we can set that over to the side for now. For now, clean your desk up, and you look like you need to sleep. You may need to remind Kardar that you're still a growing kid."

"I will." He gave me a gentlemanly fistbump. "Thanks dad. I gotta go back to work."

He hustled off the catwalk to his desk and started crunching numbers like a madman on one keyboard, and then looked up videos on how to throw a curveball. I smirked a little, the turned to see Elias smirking at me.

"You gave him an idea."

"Well, it looked like he was spiraling. He did that when he was a kid. Younger kid, I mean. He'd hit a wall and keep trying to go through it the same way. I'd have to stop him, have to give him a way around. I dunno if it's a good idea, but he'll maybe get out of this track. Kardar put him on a job that looked pretty grim."

"Well, he is shaping up to be one of the best researchers we've got."

"He's sixteen." There were all these brilliant minds stuffed into one room, and somehow he was at the head of the class. That felt weird on a few levels.

"Remind them of that once in awhile, yeah?" Elias shrugged a little, watching my reactions.

"Yeah, I'm gonna have to. How's date night looking?" It was definitely time for a subject change, and it felt like that was the best route to take.

"It's looking good. But, we have a double date." Her expression was unreadable for the moment.

"Good for them." Whoever the them were in this situation.

"Good for us." A smile threatened to make its' way across her face.

"Us?" I definitely did not like the way this conversation was going as we turned down the hallway to where the supply closet was.

She smirked again, with a little wing flap. "Mmhm. You, me, Dhara, and Sammy."

I softly groaned. "Why..."

"Only way Dhara'd agree to go. C'mon, we gotta tell Sammy."

"I object." Part of me was wanting to turn right around and head back to my room with a lot of pizza and beer.

"Objection overruled. We need that gear, badly. And if we do it right, Sammy'll throw in some extras for us."

"The last date I was on is in your dossier. The last one before that was when I asked Ann - Aoife, to marry me."

"Are we not counting the dates that your Nona set up?"

"We are not." I snorted.

She looked at me quizzically. "How many women have you dated?"

I snorted. "Look it up. Pretty sure someone here has that on file."

Her face softened a little. "Hey...take a breath."

I took a breath. "Listen, maybe it's just me, but I never really dated casually. Okay? I never thought of being with anyone but Aoife. She was there for me when I was in rehab, becoming a cop, then through our Changes, and that meant something. We just didn't click like we used to, and I'm okay with where I am and I'm just not a fan of going through that again, and dating is going down that road again. And after what we just went through, I keep having you drag me into things, first the op, now with this quarters situation, and now we're, we're dating?!"

She reached up and touched my face, gently. "Hey. We're doing this to get something we're going to need for an op. Nothing more, unless we - me and you - want it to be." She flexed and spread her wings out a bit. "I'm not Aoife. I never will be."

I swallowed, looking at her wings as they fluttered. I wasn't completely sure, but there was tension in them that meant something for a moment before she relaxed them and continued.

"We're doing what needs done, so that the world can keep being happily ignorant of everything that threatens it. Now, this is a mandatory social function, so get your mandatory happy face out and you will be mandatorily charming, pleasant, and cheerful. You will dance with all four feet happy."

I took a breath and nodded. "Got it. Let's go give Sammy the good news. But first, I'mma got hassle Kardar."

I wound my way through the catwalk to Kardars' station which was one part video game shrine and one part equation whiteboard. He'd apparently joined the no sleep gang as there were more energy drinks and several cups of coffee of various fill levels near his keyboard. It was quite likely he forgot that they were there and went to get a fresh cup every few hours.

"Kardar, you got ten seconds?"

He grunted and spun his chair a bit to look up at me. "If you've got more numbers for me to check I will smack you with a hammer."

I raised my hands a bit. "Nothing like that, but I'd like to put in a request for my kid. I know he's brilliant, and he's gonna be doing great things, but at the same time he's not used to this. If we ride him to the ground too much longer, he's going to be tripping, falling and making mistakes. You need him on his A-game, so....make sure it happens?"

Kardar ran his hands through his hair as he considered his answer. It was that or he was trying to remember how to talk coherently. "You know what we're working on right now. It's crunch time, and everyone's pulling extra time right now."

"When was the last time he left?"

Kardar paused, tapping keys and checking something. "Mighta been...uhm...huh. Looks like he came in a little after you came in and dropped that grenade."

"Annnnd he hasn't left."

"Well, he has gone to the bathroom."

I exhaled slowly. Everyones' nerves were frayed, and I would not help the situation if I beat the section boss unconscious. "That was about a day and a half ago. I got things to do today, but I would very much like to see Jere tonight for dinner. In fact I insist. He's getting lost in his head - heck I had to give him an idea to chew on right before I came to you. He's brilliant but he needs rest. From the smell in here, I'd say you all do. I promise I'll feed him, put him to bed, and then in the morning he'll be better off for it. We'll even call it a 'I owe you one' if we manage to avoid a world-ending crisis. Deal?"

Kardar considered, apparently running multiple sleep deprivation studies through his head. "Deal. Make sure it's a good meal at least, it might be his last one for awhile." He held up his hands himself as my face began assuming A Look. "The whole section's getting booted out tonight, we're getting sleeping bags and lots of eat-n-go stuff for the next couple weeks. Probably ain't nobody sleeping inside the mines for a couple weeks after today. The Elf wants three contingency plans on top of what he's got you rats working on."

It was good enough, so I nodded and scrambled back up to find my way out. It was quite likely that everyone going home was not a gesture of goodwill, more of a clean-and-rearrange so everyone could live in the mines for as long as they could stand each others' BO. I hoped the ventilation was good. Those thoughts occupied my mind to the point where I didn't realize that Elias had at some point re-asserted her position on my back and was lounging. And that I had altered my usual pace to make sure she was comfortable as we went back to Sammys' supply closet and engineering miracle emporium.

Sammy reacted to the news with a smile and a whistle as he told his boys they had a new project to go to town on, and gave them the specs like it was his own brilliant idea. The griping I heard was epic and brought me back to the good old days when I had no neck, no hair, and no idea what the heck was next.

Ah, memories.

Still, it wasn't the worst thing in the world to happen that day as we went over the floor plans and came to a realization. Mainly that the location had built most of the place with the Unchanged in mind, not Neotypes - more specifically, not my fat butt. There were fire exits, but for the most part the walkways were going to be a tight squeeze. We drew routes and re-arranged them, going for an optimal path. When it looked like we'd found it, we broke for food and a little beer.

Once that was done, Elias disappeared for a bit, leaving me alone and relaxing. Until Max's voice broke into my head.

"Brooks. Shut up and listen."

"Oh, what now?!" I took a pull from my beer and settled to watch more of this hockey stuff. Maybe that'd give me some insight on this mad woman currently sharing space with me.

"It's about Elias. You're ticked about her, because why?"

"Have you not noticed? She's pushy, decides things that involve me without me, and she's...close. Always. There's supposed to be a thing called professional distance."

"There is." Max got up, did a full body stretch, and hopped up to park it on my mostly healed section. "But at the same time you're someone worth breaking the official rules for."

"Bull."

He gave a huge chuffing sigh of some sort. "Brooks. You've been rolling with a lot of punches and holding a lot of things back. I feel it. But you are a freaking rock, even for a Centaur. She realized it without realizing it, and a lot of what she's doing is clinging to you like you're a life raft, because in a lot of ways you are."

"She needs to back off a little."

"And you told her that?"

"Yeah."

"So that's why she went for a walk after you got your gooshy food. Speaking of, beef."

"Fiiiiiine."

"So, for you two to figure it out, you give her some of what she needs, and she gives you some of what you need. But it sounds like you're already doing that."

"The heck are you, my therapist?"

"Paid in gooshy food, warm places, and skritches. But if you keep acting like this, I'm gonna want a raise." He looked unbelievably smug as he wound around me and curled up on my shoulder.

"Still, relax on that mess for a bit. Jere's coming over for dinner, and we need it to be a good one. And tomorrow I'm apparently going out with Elias on some hideous version of a double-date."

"Well, that's progress at least."

"It also means you need to move." I started to shift around a little to confirm he knew I was in fact about to move.

"That's not even a little fair, I just got comfortable."

"Fair's for board games." I finished standing up and grabbed the tablet to order up a large amount of food for Jeremiah, and after a few minutes of debate, I ordered for Elias as well.

Elias showed up first. I was in the shower cleaning up - quite honestly I needed a few minutes of quiet and the last few days had been all-go from the time I woke up with feathers awkwardly strewn about my face to the very amorphous and alcohol-infused bedtime. And I still hadn't gotten a haircut. despite all this, I found myself running through what was happening and considering possibilities, and then I realized I was humming a happy tune.

Max was giggling in my head, which was never a good sign. He refused to tell me what was up, which further reinforced the "bad things are happening" thoughts in my head. With that, I hopped out of the shower and into something that didn't have a ton of sweat on it. I came out and saw Elias closing up one of the multitude of hidden drawers that were apparently part and parcel of the design. Max was on his tree looking amused.

Elias pointed at the tablet where the food listing was. "Good choices. Jere's going to need the energy for a couple days."

"Are they going to give him time for a shower?"

"Nope. Basically everyone gets a couple cans of deodorant, a sleeping bag with an air mattress, and some noise-canceling headphones when they need to sleep."

"Ah. So this is the big healthy meal before we get run into the ground." I went to the tablet and changed Jere's order to a large steak.

"More or less. For the record, they're going to be doing the same to us, so pick your favorites."

"Noted."

Food arrived, and the kitchen had gotten the message as far as what was happening, because they took our request and doubled it. It was in fact the feast before the famine, and they'd thrown in some extras. We got it set up, and finally Jere arrived from his room, looking woeful and tired, but showered. At least he had that going for him. The conversation was almost awkward, as Jere was looking between us like he wanted to ask a question but didn't want to know the answer because the answer might be awkward.

After we finished and set the cleaned-up dishes outside, we all settled out on the couch, with Jere finally spitting it out.

"So, uh, Dad. The thing about you two not dating...is that still..still?"

It took me a few moments to sort the question before answering. Although to be honest, I'm pretty sure Maxs' cackle-chirping helped a bit. "We, haven't had any discussions, er, about it. So yeah. It's still still."

Elias, for her part, moved in while I was distracted and shifted herself to a distressingly close position, looking at Jeremiah oddly. "Would it bother you if we had?"

He looked at his hands for a bit. "Well, I mean, it'd be different. But, I mean, you're not like Mom, right?"

She shook her head. "I'm not. But your dad's - " she paused for a moment, considering what to say. "I haven't known him for a long time, but he's very good to be around. And I'm not going to make him sad or angry if I can help it." There was a pause. "He cares about you a lot and I think that's something special in your life, and you're very lucky to have him for your dad."

Jeremiah looked down. "But you've got all your stuff here. And that's like a thing. A big thing."

She nodded. "It is. Because right now we're pretty much teamed up by The Elf, so it's more efficient for me to have all my things near me."

"So it's not like permanent?"

"Oh, I think it might be." She leaned in conspiratorially. "He's scared of getting hurt again like he was with your mom. But we'll work on that."

I looked over at Max. "I am right here. Hearing this. Watching these two. Max am I invisible or have I been downgraded to an extra in my own life?"

Max cackled while they talked. "They're messing with you. Pretty sure you've already made the decision, and now you're just fighting it."

"I beg to differ."

"I've seen you for several years now. I know your good days. And ever since she wrecked the hammock and found space in your bed, you've been different. Coming back from that trip, you've been radiating the happy when you think nobody's watching. Even after researching all this other crap. Deal with it."

"I'd like to think I have something to contribute to this conversation that is in fact about me."

"Except that right now your girlfriend and your son are establishing themselves as part of each others' lives as well as yours." Max yawned and rolled over on his back casually.

"She's not my girlfriend. And I seriously doubt she thinks I'm her boyfriend."

"Oh you sweet summer kitten." Max chuffed and started washing himself.

Meanwhile, Jeremiah and Elias were wrapping up their conversation, and since there weren't any fights for me to break up, I could only presume that they'd come to some sort of agreement. Making things better, there was a tension in Jeres' shoulders that relaxed. "Okay, I'll...I should go to bed, I'm kinda sleepy."

We all rearranged and got off the couch to walk him to his bedroom. He seemed to be accepting of whatever was happening, or he'd shifted gears and was going into thinking about what was happening starting tomorrow. In any case, he sacked out pretty quickly and left me and Elias to creep back to my (my, darnit, my) quarters. It was in fact lights out and probably time for the last restful sleep the entire site was going to get for about a month. I was in my own head a little bit, enough that I only moved once when Elias moved in on my bed space. My last real thought was that I was going to need a bigger bed if she insisted on sharing.

I smelled coffee, and blinked awake as Elias was humming happily as she broke out the coffee mugs. "Big day coming Brooks. we gotta drop Jeremiah off, head for the supply closet, ignore all the stupid aches from the last gig and start doing dry runs on our infiltration run."

I yawned, flicking a hoof absently. "How could I forget."

Breakfast progressed in silence as we were both running over the plans in our head - at least until Jeremiah came in with words that shocked and amused.

"Someone...someone re-arranged my room!"

Elias smirked. "Yep. Janitorial comes into your room weekly and cleans. Where'd you think the clean sheets came from?"

"But...it...it was...all arranged already." He looked like he had when he'd lost his favorite stuffie.

I interjected a bit. "You need to get some labels on your bins then, so it looks like you have a system and not a mad scientists' lab. Put stuff in the bins so the cleaning crew knows not to mess with it."

He was apparently mollified by that. "...kay."

The rest of breakfast was quiet, until Jeremiah dashed off to work on some equations to figure out how to deflect orbital strikes (and that still felt weird thinking about) and Elias and I went to the Supply Closet to pick up some prototype gear and head up to a hangar where we were busy most of the morning. We were making good time, clearing the whole place in 45 minutes with the new gear. Until my rig broke. Elias glided down to my catwalk where I was wedged in and giggled at the predicament.

"Come on, let's tell Sammy we need the mark 2 to be sturdy."

Sammy was surprised, to say the least. "You're telling me you broke a rig made of..." he waved his hand at it. "This is ridiculous. That thing could survive damn near anything."

I shrugged. "Look, simple reality. If it ain't broke, it hasn't been given to a grunt. I'm just glad it didn't break in the field."

Sammy looked at me apprasingly. "Grunt?"

I nodded. "Airborne. Medicaled out after a thing went sideways."

There was a low whistle. "Got it." Sammy grabbed the remains, gave piercing whistle and proceeded to tell the boys that they needed to 'infantry-and-idiot-proof' the rig as we left.

Since practice was a bust, we spent the rest of the afternoon getting ready for date night. Which was only a date for Sammy and Dhara. For me it was a mandatory social event. I found a sneaky-flashy dark blue sarong that complimented Elias' wings and was reversible to a flat maroon, along with a nice sports jacket and a clean t-shirt. Good enough. To keep my tail in check, I found several hair-ties that were black and very no-nonsense. And I still hadn't been able to get my hair cut. The world despaired, and I had to spend an unseemly amount of time getting my hair back and raking my coat down so that it would behave.

Chapter 14

E lias had no say in my clothing choices, which was a pleasant surprise. Once we'd both changed and I came out with the iridescent side of the sarong showing, her eyes were...glittery from some sort of makeup work that was impressive. It complemented her dress nicely, a turquoise backless thing that let her wings move freely. There was an odd scent in the air again and I spent a few moments sniffing about before finally deciding it was perfume. I wasn't so wrapped up in locating the odd scent that I didn't notice Elias' wings extending and snapping shut repeatedly. Apparently the wings had a mind of their own, as she looked at them and brushed them off with an almost annoyed look. Max chuffed his approval as we left and went to the heretofore unseen restaurant-slash-dance club in town.

We took separate cars, which was a benefit for everyone. I didn't know the area, so I was relegated to being in the passenger side with the seat pushed all the way back, and quietly taking in a very nice sunset. Unfortunately the ride was short, and we got out with minimal fuss. The restaurant itself was astonishingly open, which brought a sigh of relief from me. It was bad enough having to go out to dinner, where most restaurant portions were insignificant enough to make me wonder if they'd ever heard of food in addition to the added trouble of having to navigate the wretched mess that was seating. Most Centaurs either gave up on the whole mess entirely or found places like Nonas' where they understood you were there to eat food, not experience whatever atmosphere was chic.

We were apparently late, and both Sammy and Dhara had dressed up for the affair like teenagers at prom and were talking over an order of mozzarella sticks. Sammy had gone all-out, with an electric blue tie and a dark green suit jacket - his genius at making custom gear pretty much overwhelmed his fashion sense. Meanwhile Dharas' dwarven form was held in check by a red dress that was doing yeomans' work at accentuating her feminine parts. Not exactly my flavor, but if that's what made Sammys' tassels twirl, who was I to begrudge? It wasn't like I'd ever had a line beating down my door for a long evening followed by a walk-of-shame morning.

The dinner itself was an interesting affair, with each of us pairing up for conversation in turn. The food was excellent, and somehow Sammy and Dhara had decided to split a huge order of poutine. This was the first educational experience of the night for me, since I had no idea what poutine was. After they brought it out I still wasn't sure what it really was. Then Elias jogged my elbow and educated me. After that I felt they were pretty bold on a first date, since fries, cheese and gravy had a tendency to make a mess. Still I wasn't going to question a first date that could turn into a second date - also, if we screwed up, there was no way Sammy would have us geared up proper when the time came to do the thing.

After food, we shuffled ourselves to back area that contained the dance floor, where I had what I would consider an unusual experience. Before I'd changed I was a fairly aggressive dancer, with me and friends from my unit going out and engaging in what was one part moving around, and one part trying to beat each other up. Now I had four left feet, and I knew it. So at the outset, I sorta swished my tail around and tippy-tapped a bit, much to the delight of everyone with me. Elias for her part was in fact an outstanding dancer.

She'd probably had a few classes somewhere - I was a little concerned about what that meant for me as I really hadn't had many reasons to dance since a time long ago when I had two fewer legs and one less divorce under my belt. Then she grabbed me and I discovered that I could move around a little bit more gracefully then I thought. Elias was almost certainly helping, as she would flick a wing out and guide me without telling me what to do. The effect was mesmerizing, to be honest, and we received more then a few cheers at the end of a song or two, before we went back to the bar for refreshment. Then the DJ decided it was a little late, and decided to slow the music down to something more suited to couples.

Before I could make an excuse, I was catching Elias' spinning form as her wings brushed my face and her face went directly into my shirt in some sort of declaration that her flag had in fact been planted. I made a mental note to deal a fresh beating to whoever was running the DJ booth tomorrow, but for just a moment, it was a world where only the two of us existed. Finally I picked her up by the waist gently so that she didn't have to suffer the indignity of five minutes with her face in my abs. It was five minutes of awkward swaying that was again far too close for comfort. At least for me - Elias seemed to have no problem with it, if her wings running along my sides was any indication. The whole room felt close. I kept my eyes on Sammy and Dhara, and from the way it looked, they were going to have the best hangovers ever in the morning.

Eventually, the suffering (or at least my suffering) stopped, and the lights came up as the DJ started to shoo us all out so they could do it again tomorrow starting at five pm. The four of us wobbled out, with Elias helping herself by hanging on to my forearm. I looked over at Sammy and Dhara, who appeared to be busy deciding who was packing an overnight bag before they disappeared in a cloud of alcohol and laughter to catch a shuttle bus back to the base because they were both far too tipsy to navigate home. Since neither of us had drank anything stronger than soda, we made our way back in amiable silence, before I popped the door to my place open to find Max lounging on the laptop. He looked up lazily and flicked his tail in what was a contented sort of move.

"Brooks?" Elias broke the silence with a glance up at me.

"Mmm?" I was feeling uptight about the whole affair. It seemed like there was something hanging in the room that was not my extreme desire to find the stiffest possible drink.

"Thanks." She brushed my cheek with a wingtip. "I haven't had that much fun in awhile. Even the part where you looked like you wanted to shoot the DJ."

"You caught that?"

"Kinda my job to see and notice. Shower?"

"You first, I think I'mma find something to watch." I settled into the couch and ditched my jacket and found my pajamas before settling in for a minute until Elias came out wearing what I now knew as a hockey jersey that was apparently made for Erinyes. I didn't recognize the logo, but it didn't really matter, as she promptly shooed me into the shower. I did not take my time there, but by the time I'd managed to finish drying myself off, she'd nodded off. To be fair, we'd had a long day, and there was going to be more of the same over the next few days. I debated for a moment before picking Elias up and carrying her to her side of the bed. After everything she'd pulled, she at least deserved to wake up in comfy bed.

I woke up to the happy smell that is oatmeal, blinked a few times to see Elias cooking up something for herself, and a large bowl of breakfast apparently waiting for me. She was still wearing the jersey from last night, and humming a bit.

"Mm. Mornin."

"You too sleepyhead. Schedules' changed a little, Sammys' group says they'll have the second version ready for us this afternoon, so we have the morning to ourselves. Which means I am being a lazy slug and watching hockey."

"Seriously?"

"Brooks, these half-days are gold. And I didn't get to catch the game last night, so shush and learn what offsides is."

I learned what offsides is. I think. Like most sports, the referees had the best view and the least knowledge of what was actually going on. Elias, on the other hand, was quite animated, spilling her coffee a few times before settling down. I did ask questions, a few of which were answered and a few of which earned me a look like I'd been dropped on my head repeatedly as an infant. It wasn't the worst thing in the world, but still, it was odd. Especially when Max rubbed along her wings and dropped into her lap. The traitor was getting no treats from me tonight. Elias' eyes went into a half-focus that meant that her and Max were talking. It wasn't a long conversation, but she visibly relaxed at some part and gave appropriate belly rubs to the small furry demon.

We finally got ourselves ready for the day shortly after lunch, where a visibly hungover but still happy Sammy gave us the newest version, declaring if we broke these, he'd buy beers. Elias and I glanced at each other to determine if that was a challenge or statement of pride in workmanship. We decided it was not a challenge.

The next week was training. While it was intense, it was very much within what we could do, and after the second run we'd almost stopped speaking to each other. There was some sort of odd synchronization with this - it felt like what we were doing was the result of years of working together. It felt weird when I thought about it. I'd never been able to act with my partner Devoin like this. When we reviewed our actions after each run-through, I was fairly certain that Elias had similar thoughts running through her head. The doctor was onsite every other day to monitor our progress and make remarks about how well we were doing physically despite the presence of a cat in our lives. In short order we got our times in the mockup down to thirty minutes from onsite, video fixing, and then out. The days flew by as I started to settle in and get ready to do this thing. Once we got settled to part one, we moved to part two. The second one was dead easy. Finally we ran parts one and two in sequence, drilling, reviewing and then experimenting to see if we could do it faster in any way. Max started getting annoyed with us as Elias and I began to talk our way through the mission in our sleep.

From looking at everyone, it seemed like they had a backup plan in case, but they seemed content to let that gather dust somewhere. At the same time, checking on Jeremiah was an exercise in checking the right room at the right time, as his normal quarters were gathering dust. The Mines on the other hand were a constant activity hive, with at least one member of the team asleep under their desk and their area being cleaned of empty cans and containers by another member of the staff. There appeared to be some form to the chaos, as one of the walls was sectioned off for who had the cleaning duty. Somehow it was workable.

Finally the night came. We'd flown in on the jet, where the pilot and co-pilot pointed out the newest amenity of a small surgical kit and once we'd landed we rented a van that Elias could drive, making our way to a crappy hotel about an hour away from the place, where we'd finished our last minute checks. Frankly, this was what I'd been waiting for. I took a few minutes to check and recheck everything we'd brought, making little adjustments to everything and finally getting ourselves geared and ready before finally stowing all the little things in the van storage.

That accomplished, I checked the clock and realized we still had about six hours of waiting before we could go and do anything.

Which meant there'd be at least one nap and one meal in all of it; assuming we could get takeout.

Unfortunately, it seemed like the area we were in was very much adverse to anything regarding decent food. It all seemed like the local four food groups were Deep-fried, Beer-Battered-and-Deep-Fried, Deep-Fried-and-Gravy-Covered, and Soda. These were not a people who were worried about heart disease. In any case, I found something that worked, and then flipped the menu over to Elias, where she regarded the options with a fascinated level of disgust.

The whole affair was depressing on several levels, because after a long look, there was no way I was getting a decent nap on the bed - an oversized twin mattress was not going to handle all of the me that was there. The desk clerk was not helpful, indicating that there was a stable about four miles down the road if I thought the accommodations weren't to my liking. It's not that I was used to it - it was annoying. But no amount of epic lung capacity was going to make the bed tolerable, and it would make things worse by making us go from "irritating" to "ejected". Nap time was going to be in shifts once we got the food thing taken care of. I made my way back to our room to discover that food had been delivered. It was enough that I could survive, but I laid down and could almost feel a ball of grease forming in my stomach. Still, I'd had worse meals. After I'd initially Changed, I tried some of my old favorite comfort foods and discovered they were no longer comforting. After all that, it was in fact nap time. I snagged a blanket and got comfortable on the floor.

Nap time was interrupted. Rudely. For some reason the local police had been summoned and were knocking. I looked down and took it all in; both of them were about six feet of muscle with blue hats covering close-cropped hair, mirrored sunglasses, and uniforms that were filled with lanyards and ribbons. The big differences were in the details, one had four rows of ribbons while the other had five. It almost like they were trying to be military without actually being military. Their sleeves were rolled up to expose a few tattoos that were well-done but disturbing in their content. On one arm was an Erinyes in a golden cage, another held a scene in a book - as if to remove any doubt the top of the book was noted as Genesis I: XXVI. I was pretty sure I didn't want to see anything else, and I was really sure that my being a cop up until recently was not going to help a bit. The one with four rows of ribbons was the first to speak, taking a deep breath and sighing.

"What a world. Got folks coming in and demanding everything, thinking just because they're bigger that they're better. Huh." It sounded rehearsed, but there was some venom behind it that was real. I was going to have to talk to some people about this, because if they decided the Elias and I were a menace to their society, we'd be spending a few nights in the local lockup, and some things weren't going to get done. This was probably a fieldwork test. In any case, it was time to play nice. Or as nice as I could.

"Just looking for a bed before we get on the road again, officers." Keep it short, keep it simple, and keep your head down. Admittedly given the height differential, it was hard to keep my head down.

"Well, you found a bed. If you don't like it, there's a stable about three miles down the road. If you're still not happy, I'm sure me and my partner can find you two some accommodations." I'd said that last line a few times myself, mainly to get someone rolling toward a health center. These guys did not seem to be so civic-minded. Or they were, and their idea of being civic minded was to figure out how to shove me into the back of their squad car than let a centaur figure out how to sleep on a bed nowhere near the right size.

I looked a little thoughtful, looking back to Elias and then regarding the police officers at the door. "Nah. This little place is a slice of paradise compared to some places I slept in back in the old days. Back before all of...well, this." I indicated my rear half and attempted to pull off a "I hate this" look. "I was in the army, had a good career going. Then this, and I got drummed out. Now'm a jumped-up mailman, living out of a box van or a rental car. Me and the missus ain't here to cause trouble, just catching a little sleep before we're on the road and gone."

The two looked at each other for a few moments of discussion before they turned back to us. The one with more ribbons took over. "Well, you understand we're going to need to check that story, so you and the missus come on out with your license and we'll make sure there's nothing odd going on." And the way he said that made my blood a little cold - still, nothing we could really do at that point.

We stepped outside, and I was cuffed and hobbled with some zip-ties. Elias got a similar treatment. Meanwhile, the two officers went through the hotel room looking for anything suspicious after running our ID's through their system. They stared at the results for a long time; I had a feeling they were getting several flags that didn't exactly mesh with their attitude, so they were going to content themselves with making us sit out here in the sun.

Finally they returned our ID's, but they took their time pulling the zip-ties off. The whole ordeal was one part humiliating and one part rage-inducing; the humiliating part being standing out in the sun slowly getting hungry and thirsty while the wind blew my clothes every which way but decent. The only saving portion of the whole thing was Elias keeping me covered after the first gust of wind let the world know far more than it needed to regarding my nethers.

With a final scowl and a reminder that while the sundown laws weren't on the books, they couldn't be everywhere and bad things could very easily happen to folks who weren't careful. That was all in all a depressing thought, and of course, we had to clean up and breathe a sigh of relief that they didn't toss the rental van where all the goods were loaded. I flopped my upper half onto the bed, letting the tension of everything that had just transpired flow out.

"Elias?"

"Mm-hm?" She had done likewise, stretching her wings and fluttering them about repeatedly before flopping.

"We really need to include this in our report. Something about Neotype operations in the G-126 friendly areas. Frankly, the only reason we're not in jail on some imaginary charge is they couldn't fit my butt in the back seat." I settled a bit more, stretching my legs and feeling a bit more confident that the local constabulary hadn't had a lot of training on how to properly restrain neotypes.

"Mmm-hm. And that is yet another reason I like your butt, Brooks. Dare I even say, I adore it."

"Okay, but why."

"You've seen it right?"

"Yes. Yes I have." And I did not like the tone of her voice as she said that. It felt like there were some feelings attached to that one little sentence, that might unpack a whole new line of questioning, and I wasn't sure this was the time or the place.

"Annnd?" The little demon in my head that had to know everything was apparently in charge for a few moments to ask that silly question.

"And, it's nice. Deal with it."

At that point, it was either argue with Elias about my butt and whether or not it was attractive, or catch as much sleep as I could. I opted for the nap. Sort of. Unfortunately, the idea that the local yokels might come back with a panel van and a plan may have kept me from going much further than a light drowse.

Finally, the alarms went off, and it was time to go to work. We checked the outside, checked out of the hotel, and hauled ourselves down the road. Elias was driving and I was checking to make sure nothing was disturbed. While the van had several alarms, you couldn't be too careful.

Once I'd declared everything fit to work, we checked in with the group that was going to make the power go away for an hour, confirmed our fallbacks and oh heck moves before getting ourselves ready. We parked and killed the lights a good hundred or so yards from the facility, took out binoculars and for the first time got some eyes on our target location while we did our last-minute prepwork of dulling Elias' wings and braiding my tail so that it didn't catch on anything. Then we checked through the windows.

Funny story, it looked a whole lot bigger than our mockup in the hangar; a converted barn made of aluminum, with a multitude of warning signs regarding open flames, explosives, and other possible dangers that could maim, mutilate, wound, and/or kill. The lighting was bright and harsh, which was not helpful for our current situation of needing to sneak in. The worst of it all was the entryways. Specifically, they were not built for a centaurs' width. This was not a good sign, especially since there wasn't time to look around for a cargo entrance. At least not that I could see. There was a sliding front door that I could have gone through if there wasn't a large padlock hanging from it. And I had not studied lockpicking.

Elias looked out through her own binoculars and hmph'ed softly. "I'll be back in three minutes. Keep the line open." She slid out the back door, took two steps and launched herself up into the starlit night. I felt very prickly and exposed suddenly. Maybe it was the constant presence of Elias and suddenly not. More likely it was that I was a centaur in a place that was probably not friendly to me, and I was in theory a courier with no real reason to be out here. The seconds warped into minutes as I checked my watch and listened for any sound other than the wind. Finally after two minutes and forty-five seconds of eternity I heard skid and gravel crunching as Elias landing. She slipping into the side door, shaking her head.

"Just the two entrances. Electronic lock on the front door'll be disabled when the power dies, alternates are locked more solidly than we have time for. So, we're gonna have to squeeze you through." Elias dug into her pack and pulled out a spray can of lubricant.

"Elias, what precisely are you planning on doing with that?"

"Spraying you. Well, the wide parts at least." Her look of innocence was setting off alarms all over in the part of my brain responsible for detecting potential shenanigans.

"Just spraying? And what's that gonna do to my fur?"

"Just spraying. I'll get it all nice and greasy so you can slip through that human-sized door with minimal fuss." And with that she started spraying. Though she did make a liar of herself by smoothing it out with her hands once she got done "For an even coat". It was a very disconcerting feeling, and did absolutely nothing for the ball of tension that started in my chest and raced the entire length of my body.

Finally with a whisper, we sent out our ready to go request, and the power went out. Part of me hoped the other team was well and truly gone and we didn't have more explaining to do once we got back.

It was a long fifteen seconds as I raced full-tilt to my spot, snuggled the cables where they needed to go to feed the "nothing here" loop to the offsite security desk, and forced my bulk through the door and closed it just in time for the backup power to come back on. From there it was frantic movement and watching to make sure we had blue flashes, three per canister, twenty-five at a time. While I was certainly trying to be quiet, the catwalks groaned and creaked with every step I took, making the whole thing an exercise in structural stability. Fortunately, the folks who built the catwalks had stability in mind, but it was still rather nerve-wracking as I watched my balance, the rig, and the next place I had to go. That was, however the worst of it.

It was amazing to watch a plan go off without a single hitch. Once we got met up in the middle, we thumbs-upped and went back down, where after a moment, we hurried out to our car and checked the time. Twenty-two minutes, a record. We cleared the area rapidly and headed to the next section where we were going to be doing a little more breaking and entering, along with what could be argued was destruction of private property.

Part two was even easier in the beginning, if that could be believed. We put our counter-additive mix in, and activated the safety mechanisms that kept the dust from rising and subsequently exploding, and finally stirred things up slowly so that we could confirm an even coating and hopefully keep people alive, remembering the ancient wisdom that a bomb disposal technician at a dead run outranks everyone. Neither of us were really bomb disposal technicians, and being in an area where one spark could very easily send us and the surrounding half an acre directly to the afterlife was never so abundantly clear.

This was going far too cleanly for the universe to accept, and so it was that something had to go horribly wrong. Everything was done, and we were packing up to make ourselves scarce when one of the rentacops found us doing things we shouldn't have been. Things began happening very rapidly. I turned to shield Elias as she moved to take a shooting position to hit the guy with fifty thousand volts of naptime. At the same time, he fired off several rounds that hit my previously un-abused left buttcheek, and I rather reflexively closed the distance between us, turned and kicked him in the head with a foreleg. Now I may have overstepped a bit by picking him up and launching several haymakers to his head, but in my defense he shot me and he'd definitely shot at Elias. I took a closer look and it seemed as though the security guard was also one of the gentlemen who'd hassled Elias and me earlier tonight. Karma had apparently arrived in the form of my hoof.

Then there was additional oddness, as Elias went over to the cop/rentacop and began rapidly hopping up and down on him and hissing something at him in a language I couldn't even begin to place. I was rather surprised by the vitriol involved so all I really did was watch for a good fifteen seconds.

Although watching Elias work him over was quite satisfying, that was not how this was supposed to go. He had a concussion, and from the look and smell, several shots of vodka before he'd started his rounds. On the one hand, it was good that we were probably not going to be identified, however it was bad in that anyone who looked too closely was going to see more than just a security guy who'd had one too many on the job, passed out and thumped his head on the pavement. Speaking for myself, I was not happy. I grabbed Elias before she could injure him even further, which turned into her grabbing on to me far too tightly for a few moments.

I gritted my teeth a bit and thought about not bleeding. "Elias...we need to find his flipping brass and clean up a little."

Elias took a long heaving breath and nodded, looking around and finally pocketing the spent casings, which she put in a pocket as we hurried toward our vehicle, me limping on three legs and once inside I managed to slap a quick bandage or three on my rump to make the bleeding stop. After all the activities, I was physically and mentally drained, which resulted in a brief period of blissful unconsciousness as Elias drove us to the airfield where our little business jet was waiting to get us the heck out of there.

On the jet, life started to suck less as I had a nice shot of whiskey and a few painkillers before the doc could tell me no. Meanwhile, Elias dug into the "bad things have happened" kit, pulling out a couple syringes and some large and very mean-looking tweezers. I was not amused.

"Elias..." This was not how the night was supposed to end. I was fairly certain that the celebratory whiskey was not going to be opened on the way back.

"Brooks, you've been shot three times at close range. We may need to do something about that." Her voice was clipped and severe. We were definitely not going to have a discussion about what was and was not overkill on the flight.

"Now?" I blinked at her owlishly, as things were not exactly tracking right for me for some reason.

"Now."

"Turbulence?" Of the many things I needed, a badly-timed air pocket while Elias was digging around my new set of extra holes with the tweezers was not one of them

"Minimal if we get this done quickly. The flight crew has advised that we got about 30 minutes of smooth flying before it gets interesting."

"But seriously, like, now?"

"It's either me or we wait several hours for the doc. Now ask yourself, who would you rather have playing with your ass?" She had donned rubber gloves at some point and had dunked a few things in non-drinkable alcohol.

"Gently." Because that was really all I could ask for. She was right, and having bullets in me well and truly was making my night a bad one.

"With you, darling? Always." And she promptly made a liar of herself by stabbing me in the butt with a syringe.

On the up side, I didn't feel much as Elias went to work and pulled out fragments from three very nicely broken up bullets, then dropped them in a baggie.

"Whassa prognosis doc?" The painkillers and local anesthetic were decidedly doing work.

"You're going to see the real doc when we land. Might be some scarring, and I think you might want to consider letting your fur grow out a little to cover it if it does wind up scarring."

I grumbled and pawed at the air a bit. Okay I was a little loopy, but still. "Years. Years on the force, nothing happens until y'all come along. Then suddenly I've been shot in the chest once, shot in the butt what, seven or eight times, yanked into the air like a bag of rice, and, and..." my train of thought stopped at Massive Painkiller Station, decided it liked where it was and promptly began to shut down.

My last truly coherent thought was "Did she call me 'Darling'?" - that thought was followed by 'nah'. From there it was just the blissful sleep of the heavily medicated.

Chapter 15

The lights came on in the morning, and with them the doc. It appeared that I'd been moved from plane to bed without waking me up, which meant that someone had access to stunningly good painkillers. The largest change was in my quarters themselves. There appeared to be a degree of modularity with these, as the bathroom had been re-arranged to a his-and-hers sort of setup so that nobody needed to wait in the morning to take care of showering and the other sundries of the morning. I started pondering this in my head regarding what exactly this meant. That particular thought seemed to be going toward places I wasn't entirely sure I liked, so I chose to consider thinking about the debriefing that was sure to be coming soon.

Since it was apparently a formal morning, Elias had a white hockey jersey with a couple patches and flannel pajama bottoms. Max hissed and swatted the air to make sure Doc knew who was in charge as he entered to check on me, while the doc flicked his fingers at Max in annoyance before slapping several patches on me and eyeing the results on his tablet.

"Agent Brooks. If this report is accurate, I would like to study you. Three bullets at close range, and you still managed to fend off your attacker and complete your mission, remaining conscious well into your flight home."

"I ain't the first Centaur you've run into."

"You may be the most resilient. As it was, Agent Elias was kind enough to ensure the bullets were fully removed, and your bandages secure. All I needed to do was clean and suture. Now then, your recovery time will be approximately two weeks;

normally I would say one but you refuse to heed medical advice. This will cause difficulty in the future." While he said this, he was eyeing Elias and Max in a "this has to be your fault" manner. Still, the air that something was not quite right was persistent.

The sense of foreboding lasted, even as we left my quarters for debriefing and a reunion with Jeremiah, who looked like he had a shiner from the land of "I fell" until I inquired further. Officially, he and another colleague had fallen. Unofficially, nobody was willing to admit. Not even Jere. When I asked him, he dug in and stuck to the official story of "I fell."

On the one hand, he was still a kid - as far as I was concerned. On the other hand, Elias did some discrete questioning and found out that he'd developed a mean left hook, and I was slightly proud of him for that. Additionally Kardar had done some re-assignment, and now they had been reduced to insulting each other through the group discussion board. This was going to be rough; on the one hand I didn't want to be overprotective, and Jere could almost certainly hold his own in a lot of ways. That said, someone had punched my baby boy, and if certain videos were to be believed, a centaur punting a dwarf was a sight to behold. Unfortunately, since I didn't know who the culprit was the options were to either dropkick every dwarf in the Mines not named Jeremiah through the door, or ask Kardar what the next plan was going to be.

I went with the latter option, as it seemed less likely to land me in the stockade. So, over the ramps and catwalks designed for us mere Tall Folk I went to find Kardars' niche. Kardar eventually looked up, saw me standing in wait, and sighed. He looked a wreck, and from the expression on his face I was not doing his temperament a bit of good.

"Brooks, you're not wrecking things. That's good." He was a little wary, and appeared to be upright through some large amounts of coffee.

"Day's still young. I'd like to hear a story. A story that explains why my firstborn and only son is currently walking around with a black eye that reminds me deeply of a barroom brawl."

"Well, here's the thing. We've been tracking Jeremiah on several fronts, since we haven't had very many newly Changed enter the system. The problem with that is, he's basically got a sixteen-year-olds' handle on his emotions. He has outbursts, especially since he feels more than a little bit like he's the low man on the totem pole. Literally. I mean as far as academic accomplishments, he's only got the single masters degree. Which is a sore spot, but he really doesn't have time to correct it. At the same time, when he's right, he doesn't know how to graciously point that out."

Kardar continued, running a hand over his head. "As far as I can tell, the breaking point was when Jere was looking over some spin rate analyses to determine the minimum rotation we're going to need to deflect whatever masses are coming down. The projection was using a smooth mass, which is admittedly not going to happen, but it gives us a baseline to work with and then we can move on. Jeremiah mighta popped off to the one doing those projections and hinted that we'd be better off if the other guys' talents were best put to use in the next Pacific Tech Smart People On Ice show. End result, two broken pairs of glasses, two black eyes, a couple teeth loosened, and no real resolution to the actual problem regarding how to make the necessary adjustments in time. I refuse to divulge the other guys' name at this point on account of you may hit harder than your son, and I need unscrambled brains working on this."

"So does mean I can kick 'em anywhere but the head? I mean I still got three good legs, and the fourth one might be a little weak but it'll do a job if it's gotta." Admittedly, I was a little cross that Kardar wasn't going to let me loose on the culprit.

"That is not what I'm suggesting." Kardar paused to run a hand through the shock of hair on his head, apparently choosing his words carefully. "Look, your kid's brilliant. Frankly he's one of the top five in this department right now in terms of raw potential. The problem is he's new, and to some he's still an outsider. But he's getting there. In order to settle this, we're doing some group work that's a little competitive, but shouldn't result in trips to see the doc. Then maybe one its' all done they can get together and figure out how to work like civilized folk."

"Details." I wanted to be sure that I wasn't going to have to step in and mete out a little of my own extra-curricular corrective action.

Kardar exhaled, looking at his desk. Either this was embarrassing to divulge or he had no idea how to explain this to me. "Three part thing. First, Robot fighting. They get one hour with a base robot kit, adjust it however they want, then we put 'em in the bathroom and they fight it out. Second, one on one video game. Shooter. Twenty minutes or twenty frags ahead. Last, chess boxing. Three minutes of chess, three minutes of boxing. Nine rounds max, ends either on a KO, checkmate, or at the end of it, judges' decision. Any questions?"

"Fine. Lemme know how it goes, I gotta go debrief with The Elf." Okay, so the dwarven mines had their own conflict resolution process. It wasn't quite what I'd expect, but then again it was a dwarven thing.

Still, I was not expecting what came next. We spent a good half-hour going over everything, and Elias and I repeatedly indicated that the whole thing could have gone sideways very easily due to the local attitudes, both of concluding with making a simultaneous recommendation that we not be put in a similar spot without a unchanged backup to play peacemaker; that startled all three of us, honestly. The Elf narrowed his eyes at us after a moment, as if we'd rehearsed that. Immediately after the debrief, The Elf had a new gig for us, which meant that we had to shift gears rapidly.

"This operation is quite simple. You and Agent Elias will be calling upon the space elevators. We know why. Officially, they have closed themselves off completely in order to devote their full resources to their newest projects. Aerial reconnaissance shows that they are ahead of schedule with the solar rings and collectors. We estimate they will be ready for completion by Neo Day. Therefore, we have two weeks to complete this task."

The Elf moved aside, allowing the briefing board to come to life. "The two of you will board the Poseidon platform. There you will locate the fire control system for the railgun, and introduce multiple re-calibrations to the systems in order to allow a safe dispersal of any accelerated earthbound projectiles via their secondary ground-based targeting systems. Those re-calibrations are being efforted in the Dwarven mines, and will ideally be able to be completed prior to boarding. This will be done quietly. However, owing to reality, you will be issued non-lethal munitions in order to ensure task completion at the expense of exposure. Agent Brooks, you are tasked with the initial insertion and boarding operation. Agent Elias, once on the ground you will be leading the location and distribution of the re-calibration payload. Agent Brooks, proceed with your silly questions."

"Are you aware that I got shot less than a day ago?"

"I have read the report from Agent Elias, as well as the doctors' prognosis. He has indicated that you will self-evaluate as fit for duty no later than two days from now, and that he would recommend otherwise. The Doctor has also advised that Agent Elias refrain from indulging in any frivolity." I glanced over at Elias, who had a "Who me?" look. I decided that we could have that discussion without The Elf looking peeved at us, and continued.

"Listen, I don't know how many times you've had to do covert insertions, but between Elias' wings and my entire body, covert is generally not on the menu to be selected. We're quite noticeable."

The Elf pursed his lips for a moment. "I suppose then you will have to allay those concerns through your own ingenuity. You have the mission. I expect a preliminary mission plan tomorrow."

Thus thoroughly dismissed, we left and I waited until we were out of Executive Alley before ranting.

"What the actual hell is he thinking? Covert. Against all of that. I got half a mind to go back in there with a breathalyzer. I need to go punch something, that's absolute bat-crap loco and everyone knows it." I turned hard toward the gym, as there was a lot that I needed to work out, and it wasn't just my leg.

"Brooks. He gave you minimal instructions, and left most of the planning up to you." She lowered her voice. "That means he trusts you. I didn't say anything, because I trust you." She flicked a wing out to smack my unabused lower left shoulder.

That brought me up short for a moment. "Well, I guess that means I need to come up with a bang-up plan."

"You do." And that brought a new urgency to the walk to the gym, as I was going to need some post-workout clarity in the worst way.

"Alright, we need every scrap of data on that platform. Also, do we know if they're doing anything with the other two platforms, or is this one a capabilities demonstration?" I started ticking off things on my fingers to keep track.

Elias glanced down at her phone to access a few things before answering. "Just the Poseidon one that we know of."

"Are we sure?" Something like this had to have a backup. I mean I could see the need for a backup, and I wasn't anywhere near an evil genius.

"They're not building rings around the other elevators yet."

"We know this how?"

"Through a brilliant innovation called the telescope, Brooks. If there were others, we'd have other teams. Now, we gonna plan or borrow trouble?"

I opened the door to the gym. "Before we do either, we gonna work. Two miles on the run, and then upper body and torso."

We spent most of the next hour in silence, throwing iron plates around and then finishing with a long run. Elias hated running, as the wings that were her pride and joy kept slowing her down or trying to get her into the air. Meanwhile, even on three legs I could still run like a marathoner. It was all in all a good way to get the mind clear for what was coming.

Post workout, we returned to our room and settled. Unfortunately, as I kept looking at everything, a plan would form and then fall apart. The biggest hurdle was the location. It was isolated on the open ocean. And reading the reports, the Pacific Ocean was nobodys' friend at any time, and we were coming into a time of year when the weather was highly unpredictable. Not fun, and with a hard date for when things were going to happen, we didn't have time to wait for a nice day to arrive.

Looking at everything that needed to be done, I exhaled. "We need to get the planning juice out."

Elias nodded. "Right then. Liquor store?"

"We can charge this to the planning budget, right?"

"If it succeeds. If it fails, who cares, right?"

We went to town, where the liquor store was well stocked with multiple varieties of eighty-proof thinking juice. For me, it was peanut butter whiskey, while Elias grabbed something with a maple leaf on it. Curious, but we grabbed several bottles of each, as it could be a long night and perhaps an early morning. Then we hit the pool for our mandatory therapy session - we checked with the doc, and he determined that our previous hour in the gym didn't count. That said, there was a bonus of sorts; I saw the pool and paused. I had an idea.

I promptly scrambled up to the diving platform, took a breath, and belly flopped into the pool before scrambling up and doing it again. I was not doing my butt any favors with this, and it let me know. Maybe the doctor was right. After the second time, Elias climbed out and gave me a look.

"Okay Brooks, what the heck?"

"I got an idea. We call it here?"

"Yeah - otherwise I think you'll drown yourself or hurt yourself. Probably both. And I am not a fan of trying to save your butt from drowning."

I changed into a loose wrap, and hurried back to our room without even drying off. Elias was looking at me confused while I was pulling things up and pouring a shot, and a second to help the first find its' way home.

"Brooks, what kind of idea you got?"

"Simple. We'll do a high altitude low open jump. We know they're gonna lock onto anything close so we drop with an inflatable raft. We jump at thirty thousand, pop chutes at a thousand, cut the raft loose five hundred, hit the water and go in low and slow. Hit the platform from the west at twilight when they're blind, give it an hour for full dark, we go in and do the deeds, take the raft out or liberate a boat, get the pickup and be home in time for last call."

"Small problem Brooks. I've never done any sort of parachuting jump. I can glide in." Elias fluttered her wings a bit.

"Hmm. You show up on radar?"

Elias grimaced. "I think so."

"I'll definitely show up on radar then. Can we coat the bottom of the raft to scatter the radar? Maybe see what kind of radar they have and do a test jump separately to see if you can glide while I fall?" I was pacing a bit while thinking, which was starting to cause an ache in places.

"Probably, but can we take a sub? Skip the whole jump out of a perfectly good airplane business?"

I scrunchfaced a bit. "We should ask."

We asked, and The Elfs' assistants were grim as they advised that there was exactly one sub available, and that it would be detected at extreme range due to the anti-piracy measures on the platform. That left us with going in through the air.

We left Executive Alley again, feeling grim. "This does not look promising for a surface or subsurface attack. We're - I hate to say this Brooks, but I think I'm going to have to learn how to jump out of a plane like you in two weeks."

I considered. "Nah. We'll do a tandem jump. You hop on my back and strap down, I jump and take care of everything.

"Well, crap. Do we need to drink all this then?" Elias pointed at the mostly untouched bottles.

"Yes. Tradition dictates that if this is good idea sober, it'll be a great idea drunk. We're alcohol-proofing this sucker. And, you need to figure out what we're doing once we hit the platform, yeah?"

"Yep." She knocked back a shot. "And you need a shower."

I didn't disagree, however I came back out of my shower to see her wearing my favorite football jersey. There was a moments' discombobulation as I tried to sort out what was what, but it seemed like I was missing something. I don't want to say I showed her up by putting on her favorite hockey jersey, but after I looked in that direction Elias gave me a look that promised something. Not sure what, but the solution obviously more whiskey and my second favorite jersey. For her part Elias had eschewed the pedestrian shot glasses and was taking her thinking juice straight from the bottle. She was going to get wrecked. I started putting my fingers to work on my tablet, getting specs and requirements, as well as data feeds for what we'd need to get everyone there in one piece. She finally looked up and declared that she got an idea. Except that it came out as "I gawdid."

I glanced at her, as she stumbled to the big screen and started tapping out things. She took a deep breath to explain.

"So...this section here. S'all marked as secondary security depot. But here's the thing. They already have primary and secondary security here, where you'd expect them." she pointed at another section of the layout. "So I looked, and there's some of their promo videos, showing off their security teams to ward off pirates and stuff, so this has gotta be a fire control or something that they don't want us to know what it actually is. So if we go in there, we'll find what we need to dump the updated target data into. And then I checked, and cross-referenced the plans for the other two, and this is the only anom..amon..weird thing on all three plans. Ever'thing else matches like they're machine-stamped." She was swaying at the end of her chain of thought, but pointed a finger and a wingtip for emphasis. "It's where it is. Now we gotta get there. Which is your job, Mister Brooks."

I scrunched my face a little and knocked back a few more shots to see how much sense the plan made. It seemed to hold together, but the concern was other people we'd meet. Still, it sounded like that was why we were being sent. It looked like we had solid plans, which meant the whiskey turned from thinking to drinking. We even traded bottles at one point and both made weird faces at the others' preference. Her bottle tasted like alcoholic maple syrup. She in turn decided that my preferred drink was a declaration of war on the nation of Whiskey. We eyed each other for a moment before dissolving into a fit of giggles, and I finally realized something that had actually been on my mind but I hadn't been able to fully vocalize.

"So Elias."

"Mmmmyeees?" She cocked an eyebrow at me in anticipation.

"So...like you know my whole life story, right?"

"Mmmhm." If she'd lost the power of speech, this was not going to end well.

"So." I paused to force thoughts into words. "How'd you get here anyway?"

Elias scrunched, pausing for a long time before answering. "So I was born in Montana, on the Blackfeet reservation. The main occupation there is 'unemployed', and there really wasn't much there. So as soon as I could I left, got through some years in the army, and came back to become a teacher after being a door-gunner turned out to have fewer long-term prospects than I originally thought. Then those plans got derailed when I Changed - like you I was one of the first. Most of the tribe who changed became...well, not Erinyes. Overnight I was suddenly Thunderbird reborn. It was odd, since I really just wanted to teach and get used to having wings."

She paused for a long swig of whiskey. "It didn't last. Some of the elders were impressed, wanting me to quit teaching and be a tour guide to help the tribe, as I was still a bit of a novelty. Others though, they...well, they didn't think that someone who'd left the reservation would have been so blessed - even thought I came back, and instead of Thunderbird, they thought I was Coyote come to trick them. It was rough. I'd go to the grocery store and after I came home, I'd have to go over my feathers for spit and burns."

"The Coyote group was vocal and angry enough that a vote was called among the elders. The vote was split, but the message was pretty clear. I could stay and gamble that there wasn't someone trying to kill me every day, or I could leave and never come back. I decided to leave, and....well, several members of the group who thought I was Coyote decided to help. They broke into my house and stole everything useful, and then they proceeded to burn everything else down. They left my car alone so I could actually get out. Thoughtful little dirtbags."

She paused, while dredging up some painful memories. "They burned my Grandmothers' fancy dance dress. It was supposed to be my daughters and her daughters after, if I'd had one." She paused again, forcing herself back on track. "Anyway, I could see a few headlights nearby, so I really didn't have a lot of time to figure out where to go so I basically went west for a couple hours and then stopped to take a nap. When I woke up, I was looking at a flashlight from a tribal cop. I had managed to stop on Flathead land. In case you're wondering, that's not a good thing. Our tribes would go to war with each other often back in the day, and even now there's a low friction. I explained it out, and what was officially house arrest but in reality it was a hotel room."

"Things changed a bit after that. I was still looked at weirdly, but there was a bit more acceptance. I couldn't get a job as a teacher - well, I was a substitute teacher, but I really started finding myself doing more and more dancing. I was able to get a loan and start a school for it."

"That summer, everything was going well. Then a few odd things began happening. It was like I was being watched. Then someone mentioned that the Blackfeet wanted to make peace with me. The elders were still infighting, but after some looking, the leader of the group claiming I was from Coyote had laid claim to my family lands - ostensibly to purify, but a few of the elders checked and he'd built an awfully nice lodge for himself." she paused for a moment, lost in a memory for a moment. "Our whole family'd go out on the lake, go fishing and then stay up late to watch the shooting stars and tell stories of the old days, so that I could tell my kids." She took a breath and exhaled. "Anyway, I got the invitation to dance and I said sure, partly out of pride really. Like you could put me anywhere, even send me away from the tribe, but I'd still represent the best of us anywhere I went."

"It was a beautiful time, and I didn't win the dancing portion - that was someone else who was better than I was by a long shot - but I did win best costume. It was all the bells on my feathers that did it. Anyway, I decided that while I was here, I should go home one more time and because I could, I'd fly over. It was dusk, but I saw my where my home had been, and then a little further up, our fishing cabin. And then the people there. It didn't look right. I saw there was a lot more boat activity, and I was able to move closer and see a lot of things I shouldn't have. Buncha people, and I took the time to memorize their faces. And they were moving all sorts of things over the border to Canada - looked like a good trade in cigarettes for whiskey. Since I didn't have a gunship handy, I had to go to the local Indian Affairs Office. Lo and behold, one of the people who was moving smokes and whiskey had his picture on the wall as the local head of the office."

"So I couldn't do anything the normal way. But I still had a friend or two in the Army, and I went to see them. I took a training flight to my old commanders' place in Virginia. We talked, and I told him what I'd seen. I showed him how to grill fish properly, and he promised to do something. The old man was as good as his word. About a month later, the news lit up about a cross-border smuggling ring that was moving more than just smokes and booze, and my old CO was named as part of it, and he'd gotten an anonymous tip from one of his old troopers, and he'd gone to several folks in Washington for an investigation. I was a little unhappy about it because of course, brass takes the credit for the grunts' sweat."

"I was more unhappy when I found out he'd been killed a few days later. He was a good man, doing the right thing. After that, I decided to pick up a knife and a small pistol. Just in case. Just in case was right on the money, as the next day three unhappy men who claimed to be with the FBI were at my apartment, asking me to come with them and make a statement. The problem there was that, ah, feds don't generally have silencers on their pistols." She shrugged and went on after another drink. "I grabbed my pistol and fought for my life, and won. Still, I called the police, and they took me for questioning. And arrest because, well, I shot three people. Even if it was self-defense, I'd have to go through the process. I got bailed out, and a lawyer I'd never seen before introduced himself, told me two things. One, that the people I'd busted were not going to stop until I was dead and set as a warning to anyone else who thought interfering with them was a good idea, and two - that he thought I was good enough to join a group he called Jacks' Friends. If I agreed, I wouldn't have to worry about the other people ever again." She finished off her whiskey. "He forgot to mention I'd have other problems. Still a good trade. The next day, the district attorney dropped the charges, and I was free to go to an airfield in the middle of nowhere to learn all about my new life."

That was in fact one hell of a story, so I took a long swig from my own bottle and leaned into her in companionable silence. Elias didn't cry, that I'd saw, but I had a feeling that it was a near thing as she buried her head in my side and was indulging her inner horse girl. It was a tad worrisome, but there was a question on my mind that wasn't exactly proper, but it had fought valiantly through my alcohol-soaked brain and thus deserved to be asked.

"So Elias. If you don't mind my asking."

There was a muffled "Mm?" from her general direction, which I took as a what-do-you-want.

"I have two questions."

"Mmm."

"First, what's an 'Ohpa'? I know some places it's like, grandad."

She blinked at me, apparently missing something. "When did I call you ohpa?"

"While back when we started this whole thing, you were talking to Kardar and called me ohpa or something, and then you were kinda lost."

She blinked and blushed a little. "Oh. That." She looked around a bit. "I was actually calling you 'ohpatoom'. It means, well...the closest translation would be boyfriend, but the usage implies that there's intimacy."

It was my turn to blink. "But."

She nodded. "I know. I had a lot on my mind and I couldn't think of the word at the moment. Slip of the tongue, I was a little frustrated and cranky, y'know?" She looked a little embarrassed and if I was reading her right she was actually scared.

I had no intention of riding that train to any conclusion, logical or otherwise. Something in the back of my head was sounding all sorts of warnings and cautions. Time for burning question number two. "Okay, never mind that. So, what exactly, is this 'fancy dance' thing?"

She lifted her head up to regard me as if I had not only been dropped on my head as an infant, but that said head-dropping was a family sport. "It's - wait, you've never seen it?"

"Uhm, the half Italian, half Irish Centaur cop never had the opportunity, no."

"Well, that makes sense then. Le'me try." She got up, and first went to the door separating my room from Jere's to make sure he wasn't conscious, then went to the front door to make sure the hallway was empty. Then and only then did she go to her tablet and search a little, finally queuing up something that was made up of drums and chanting. It didn't exactly resonate with me, but at the same time it changed Elias; she started bouncing on her feet in rhythm, before she suddenly exploded into a whirlwind of arms, feathers, and kicks that hit the floor and propelled her to doing something that somehow blended with the music.

The fact that she was in fact fairly drunk at this point finally caught up to her, and she almost faceplanted into my butt where she was going to hit something that hurt. I saw this coming - sort of, and was able to catch her with my lower ribcage. Painful, but not the worst place she could have landed. She wobbled to her feet and killed the music, looking much more herself than before the dancing part started. She looked at me and looked to the door. I was probably going to have to be the responsible one here, but we packed our respective bottles with us just in case and left to get some air.

Chapter 16

The next morning started in the afternoon, as we sorted out the remnants of our planning session. I'm not sure what happened, but Elias was wearing a traffic cone on her head as she snored laying crosswise on my lower ribs, I had a traffic sign under my side, and the room had been redecorated in College Sophomore Explosion. It was not good. I scooched myself out from under Elias so that I could clean up a little and not disturb her, finally showering up for our meeting with The Elf.

Once Elias came around, I offered her the awful but can't-miss hangover cure. Several aspirins blended into two raw eggs and subsequently poured into a brandy snifter. Normally I'd add a shot of brandy to make it palatable, but since I was lacking brandy, I added some of that hideous maple whiskey. She was grateful for it, and we managed to be somewhat presentable as we went back to Executive Alley, where The Elf was looking exceptionally pinched.

"I have here a report of unusual activities reported by security last night." He turned a page. "Stolen Road Sign." Another page turn. "Stolen Road Cone." Page turn, "Indecent exposure, 'mooning.'" He turned the page again. "Indecent exposure, public urination. Two counts. The second incident was performed by someone was quite perversely skilled, writing 'Airborne' on the side of a building. Now, I'm quite sure the two of you had nothing to do with this, I simply note it as to reflect my mood this afternoon. Where, is the plan I requested."

Once we'd run him through the plan, he seemed to slip into a gaze of neutrality. "It seems effective. Submit your equipment requisitions by the end of the day, we'll begin training tomorrow.

Arrive at hangar one sober. And I do not wish to see any further reports that even hint that the motor pool repair logs have been updated to reflect that the Master Arm switches have been relabeled in any way, or that any hyperdrive motivators have been damaged."

Elias nodded. "We'll find new ways to assist the crews responsible."

The Elfs' eye twitched. If my old boss was any indication, it meant he was hoping for a meteor to hit us. We scooted out.

We quickly requisitioned everything we needed from Sammy, who was all too happy to help and even find a few extra items. Then I put in for several more things just in case. And then we went back to my quarters to clean up. There were several messages waiting for us, mostly of the "Well done, don't ever do it again" variety. There were a few other requests, asking if we were available for special requests, because there were a few people in Executive Alley who were roundly disliked. As a final note, we received a brief video of the mooning incident, with a note that the Christmas party was going to be awesome this year.

There was one more surprise, in the form of a package at the door. First off, I wasn't aware that we could receive packages. Second, it was for me. I opened the box so Max could have a new place to sit, and looked at it. I didn't remember ordering a shirt. It was large, red, and upon review, it looked a little hockey-ish. The number was ninety-nine, and the name on the back had a consonant-to-vowel ratio that was heavily weighted in favor of Team Consonant. I looked at Elias with undisguised confusion.

She was bouncing with happiness as she went back and forth. "Try it on."

I did and it fit. "So, uh, who's Gret-suh-kee? Hockey player, right?"

From the look on her face, I'd committed some form of sin. Quite possibly a major one. "Grets-kee, how do you get through life not knowing this? He's The Great One, retired over two decades ago - still has sixty records to his name." She took a breath, holding back something obviously, but not going further out of apparent respect for the terminally ignorant soul in front of her.

I filled in the silence after a moment. "My turn. That jersey you keep accidentally borrowing is Number Seven. *The* Number Seven. Held or shared forty-eight records in the league when he retired after back to back championships, showed the entire league how to play the position. Changed the way the game is even played, to the point where up-and-coming players wore seven because it was his number and they wanted be like him. You were wearing that jersey. So...neener."

She dissolved into a fit of giggles. "Neener?"

I nodded. "Yeah. And since you been educating on this hockey thing, my turn. Best game ever, we're watching it."

Elias nodded, apparently amused. "Oh, this I've got to see."

So we parked it on the couch, with her taking a few moments to find a lounging spot that wouldn't bruise or ding either of us as I went searching for the one specific game that would show Elisa what the football thing was about. As she lounged, there was some sort of mental tension that seemed to be flowing away. It felt like we were a small bubble of calm in what was rapidly becoming a storm of chaos. Starting tomorrow, we'd be in the chaos, but for tonight there was just football and us. And Max in the cardboard shipping box that had up until recently held a Gretzky jersey.

The next morning, it was my turn to surprise Elias with the days' plan. We were going to practice the tandem jump thing, first with minimal gear, and then in full kit. Elias was not amused.

"I remind you that I can fly."

"And yet, not parachute qualified."

"Because I can fly."

"We're falling from over thirty thousand feet. It's about a three minute fall, and then we pop a parachute and decelerate from three thousand feet to hit the water gently. Now I can cut you loose a couple hundred feet up along with the raft, but we're going to need to be together for as long as possible to beat any radar return they might have."

Elias chewed her lip for a few moments, weighing various things in her mind. "Fine. When do we start?"

"Soon as you get your wetsuit on. I'mma go get mine on now. No you cannot watch." And with that, I headed over to the locker to gear up. In truth, I needed to take a leak as well. Gearing up was both familiar and awkward, as I hadn't put anything like this on before with a horse half, but the human half was like riding a bicycle. Still, memories came flooding back, some good, other distinctly less so. This was going to be an emotional ride.

Getting into the wetsuit was an ordeal in and of itself. It was a single piece of material that was supposedly going to form fit once I'd gotten into it. Basically I had to bunch it up and slide into it with my back legs first while laying with my stomach in the air. With that accomplished, I had to roll over, stand up, and pull the whole mess forward to get my front legs in, and then finally yoink it up and around for my arms and neck. My fur was going to look awful when I got out of this rig.

As I emerged from my locker, carrying a lot of gear and goods that we were going to need for this first jump. I was checking and double checking everything I was going to need, while Elias had a wetsuit, helmet and oxygen mask.

"Alright Elias, here's the drill. We get up to altitude, and the pilot's going to pop the red light. That means we got one minute. Hook up to me here and here at that point. Be quick, because the next thing he's doing is hitting the yellow light. Turn on your

O2 when you see the yellow light, because he's going to be depressurizing the cabin and opening the back hatch. Once he's done that, hop on my back and hook up to me here, and here. Light goes green, that's our cue to get the hell out. Whatever happens, don't fight me. If I twist or move, shift in that direction. Then sit back and enjoy the ride until three thousand when you get the shock of your life. I'll cut the harness with you and the boat loose at a couple hundred, you glide down and get the motor started, I'll be with you as soon as I hit the water. Got it?"

To my mild surprise, she nodded, her face the all business look.

We entered the plane from the cargo door because there was no way I was going through the regular door with the large parachute and other assorted gear I was going to need. Not going to lie, it was weird watching what looked like an executive "Behold for I am important" jet opening up like a military cargo transport. Maybe it was nerves coming back, but I found myself singing a little song about Bo Diddley and jumping from a big iron bird. I didn't see Elias' face, but I'm pretty sure she was amused.

The ride up was in silence until about 10 minutes. Then things started happening. The pilot killed the cabin lights, and after a moment the lights came back on in a refreshing shade of red, and Elias clambered up and locked herself to the harness. And that's when the shakes started. I heard Elias' voice in my ear.

"What gives?"

I remembered that while she'd read my record, she'd never experienced it. So there were details that had to be filled in. "I'm always like this before a jump. S'normal. Remember, we're about to toss ourselves out of a perfectly good airplane. On purpose."

"And this is somehow normal for you?"

"If you wanted to live the quiet life, you shoulda joined the Air Force."

"Point made, point taken."

I looked at the light. "Yellow, go to your oxygen, strap on and make sure the mask is tight. Breathing's important, and oh by the way it's about to get cold."

The light went yellow, and I started quivering as I checked my own oxygen supply, as all the bad memories tried to force their way to the front at once while the cargo door opened and filled the cabin with light. Finally the light went green, and I was out the back with a ton of gear and Erinyes strapped to me.

It took a few moments for me to realize we were clear, and Elias was having what felt like an absolute panic attack with her thrashing, which was pulling us way out of position. This was bad for several reasons. If she was panicking, she could throw me off when I needed to pull the chute. Which was the exact worst time to panic; with only three thousand feet to play with, seconds were the difference between a harsh but manageable water landing and hitting the water at a speed relatively close to terminal velocity - at which point we might as well be hitting concrete. My options at this point were limited, so I reached back and grabbed her hands, which sent us into a rolling tumble as we fell.

"Elias! Get it together, and stop squirming back there - talk to me, tell what you're feeling, and we'll work it. You're in my part of the air now, this is the part where you trust me to get us there. Think of me as your friendly Irish-Italian taxi driver, huh?"

"Oh-god-oh-what-was-I-thinking-BRRRRROOOOOKS! We're tumbling! I'm freezing and we're tumbling, do something!"

I had to let go because if we kept tumbling like this, we were probably going to barf, and that would make jump number two more fun. I put a little cop in my voice to get her attention. "Elias. You can do this. Seriously, I'm doing all the work here - your job is to stay still for ten seconds, and we'll go left." She stilled, whether that was because she'd passed out or something else, I wasn't sure.

Still, I'd take it. As I demonstrated going left, going right, and altitude checks, I heard her softly say "Holy crap..."

Eventually we got to the magical altitude of three-thousand five hundred, and I gave Elias a final warning to hold on, and said a prayer to Bo Diddley as I popped the chute. The chute flared and downward motion was arrested, severely and suddenly as all manner of weight including me was held back by the parachute harness, and there was one more horrific thing that I'd hoped to avoid.

Me tenders was pinched. And I ain't gonna lie, the only thing that kept this practice going was that I didn't want to deal with a soaked Elias, who was currently screaming over comms to cut her loose. I did not, given the altitude. Finally at about five hundred feet, I cut her loose; at fifty the raft suffered a similar fate. It started inflating as soon as it hit the water. And then I hit the water, and all manner of things started happening.

The first was an epic splash as I hit the water, then I hit my parachute release to get what was now a sea anchor off of me, and finally I swam up and into the boat where Elias was waiting to get us to shore. She hadn't even gotten damp.

"So...chute recovery?" I wasn't entirely clear on that.

"We'll have some teams hit the water tomorrow while we're practicing phase 2. Now, explain what the heck was going on there Brooks you, we didn't, I, we..."

I put a finger over her lips to stop the stream of nonsense. "Elias, you wanna fly in a plane, join the Army. You wanna land with the plane, join the Air Force."

Unkind words regarding my parentage were said all the way back the dock, where we deflated the raft and I squished my way back to the recovery truck, a nice big deuce and a half that drove us the half an hour to the hangar, where the plane was waiting for us to enter and do it all again. We did a quick debrief and checked our approach on a mockup of their targeting radar. Good news, the radar didn't pick us up until three thousand. Bad news, it did pick us up until fifteen hundred. That was bad. And a quick discussion regarding stealth versus detection, it was agreed that I couldn't cut everything loose until fifteen hundred. I said a quiet prayer to safeguard the tenders.

The second and third attempts were, dare I say, routine. The fourth and final jump of the day was spectacular in that Murphys' Law decided we had been having entirely too much success. It started in the plane. We were sorted, checks completed, and then finally we got the proper signals to strap Elias to my back, strap a raft to my stomach, and waddle to the back cargo door.

The door stuck. I should have taken that as an omen, but instead I took it as a dare. I talked to the pilot who told me to just boot the darn thing. I don't think he anticipated that I have a very solid boot. What transpired next was written up later as an uncontrolled exit. To wit, we fell out the ass end of the plane, which caused the pilot some problems. That's what they paid him for, so it was time to do what I was paid for, fall over six miles toward the ground, cut Elias loose, pop a parachute, and then cut a raft loose, and finally land safely.

There was tumbling, but I managed to straighten us out with minimal trouble. Then I realized Elias was beating on my shoulder blades severely. I looked back and saw her oxygen mask/ communications lines leading back to absolutely nothing. We'd lost her stuff on the way out apparently. Which was a bad thing in many ways, in that I did some quick math and realized that while we could make it to ten thousand feet with a rapid (and not recommended by any sane folks) descent, it was going to be very close.

First things first though. I took my mask off and shoved it under her face, and then I waved my hands a little to hopefully give her the idea to hold on. And then I put myself in a facedown position so that instead of the usual calm-ish descent, we were diving straight to the ground and picking up speed rapidly. It was not fun because I was having to remain in a downward orientation, holding my breath, and taking the express elevator to where I could get oxygen into my lungs. After a minute and a half I was not having a good time, and according to my altimeter, we were at about thirty thousand feet.

That couldn't be right. I tapped it a few times, and the needle didn't move. We were definitely below thirty, but without any real way to gauge where we were, I was going to have all sorts of fun trying to figure out when to go through the release process. Time to trust the instincts. Except that my instincts were telling me to breathe, and the air was not cooperating with the plan. I leveled a bit to slow my descent, tried breathing and didn't like the result in the slightest, and finally gave my hose a tug. The hose came back, but the mask didn't. At this point that was a teacup in a tempest as the problems began to mount. Ten quick breaths and then I passed the hose back to Elias. Except that she didn't take it. Whatever it was, lack of oxygen or whatever else, Elias was currently dead weight. Figuratively, although quite possibly literally if I didn't herd us back to the ground with a quickness.

Back to a power dive I went, working awkwardly to make sure Elias was still secure and could breathe, and eventually the air became breathable. One problem down. New problem was that I was going to have to do a tandem water landing and get us both to the raft. And I was not exactly graceful with that yet. I watched my altimeter stubbornly insist we were at thirty thousand feet all the way down to what I gauged to be the right altitude - after all, this whole mess could be a nice live training exercise. Would be their style at this point. I eyeballed the altitude, and when I thought it was right, I popped the parachute and braced.

Friends, you can brace all you want, but it still hurts where it counts. The raft thankfully cut loose and inflated, but the landing was harsh on my everything. No real time to think about my own bumps and bruises, I just cut Elias loose from the harness where she was still passed out and swam toward the raft, which decided it hated me and drifted away. Fortunately, I was swimming faster, and finally I slung Elias in like a sack of potatoes with wings and followed, getting the motor started and guiding us to the dock where our ride home was waiting.

I was no doctor, but once we got in the truck and lurched rapidly forward, Elias finally responded to my impassioned yelling and giving her the last dregs of oxygen from the bottle and sat up blearily.

"Whu...where we?" She wasn't entirely focused, but when she recognized me, she grinned a little.

"Truck. Heading back. You passed out."

"I'm...fine. Just a little dizzy. I don't think your mask was working right on my face."

"Mistress of the Obvious."

"How'd it go?"

"We ain't dead, which was not a guarantee."

"I owe you a beer, Brooks."

"Hold you to it." I finally relaxed a little.

At least until we got back, where the doc looked at both of us and threw his hands up at the both of us. Apparently I was supposed to abort the jump when the cargo door jammed. Speaking of the cargo door, the pilot was highly displeased that I had killed me a cargo door. He could send me the bill later. Finally, there was the debrief. Apparently my internal altimeter sucked, as according to the ground instruments I'd pulled the chute at about seven hundred feet - far lower than anyone sane recommends. The replay was hilarious now that nobody was dead. The fact that there were no serious injuries was a damned miracle. We were dismissed for further discussion and plan revision tomorrow before throwing ourselves at part two, getting in and doing the rest of the thing.

We dragged ourselves to the respective lockers to change and dragged our abused bodies for food and restorative drinks. And more than a few painkillers. I couldn't speak for Elias, but I had an impressive amount of dings and bruises throughout my everywhere. The conversation that night was sparse and mostly consisted of new pains being found as we moved about. On the up side, Elias did bring me a Guinness as we watched highlights of this Gretzky fellow.

That night was full of not-sleep. It was a long chain of nightmares - the Change, my last active mission from the army, and then it melded with the last jump from today where more went wrong than actually went wrong, and instead of the wind, it was my drill instructors berating me for not checking every last thing that was checkable, declaring me to be a weak little mistake who should have died a child and spared them the agony of watching this failure. Jeremiah and Aoife were there, pointedly discussing how stunningly pitiful of a father and husband I was, and cheering for me to die so that they could find a decent replacement. Falling forever as Elias died of oxygen starvation while I couldn't do anything except hold her. The worst of it was Elias' face, looking at me with dead eyes but still talking, asking questions that had no answers.

I woke up with a start, a shout still echoing in my ears as Elias was...hugging me from behind. Max noticed I was awake and loped over to lick my ears. I rolled over to my stomach to disentangle myself from the everyone; there was just too much too close, and I needed a minute and some coffee. Max's voice was in my head first as I stumbled for the bathroom and coffee.

"Brooks. We need to talk."

"I know, crunchies and gooshy food. Gimme a minute." New pains asserted themselves as the necessary was accomplished.

"No, last night. Both of you were bad off, but you were worse. I think she might have been feeding off you a bit."

"Look, analyzing it is not going to help. We're working on stage two today, we'll deal with it tomorrow, rest day before we do the whole thing and start ramping up."

There was a feline sigh in my head. "Brooks, you need to work on this 'I'm Fine' streak you have. You are not fine, and if you wait, it gets worse."

"Tomorrow."

"I'll be waiting for my 'Max was right' catnip. From both of you."

I grumbled and finally looked around. Elias was not doing better than me, hair and feathers askew, and impressively dark circles under her eyes.

"Coffee?" I offered her the mug first, which was half gone before I finished getting mine sorted.

We ate and drank quietly before slugging through to our next practice area, where we had to sprint from point a to point b, open a door as politely as possible, then get our asses down an elevator shaft to the anomalous section, deliver the goods, and finally get the heck out of there. We were working through it all quite nicely when there was a chime on our comms and we were summoned to Executive Alley, where The Elf was waiting for us with an extremely nervous-looking Jeremiah.

The Elf steepled his hands. "We have encountered an issue that requires resolution."

I glanced at Jeremiah. He didn't seem to have any bruises or bumps, so it wasn't another fight. "So what's the issue?"

The Elf kept his fingers together as he ran through. "Analyst Brooks has made a fascinating discovery, in that the local networks that appear to have fire control function have been removed from any form of remote access. In order to make any adjustments, it will be necessary for him to be on site."

I was going to kick Kardar in the teeth. Hard. "Sir, why him?"

"Senior Analyst Kardar made the decision based on multiple factors, which I concur with. Firstly, despite his relative youth, Analyst Brooks is above and beyond the majority of his group. That is a requirement, as he will need to make rapid calculations and execute them properly in order to make corrections in real time. Secondly, he is light-weight and reasonably fit. Adjustments to your proposed plan will be minimal. Thirdly, he is unique in that his non-traditional joining has caused a social rift. Assuming the plan is successful, this will, according to Senior Analyst Kardar, cause the rest of the analysts to look upon him more favorably. I will now hear and dismiss your objections."

I started ticking the objections off on my fingers: "First, weight. Second, the tandem rig. One is tough but doable, two is exponentially worse. Three, swimming to a raft in any sort of seas is going to be problematic. You cannot teach and have someone prepared for all the contingencies of what we're doing in under a week. And I'm bringing this last point up for the sake of completeness, because this should be front and center of this entire thing - standing right there is my baby boy. The one thing I will protect above all other things on this miserable little dirtball. And you want me to carry him into combat. On purpose. That is the sort of request that tends to end in violence."

The Elf extended a spidery finger to begin knocking down the pegs that I had set up. "Determine the new parachute size. Adjust the training schedule accordingly. Utilize Agent Elias to assist you. Prepare him for as many contingencies as possible. To your final point, Senior Analyst Kardar has sent multiple scenarios to my desk at my request. The range of extrapolated possibilities begins with initial death tolls in the millions, and secondary death tolls an order of magnitude higher. If there were someone more suitable, they would be here and not Analyst Brooks. A very large number of lives are depending on your actions, Agent Brooks. Do not fail them."

That sounded an awful lot like "Embrace the suck, or the suck's getting worse." I took a deep breath, realizing that Jeremiah being here was probably going to work simply because I was highly invested in his well-being. Or it was going to go severely sideways because I was too worried about him and not anything else. No middle ground, and The Elf was definitely rolling the dice on this. I took a deep breath before nodding. "Understood. However, this leaves us five and half, six days to get spun up. We're going to need multiple planes and multiple jump rigs for training. We take off, jump, land, and go straight to the next one for take off. Build a damn runway next to our drop zone if you have to. Medic on standby for anything going wrong." I thought about it for a moment before pulling a schedule together in my head as I continued.

"So here's the schedule that's going to happen - rest of today, we're doing weapon familiarization. We're going into combat, I do not want him defenseless. That's going to be the rest of today. Meanwhile, I'm going to be putting in an order for a tandem rig for the three of us, we're going to need several. Starting tomorrow, two straight days of jumping out of airplanes. Get lots of parachutes. Day three - half-day for rest and medical evaluation. The other half of the day and the entirety of the next day is going to be picking up where Elias and I were before we got called in for this. This is not an argument, debate, or negotiation, this is what is absolutely necessary to carry this thing to completion. And it is the bare minimum that I will consider." I spread my hands slightly.

The Elf considered things. "This training schedule includes weapon familiarization."

"Yes it does. Like I said, I want my son to be able to defend himself." My expression was set, daring The Elf to say no to it at his own personal peril.

"You may not perform weapon familiarization in my office. You should be elsewhere for that task."

"Understood." In short, I'd just been given a blanket approval on everything I just asked for. Oh, there were going to be some miserable lives as a result of this. The full force of what was coming hit me once we'd made it five steps out of Executive Alley. Quite honestly, it staggered me. A helpful wall was there to keep me upright, and both Elias and Jere looked concerned for their own safety. I didn't blame them. I took a breath to steady myself a bit before looking back at the two of them. Jeremiah actually spoke up first.

"Dad. I want to do this. I can do this. I have to do this."

"Why? Because someone said? This is insane. There are rules against this - even in the army, where rules are pretty much polite hints most of the time. Family members don't go into combat with each other. It's dangerous. It's a bad idea. It's...how is this even going to work? I mean, I, I..." My words started to fail me, so I looked at Elias for some backup on this. Elias, regrettably, was not picking up what I was putting down.

"Agent Brooks. You came up with the schedule. So now we're gonna follow it. Come on. Range time. We have to find him a sidearm that he can use. And we need to teach him how to use what we're going to be carrying." She nudged my lower shoulder. "Right now, this is where an entire organization rests. Because this can carry the load. There's no backup, no plan B. We are it. Now, are we going to stand here and complain about it being impossible, or are we going to do it and make sure the world keeps spinning?"

Sadly, she was right. It was not fun for at least an hour. We ran to the armory, and finally found a pistol small enough that he'd be comfortable with it. And then we told the range officer to just keep the spares and ammo coming because we were going to be training a lot. The down side of it was that owing to his size, the only pistol we could really find for him was something that was normally used for concealed carry purposes. And that meant he didn't have much ammo. Hopefully we wouldn't get to the point where he needed to do anything because while Elias and I had seen war zones and fighting, Jeremiah was an unknown. We took a break only to get Jeremiah fitted into some body armor, and then we wore it back to the range for several more hours. Finally, we were strongly advised to go to our quarters, on account of the range needed to be cleaned of all the brass rolling around, and Jeremiah was looking a little sleepy and nervous. His marksmanship had improved, but that was no real comfort to me. We put him to bed before Elias and I retired to my quarters.

"You know he's scared, right?"

I nodded. "Yeah. Me too. I mean, who willingly puts their kid in the line of fire? My job's to protect him. Make sure he gets what he needs and make sure he gets to have a family of him own." I flopped on the bed, groaning. "We are in so much trouble. And tomorrow, we're jumping out of a plane with him. We're going to need a harness, strap him to my back or something, and then you're going to have to be right behind him, chute on my chest, and then the reserve, we're gonna need a lanyard so I can pull it to us." And unspoken were all the things that could go wrong, which had been multiplied by a large number. Elias then did an odd thing. She put her head on my chest.

"We're gonna make it. Because even after everything that happened, you're worried. And that worry means you see the problems, and you're going to solve them. Now come on, get up, shower off, and get some sleep. We're gonna need it." She wasn't wrong, and really this wasn't the first time I'd had last-minute changes thrown at me. That said, last-minute changes usually did not bode well, like the time Intelligence changed the drop zone to one that was more 'strategically advantageous' and my entire squad was out of action for a month. Strategically Advantageous was code for "chock full of folks who wanted to shoot me", apparently.

It was not a happy memory that sent me off to sleep.

Chapter 17

The next morning started bright and early at Sammys' House of Making Stuff. There was a fitting to be done, and everyone there was looking a little bleary-eyed. We'd definitely made the coffee suppliers happy, as it looked like Sammy and his gang of madmen had only gotten a few hours of sleep while they worked out how to fit things together. Overall it was concerning. The rig they'd build for me to get into was one part draft horse rig and one part torture device. The boat and other assorted parts were supposed to sling under my lower torso, and connected to the main rig with some heavy cord with a pull-ring to release them at the proper time. Meanwhile, attached to my chest were the parachutes and personal weaponry I'd need. All of this meant my back was free for passenger space, with Jere and Elias riding behind me. Jere was in what was effectively a backpack, and I made sure he was snug but ready to get cut loose by a quick-release. That gave Elias a lot of room behind Jere to move and shift around. On the up side, they'd maximized my carrying capacity. On the down side, maneuvering in the air was going to be difficult. It was time to test it. First test, the pool.

On the up side, we didn't have to climb the steps to the ten-meter platform for our first test series. The idea here was that I would jump off, cut the boat and Jeremiah loose, and then we would all reconvene in the boat. The down side of this was that the way everything was held together, I would not be moving with any sort of speed or grace. Still, there were worse ways to make a living. I waddled toward the edge of the platform and looked over it to where the water was waiting to catch us. And jumped.

The good news was that gravity still worked. The bad news was the same. I barely got Jere and the boat loose before the splashing commenced, and while Elias was in the boat as it was inflating, Jeremiah was bobbing in the water and flailing to grab something solid. Specifically, me. This did not bode well, and it was time to adjust some more. Once we got into the boat, Jere was sneezing and burping a bit - apparently he'd landed belly first and when trying to right himself, he caught a face full of water. This was not good, and called for a poolside equipment re-calibration We got him a full face mask and a thirty-minute supply of oxygen so he didn't have to risk getting his face wet. In addition we reconfigured the quick-release tabs so that I cut both Jere and the boat loose at the same time. After that, we jumped into the shallow end to get him used to having everything on, and he discovered that he could trust his gear. After that realization, his life became pretty swell, and we felt like we could move to stage two of this, actual jumping out of a plane. First at low altitude, then if all went well we could go up a few notches. The training schedule I'd laid out wasn't impossible, but it didn't leave a lot of room for down time. Well, we could sleep after everything was done.

We dried off and collected our gear, and then it was time for our first jump of the day. An easy, low altitude ride, followed by a nice casual hop out and a landing. Lunch was going to be on the ride back. What could possibly go wrong was a list of many items I had in my head. Jeremiah and I were going to hop out at low altitude first, then we were going to try the whole group at low altitude, then finally we'd wrap up the day by trying the whole thing. High altitude, low open, and hit the water for a quick swim and boat to the shore.

The problems began asserting themselves shortly after we took off, when Jeremiah's second airplane flight ever began with him making swift use of the barf bag. I made a note to see if there was something we could do about that. On the up side, if the worst thing that happened was a call to Cousin Ralph, we were definitely ahead of the curve. I checked everything over, checked it again, and Elias was polite enough to get Jere situated where he needed to be and buckled in, after which I did run through a quick list of things to be careful of, including the tenders. The weight wasn't physically heavy. It was however, a stark reminder that anything going wrong would have severe consequences. Even more than the previous jumps with Elias, since if that went wrong I could cut her loose at altitude and she could glide herself down. If something went wrong here, it would be far more problematic. Still, I checked to make sure the comms were working, and for my trouble I got a very weak "Hokay" from Jere in return. The ramp went down, and the light went yellow. It blinked, blinked again, and then it went green.

Once out in the air, I heard a gulp from my passenger and then a little "whoa" from him as we started to freefall. I checked the altimeter, then the backup altimeter, and since this was a first run to get him used to what was going to happen I gave him a three-second warning before I pulled the chute. For me, the shock was familiar. For Jere, it was not. To be fair, I warned him. But the pained wail that came through the comms left me highly doubtful that I'd have grandchildren. On the other hand, I'd jumped out of planes for several years, and Jere was around. The rest of the descent was uneventful, as such things went. I cut the raft loose, it inflated nicely, and then when we hit the water, I cut Jere loose so we could reel the raft in without too much trouble. Elias landed and made no effort to hide the smirk as she bodied Jere in and gave me a spare arm so I could climb aboard and get situated for the ride to shore.

Jere was disconcertingly silent until we made it to the truck where the recovery was waiting to deflate, drag parachutes in, and get us loaded up for a short drive to the very temporary runway.

Then he waved me over for a conversation I could only assume he wanted to have very quietly.

"Dad?" His voice was all manner of uncertainty as far as how to ask the question that I knew was coming, so I spared him a little of the indignity.

"Get the leg straps tight, and lean back a touch. It'll hurt less."

"It's gonna hurt?" He looked like I'd just told him we were going to volunteer as tackling dummies.

"Yep. Get used to it. We're doing two more of these today. Next one's gonna be high up."

"This was a bad idea."

"Yep. But it's still the best idea around. We're gonna have to talk and eat on the way up to our next jump."

"We're doing it again?"

"Two more times today, to be exact. Then, we're going to be doing several more jumps tomorrow just like the last one we're doing today."

"Oh." He did not have the voice of someone who was going to enjoy the near future.

"Hey. Sometimes, you gotta look past the ouch to the good."

"But, I don't have a good. You got Miss Elias. And mom."

I scrunched down onto my stomach and leaned into him as much as the size difference allowed. "You still got Mom. And all the people we're gonna save? Maybe your someone's there, y'know?"

He knitted his brows together in what I'd come to recognize as his "doing the math" face. "The odds are better if we save the world."

"So, let's do that and then worry about your social life. Just remember, lean back."

The second jump went frighteningly well, all things considered. On the way up, there was more air-sickness from Jere. To reiterate, it was not fun watching him send the army version of beef ravioli back to whence it came. Still, they could have given him chili mac that they served me. The culinary mixture of ground beef, elbow macaroni, and various harsh seasonings was the international "we want to see you puke" meal. The folks in charge of meal prep were not happy that I could handle it. That said once we'd jumped out of the plane, there were no oxygen mishaps, faulty doors, and barely a yelp at the opening shock. Jere did however mumble a bit all the way to said opening shock. It sounded like he was doing the math to figure out how long we were going to be in the air. And then after getting over the ouch, there was a sound that might have been disappointment. He was probably off by half a second.

Still, it was nice to just ride down for a bit and finally cut everything loose before hitting the epic belly flop. That stung, but it was time to swim and reel everything in. And after checking the sun, we were running low on time. One last jump with everyone, and we could spend the night sorting out the bumps and bruises and figure out what went wrong.

Finally, it was time for the last test, and we were in a hurry. I stood up, strapped everything to myself, and waited. First for Jere, and then Elias. This whole thing was cumbersome and annoying, and movement for me was down to a slow waddle. On the up side, the door dropped nicely for our exit, and when the green light went I honestly fell more than jumped, which brought a few seconds of everyone getting a little green in the gills before I could right myself and therefore my passengers. And the comms channel was filled with unkind words. Elias hinted that the Air Force could have done a better job, while Jere was mostly filling my ears with the science of air stability. I took it all in stride. After all, this was the first time I'd ever had a double tandem jump, and quite honestly this was a level of insanity that made me think that the folks up at the top were just happy I'd had any sort of an idea at all.

These were the thoughts that occupied my mind as we fell for several minutes, with Jere in the background having settled a bit, he was running through some more calculations in his head to figure out when the ouch was going to arrive and prepare for it. I cut him off when the altimeters hit the magic number - he was off by about twelve seconds - and then opening shock hit and everyone got slowed rapidly. In the fading light I counted up everyone, and then cut Elias loose so she could do her glide thing. As soon as I did, she gave me a light slap on the rump and started a lazy circle so that she could hit the boat as it was inflating. On the up side, that was the worst part of the whole thing. Still, I wasn't too keen on getting my butt smacked while having a second passenger.

It was distracting, almost to the point where I was late cutting everyone else loose. The boat went and hit the water, inflating almost instantly to get all three of us in, and the worst thing was everyone and everything made the boat ride low in the water. We were going to have to do something about that. Overall, the chute was workable, but we needed more room for the boat and motor. All that done, we took the truck around town and back to the base for a quick checkup from the doctor and a sleepless night as my thoughts kept coming back to everything that could go wrong. It was an extensive list, and Elias' wing draped over me like a second blanket was not helping. Eventually I got to a half-doze sort of rest, and the night passed in some sort of awkward fashion.

The next day was a blur. Having requisitioned a larger inflatable boat and a few other small things, it was half a day of jumping out of planes with Jere dry-heaving from his spot, cutting everything loose, and finally dropping into the boat in relative comfort for a quick ride back to the temporary landing strip for another ride to high altitude. After that, we started part two wherein we went to a hangar and used as many plans as we could to infiltrate and make the world safe again. In theory. This was the part we brought Jere for.

During lunch a small package arrived for me from Sammy. It was one of the other things I'd asked for - two sets of jump wings, one for Elias and one for Jeremiah. They'd each made the minimum number of jumps from an airplane - we'd skip the part where they were basically baggage. Jere was all kinds of giggling at the idea, while Elias was feeling bold - she took a deep breath and invited me to pin the wings on her chest. I declined.

A few people had made up some security measures for us to get through, and the most difficult part was giving Jere a boost so he could actually see the display. And in something that eased my mind tremendously, he had a small toolkit with him so that he could physically access things that were hidden. Still, there were problems. We looked at stair access, but it seemed like that wasn't going to be possible. According to the plans we'd found, they'd secured their stairwells by the clever trick of making them too damn skinny for me to get through. I suppose for safety reasons this was a no-centaur zone, but at the same time it forced us to use the elevators.

Again, this was why we were bringing Jere. We broke and entered, reset, and did it all again repeatedly. Finally we called it a day on account of we were getting very sluggish and sloppy, with the last run ending in bruises and bumps that were not expected because we were rushing and taking shortcuts. Still, it was a productive day.

Our last day of training was the worst. We were running the entire mission in one fell swoop, and someone up high decided everything was going entirely too well. Not one of the five attempts went perfectly. Airplane didn't get high enough, engine flame-outs, door failures, and the cherry on top was a parachute failure that could have very easily resulted in a catastrophe had I not instantly cut it loose and gone to the reserve - as it was, the landing was harsh enough that I dislocated both of my right shoulders and limped it until I got to a nice solid wall where I could perform an emergency re-seating. Twice. It was not fun and I saw stars and a pair of highly concerned faces until I waved both Elias and Jere off to hurry up because the clock on the exercise was still ticking.

Once we wound up for the day, the doctor looked over all three of us and was not pleased. Somewhere along the line, everyone had gotten a ding or a bruise. In addition to my dislocated shoulders, we had a list of injuries that was impressive. Bumps, bruises, strains, hyper-extended knees and ankles, and a few chipped teeth rounded out the list. Not entirely unexpected, but still damned impressive considering not one of us asked for a medical timeout. However, the doctor insisted that the last day be scrubbed in favor of us taking a day and recovering. It would be the last day before the actual mission, and The Elf agreed with the doctor. We'd already run through as many simulations as we could, and now it was time to rest and recuperate from our problems. The day after tomorrow was Neo Day, and we were going to need to be as rested as we could, because that was where we put all this training we'd done into practice.

I did not like it at all, since resting gave me time to consider all the horrible things that could happen. Also, it gave me time to think about things that we hadn't quite addressed fully. We were on the couch when the big one hit me, and I nudged Elias with a hoof to address it.

"Elias, quick question. Has anyone, us included, given a thought to how we're going to get the hell out of there once we've done the thing?" I was rather focused on getting in, and the curveball that had been the addition of Jere threw off my personal mission planning quite a bit.

"Yep. Lilbit."

"...And? Tell me we're not doing that skyhook thing again. That is flat out insane." Also, I was fairly certain the Jeremiah would puke up his everything if we tried that with him.

"We're not." I heard a slight tinge of relief in her voice as she said that.

"Then what are we doing?" Whatever plan she'd come up with was going to be the worst kind of fun, if previous missions were anything to go by.

"Taking the boat due south as far as it'll go, then hitting a button."

"And then?" That sounded rather simple. Too simple.

"We wait. we'll have pickup by dawn."

"Pickup by whom?"

"Submarine. Then we go to the retirement village in Hawaii, and then we get a boat to the big island and fly home."

"That's nuts."

"Yep."

"How many submarines do we actually have?"

"We have three submarines, to be exact. We use them to carry people from place to place. Most of the time it's covert luxury travel. It's like a cruise ship, but underwater."

"Has anyone considered the possibility that my ass won't fit in a submarine?"

"Yep. It was discarded. Worst thing that happens, you get stuck in the tower and your butt gets a free power wash all the way to Hawaii. But we've confirmed you'll fit. I took measurements and forwarded them."

I blanched. "You measured. My butt."

Elias smirked. "Yes. Yes I did."

"When, dare I ask?"

"When you were sleeping a few days ago. We cross-checked them against your initial measurements when you got here. You've gained some muscle mass since this started."

Time for a new topic. "So how long is this trip supposed to last?"

"Mm...probably around thirty or forty hours."

"Which is thirty or forty hours longer than I ever wanted to be in a sub. Those things are dangerous."

"Says the fella who jumps out of planes on purpose."

"For good reason - if my chute fails, I've got the rest of my life to figure out what happened and how to fix it. Submarine fails, what's the plan?"

Elias shrugged. "Hold your breath and look for a way up. Just remember, I go in first. Jeremiah goes second."

CH17

The rest of the day was a forced kind of routine, but not. The cafeteria knew what was up, and they sent the three of us a five-course feast with everything except poultry. According to the urban legends, Erinyes were not fond of eating anything bird-ish. My observations didn't really bear that out, since I had seen Elias eat eggs, so maybe there was a cut-off of some sort. In any case, it had something of a last-meal-for-the-condemned feel. I for one was going through fettuccine alfredo and I could have closed my eyes and heard Nona asking when I wanted seconds, because I was a growing boy and I needed my strength. Elias was going through salmon and rice plates at a rate that would have frightened a lesser man. Jere was almost the same, as triple-bacon-cheeseburgers were going into his mouth like they were going to be illegal tomorrow.

"Hey." I nudged Jere a few times with my foot while we were sitting back with drinks in hand and waiting on our respective third helpings.

"Dad, I'm nervous. What if it doesn't work? What if there's something we missed? What if I made a typo?" The training had taken its' collective toll, and he looked rough in the hair and beard department.

"Did you check your work?"

"Three times. And Kardar checked it too. But we won't know until you get there, and you could get hurt. What if..."

I raised a hand before he could spiral. "Jere. M'man. Take a breath and listen. Before you were born, I was doing things like this. Miss Elias was too. We know that things can go wrong, and sometimes they do. When they do, we'll come up with something. We don't have any options otherwise. We can only do as much as we can. Okay? Don't borrow trouble, tomorrow's gonna have plenty of that for us. But for now, we're going to stay up a little late tonight, relax, watch a movie, and then we'll get some sleep." Elias took the opportunity to disappear and change into sweats and a hockey jersey of some team or another.

"Dad?"

"What's up?"

"I dunno if I wanna be alone tonight."

"S'okay. I'll keep the door open for you." I smiled at a memory for a bare moment before other memories intruded and left Happy Memory weeping in the corner wondering what it had done.

"Okay. I'mma scoot and change before movie time."

I put on my lucky jersey and somehow it didn't smell right. I sniffed again and realized I kinda liked it, so I left it on. Max looked pleased at himself for no reason, and we finally arranged ourselves on the couch, with me serving as the backstop for everyone. Elias wedged herself in between my forelegs and arms with her wings up high and acting as a blanket, Jere sprawled on my lower ribcage and promptly fell asleep, and Max kneaded on the un-dinged parts of my butt before curling to snooze. Elias' eyes sparkled a bit as I planted Jere in his bed and came back.

"You're a good dad."

I grunted. "M'alright."

Of course, such a nice moment could not go uninterrupted. Thus it was that there was a knock at the door. Elias sighed in annoyance, getting up and opening the door. It was Lambert, who smiled a bit as she came in.

"I apologize for intruding at this late hour, but I wanted to talk to both of you before you went out tomorrow."

Both Elias and I looked at each other, then back at Lambert. Elias took the lead with the reply. "About?"

Lambert seemed nonplussed. "Your mental states. Both of them. How are you feeling?"

Both of us answered "I'm fine." - it was a nice stereo effect, which caused Lambert to quirk her eyebrows up slightly.

"Would you both consider yourselves under stress at this moment?" Lambert somehow managed to make the question seem like it wasn't silly.

Elias snorted. "If dumb questions had a Hall of Fame, that'd be in it."

Lambert cocked her head. "Would part of that be me?"

"Yes." Again with the stereo response from both of us. A detached part of my brain noted this and seemed to file it under 'Stuff Max is going to bring up later.'

"Why?"

I took the lead on responding to that particular query. "We're about to do a thing. Dangerous, untested, and to make things worse, we're bring along a kid who's greener than the greenest butterbar to ever butter a bar. And, he's my son. If I wasn't stressed, I'd be psychotic."

"Continue."

Elias continued. "We don't need analysis. We need downtime. Tonight'll do. I'm planning on splitting a six-pack with this gentleman, watch something mindless, and find a way to actually fall asleep without having my brain turn over every possible bad thing that could happen and then invent several others. The only reason I know I have a decent nights' sleep is because I have this big fuzzy to put my brain at ease. And I'd like to have that happen without the company of a company shrink, thank-you-very-much."

Lambert smiled. "Very well. I'll leave you to it." She stood, leaning her head slightly and maintaining a very detached look for a moment, before turning and exiting in a very economical manner. It was quite possible she was worried about possible angry words being thrown at her.

After that, Elias made good on her promise, breaking out a bucket of ice and depositing six bottles in it, hauling it to the coffee table where we were both presumably going to watch something.

"So, what sort of bizarre sports thing do you have in mind for us tonight Elias?" I was becoming accustomed to some of her odd behavior and was readying myself for more.

She chuckled softly, leaning into me dangerously close. Still, comfort was taking precedence over protesting that she was well inside the zone, and finally we settled in to watch-but-not-watch a series of hockey fights. Apparently this was a tradition of sorts, and I was willing to go along with it. Still, it was a little fuzzy even with the TV being a fairly high-end deal. I had to as a silly question to start everything off.

"So, uh, what are we watching?"

"The Punch-up in Piestany."

"The what?"

Elias eyed me like there'd been a serious deficiency in my education. "Punch-up in Piestany. You've never heard of it?"

"Do I look like someone who's heard of it?"

She gave me a look that indicated I was about to get educated. "So in the mid-nineteen-eighties, there was a junior hockey tournament in Piestany, in what was then Czechoslovakia. There was a brawl between Canada and the Soviet Union that lasted twenty minutes involving both teams; got bad enough the arena officials turned the lights off. Funny story, it did not help. Both teams were ejected from the tournament, and well, nobody was happy. Still, Eighteen minute bench brawl. Shush and watch."

I shushed and watched while Max kneaded on my back and kept rolling around contentedly. After that one was over, we went to a different clip with different uniforms.

"This isn't the same teams, right?" I was pretty sure I was right.

"Penny for smart lad. This one's the Saint Patricks' Day Massacre. It a spirited affair, and, well, pretty standard stuff - it was the Norris Division, which in itself was basically a decade-long pit fight on skates with the occasional goal thrown in to keep it interesting."

"They do this a lot?"

"Not really, this is just kind of a best-of tonight. After this it's the Good Friday Massacre, and then the Brawl in Hockeytown, which is one of my favorites honestly."

I opened my mouth, closed it, then opened it again. "Do they all have names?"

"Just the good ones."

I didn't really have anything to say about it, so we basically sat back and watched a good hour of lead up, fighting, and then a few instant replays when something truly confusing happened. Overall, it wasn't the worst evening I'd ever had. Certainly not the best, but one of the better ones definitely. Once everything was done, I thought about it and realized that I hadn't worried about the mission in the slightest.

Morning arrived, and the mission thoughts began. Quite honestly, I barely noticed who was where - for myself, I spent an extra-long time in the shower rinsing off and getting my head in the right place. Then I got dressed in the brown t-shirt and standard battle dress top, which went unbuttoned for the time being. I didn't want to change again until everything was done. Unfortunately, I couldn't wear the standard pants, as my pants area was not standard. For this one it was a kilt with a under-liner and a strategic split for my tail. With that, we were ready for the day. We gave Max skritches and a little catnip on the way out.

We went to the cafeteria for breakfast because it was apparently some sort of tradition for the folks going out on important missions. Though there were a lot of folks there, the conversation was almost non-existent, with most of the talking being centered around condiments. The line cooks didn't even ask us what we wanted, they simply handed us steak and eggs to start off with. Elias and I shared a glance, but Jere was a little confused.

I nudged Jere and crouched so as to not break the library-like silence with the whisper. "So back in World War Two, when aircraft carriers were preparing for large engagements, they'd serve the pilots and flight crews steak and eggs for breakfast. It's a good thing, but not at the same time." Jere swallowed and nodded, keeping quiet. We ate in silence, each of us in our own worlds as we ran through our parts in the coming hours. Then we packed up and headed for our final brief before we left.

Quite honestly, I'm not sure who was more nervous in the briefing room. We got our final loadouts, armor, and other accouterments of making the world a better place through discrete violence. Someone had taken the phrase "better to have and not need than need and not have" to heart. Nonlethal shock munitions for Jere while Elias and I were given significantly more lethal loadouts. I had a pistol, battle rifle, and a special present from

Sammy - a very large double-barreled shotgun with rounds that were variously lethal, non-lethal, and door-breaching.

Along with that was a baton, wetsuits, body armor, and a boat with a special coating to prevent radar return, along with the sundries such as oxygen, emergency oxygen, a couple knives, 3 days rations, water, and a small technical kit filled with about a dozen things to overcome the unknown. Just in case we had to improvise. After that was radio frequencies, check in times, and our callsigns. Elias was renamed Tisiphone for the purposes of this, and I was dubbed Secretariat. There was a heated discussion immediately after that. I did not disagree with Elias being dubbed for one of the Furies who punished murder, but several years of horse jokes did not endear me to this particular callsign. Also, Man O'War was right there. It wasn't that they had no sense of humor, but that sense of humor was skewed toward annoying me. I wondered if they'd done a psych profile and determined I was more efficient when I was grumpy. Jeremiah blinked a little as he received the callsign Blackbeard. Well, it fit, since what we were doing was probably piracy in some way. Also, if this mission lasted more than thirteen hours, he was going to need a shave.

Lastly was the whole reason we were taking this trip. A nice rugged laptop for us along with a spare laptop, tons of connectors to fit into anything they might have, and it also had wifi. Hopefully, that along with Jere's brilliance would allow us to readjust the spin rate of whatever was coming down the pipe and send it elsewhere. Worst case scenario - well, worst case scenario involved a lot of death. With that, Kardar dismissed us to the hangar, where we'd get our wetsuits on, boots adjusted, and load up for a long flight to an uncertain future.

In the hangar, a rarity. I had two people to help me get dressed. Apparently they didn't trust me to dress myself properly - looking at what they had laid out for me, they were probably right. Most

daily wear was set up specifically so that the act of dressing was a
solo operation - even the wetsuit I'd had in the training runs was
situated such that I didn't need any help getting it on or off. This
was not that.

First, there was a body stocking that hugged my everything
and was there to prevent muscle strains. Then, the wetsuit because
the ocean was going to come into play here. After that, a rather
modified battle uniform with some urban camouflage in a
predominantly gray color. Loads of pockets for everything, and
I felt myself going back to the good old days. The uniform itself
had a multitude of secondary pockets where they slid in some
high-grade armor to protect my most vital of vitals. The upper half
was interlocking and only a little cumbersome. Once I was done
and got a chance to look myself over, I was doubly unhappy that
the Man O'War callsign was not in use. The entire look was one
part pack horse and one part commando. I did have one additional
question once I was all geared up, given that I was going to be
wearing this for a significant amount of time. How exactly was I
expected to take a leak in all this.

The two assistants shared a look of "We didn't think about
that" that rapidly turned into a panic when they realized that it
could get severely nasty if I was in there for an extended timeframe.
There was a huddled conference, and adjustments were made in
the form of a pair of velcro closure to allow for me to let things
out. It wasn't perfect, as I couldn't complete the production by
myself while fully geared up. I could hear Elias volunteering to
assist from the other side of the hangar. And that was an awkward
thought. The solutions were to not take a leak (not happening,)
find a workaround with some modified gear (possible but
potentially painful,) or have Elias help (most likely, but also
awkward as heck.) I sighed inwardly as I prepared to inform Elias
of her new additional duties on this trip. She was geared up, but not

nearly as heavily as I was - she still needed to glide at least a little on this trip. She simply nodded her acknowledgment before going to my rear and braiding my tail. That said, I did see her wingtips flutter.

Finally after all of this, we both went out to inspect Jeremiah. At my insistence, he'd been given gear for every thing I could foresee. He was swaddled up and looked almost comical - the scaled-down gear with a flotation device, sidearm, laptop, backup laptop, and toolbelt made him look like the worlds' most dangerous handyman. Well, the second-most dangerous. There wasn't exactly a fanfare as we boarded the plane and strapped in, but we were walking through a heavy cloud of tension and exhaustion.

The plane had been fixed, and the interior had been stripped to the barest of essentials. We had several hours of flight time ahead of us, and unfortunately for Jere, minimal network access. It was going to be a long flight as we settled in with the mission plan for one final look-see. We'd been told there would be an inflight meal, and we also had three people on the flight crew instead of the usual two, with one being tasked to keeping us updated on our progress, giving us a headsup when we were about an hour out to give us time for last minute prep, and acting as the jumpmaster. The flight itself was shaping up to be the easiest part of this. As soon we we were clear to move, Elias was leaning on me and looking at me like she wanted to say something. Whatever was going on in her mind was unspoken, and she decided she'd rather re-braid my tail and comb it out with her fingers for a couple hours. Jere for his part was plugged into the planes' systems, and he was apparently listening in on something.

Chow was military grade rations, and they were just as awful as I remembered. After that, there was nothing to do but go over the plan and get our faces ready to fight our way in. Eventually, everyone took a nap. Even Jere, who had hated naps since the concept had been invented. The sun was just getting starting to get low when the jumpmaster kicked us up to get ourselves ready for last prep. We stretched, getting the kinks out and went over all our gear one last time, ensuring it was in fact stowed and secured properly. Then came the awkward time of "Everyone go to the bathroom". It was awkward. Elias was quite professional in her face, but her grey eyes were sparkling with mirth as everything was unseated and reseated. The lights went yellow to alert us to go to our individual oxygen supplies. There was a flurry of activity at that point, with everything being stowed, Jere getting secured to my back, then straps being secured tightly so I could make the ten-foot waddle out the back of the plane. Finally Elias checked everything one more time before she touched her forehead to mine, whispering "For luck" as she got onto my back and secured herself to me. Okay so it wasn't actually a touch, it was more of a headbutt. Still, there was a sense that if everything went well, we were going to have a long conversation.

The door opened, and the light went green. The jumpmasters of my past exhorted me to move my ass, and so I did. As I leaped out, I was startled. I could see the space elevator from where we were, and it was so indescribably large - how they did that without anyone knowing was a miracle in itself. And that they could turn it into a weapon was frightening. But back to business. My oxygen was good, and after a quick comm recheck, Elias said hers was good as well. I could hear Jere over the communicator making noises of amazement. No trouble in the first thirty seconds - this could be a miracle. Jere, for his part had gotten over whatever stomach ailments had troubled him in previous jumps and was making some odd humming noises and muttering half-sentences over the comm channel. Finally he actually managed a full sentence.

"Hey Dad?" His voice carried uncertainty in it.

"Secretariat, whatcha got Blackbeard?" I didn't want to overtly remind him that at this point, we weren't Dad and Son, but teammates on a mission.

"Oh. Uh, I'm not receiving any sort of transmissions from the space elevator."

"Blackbeard, advise in detail."

"Well, I've been monitoring transmissions around the Poseidon tower. Normally there's traffic between all three. About ten minutes before we jumped, the traffic's gone to zero. What, uhm, what's that mean?"

I thought for a moment before replying. "Blackbeard, it means they're done talking - they're about to start doing. It's not a good sign. Continue to monitor and advise if anything changes." Hopefully he'd be occupied by the space elevator and a job to remember that he might want to barf at some point. I switched the comms over to a private channel for myself and Elias.

"Tisiphone. Blackbeard reports the target's gone radio silent. We're sixty seconds from release, we might want to get ready for anti-air. Just in case someone on that platform has good eyes."

Her reply was not a positive one. "Make sure you're loaded for bear when we board the platform."

With that, we both went quiet until it was time for parachute deployment. Then there were the accompanying ouches and suppressed noises of pain from everyone as we decelerated rapidly. I looked up, confirmed the parachute had in fact deployed properly, and started steering us toward the platform, which started looking ominously large. Finally we separated out, first Elias, then the boat, and then Jeremiah right as we hit the water.

This was not the calm lake water we'd been jumping into, this was the freezing swell-filled Pacific Ocean. And it was not going to cooperate at all with our plans. Fortunately for us, we'd confirmed everything was tied together, so it was a theoretically simple matter of bringing four objects to the same spot. It was nowhere near simple in reality, as Jere's mask had popped loose and was dangling free while his face was punched by the ocean a time or twelve before I could body him up and into the boat, at the cost of my own face getting bashed against the side. That did not feel good, especially when both Jere and Elias looked at me with concern. I rubbed my face and my hand came away wet and red - joy, I'd broken my nose and hadn't realized it in all the excitement. Well, this was certainly starting off in and epic fashion. We sent Jere as far forward as we could get before I sat in the middle and faced backward so Elias could set my nose and then start driving this party of three to our reservation for mayhem. The nose setting was a painful process, even with a snort of anesthetic from our medical kit. Still, I wasn't going to let a little thing like a broken nose slow me down. Okay it wasn't a little thing, and it hurt like the dickens, especially when the salt water tried to go up my nose. And honestly, it was probably going to put me off my game just a skoche.

Still, we were underway - checks were redone, Jere continued to monitor what was ahead to see if we'd been detected or we'd become the target of folks who objected to our arrival without prior announcement. The space elevator kept getting larger and larger. And the ocean was getting rougher and rougher. It was like we could get there, but it wasn't going to be easy. Fortunately, we had plenty of power in the motors to get us there. The getting out was starting to look dicey. We were going to have to find somewhere to recharge the batteries on this thing if we planned to go more than a mile out.

Finally we hit the docking berths on Poseidon Island, and life was good for all of fifteen seconds after we secured our way out. We picked our way across the outer tarmac and finally hit the entry tower of the elevator proper, and finally called up our schematics to find the door. It was odd - there weren't any guards anywhere, the place was deserted. I started getting twitchy. All the people we'd seen before, all the activity was nonexistent. It was a technological ghost town, and while it (probably) wasn't haunted, it felt haunted. Jere unslung his laptop from its' place and was able to forge a keycard for us to get in, at least as far as the door. from there, we were hauling ass, when a speaker came to life with an announcement "Ten minutes; all personnel stand by for an announcement from Gerald in ten minutes."

Well, that was certain to be an announcement filled with good news. It did however punctuate the fact that we were under a time crunch; we rechecked the maps to make sure there hadn't been any changes since last time we were here and started hauling ass to the elevator shaft. The lights changed to a deeper shade of yellow and there was even a gentle melody being played, interspersed with a request for security to report to a specific section. We checked where we were, and it was indeed our section. Nothing for it but moving as fast as possible. Quiet was optional, really. And now it was really time for me to earn whatever pay I was making. We found the elevator door and opened it. Well, to be specific, I wedged a hoof in the crack and pushed the door aside while Elias hooked a few things to the door so we could rappel down. Here went nothing. The rappel down was easy, and as we hit the floor we needed to get to, the speaker chimed again, announcing five minutes until Gerald was going to make an announcement.

The second elevator door did not want to cooperate and open - the alert we'd triggered had also sent all the elevators to a neutral station, and also prevented us from opening the doors gently. We glanced at each other, having a conversation that consisted entirely of shrugs and gestures before we settled on a plan. Elias dug through and found a very small cutting torch, and with a little help from Jeremiah found the three things that needed to be cut.

The door decided to stop fighting us after that, and a couple quick glances ensured that we were apparently clear.

Finally we all tumbled out to a nice wide well-lit hallway, and that was the good part. The bad part was that we were most certainly not clear, and they were not bound by any niceties such as not killing and approaching from one angle. We went back into the shaft and I slammed the door shut as a grenade landed right in front of me and went off impressively, followed by a second. After a beat I reopened the door to smoke and chaos; Elias took two steps and launched herself to a ceiling-scraping flight going left, leaving me to deal with the second group on the right. I chucked a grenade of my own and picked most of them off before checking to make sure I was going the proper direction with Jere. Unfortunately, someone who was supposed to be unconscious refused to follow the script, and one last grenade floated my way, exploding and sending shrapnel fragments all over. Including the parts of me that were not covered in body armor. I was having a conversation with someone when this was done. I tapped my ear to get a comm channel to everyone.

"Tisiphone, start talking. Which way is up and which way's our destination?"

"Fifty meters north, then twenty east."

"Anything interesting between there and here?"

"A lot. Looks like ten to fifteen, they know where we're going, and they got a good chokepoint set up."

"Watch your wings darlin', these folks have no respect for well-groomed fur or feathers."

The surprise in her voice was evident. "What-da-duly noted."

"Blackbeard, can you kill their comms?"

"Uhm, uh, no. Not without a couple hours. Their stuff's good. I'd take theirs, but you kinda broke them."

Well, there went that plan to cause mayhem in the ranks. I debated for a moment what the next step would be as we held our spot for a moment. While I could certainly prefer to keep this clean in deference to Jere's presence, it was going to be difficult.

"Blackbeard, call up a floorplan - find us a secondary access route. You and Tisiphone take that route, I'll be here to keep 'em busy."

"You can't do that da-er...you can't! That's fifteen of them and one you."

"I'm not planning on dying. We can't take the straight route, and time's ticking. You find the route, and you do the job you're here to do." I knelt down to give Jere a hug. "You'll do good. Find another way in. Take Tis. Make the world a better place."

Jere swallowed, nodded and got after it. Elias gave me a look as they retreated away.

"Hey Tisiphone?"

"This better be good Secretariat."

"I need a lot of ammo and some weapons, think those unconscious guys could spare me theirs?"

My response was a rattle and slide sound as two assault rifles and multiple ammo bags came flying at me. It wasn't bad, but I was going to have to keep them entertained.

So I did. I set the liberated rifle to burst, and my own to single-shot fire, tossing smoke and gas grenades first to let them know that I had come to make their night awful. While pausing in the shooting I was more than happy to catcall them about how many people we had (more than three), their ability to shoot (so poor one might think they were getting paid to miss), and their mothers' life choices (poor with the singular exception of their choice to have a meaningful overnight relationship with me.) All the while I was picking off the most mobile shadows and dodging return fire, which included the occasional grenade that had fuses long enough for me to have half a moment to aim before throwing back. Meanwhile I was getting updates on Jere and Elias' progress, with the occasional cough from Jeremiah when I said something to the guards that would have gotten his mouth washed out with soap.

They tried to shout insults back, but they didn't have much in the tank. Apparently I was not dealing with the best of the best, and it showed. After one particularly unkind comment hinting that they were quiet because they had to look up what I'd just just said in the dictionary, they all gang-rushed me and it was straight pandemonium with a blur of my hooves, their horns, and shots fired. Finally I'd taken the last of them down and silence reigned supreme. I let them know that I was clear, and proceed to stack the generally unconscious forms neatly so we could get out at a dead run if we had to. Even with my earbuds protecting me, it was still hard to hear after that exchange. A final chime from the speakers was barely audible to me, before Geralds' voice came over the speakers.

"Hello everyone. Since I'm talking to a large number of people both the Unchanged and the Neotypes, I do apologize if this sounds odd."

My comms crackled a bit in my ear. " - to Secretariat, come in."

I bristled a bit. "Go for Secretariat, over."

A new voice broke in. "Da-Secretariat, he's on all the channels everywhere, and looks like it's real-time. We're on station, and I think I can do this. We were right, this is the secondary fire control. Are you okay?"

I checked over my body for anything untoward or life-threatening. There were a lot of dings and scrapes, and I'm pretty sure there were several cuts from the grenade earlier, but definitely better than it could have been. "I'm fine, get back at it."

The door to Gerald continued as I kept the hallway clear. "Celebrating Neoday has become a tradition, where we see the beauty in the diversity of what we all are, what we can become, and most importantly what lies before us all. However, there are those who wished to use this celebration to cause a great harm to all of us. A group calling themselves Genesis One Twenty-six created a carcinogen from research begun in my own labs, research that has since been halted. It was- " Gerald paused for a moment to gather himself before continuing. " - It was research that was supposed to end cancer at the genetic level. The research was taken, and subsequently altered to further their own cause - specifically, the death of every Neotype in the world. This carcinogen would have doomed every Neotype to a slow, painful death from multiple cancers simultaneously attacking the body. I am pleased to say that effort was thwarted." He paused for effect, and I was cranky. The twerp was claiming my work was his doing. Mine and Elias', but still.

"However, such an act of unprovoked, naked aggression cannot stand alone. The scales must balance. And so it is that this response is necessary. To remind those who demand our death for the crime of existing that there will be retribution."

There was another pause, as something apparently changed. "Here. Here is where retribution begins, and here is where the folly of such misguided action will end."

A radio blip came in. "Secretariat, he's showing the Bay of Bengal, the Med, and the Gulf of Mexico."

I exhaled. "Less talking, more trajectory-altering. I can hear backup coming." And they were, and thanks to the first security group acting like they were the personal favorites of the Ammo Fairy, I really didn't have a whole lot left to greet them with. It was time to conserve ammo as much as I could. I bunkered down and gave them a polite but firm warning shot. Just one.

"These three locations are where the hate has found it's most fertile soil, and it is here that we shall strike back first. I want there to be peace, but if peace must be purchased with lives, then so be it - but always remember as you mourn, that you, the Unchanged, could have prevented this." The folks who didn't want us here disregarded my warning and charged in en masse. No real tactical thinking on their part, they were just trying to use numbers to overwhelm.

It was a mess in every sense of the word - there were many of them and one of me, however it took about three of them to make one of me. That said, these Oni were definitely better than the previous ones. Not great, but not bad. It made me wonder if they were saving the best for last. Unfortunately the numbers were beginning to take their toll, and I was wearing down. It was time for tactical retreats, particularly when I felt a stab in my lower left shoulder. I looked to see that someone had in fact put a knife where a knife ought not to be.

I backed up a bit but I didn't leave the door too far away. That would have been the worst thing I could do. If I left the door, both Elias and Jeremiah would be in significant peril. And that would be something I couldn't live with. It was a rough time of it, and I was in the middle of a mess. I broke out the shotgun and began making good work of it. The casualties began mounting as they would surge and retreat from each direction. During the retreats I did as much as I could to make the following surge as difficult as possible. I was grim work, but I stacked the bodies of the dead and wounded to form barriers I could us as cover for my legs - there weren't enough for me to make any higher cover and for that I was marginally thankful.

Elias' voice came through my earpiece. "Secretariat, Gerald's got trajectory lock on all three sites, looks like he's about to start doing something massive. We've got the altered numbers in and according to Blackbeard the numbers are good. All we can do is wait."

That was music to my ears, but the rest of my body was in some peril. A third group was peeking around the corner and making moves to split up and try attacking from both directions. They saw the results of the first and second en masse charges, and two directions was their best option under the circumstances. They came at me again, and it was their dismay after a few moments - I bucked forward firing my hooves at both of them in rapid succession, demonstrating for anyone who was paying attention why you don't get behind a horse. The lesson was not lost on the rest of my assaulters, as going hand-to-hand definitely favored the guy with four solid kicking legs, at least at the outset. They decided it was time to regroup and possibly find new ways to come after me. Which honestly was just in time, because I was running out of energy. Adrenaline was still surging, but parts of my body were making themselves known in a hungry-thirsty-painful manner. Some things I could fix, and I chugged some water while checking the downed guards for communications I could use to listen in. I was able to find one, as the lights dimmed three times in succession, and a few moments later the entire structure shuddered. It was not a pleasant feeling, really.

At that point, everyone stopped. Both the assaulters and myself looked up and around. We all had an idea of how large the space elevator was, and for something to make it move at all was large and-or fast. I closed my eyes and hoped that we'd been able to complete everything. The ones assaulting heard something in their earpieces and retreated rapidly. At that moment, it felt foolish. The whole of civilization was riding on a sixteen year old newly changed Dwarf who was currently speed-running through puberty. I would have laughed at it, had the whole of civilization not been riding on his typing speed. It was a silence that stretched through eons before there was a static crackle in my earpiece.

"Tisiphone, Secretariat, this is Blackbeard. We're clear for evac. Two of the projectiles scattered and the third one is on a decay orbit, it's probably going to hit the sun next year." There was a pause. "It was supposed to deorbit to the sun in less than a year. Darnit. And, uh, I grabbed some stuff so the system thinks we're security, and uh, I mighta forged some stuff to make the security think we're going in another direction and trying to sabotage some stuff. That might keep 'em busy for about twenty minutes so we can take elevator out."

That's my boy. The door opened and Elias whistled lowly at the carnage I'd wrought in the hallway. I grimaced a little, realizing that Jere didn't really know this part of me and it might be a little shocking for him. It was, as he looked down, looked up, and promptly turned around and deposited his last several meals into the nearest trash can. I couldn't blame him, as I checked myself over there was blood pretty much everywhere. Even on the ceiling, which was impressive in some ways. I pitied the cleaning crew for a moment before I glanced at Elias.

"Tisiphone, I got five rounds left. Total. Nothing to scavenge here so, maybe we get gone?"

Elias nodded, and Jere finally finished filling the trash can. "C'mon kiddo. Let's get ourselves somewhere safe." She picked him up and we started moving slowly, backtracking to the elevator shaft as Geralds' announcement concluded.

"I and the Power Company will be taking our leave of you. We will be watching. When you finally take your first steps outside the lunar orbit, know that we will be there and will treat you as you have treated us. The decisions you make, will be made." The speakers went silent, and Jere finally looked up once it was clear.

That sounded tremendously ominous. But we still had problems. To wit, getting the hell out of here and to the rendezvous coordinates. If all was right, that was going to be a smooth ride.

It was not. We were about halfway to the elevator, when Jere cleared his throat. "Ah....Ah Da-Secretariat? I gotta pee."

I cursed a few times. Once because the parental 'now?' question was right at the tip of my tongue, and a second time because, well, I kinda had to go too. Great, so now the new mission was to find the nearest latrine. It was a bit of a maze, but we found it and subsequently had to take turns - one of us utilized the facilities while the other two stood guard. Until it was my turn, at which point Elias was professional. We were still on the clock, otherwise I would have ditched and taken care of everything without any assistance. Also of note, multiple pains from all my fighting in the hallway were beginning to assert themselves aggressively. It was chancy if I would have been able to manage everything by myself even if I had my normal unarmored range of motion.

We exited to see Jere doing a "holy heck this is important" wave at his laptop. "I found her! She's here, she's here, she's heeeeeere-" I finally waved him down.

"Who's here?"

"Becks. I looked for Mom too, but...she's up. She went. But Rebecca's here. she's here and it looks like she's in some sort of detention thing. We gotta get her."

I shared a look with Elias. The longer we were here, the worse the odds were for us to get to a happy ending. That said, if we bailed on Rebecca when we had a chance to get her out, there was no way we were leaving with Jere. At least not conscious. If it came to it, I could hogtie him and toss him where he needed to go, but at the same time it was not a pleasant thought. Elias scrunched up her face and seemed to be debating.

Whatever we had to do, we had to do it quickly. I shouldered my liberated weapon and touched her wingtip. "If I were in a bad spot, would you come get me if you could?"

Elias swallowed, nodding. "Even if I couldn't. Let's do this."

We both looked at Jere. "Okay Blackbeard, where's this detention area?"

He started typing rapidly, "Level twenty-one, room eighty-seven."

I paused for a moment. "Okay, does that mean we go up or down?"

There was more typing and a pause. "We're on level forty-two, so the answer to the question is 'down'. Far down. There's a locker down a few levels that we might be able to raid for stuff."

"Do we have elevator access? Unless you want to hop on while we go." I paused. "The elevators in this place aren't exactly reliable, and if security has them locked down, we're hosed." I glanced to Elias who nodded her agreement.

First things first before we did this rescue thing. We took stock of the situation for ammo and a quick check for dings and dents. There were a few, but nothing major. Ammo was a problem of sorts. We checked the map for security stations and found that one had been set up at level twenty-one. Right where we needed to go. This day was turning out glorious.

I thought things over for a moment, and heaved Jere onto my back. That wasn't exactly a mistake, but he'd gotten dense, and my back wrote a stern letter to management regarding recent treatment. My back was advised to deal with it, and we started down the stairs to our first goal, to wit getting some more gear for this fight the was going to happen.

Shockingly, the stairwells were clear of anyone who would want to hurt us, but at the same time that made it worse. Presumably whoever was running security had decided on a strategy of bottling us up and forcing engagement where they had strength, rather than sending two or three at a time after us. A good strategy and while I certainly approved of it in an academic sense, it was going to make my life more difficult.

Twenty flights of stairs and unholy tension later, we found the fight we we looking for. Jere hopped off and bolted back up for cover while I charged forward, not wanting to use my ammo up on these unhappy campers. Six of them and to of us would normally be bad odds, but somehow Elias and I knew exactly who was doing what and where we were going next. It was breathtaking, and the small logical part of my brain noted it as something to be reviewed later.

The second part of this came when we found an undamaged comm system that they were using. Life was good. Jere listened in and made some reports to send troops off in another direction - hopefully that would buy us some time. meanwhile, Elias and I went through their pockets for ammo and various other things that would help us in the next few parts of this where we would be going up and then out.

But other things needed to be attended to first; namely where Rebecca was and how we got her out of wherever she was. Our first real problem was that there was no level twenty-one. We went from twenty to twenty-two. We went right back up to level twenty and Jere found a computer that was attended by someone who made a bit of a fuss about security right up until I smacked him with the blunt end of my rifle. He cooperated after that, and Jere gave me a look that spoke volumes about how he was seeing me.

The security office itself wasn't much - a single monitor, a large safe, and a few readouts showing power usage, power generation, and net gain/loss. Once again I admired their commitment to their core mission, even if their secondary mission was a bit off the rails. The impressive part here was the design. The cells were clear plastic, and highly resistant to physical damage if the readout could be believed. Access to the twenty-first floor itself was a single port that would rotate down to create a ramp, allowing for someone to come down to provide food or allow someone to come out.

The cells themselves had three modes: Unpowered, socialization, and isolation. Unpowered was the default, with the cell being unused. Socialization mode appeared to be a large video chat of sorts, while isolation was a minimal-power mode with all the walls opaqued. That appeared to be a punishment, as along with the dimming of lights they would also activate speakers that, if I was reading it right would alter the occupants' mental state to one that was relaxed and willing to accept suggestions. High on the suggestion list was "Don't do that again". I glanced at Jere as he was absorbing a lot of information regarding what was happening to Rebecca and he was not liking any of it.

Chapter 18

Jere began punching buttons furiously before the ramp lowered. Then he began punching more buttons to open the locks. Unfortunately, it seemed like there was not a remote-open option, even after a few minutes of very loud typing. Finally with a very angry sound, Jere did kill the keyboard. And the monitor besides. And there was nerd fury in his voice while he was speaking something under his voice. Time to get him re-focused. I nudged him with my shoulder.

"Hey. easy. This is your party, but we're all here. She the only one in here?"

"Yeah. Looks like everyone else went up."

"Find out what she was in for?"

"Officially, fighting or assault or something. Unofficially, someone wanted a date, she said no, he didn't get it, and there was punching."

"Ah. Let's go find her then."

We hustled up a flight of stairs, down a ramp, and followed Jere as he beelined through the complex and then stopped at one cell that had been opaqued, looking at it and then feeling around the edges. Finally he found what he was looking for - a nice shiny keypad - and started tapping in numbers. There was frustration evident as it didn't work the first four times, and I could see him making a fist. I tapped him again to get his attention.

"Hey. Blackbeard. Think for a second. Does this thing have any wires or anything you can see?"

He paused to look it over. "Nuh. But I can't see anything."

I nodded over to a clear cell. "No wires there either, though, right?"

He looked, pulling out something from his bag of gear. "No...looks like it's a inductive wiring system of some kind. Which...wait. I got something for this." He yoinked out his laptop, connected a little rubber sucker to the wall and started pounding keys furiously while Elias and I took up station to ensure that Jere was undisturbed. Finally the walls went from opaque to clear and doorway slid down, revealing Rebecca.

Her time at Fisticuffs had done her some good. She'd put on muscle, and looked like she'd have a few suitors at hand in a very short time. Her face however, was a different story. Her eyes were empty of emotion, and it looked like she'd gotten more than a few extracurricular punishments while she was here. What she was wearing seemed to be meant to embarrass her rather than cover her with any dignity. She looked flatly at Jeremiah for a long moment.

"Aren't you a little short for a -"

Jere tippytap danced on his feet, not letting her finish the line. "We're here to rescue you! C'mon, Da- er, Secretariat's here, c'mon we're going to go - hurry hurry hurrrrrryyyy - we're running out of time before it gets bad."

Rebecca blinked at Jere a few times, finally recognizing and slowly shuffling forward to touch his face. "J...Jere-bear?" He nodded leaning his head into her hand.

There was a moment before she all but crushed him in a hug. I felt bad breaking it up, but this was not the place for a happy reunion. So I only coughed a little.

"We, ah, we gotta get out of here. Then we can talk. C'mon, we'll find you something to wear."

Rebecca looked at me; "Mister, Officer Brooks?" And finally she looked at Elias. "This isn't a dream, is it?"

Elias shook her head grimly. "If it is, it's a rather awful one. Come on *aakíikoan*, let's get you where you can breathe free."

I made a mental note to ask Elias what the heck that translated to as we headed out and up. From the look of things, Rebecca was limping and the stairwell up was not an option Jere had noticed it too, and pointed at a door. "Here, cargo elevator. I got it secured while I was opening the door."

Why that little scamp of a genius.

We hit the cargo elevator and took stock. I had five rounds left, Jere had a lot of ammo but I was not going to take anything from him, especially since his ammo wouldn't fit in my rifle. Elias was down to two from what she'd scavenged, abut she seemed more comfortable with her baton. Still, the way up seemed clear which gave us better than average odds of getting to our boat and getting the heck off this heap without anything else bad happening.

Friends and neighbors, I am nowhere near that lucky. The four of us stepped onto the platform where our boat was, only to find a loose circle of security forming a ring about twenty yards around. Along with that was the biggest, ugliest Oni I'd ever seen with a tremendously large sword to overcompensate for something. And even with only five rounds and collectively outnumbered two to one, I was still pretty confident. Taking a sword to a gunfight usually worked out pretty well for the guy with the gun once there was a certain distance involved. On the down side, it was still the dead of night and the ocean was making itself known by crashing against the side of the platform, throwing spray everywhere and making visibility a wreck. Also, the saltwater was doing my broken nose absolutely no favors. He pulled the sword out as I raised my rifle. I spoke first.

"Don't make me pull the trigger, friend. There's nothing to gain here. Nobody else has to die today."

The reply was filled with fury. "We were going to make the world a better place. Neotypes were going to be respected. Do you know what it's like, becoming Oni? Filth, garbage, divorced by my wife while I was still in the hospital recovering. Nurses sneered, and the doctor showed himself behind glass so that I didn't contaminate his air. My children visited me in the hospital long enough to spit on me and tell me that their father was dead. My country declared me dead, and they promised they'd give me new papers if I went to the proper channels. 'The proper channels' was one single old man. He told me that it would be years while he trained his replacement to do the paperwork. And then Geralds' recruiters came through the slum where we worked. Gave us food. Water. Medicine. And pride. All we had to do was come work for him. We did, and they found out I had skills, and I became second in command of security here. And you took all of that. You. The Dwarf. Your wife." He nodded at both Jere and Elias in turn. "Accept your shame and die with honor." Then he looked at Rebecca. "Prisoner. You will return to your cell, or you will be returned, and you will serve the remainder of your time until you are deemed fit to work."

Well, heck. He was psyching himself up and focusing that was bad in world to a single point - to wit, me. Maybe I could mess with his head a little and talk our way into a better position. Also, I was not keen to expose Jere to more violence. He'd already barfed when he saw what I'd done in the hallway, so maybe if I was able to get this guys' guard down we could end it with a minimum of violence. Perhaps even no violence.

I lowered my rifle and raised my hand to break up the speechifying. "Point of order. Not my wife. My wife divorced me, took our son. I managed to hold a steady job, but the court still thought her bouncing from job to job and whatever to wherever was better. Only got custody after she completely dropped off the map and they didn't have a choice. So, yeah - times are rough for all of us. But killing me won't bring your wife back, or your kids. It won't make any of what happened un-happen." Okay, so there was some doctoring of the truth there, but I was trying to talk him off the ledge of "try to kill me" - nobody would blame me for skipping a few parts.

Except Elias did - pretty sure she caught on to what I was pulling. "My tribe threw me out. I had to sleep in a car in the land belonging to ancestral enemies. I never had a chance to have children. I never even thought about a husband until I met him." She nodded at me. "You've only seen the part of him that hurts others. You've never seen the part of him that calms, chases the demons of the night away so I can sleep. The part of him that looks oddly at new things when we're on dates. Maybe, if you make the right choice here, there's a better world for you."

Okay, it was my turn to get caught sideways. "Wait, are we dating now?"

Elias cocked her head. "We're not?"

"Well, I mean, we never talked about it, so forgive me if I'm a little confused. Also, blood loss and y'know. Broken nose. Gimme a minute for my brain to catch up."

"We did talk about it - that one night when you hammered down an insane amount of that peanut butter whiskey. Which is awful by the way." While she was talking, she was also moving herself to a better position to fight, assuming it came to that.

"And refresh my memory as to what you decided for us, because I was certainly not present for this conversation. And if we're talking about whiskey, that alcoholic maple syrup you seem to think is good is not. Seriously, when we kissed after shots, I didn't know whether to keep kissing you or go get a fork to tuck into the big stack of pancakes that was coming."

She pointed at me with both her arm and wing. "You remember the kissing but not any of the conversation? Mister, we are gonna have a talk when we get home. You're lucky you're a good kisser."

She still wasn't in prime position, and the Oni was still distracted by our faux argument. Time to add a little more. "I remember more than that - I remember you were wearing my jersey, and I had half a mind to make you take it off - that jersey was game-worn and an absolute treasure from my collection. You can't just wear something like that."

Meanwhile, the Oni was looking at the four of us with varying levels of confusion, like he wasn't sure if he was going to fight me or Elias was going to beat him to the punch. It was a near thing, really, since we were both weaving a little truth into our fiction. Still, we'd talked enough that Elias was in prime striking range, and the Oni's look was not one of someone who was ready to fight. And following the ancient wisdom of "never give a sucker an even break", Elias went low to cut him down and I raised my rifle to go high and fire.

The only good news about this whole thing was that we outnumbered him. The bad news was that we really hadn't trained as a group for this situation, which meant that things could go very wrong very quickly. Also, there were a good dozen or so security guards who were quite happy to wade in and make our collective lives miserable. Jeremiah was definitely the wild card in this situation. Luckily or unluckily, he was in a very similar state to the Oni, processing Elias and I's argument. The Onis' face hardened as he finally made the executive decision that we were distracted by our argument to the point that he could make a move.

He closed the distance rapidly, ignoring the three shots I put into his stomach and legs, with my last two rounds sailing off to somewhere that was not him. I twitched out of the way of his sword, which was again both good and bad. His attempt was to stab my throat, which failed; however the sword buried itself in my shoulder up to the hilt. Then the fight became a blur of motion, as I used my limb advantage to get us on the ground. He was trying to free his sword by sawing through the rest of my arm, but I grabbed his wrist to keep that from happening. Against all logic, the best place for that godless hunk of metal was right where it was. Unfortunately, I was in no position to take further notes on how Jere and Rebecca were faring, since my field of vision was highly obscured by an acre of trouble in the form of the second in command for security.

Finally I rolled to my back and used all my legs to hug the ugly son of a goon in a really tight hug, or it could also have been a chokehold - I shouted for anyone with bullets to flipping shoot already, and I was rewarded with a hail of shots and fresh pain. The Oni went limp, and I looked around for more bad news. There wasn't, but Jere was lowering his pistol with an ashen face.

"I'm sorry Dad, I didn't mean to I was aiming for him but...but..."

And then I felt it. My son had shot me in the ass. Repeatedly. The gods had a sense of humor. It was certainly a twisted sense of humor, and apparently focused highly on my rear. Elias was on me in a flash, pulling the Oni off of me and putting herself in his place. I grunted, rolling to my feet to see that a lot had happened - the rest of the security team that wanted to cause us grief was themselves aggrieved. Rebecca looked rather pleased with herself, and Elias was smiling grimly. Rebecca was finally fully decent in some gear she had liberated from the security team

"We go'a go. Call him a medic, let's get ourselves to our. Boat. We gotta go." I was woozy and definitely needing a doctor. I forced myself toward the boat, and finally I was able to wipe my eyes fully clear before Elias stopped me from getting in the boat.

"That's gotta come out and get secured."

"What does?" I blinked a little.

"That." She pointed at my shoulder, where the sword was still stuck.

"Oh. Holy crap. Who put that there?" Okay, so I wasn't exactly in a right frame of mind. In my defense, it had been a long couple weeks, topped off with bullets and grenade sprinkles. If I paused to think about it, there were exactly three places that didn't hurt. My right shoulder, my left front hoof, and base of my tail. I was considering this when Elias yoinked the sword out and stowed it in the scabbard that she had apparently looted from the Oni. I looked at her dully as she threw a bandage on it to slow the bleeding. If memory served, the previous owner of the sword was responsible for some annoyances the first time I was here, so really this was just karma. Or something. They poured me into the boat, and actually took care to not move me much as the engine was fully charged and fired up, to send us south at what felt like a rapid pace, but was probably pretty slow. Oddly, we weren't pursued. It seemed like either they had no orders to pursue, or Gerald had seen what we'd done and decided that sending additional forces would be a net loss.

The trip to our rendezvous point was not without trouble. There was a bit of a fuss as the Pacific once again decided that we as interlopers should suffer deeply for our transgression of taking a six-person boat and attempting to go anywhere in a respectable amount of time. Also, the main reason I was conscious was because salt water and open wounds mix about as well as you'd expect - it was worse when I tried to inhale through my still-broken nose. That said, it was kind of cute watching Rebecca wrap herself around Jere to protect him from the worst of it. During the last fight with the security team, he'd gotten a respectable ding or five, along with a twisted knee and dinged ankle. It was going to be fun explaining all this later.

It was about two in the morning when we finally got where we needed to be, and we sent a few signals. Then we waited. And waited. Our wetsuits kept us from freezing, and we huddled together to stay warm-ish as we received notifications on the sub arrival and bearing, so we decided to try to meet them. It worked after a fashion, and it was just past sunrise when our ride surfaced. Finally, we could get some decent food.

There was in fact a small problem, in that the sub was a refurbished job from a country that had a lot of them to spare, and someone forgot to make the entry wide enough for me to squeeze my everything through. Jere went through easily, while Rebecca had a slightly difficult time. I was down to my wetsuit before I was finally skinny enough to get into the damn thing, and there were looks from some of the crew as I hit the deck with a significant thump. Then my gear came down, followed by Elias. Lastly, the deflated boat and the chief of the boat - who was apparently responsible for keeping a level head while the sub was being boarded by three folks who didn't know port from starboard, were very much unshowered, and all in various states of wounded. He snapped out a few orders to get some fresh gear from the biggest centaur they had on board. The medical chief wanted to lead us all to his domain first to get checked out. We needed showers. The debate was settled when I squirmed out of the top half of my wetsuit and let him catch a whiff of my shirt. The doc recoiled and we were shown where the showers were.

Unfortunately, the showers had not been fully retrofitted, so I had to wash one half at a time. This caused a few folks on the crew to pass through the showers more times than was strictly necessary. Elias gave a few of the more interested personnel a look, which caused them to go look somewhere else. Finally everyone was clean-ish, and we were in due turn poked and prodded. Jere had a tweaked ankle from taking the alternate route and falling, Elias had scrapes, bruises and some wing damage from grenades. Meanwhile, I was apparently Fates' punching bag - my broken nose was set properly, bullets were pulled out of my rear yet again, and shrapnel was removed from my equine torso. In addition to all that, my entire upper torso was one huge bruise from where I'd been catcalling the hallway security. They were lousy shots, but when you turn an area into eighty percent flying bullet by volume, you're gonna get hits just by sheer chance. Still, I'd been flipping lucky. And finally, the hugely impressive stab wound was tended to. My arm was put in a sling so that I wouldn't move it and make things worse accidentally, and I was handed yet another bottle of painkillers. Even Rebecca had a few bumps and bruises from her time in detention as well as taking part in our exit.

Our next stop was to get some fresh clothes. With all the damage they had received, the gear I'd brought on board was deemed a total loss, but they had a few spare outfits donated by the centaur crew. After all that, we were shown to our quarters. Technically it was the XO's cabin, but it had been decided collectively that I was not going to fit in standard crew berthing, the centaurs among the crew were already sharing a section, and even the officer and visitor cabins (normally where the weapons stowage and firing sections were) were not going to work. That left the captain and the XO's cabins. The captain, being the captain, pulled rank.

The captain also was very put out that there were four of us when he'd been advised that there were only three. There was a discussion of sorts that lasted right up until I took a deep breath and explained the situation in detail. The captain seemed calm about it, but the XO was very fussy about it and demanded that we all be re-quartered, which began yet another round of discussion.

The argument was getting heated to the point where I was going to raise my voice to levels that would be outright criminal on a noise-conscious submarine. The debate was finally settled by the Chief engineer offering up her cabin for Rebecca and Jere, since she was basically going to live in the engine space for the next few days. Which was good for everyone involved, as I had declared that any separation of Jere and Rebecca would be taken as a personal insult to be settled with any and all comers as soon as we hit land. I strongly hinted if folks wanted to settle accounts sooner the integrity of the tin can we were riding in could not be guaranteed.

The captain was very dismayed with the implied threat, and after settling the department heads down, we had a discussion that was admittedly brief but also quite meaningful. I was very specifically forbidden from giving the XO any amount of grief. The number four was forbidden. Also of note, despite the cabins being separated by age and not gender, there was to be no canoodling, snogging, shenanigans, or tomfoolery. By anyone. Those were activities that would be reserved for the beach. And with that I was dismissed in order to acquaint myself with the XO's bed.

Elias and I piled into the cabin and collectively fell asleep. I collapsed on the available bunk, which was amazingly soft. I felt a slight movement as Elias crashed out on me. She was kind enough to avoid the areas that would be painful.

We were awakened by the XO, who was apparently not pleased he'd been kicked out of his bed by a pair of interlopers. And worse, Army interlopers. To be fair, it was probably going to be a week before the battle funk came off the mattress. I checked my watch and found that it had only been three hours. I groaned softly and nudged Elias, who responded by curling up and inviting me to do the anatomically impossible. The XO was unmoved by our plight.

"Message traffic for you two. Go forward to pick it up. Chow circuit starts in an hour." My stomachs growled as I realized that I

actually hadn't eaten anything since we'd left the plane, which after
doing some math I realized was eighteen hours ago - which was
definitely a recipe for disaster. Elias was already stretching as the
XO left, muttering about godless disrespectful Army punks who'd
defiled his lovely bunk.

"Elias?"

"Hmm?"

"Remind me to defile the bunk some more before we leave."

"I like the sound of that."

"Not like that. Wake Jere, he'll ruin our day if he misses
breakfast."

Jere was tough to wake up. Apparently the activities of the last
day were roughest on him, despite him taking almost no battle
damage. We all squirmed forward to communications. Per the
message traffic, we were being given gold stars for the successful
mission work, and as a reward we were being given a free ride on
the sub to enjoy a full weeks' R&R at Jacks' Retirement Residence
on Lehua Island in Hawaii. The post-mission debriefs would occur
there. We glanced at each other, figuring The Elf had found an
excuse to take a week off himself and we were the convenient cover.
After that, we were to return to home base with haste, because the
world wasn't going to save itself, and Geralds' actions had stirred
up a bit of a hornets' nest. As for Rebecca, she was going to be
fully debriefed in Hawaii, and from there decisions would be made
regarding her future.

Once that was done, we lined up for chow, and I immediately
recanted my previous thoughts about good navy food. Still, word
had passed - quietly - about what we'd pulled off, and after we'd
eaten enough to take worst of the edge off, we were summoned
forward and presented ships hats showing the name of the ship
(Ocean Pearl), and the crew gave the softest of cheers as we looked
awkwardly around; apparently this was what passed for a hell of

a party in the world of subs. Still, we had about a day to kill, so Elias and I spent our time holed up in the XO's cabin. We were passengers on the taxi, the least we could do was be good passengers. No such luck for Jeremiah, who had zoomed off as soon as he could, who was small enough to get everywhere, inquisitive enough to ask all the right questions, and smart enough to ask permission to fix a few things. Rebecca came in to tell us that Jere was behaving strangely - he'd come into the cabin, grabbed his laptop and promptly headed for Engineering.

According to a few section heads, Jere had re-written a few operational programs well enough to improve the ships' overall efficiency by five percent. And that was only with a few hours of poking around. The captain ordered a change of course to divert around some marine wildlife. This also had the added effect of putting a couple more hours on our journey, so that Jere could do a few more things. Once I found out about that, I went forward to Communications and asked if we could loan Jere to them once vacation was done, otherwise the captain was going to eat up all our R&R time with minor course corrections.

The Jere loan was approved, and I had a feeling that we were going to get some more requests. In any event, I was rather politely told to sit down, shut up, and start writing my notes for the debrief. And also report to the doctor every twelve hours for evaluation. Overall, I spent the entire trip cooped up and annoyed. For some reason they couldn't do the debrief via radio, telecom, or signal flare. So I wrote down what I remembered, and let Elias lean against me after the painkillers kicked in. The ships' doctor was about as impressed as the regular doctor, as my nose had already healed and the bullet wounds were well on their way to being minor scars. The stab was a problem, but if I was smart and kept my left arm movement to a minimum, I'd be back to normal in a week. Possibly less. He did also recommend I let my coat grow out to cover the growing collection of scars I was picking up from these jobs, which was a bit disconcerting. I mean it was possible, but then I'd look shaggy. Or worse, like some middle-aged goob trying to hold on to his youth. I let him know that I'd take care of my own fashion choices. I did not let him know that I'd had my current haircut more or less unchanged since I was Jere's age, and I'd never actually let my fur grow out to any appreciable length. Nothing else felt right.

Once I was declared fit to go sit in my cabin, I found my way to the chow hall, where there were a few stragglers trying to wheedle the cooks for a spare sandwich. I was more of a mind to cook my own food with both hands, doctors' orders be darned. Regrettably, I was noticed walking into the kitchen and was promptly chased out. finally I caught one of the other people and asked where Jeremiah was. Apparently he'd become the mascot of engineering, and worse, I was not going to be able to get in there. I was able to get a message to him that he needed to eat. He came forward from engineering, looking greasy, messy, and happy. And also hungry. I passed a message to engineering - to wit, he was still a growing boy despite the dwarven beard, and his father still believed in meals and bedtime.

There was a discussion with the engineering chief and the doctor. Jere's injuries were minor, and Jere had reportedly made a nest of sorts in Engineering where he slept for a few hours at a time, but not exactly well. Still, he was productive enough that if he hadn't already been in the Dwarven Mines, they would have snagged him. Still, I had a feeling he was avoiding me and Elias. After discussing the situation, it was agreed that he'd be sent forward for a shower and a meal, and he was not to return to Engineering without my say-so.

Jere was a wreck, of sorts as he walked in. Even after the shower, he still had grime in a few places. I wiped a few places with my good arm, eliciting a grunt from him. I put the washcloth down and regarded him. Elias gave us the room.

"Jeremiah. What's on your mind that you're not wanting to talk about."

"I keep dreaming that we messed up. And you, you were different. Angry."

"In the dream or not in the dream?"

"Dad...you shot those guys. You killed them."

I nodded. "Yeah. I did. I didn't want to. I didn't want you to see it. It was one reason I didn't want you to go."

"But, but why? Did they have to?"

"No. They didn't have to, but if they were anything like the head security guy, they probably didn't think they had another choice. Gerald picked them from bad places where the Genesis types are the rule, not the exception. I got a feeling that if we look, we're probably going to see that as a common thing - that everyone there was desperate, for one reason or another. And that desperation is what led them to do whatever they were told, even if it was going along with a plan that would have led to a lot of people dying."

"So why'd you? Were you desperate too?"

I had to think about that one for a minute. "Yeah. You could say I was. But in a different way. I wanted to protect you, and keep you safe. If they got past me or knocked me out or whatever, they woulda gotten through the door before you could do your brilliant thing, and they woulda hurt you and Elias, and then they would have let an awful lot of people get hurt or die. I didn't want that to happen."

"But the security guy...he stabbed you after. We were leaving. He didn't have to."

I nodded. "I think he saw that Gerald wasn't entirely right. And we weren't entirely wrong, so he maybe fell back on what he did best, which was fighting. I didn't really have a chance to ask."

"You kept his sword."

"Yep."

"Why?"

"Well, it kept me from bleeding worse. It's a weird counter-intuitive thing, but if I pulled it out in the middle of the fight, it would have been a whole lot worse." Jere flinched a bit as I spoke, so I tried to keep it as soft as possible. "And as long as the sword was in my shoulder, he couldn't hurt you with it."

Jere seemed to take this into consideration, finally nodding but keeping his eyes toward the floor. "Oh, kay. It's still, uhm, you're still kinda scary."

"Yeah. It's something we have to accept about our job. That sometimes we're going to be hurting people. And sometimes we're going to get hurt. It's backward thinking, and I still have sleepless nights about it. But I got an idea that might help."

Jere looked up finally "What?"

"Well...once we hit land and get a decent network connection, take a look at the target areas and figure out the damage those three things woulda done." I shrugged a little. "Gotta be pretty big, right?"

Jere nodded a little and I continued. "So, y'know. Remember the people we don't see along with the ones we do, and I dunno. Maybe it'll make it easier to live with. Still, pretty sure there's a few people we can talk to if you keep having bad dreams. Spending all your time doing work only delays the bad dreams that are coming." I leaned in conspiratorially. "Trust me, I tried it. Pretty sure if you asked Elias, she'd say the same."

Jere nodded again.

"So, we get back to base, we do all the stuff they ask us to, and then, we take a week off. We'll go...find something to do. Maybe we'll go fishing." I shrugged, letting him wrap his head around the idea. "Maybe have a late Neoday celebration or something."

"Did you ever celebrate that?"

I shook my head. "Nope. Was always working that day. We'll do something better next year."

Jere looked around a little more before looking down. "I...uh. I might have been looking in on Rebecca a little before all this happened. Do you think that...she'd still like me if she knew everything?"

"Well, you did just do things that saved a lot of people. Jumped out of an airplane, and now the two of you are getting a free submarine ride to Hawaii. I'd say if she knew that and didn't like you, she probably never liked you. That said you did kinda sorta rescue her. On top of that she called you Jere-bear, so I'm pretty sure you're alright in her book. Just, y'know. Try not to shoot her in the rear. You can only do that so many times before folks start taking it personal." I grinned a little.

Jere turned a little red. "I'm sorry."

I leaned on him a little. "Don't be sorry. You did what you thought was right, and that's good enough. But we are going to work on your aim when we get the chance."

Jere finally nodded a little and settled in, looking a little calmer than he had when we'd started talking. He was quiet for a long time, apparently thinking over the questions of morality and trying to square what he'd seen with the fact that it very easily could have been worse. Much, much worse. After a bit, his head sagged forward to rest on his chest, as he needed sleep a lot more than he needed thinking. I snagged a blanket and laid him on the bunk, which was probably not going to give the XO an ounce of joy. I was okay with that, but I checked my watch to see if we were close to chow time. Luckily, we weren't, but I felt like stretching my legs and letting Jere sleep.

I visited the Chief Engineers' cabin long enough to tell Rebecca that Jere was sleeping in the XO's cabin. Her eyes sparkled as she went to test the limits of the captains' no-shenanigans edict. I wandered where I could, and found myself forward with Elias, who leaned into me a little. "He'll be okay. We'll probably need to get him someone to talk to once we're back from Hawaii."

I nodded. "Yeah. I really want to deck some people."

"I know. But on the up side, we're about an hour out and we're at periscope depth. So if this tub breaks, we're okay." She leaned in conspiratorially. "And we'll have real food tonight."

I snickered despite myself. "Don't say that too loud. Captain might think keel-hauling is still allowed if you insult his cooks."

We stayed forward until we were shooed away so that the sub could dock. Back in the XO's cabin, we woke Jere up so he could get his gear together and blink the sleep from his eyes. Once he did that, he staggered to Engineering just long enough to get an oversized cup of what he claimed was coffee. I closed my eyes for a moment, letting the thoughts of smacking the heck out of someone go because, well, he was going to learn about coffee sooner or later.

Finally, we hit land. Or more precisely, we docked and secured from all stations. A relief crew was brought on to watch over the important stuff while the XO announced that the entire crew was receiving a seven day liberty on the island, and that they would be dismissed by their section chiefs within the hour. Our gear had already been thoughtfully packed (probably at the XO's hint) and we were the first ones off. Getting out was still a chore, particularly since I was down an arm. That said, I had never let a small thing like being wounded keep me from a weekend of booze and sun, and I was not about to break tradition. Tradition also dictated that we salute the colors as we left. In this case, the Jolly Roger was hung proudly from the conning tower for our benefit. We and our gear got off, and whole crew erupted as they were dismissed.

We made our way down the gangplank first - apparently not exactly in line with tradition, and for that we were gently chased off, as Army pukes had no right or business being on hallowed naval grounds. From our perspective, it was only right that the taxi let us out first. Waiting for us at the bottom was a group of retirees all glad-handing us and welcoming us to the island with lei's and kisses on our cheeks. At the end of that was a large flat-bed pickup for us to ride on to our vacation quarters. As if to prove that this was to be a working vacation, the vehicle was driven by none other than The Elf. Even in the warm tropical weather, he wore a pressed charcoal grey suit. His only deference to the island was a printed pocket square.

"You may utilize the back of the vehicle for your equipment and selves. Jeremiah may sit up front."

I was still in a good mood. "Hey, we need to tip the taxi driver. You got ten bucks? He did good." Elias giggled a bit at the thought.

"You may not tip the captain of the Ocean Pearl. He would not be amused." The Elfs' nostrils flared slightly, as if he was already annoyed by the children he was babysitting.

I raised my good arm, filling my face with an innocent-ish expression. "The Air Force accepts tips, I just thought that these guys had the same tradition."

"They. Do not." I got the sense that if I pressed the issue, I would be put in the corner to think about what I'd done. I did not press the issue.

Still, the ride was gentle in deference to our collective aches and pains, and we were deposited at the steps of a single-floor bungalow. Lawn care was not a thing, as the front was landscaped with natural plants and sand. Apparently retirement meant never doing yardwork. I was okay with that line of thinking.

We walked in and it was...spacious. I walked through, checking everything out - the living room and kitchen were separated by an island counter, with the kitchen being fully stocked with a little bit of everything. There were two refrigerators. One was stocked with the things near and dear to our collective hearts, while the second was full of Guinness, chilled whiskeys for both of us, a few bottles of rum for variety, and "I'm too drunk to taste this" beer at the bottom. Outside on the back patio was an immense hot tub to soak the aches away. Looking around more, there were three bedrooms, with two shared bathrooms to separate them. Maybe this vacation wouldn't be so bad after all.

Jere flipped open his laptop and found the wireless connection, tapping a few things and getting a connection after a minute. Even money whether or not he'd found the password or hacked the router and changed it. Either way, he was catching up on the couch - the only thing that pulled his attention away from his monitor was Rebecca, who had been found some clothes that fit her better than the loaner gear from the ship. If Jere's face told the tale, they fit her quite well. Ah, young love. Or something akin to it.

Elias, for her part, was enjoying the open air and being able to fly again, finally. I saw her circling a bit to test her wings before she did some aerobatic maneuvers that were surprising in their grace and speed. I glanced at Jere and Rebecca, and he seemed to be relaxing and telling her more about what we'd been doing for the past little bit. Which left me to check everything out and make sure nothing was out of order or needed to be put right.

I checked the closets and found that I had been assigned the largest room and attendant bed, and I also found that a few items of clothing from my closet had accompanied The Elf here. In another closet I found a selection of Elias' hockey jerseys and some additional items that would be considered indecent anywhere but Hawaii. Meanwhile in the second bedroom was Jere's stuff, and finally a few basic centaur items with a properly sized bed in the third room. Apparently the Ocean Pearl had communicated that the passenger list was heavy by one teenage female centaur, so they'd gotten the basics up for her. Well, at least the Navy was that smart. I threw on a wrap and my most favorite football jersey, walking out to find that Max had also made his way here and had come inside to find a patch of sun to warm his belly. He blinked one eye at me as his voice blinked sleepily into my head.

"Took you long enough. I had to deal with that elf putting me in a carrier. The only reason I let him was he told me you three'd been successful. I found someone for Jere while I was at it."

"Wait, Jere? Seriously, he does not need a girlfriend." I nodded toward the couch where Rebecca and Jere had stopped talking and were just looking at each other. That in and of itself was surprising, as Jere hadn't had full internet access since we took off from our base a good three days ago. I paused for a moment. "And before you ask, neither do I."

"I know. You got Elias. And I didn't get a girlfriend for him, I got a kitten for him. He's gonna need it." Max rolled onto his back, letting the sun toast his belly. "Kitten needs a name, and that's going to be the first job."

"Well...where the heck is this kitten?"

"You are in a rush, aren't you. Sheesh." Max rolled over and padded back outside. It was a long beat before he finally returned, herding a kitten toward the couch. Said kitten was a mottled grey and white thing, and was awkwardly much larger than a normal kitten.

"What the actual heck is that?"

"It's a Maine Coon. Brooks, you're just not that brilliant, are you." The kitten, for its' part, was investigating, and finally found Jere, who looked very confused for a few minutes before settling and skritching into it. Jere's typing slowed, stopped, and then there was some sort of discussion happening. They both nodded, and the kitten squirmed into Jere's lap, moving the laptop a bit out of the way. He didn't seem to mind.

Max began weaving his way around my legs a few more times before settling on my flank. "Kitten says her name is Northbridge. What's that mean?"

"A bridge that goes north? I unno."

There was a pause before Max rolled and pawed the air. "Apparently it's a computer thing. I don't get it. Anyway. You need to corral Elias before the big meeting thing."

I snorted. "Right. Like I can manage that. We're probably going to have to start without her."

As if to confirm that, there was a knock at the door, and I was greeted by several people all dressed in nearly identical suits. To be specific, a regular human was leading, flanked by two large centaurs, and bringing up the rear of the group was The Elf. None of them looked happy to be here. Both Max and Northbridge hissed and swatted the air at The Elf before leaving through the patio door. It was highly unusual, and it only got awkward when the human and one of the centaurs tried to frisk me. I backed and raised my fists - overall, the day had been going pretty well, and if these guys wanted a fight, I would definitely, well, I'd definitely lose. But at the same time, this wasn't quite right.

The tension was broken by a cane tapping, and a reedy voice saying something quietly. The group broke rank and busied themselves by invading the kitchen and making a large pot of tea, as a very old dwarf walked in and inspected the room before settling in one of the chairs. The Elf took my good arm and began whispering urgently. "That, is Jacques. The one and only, Jacques. Not to belabor the point, but our leader has always been named Jacques. He has flown here himself to debrief you personally. I will be translating. Locate Agent Elias that we can begin the debriefing."

Since I didn't exactly know where Elias had gone off to, I went back and found my phone and a speaker to bugle Assembly at a significant volume. Elias showed up rapidly. God bless the Army reflexes that she still had. I filled her in, and she stiffened slightly. We left the phones outside, and came if to see Jeremiah and Jacques talking, after a fashion - Jeremiah was using his laptop to translate, and subsequently reply to all the questions that Jacques had, while The Elf was listening to the translations with a pained expression. Apparently machine translation still hadn't caught up to the nuances of the spoken word. Rebecca for her part was very much standoffish during all this. Her world had been upset repeatedly in recent months, and somehow I seemed to be around for most of it. Hopefully she wouldn't take it personally.

There was a pause, and a slight clearing of the throat from The Elf brought both Jacques and Jere to the rest of the world. There was some rapid, albeit apologetic verbiage from The Elf, while everyone found a place to sit. I took up most of the couch, with Jere on my right and Elias sitting theoretically on my left, but she was mostly positioned on my butt. Rebecca was in a separate seat, since she wasn't part of the group proper, however she had been exposed to significant information. Tea and coffee were in front of us, and with that polite veneer, the conversation began.

Six hours and two breaks for bathrooms and doctors' checkups later, Jacques had exhausted his lines of questioning for all of us, and included several speculative questions for which we could only make guesses. We all sort of followed the same track, confident at first, and then as the questions grew deeper, we were left hemming and hawing, finally reaching points where we couldn't answer without several hedges reiterating that we were guessing at a certain point. The Elf translated Jacques' questions for us but it seemed as though Jacques could understand English quite clearly. Apparently it was some sort of point of etiquette that I was unfamiliar with.

At the end of it all, there was a pronouncement of sorts. Specifically, that all the accolades and whatnot that we had heard about were in fact true and correct. Also, the Power Company had been disbanded, and was in the process of being reformed; whatever ill Gerald had done, the fact remained that the space elevators existed, were brilliant, and also generated electricity for folks who desperately needed it at a minimal cost. Therefore, bids were being accepted for management of the three facilities, including the power generation and launch capability. We all looked at each other, knowing that the Friends of Jacques would pretty much be running that show whether the UN wanted it or not. More than likely it'd be under a few shell companies, but it'd definitely be efficient, and far less likely to cause trouble for the planet. I glanced at Jere's laptop briefly, and it looked like he'd already started plans to turn the three into essentially orbital defense platforms. Given that Gerald and the Power Company were probably going to set up for a second try, it seemed like a smart plan.

The next problem was what to do with the personnel. It seemed like we could keep most of them on the job, but it was also quite likely that some of them would need to be worked with. Given my initial reports during the debriefing, it seemed quite likely that Gerald had culled most of his employees from the Neotypes who were specifically in desperation mode of one kind or another. I made a few inquiries, and it seemed as though Aoife was one of the ones who'd gone with Gerald to their brave new world out between Mars and the asteroid belt. Finally after all that, we were released, with the fulsome thanks of Jacques and his security detail.

After all of that, we raided the fridge for some things, and we had a few things laid out on the barbecue in short order. Jeremiah and Northbridge were bonding, when he was approached by Lambert the Demonic Interrogator Faun Counselor. I had a bad feeling like she was going to be coming for Elias and me later. But for now, she seemed to be very engrossed in her conversation with Jeremiah. I couldn't hear what was being said, but there were the occasional moments where I could tell he was struggling to put words to his thoughts. I did not like where this seemed to be going.

Rebecca sidled up to me. "Officer...uhm, Mister, uh...Mister Arthur?"

I grinned a little. "Just call me Brooks. We'll get the specifics later, but yeah?"

She glanced at Jere and Lambert. "Who. Is she." From the look and tone, Rebecca's undercurrent of "Do I need to put a violent beatdown on this hussy" could not have been clearer had she outright stated it.

I chuffed. "That, is our groups' headshrinker. If you asked Jere, he'd rather be with you, but for now, whatcha say we take a walk, huh? I know you have a bunch of questions and Jere can be...scattered when it comes to answers."

She blushed a little. "I, uh, wasn't paying attention. He's just got this cute nose, and his eyes are so, so full."

Oh merciful heavens. I called Elias over to run the grill for a bit while I had a quick stroll on the beach with Rebecca.

It was all of ten yards before she got her first question out. "So, who else knows? Nona, or Mister Paulie, or..."

I shook my head. "Nobody knows. I can't say it's better that way, because to me it's not. That said, this...this group has a mission, and it needs folks like us."

Rebecca paused for a moment. "But. Why were you even there? I asked Jere a few times and he didn't seem to want to talk about it."

I grimaced a bit, thinking about it. "Well, The Power Company was planning on using their space elevators to, well, damage parts of the world. Maybe it started out as a good thing, and it can still be a good thing, but at the same time, a lot of whether something is good or bad depends on who's in charge of it."

"Are we going to be in charge?"

I shrugged. "Probably. That said, we're definitely not going to be using it to destroy countries. You start destroying the good with the bad, and eventually everything starts looking bad."

Rebecca nodded. "So, what'm I gonna do?"

That brought me up a little short. "Well, they're probably going to run some tests to see what you're good at. For me it was kinda easy because they had my records and what I'd done before. For you though...I dunno. Maybe they'll get you to that physical therapy thing you'd talked about before. We, ah, sometimes get hurt doing stuff and not everyone heals as fast as me."

She smiled a little at that. "Maybe if I asked them...I could do what you do? I mean, if, uh, if Jerebear goes with you, someone should keep him safe."

I nodded a little. "Yeah. Someone should, but there's a lot of training and sweat that goes into this. Like, several years. And it's not all fun and games."

She nodded seriously. "Okay. So what's the first thing I gotta do?"

I wasn't exactly an expert, but I was very much leaning toward her and Jere having a serious case of the Instinctive Compatibility mess. Both good and bad, but we'd launch ourselves out of that airplane when the time was right. Part of me wanted to warn her against hurting my baby boy, but then another part of me realized that such a warning was probably unnecessary.

"For now, we turn around and head back. Elias might be trying to burn the hell out of the burgers." I elbowed her gently. "And Jere's probably done with Lambert, so you can have him to yourself for a bit."

At that, Rebecca wheeled and galloped back down the beach toward our vacation home. Ah, youth. As expected, Lambert had left us to our own devices. For the moment. She had a bad habit of showing up to ask awkward questions, so she was probably slated to tackle Elias and me within a day or two. That said, Jere seemed to be doing better once he left her company. And subsequently much better once Rebecca was within a range that could be described as 'danger close'. They moved away for a moment, then rejoined us on the patio. Between Jere, Rebecca, and Northbridge making himself comfortable, there was a sense of looking at a mirror in some ways.

Jere eyed the stack of burgers on the plate for a moment before saying anything. "Dad, Miss Lambert says I'm, like, normal. Like, what we went through. I'm sorry I was mad at you, but she said it was normal and we'd talk a few more times this week before we go back." He was smiling as he grabbed several hot dogs and made a quadruple hamburger. Northbridge began investigating as we all settled comfortably in some lounge chairs. I had a small-for-me plate of two hamburgers and a beer.

There was a new voice in my head. "Hi I'm Northbridge and Jere says you're important to him so you must be important jeez you're big you and Miss Elias are big what's it like kissing her I think she smells nice hey that smells like food can I have some it smells nice." The kitten that wasn't a kitten walked up and down Rebeccas' back for a moment before hopping down and getting close to the grill, sniffing toward the goodies.

Max hopped up and re-asserted his position as Head of Household, squashing the kitten and settling himself in where Northbridge had been. "Burger. Gimme."

I shooed them both away. "You two have gooshy food and crunchies in the kitchen. No mooching until later when we're full."

The cats conversed with themselves for a bit, finally retreating into the kitchen. Apparently they were plotting to grab leftovers once the larger folk had gotten fat and happy on barbecued burgers and hot dogs.

We quickly broke up into our own little groups, the younger ones on the beach enjoying life and being together, while Elias and

I turned to the serious business of eating and emptying the beer fridge. I lounged a bit, as Elias curled her wings around herself before taking up what was becoming her preferred spot - behind my foreleg and leaning into my lower chest.

She nodded toward Jere and Rebecca. "They're gonna get married."

I groaned softly. "Don't remind me."

She looked at me with concern. "That doesn't thrill you? I mean seriously, he's...it looks like they both found the love of their life, and if they don't mess it up, it'll be better than anything we've ever seen."

I nodded. "Yeah, but still. I look at Jere, and...y'know. I remember changing diapers. Walking. Taking the training wheels off his bicycle. Christmas presents with fifty Science Experiments You Can Do At Home. He's growing up and it's hard because part of me still sees him as..."

She finished the sentence; "...your baby boy. Even if he's going to be one of the best we've seen, accolades and prizes all over, you're still going to see him like that."

I smirked around my beer. "Curse of being a parent." I glanced at her. "How do you see him?"

She chewed her lip for a moment. "He's growing. I can see how you see him. Dark blue bike, orange stripes - you saw him winning a Nobel Prize for something."

I broke in, eyes wide. "How do you know?"

She shrugged. "It's what came to me."

I scrunched. "That. Is exactly the bike I had for him. I repainted it because the store didn't have the right colors."

Elias shifted uncomfortably, considering something. "So, if you think about it, what was my childhood like?"

I paused and closed my eyes for a moment. "Learning about the stars. Which ones were important because they'd guide you home.

Which ones were important because they were heroes raised to the heavens to show you how to live. Dirt, fishing, and dancing. Dreaming about adding eagle feathers to your grandmothers' dress - "

She looked at me with some unknown expression. "Nobody. Knew about that. You can't tell anyone you know. That, that, that...you can't know that."

I shrugged helplessly. "I don't know that I know. Or how. But another couple rounds seems in order, yeah?"

She nodded, beating me into the kitchen and coming back out with the bottles for both of us. We both partook, looking at each other guardedly. Whatever was happening, there were mental alarms for both of us, and Lambert was going to have a field day - which was nowhere near as bad as Max. He'd never let us live it down if something did happen. Emphasis on if.

It was getting on toward sunset, and from the patio I could see fires starting as the sub crew and the retirees got together to swap stories and lies about the recent past and the distant past. I could smell meats cooking, and my stomach reminded me that it was certainly about time for something to be done about that. But first things first. I stripped off my clothes and went to check the shower out. It was Olympic sized, and the very definition of luxurious. The retirees had it good. I relaxed and leaned against the wall, letting the hot water flow.

The shower door slid open and Elias stepped in, wings wrapped around her torso. She moved closer, got on her toes to get her arms around my neck, and whispered to me as she wrapped her wings around me to pull us together closely.

She told me her name.